THE JÄGERMEISTER'S APPRENTICE

By Jonzy Wandelaar

Published in 2017 by FeedARead.com Publishing

First Edition

A CIP catalogue record for this title is available from the British
Library.

CHAPTER 1 – VOODOO LOUNGE.
"It is all in your head!"

Allow me to introduce myself. My name is Buddy Rioux. I'm 23 and need a job. My brother points out a new bar that's opening up in town. I decide, without delay, to give it a shot.

It's July, 1999. I walk into town with a determined step. I go straight into 'Voodoo Lounge' and ask to see the manager. The gentleman I'm speaking to booms aristocratically: "I'm the landlord. What can I do for you – if I may inquire?" Seems to prefer to be called a landlord, even though he's just a manager. "I'm looking for a bar job."

"Full-time or part-time?"

"Full-time."

People also refer to the blue-blooded 'landlord' of Voodoo Lounge as the Jägermeister. This black, herbal, alcoholic drink is his nickname. It's his favourite tipple. He always has a soothing bottle to hand. He's a robust and compelling character who appears altogether explosive. It's as if he's attempting to take on the world.

"What experience have you had of working in this licentious trade?"

"I worked in a wine bar. On Lavender Hill in London. I've just got back from Val d'Isère in the French Alps and…"

"Oh Val d'Isère! The winter playground for the rich and famous hey!" The Jägermeister is suitably impressed.

"There might be something. But I'm busy right now. Come and see me later for a chat." A weary looking workman interrupts us. It's an appropriate time to leave.

There's still work being done on the bar and disarray in the air. As I stride out through the iridescent doors into a sticky summer's day I'm disappointed I've not secured a bartender position. I feel sweaty. Slothful. Also feel bizarrely mesmerized.

My former life in Val d'Isère was anything but glamorous. I washed pots to earn a crust. The English-owned hotel paid me a drop of 300 Francs per week; an offensive £30. Those six months were grimy and cuttingly cold. I'm still a bit of a woolly-minded mammal, but I'm a little wiser after my snow-capped adventure. My time spent buried in the mountains was both wretched and wonderful, but that's an entirely different story altogether.

I'm in unspectacular Liechester now. Whilst I'm skulking around town I think - *better try a few more places for work.* My parents don't mind me staying under their roof for the moment. They'll soon be on my back though if I don't get a job. Gotta contribute at least something towards my board and top-storey lodgings. So, I wander around town, aimlessly looking for employment. With my head down I notice the pockmarked street. The pavement is chaotically scarred with bubblegum splotches and stains. You can avoid the cracks in the pavements, but you can't avoid the masticated gummy remnants, that's for sure. After hours of being seared with demeaning looks and accepting knock backs from people so clearly above me, I feel worthless. With nothing but my dignity to lose I return to see the lordly Jägermeister in Voodoo Lounge.

As I approach him he bellows, in Jägerbombish fashion: "I dare say I could find room for you. Start tonight. Be here at 8 o'clock. Prompt. Make sure you are fully charged. It's our opening night. Everyone needs to be looked after. Entertained. Do you understand?"
"Eeeerh...Completely...yes...totally. Eeerh Cheers."
"Oh and do be ready to have a lot of fun!" Looking me up and down, he adds in a highborn voice: "...And make sure you look respectable."
What I think he really wants to say is 'neaten yourself up you scruffy scamp,' but he's a man of repute and so he speaks in a well-to-do way.
"Eeeerh yeah – will do. Eeeerm…yeah…catch yuh laters."
I am a bit of a scruff but I've other diligent qualities. I leave feeling apprehensive, but relieved and less vacant. *Got meself a job.* My parents will be pleased.

In stature the Jägermeister is like a walking sculpture. His confrontational attitude towards life fascinates me and his sense of urgency rubs off on me. In a couple of hours I will join the Voodoo Lounge fellowship. I've just enough time to: grab a bite to eat, freshen up and make myself look as respectable as possible.

Pass a splodge of Brylcreem through my in-need-of-a-cut hair. Have a rare meeting with my best-a-man-can-get Gillette. Spray 'activist' eau-de-toilette all over my raw neck. That opening night I'm on display to an insatiably thirsty world.

20:01: hordes of debonair and parched customers start streaming through the bouncer-defended doors, curious to find out

4

what's in store at Voodoo Lounge. The air is fervent and filled with a metallic dust. The Voodoo venue has only just been erected in time. You can still feel the workers' exertion in the atmosphere. The place smells woody and tinny, just like a carpenter's workshop. Could have done with at least another couple of hours to sort stuff out behind the bar, but I kinda like the fragmentary chaos of the whole situation. I can tell by its muddled inauguration that working here's going to be a turbulent, if not an entirely riotous affair. Voodoo Lounge's well-groomed front man is as unpredictable as they come. One minute there's an 'anything goes' kind of atmosphere, the next minute the Jägermeister's running the place with an iron fist.

Suddenly and unexpectedly a cagey man wearing a long beige trench coat points out: "You won't meet many people like him in your lifetime!" Evidently he's referring to the unassailable Jägermeister. The man in the trench coat is called Les. Never ask Les what he means, but as time rolls by, his judicious words begin to make more and more sense.

Les. Late forties. Plain-clothed detective. Becomes a regular at Voodoo Lounge. Seems concerned about my welfare. Above average intelligence. Attempting to teach me something. Know there must be other sleuths on the prowl, but who are they? And where are they?

During the opening week a talented mural artist approaches the Jägermeister. Wants to do some creative wall paintings in the Voodoo basement bar. Wears Converse baseball boots and colourful casual layers. Has a touchy attitude emblematic of modern-day artists. Has a couple of inventive concepts of his own but the Jägermeister insists on a fresco of Sean Connery. The Jägermeister identifies himself with Connery. To be fair there are stark similarities between the two men. Indeed, the Jägermeister is unmistakably Bond like. The multihued mural artist appears somewhat perturbed. Stands there flexing himself like a sore contortionist. He argues. Expressively: "Portraits are normally part of my repertoire but on this occasion soz. I apologise profusely. Can't do a Connery. It just ain't in meh bag baby - if you get meh! Sorry...soz meh ducky." After much deliberation and honey tonguing from the Jägermeister, they come to a compromise. The gifted artist does a superb frieze of Roger Moore. Ultimately it isn't so much about who the image is of, but what the image stands for. The Jägermeister wants the mural painting to be a cryptogram signifying counter-intelligence; a work-of-art with an 'I've got my eye on you message'. This insidious gesture is intended for Mo's eyes-only. Mo is the proprietor of this drinking hole. Voodoo Lounge is *his* menacing creation.

Here handshakes mean nothing. Artificial allegiances are struck. Twisted. Broken. At Voodoo Lounge I witness the constant exchange of furtive glances between the Jägermeister and Mo. Their fleeting looks are enough to convince me that something extreme is going on. When Mo isn't around, the Jägermeister refers to him as the witchdoctor. The tension between the Jägermeister and Mo is undeniable and it's swelling. They're of radically different political complexions. The Jägermeister...white and western. Mo...black and Islamic.

Mo and the Jägermeister strut past each other in Voodoo Lounge one day. They joust each other's shoulders like medieval gangsters. Blimey. But who is the most masterful? At this stage it's difficult to tell.

Voodoo Lounge is a hideously decorated lair. The brassy bar stools are adorned in fake leopard skin. The walls are painted a garish salmon pink. It's as far removed from the image of your archetypical traditional local boozer as you can get. In an attempt to create a cutting edge cocktail bar Mo has failed. He tries to make the bar appear sexy and glamorous, instead, he achieves a sleazy manifestation. The business name of the bar 'Voodoo Lounge' couldn't be more fitting. There are symptoms of iniquity embodied in Mo's entrepreneurial trademark. Let there be no doubt, Mo has ambitious plans, but whatever he's up to, it's a dangerous game he's playing.

There's menace in the air as Mo hovers around. It's as if he doesn't know what to do with himself most of the time. Even his walk suggests he's a man with a burdensome soul. He shuffles to and fro in a noxious state of self-absorption, covering every inch of his Voodoo establishment. I think - *perhaps this is how all men act when they're up to no good.* There's something of the night about Mo and I decide, without delay, that I dislike him. Mo's an immodest beast, with too much money and too much hair. His black locks cascade in long twirls down to his shoulders. Looks like sopping tarmac plastered onto his skull. His undignified hairstyle is outmoded. Makes him look like he's still trying to be young, even though he's well into his forties. He tosses his greasy tarmac mane to and fro in an attempt to make an imposing statement to the world that he has presence. He wouldn't look out of place in an 80's hairdressing magazine.

Mo routinely wears a black suede suit with a feathery yellow shirt bulging out from underneath it. As I take the time to look at him I see nothing but a fake facade. To put it succinctly, he makes me think of a wasp. In particular I notice he has an unconvincing smile and a huge shiny nose. *Glad I don't have such a large polished nose like this* I think. He isn't a good-looking man. By any means. Thinks he is though. And we all know somebody like that. To be sure, Mo's every bit in love with himself. He drives a red Lotus. He wears expensive jewellery. He likes to think he's a bit flash. Really though, he's a counterfeit-creature. In his oily vanity, Mo's certain he can outwit the police.

Think hard to myself - *what kinda obscene world am I working in?* Of course, I've chosen this Voodoo path, haven't I? Well I've always been a bit of a drifter, but this time, reckon I've drifted into *completely* the wrong place.

This is what I see and hear and think. Fear exists here. If something bad hasn't already happened, then something bad is going to happen. This place makes me have ugly thoughts. There's some kinda corrupt power at play here. I can see it. Hear it. Feel it. Can even smell it. 'It', whatever that is, seems destined for defeat.

I have an aura of invincibility. Still young 'aint I. Reasonably well educated. Done a bit of travelling. Still easily influenced though. I suppose. Quite an impractical person aswell. I guess. Nonetheless, I can see and hear well enough and it's clear I've wound up in a jeopardizing position. Consider myself to be streetwise...but don't we all? I become entangled in an unusual situation. One which enlightens me, terrifies me and worse still, exposes me to real life dangers even the most hardened of characters would find difficult to deal with. Yeah I'm impressionable. Bit of a maverick. A susceptible odd-one-out. Think I'm unconquerable but I'm a fragile spirit really. Have foolishly floated into this nightmare. If truth be told, I'm recklessly close to the gutter. Just trying to survive in a puzzling world. I guess. Wanna live to tell my tale - don't I?

Each evening at 23.00 I descend into the Voodoo under house. It's a steamy underbelly; an extension of its owner's hideous bad taste. This is my place of duty. The Voodoo nights come quickly. The air's always warm and thick. Mo dims the lights fixatedly. Every couple of minutes or so he slinks over to the dimmer - readjusts the gloom. "Just trying to set the right scene Buddy boy! Know what I mean?"
"Yeah."

The Voodoo basement becomes swamped with a concentrated murky shadow. During the evenings it's as if Mo wants to be consumed by a defensive darkness. Indeed, his keenness for obscurity is glaringly apparent. At least to me it is. Nobody else can see his Voodoo fanaticism, for I'm the only other being here. It's just Mo and me. How cosy. Yet he can do as he pleases. Can't he? It's his territorial patch. After all.

This one particularly oppressive night Mo disappeares for an instant. Reappears minutes later with his trophy girl. "Mo you're like a God – hee, hee, hee, hee, heee." She clutches hold of him. Giggles. At *everything* he says. *Oh my days!* I think.

"Turn the music up." I turn the 'Music to Watch Girls By' CD up a notch.
"Make us a couple of cocktails Buddy. One for me. And one for this bombshell." Puts his arm around her waist. Thrusts her towards him.
"OOooooh....Mo. Hee, hee, hee, hee, heee." *Oh my days. There it is again....*I cringe. Obligingly. I do what he requests. Within minutes I'm positioning two freshly blended margarita cocktails in front of them. Seconds later...she saunters off towards the toilets. As soon as her back's turned Mo pours a white substance into her cocktail. How low can this man stoop?

My effervescent mind begins reeling with unanswerable questions. Does Mo fancy himself as a bit of an alchemist or something? Is that a poisonous powder he's put in his partner's drink? An amphetamine concoction? A date rape drug? Or is it just an innocuous substance...a red herring to test my allegiance? Does she know about this? I don't think so. He's spiked his partner's drink. Right in front of me. Like he has nothing to hide. Feel offended. Mo stirs the cocktail with his finger. Clicks his tongue. Lustfully. Pronounces: "What I call.....'a mixed blessing!'"
"Yeah. Eeerh ok then. Eeeeeeeeeeeeeeeerm."
There's a waspish lilt to his voice. In fact, come to think of it, his voice is thoroughly spiked with menace. In Mo's mind no woman is unattainable. He just stands there. Right in front of me. With a villainous Voodoo smile smeared right across his face. Like a slice of iniquity it is. Wanna wipe it clean off his face. Right then and there. Sadly, I lack the audacity. Eventually Mo's titanic smirk disappears of its own accord. He begins surveying me with a lecherous air. My conscience whispers - *Coward. Yellow belly. Do something!* But I do nothing. Absolutely nothing. Been stung. Voodoo style. She's back

within minutes. Smiles happily as she sips her dicey cocktail. Mo's impatient. Smacking his lips together. Hungrily. Starts shuffling. Twitching. "What's with the birdlike sips? Come on....take a good slurp. Swallow a mouthful!" Is he planning to rape her?

By Jove! Absolutely scandalous. Unpardonable. Feel like a Voodoo guinea pig after witnessing this drink spiking occurrence. Feel all alone. Left wondering - *where's he going to take her? Is he going to take her to the flat above the bar? Down into the cellar perhaps? Or is he simply going to take her into the toilets to do his business?* Truth is, all I know for sure is that he's put something in her drink and disappeared with her into the murk. That same evening the basement bar is characteristically swamped with punters. Once Mo gives the signal for the upstairs armed barrier to be lifted, countless indistinguishable figures begin stumbling their way downstairs, looking for a dishonorable fix. This is how it always is. Scores of people ask for Mo. I never know where he is exactly. Know he's slithering around somewhere. Inhabiting the night air. Dashing in and out of the darkness. Creating an accursed Voodoo atmosphere of his own. By midnight the underground bar is full of punters and their flickering shadows. The tables and chairs become fixed obstacles. The punters themselves - like phantom night figure impediments. It's almost pitch black down here towards the end of the night. I serve liquor. In this obscurity. Long after 02.00am. Am I doing something unlawful? Sure as hell seems crooked. I become befuddled. Jittery. On that poisonous night.

During these early hours, most punters are busy lacing their beer bellies with pungent cocktails. The Voodoo underground room is also a place for grown-ups with other bad habits. Often hear remarks such as: "Coked up to the eyeballs mate...coked up to the eyeballs." As well as: "Buzzin meh tits off me...buzzin meh tits off." And "I feel-a-rush! Oh fucking yes!" Later still...the boastful banter becomes incomprehensible and there's just a lot of laughter and leering in this hot hedonistic smokiness. The gloom of this night box cavity reflects Mo's own mood of murkiness. Is he our enemy? Should he be *my* enemy? It wouldn't be difficult to be his adversary. That's for sure.

Mo's hair swishes from side to side as he saunters away. Like a monstrous human rat into the shadow he goes. With Mo gone and darkness still on me, I do what he pays me £3.20 per hour to do - shake cocktails and crack open bottles of champagne. I go about my business, with big question marks in my open ears.

9

Later on, whilst I clear up the rancid mess Mo and his blustering punters have left behind I find myself wondering - *what other Voodoo deeds might Mo commit? Where will he go and what will he do? Which woman will be next?* His flagrant presence hangs in the air like a wisp of sin. The atmosphere: muggy and pregnant. It's too dark. Too hot. I go about my laborious chores anyway. Now I need a drink myself.

Each time our paths cross it feels like a face-to-face meeting with evil. I've caught Mo's interest. Not sure why. He's caught my concern. I'm concerned about the culpability of this man....concerned about the safety of others in my neighbourhood. Inside I've an urge to protect my community....don't really know what to do though.

Witnessing this undertaking has tied me to the devilish deed. Feel like a co-conspirator, an accomplice if you like. May sound strange but it's as if Mo is somehow testing my loyalty. How long will I be shadowed by this 'in your head' curse? Plagues my wits it does. The sooner I can leave this shameful place the better.....

Few days later we're having a bit of a lock-in after work, as we often do. Les and I are chatting over a Grolsch flip-top and a Jäger-bomb or two. The Jägermeister's alone at the other end of the bar.
"What do you make of this Jägermeister chap?"
"I think he's a good manager."
"Behave yourself! Huh…oh yeah. Mmmm!"
The Jägermeister's fine-tuned antenna catch my just-within-earshot-compliment. He lunges over to us.
"By Jove! Nothing wrong with your hearing then! Unbelievable!" All buoyant and eager he is....like as if he's found some new friends.
"Let me tell you something. Mo's an utterly perverse man. He's not the tribal idol he thinks he is. He should not be worshipped. Not by anyone in this neighborhood. I can take this lowlife on but I can't take the whole world on alone. If you think this place is primitive Buddy – well let me tell you – you haven't seen anything yet!"
"Hey…I've seen some stuff in my time. I'm not such a dope you know?"
"We shall see about that little Buddy. Now listen: I will instruct you. Ok?"
"Yeah"
"Oh and by the way, you do look like a bit of a dope with that grungy mop of hair!"

I don't think the Jägermeister is a *'good'* manager, but I want him to think that I think he's a *'good'* manager. If you catch my drift? I'm doing a bit of scheming myself. I won't deny that I find him a fascinating character and he is, I have to say, a marvelously patronizing mimic. Anyhow, my cunning words are spoken just loud enough to reach his ears. He's meant to hear them but he thinks he isn't. It's enough to convince him that I'm devoted to him (*what an actor I am!* Should have done expressive arts at school – would have excelled in that). That night I earn a place in the Jägermeister's conniving plan. To a certain extent I delude him into thinking he has my trust. Yet he's already begun thinking about ways in which he can manipulate me. As for Les...he just thinks I'm utterly naïve.

I've got the keys. Feel nervous being responsible for locking up Mo's den. Doing one final tour of the place. For the umpteenth time, I go to check the toilets. Just wanna make sure there's no inebriated or over-dosed customers lying comatosed on the floor, you know anything like that, when, without warning, I hear a glass 'Tlahtch shing!' smash behind the bar. I almost shit my jeans. I call out: "What's that!?" Receive no response. Call out again: "Is there somebody there?" Again, no response. Here I am, late at night in this lair, thinking I'm all by myself, only to suddenly realise I'm not alone. There's an intruder. I turn to face the noise. There's nobody to be seen. A big sigh of relief channels through me. I come to the conclusion a glass has somehow just slipped off one of the bar shelves. I go behind the counter to investigate. To my astonishment, the Jägermeister's sprawled on the ground behind the bar. A Basement Jaxx artwork-logo catches my eye. There's CD cases scattered on the floorboards all around him. Looks like he's fallen asleep hugging the hi-fi system. "Corfu...sncZzzz...corfu...sncZzzz...corfu...sncZzzz." He's proper in the land of nod. The floor is tacky and hasn't been mopped after the evening's boozy shenanigans. There are splinters of broken glass everywhere. The beer stains are gooey enough to take your shoe off in a second and are splodged all around him. The place hums of alcohol and iniquity. The Jägermeister stirs, but says nothing. Just lays there like a wounded British beast nursing its hurts. "Are you ok? What's up? Are you going to be comfortable enough sleeping there?" He groans an indecipherable set of words: "Aaaah-ooooooooooh-fhaaah-hummm-caaam-heh-ssssssh! CorfusncZzzz.CorfusncZzzz.Corfu..." Bit of a struggle going on there I figure. His voice is fuzzy with slumber and booze. He rolls to one side. I notice a gun poking out of his

11

pocket. *"Whatthefuck!"* I leave. Immediately. In a whirl. Now I'm absolutely cacking my pants.

I make my way home feeling dismayed by this man's apparent inner state of turmoil. I make my way home thinking - *Why in God's name has the Jägermeister got a gun? Hope I locked the doors properly.*

The Jägermeister is like a lovable rogue.......one can forgive him for his drunken and haughty eruptions. For some reason he mimics the actor and infamous drunk Oliver Reed. He often does this when he himself is drunk..."ROAR....I like the effect drink has on me...ROAR." The roars and bellows that come out of the Jägermeister are quite remarkable and have to be heard to be believed...."ROAR....What's the point of staying sober...ROAR." When he erupts it's a theatrical audition for all to see..."ROAR...I like to give my inhibitions a bath now and then....ROAR." On occasion he sustains his sensational performance all night long and sometimes even into the next day...."ROAR....I do not live in the world of sobriety....ROAR." It's as if he's happier under the illusion that he's Reed. I don't know what compels him to do this. Is it some sort of cry for help perhaps? Has someone told him that he behaves like Reed or did he imagine it for himself? Perhaps he just idolises the man? Whatever the reason, his play-acting really is quite extraordinarily masterful.

The Jägermeister often falls into other people's ways and adopts their voice pattern. He can talk pure Cockney for instance....as if he's been born and raised on the streets of Shoreditch. "Buddy - obey your lath-and-plaster." To be candid I'd say he's the most convincing imitator I've ever seen.

I work alongside the Jägermeister for two months at Voodoo Lounge. It's a tumultuous time. It comes to a point when Mo and the Jägermeister scuffle like stags at the mere sight of one another. I'm predicting an 'antler clash'.....

One time the Jägermeister stumbles into the bar, toppling various leopard skinned stools as he goes. "Well, I wouldn't sit on them, would you? Hiccup." He's drunk. At least I think he's drunk (possible he's just play acting). In any case he makes quite a spectacle of himself. Mo reels back. He's scowling. Showing his teeth. He's in 'let me at him mode'. Mo ejaculates: "What the hell do you think you're playing at? This exhibition you're making of yourself is bad for my business."

"Excuse me! We've had enough of your Voodoo nonsense. This may be your bar, but this is my country. Now, what on earth do you think you're playing at? – if I may inquire?" That's enough for Mo. All of a sudden he turns on the Jägermeister with all the fear and willpower of an unchained wild animal. His hair flickers about womanishly. Mo grabs the Jägermeister by the throat. I watch in agitation as he holds him by his Adam's apple. He holds him there as if he's a naughty schoolboy for all to see. Tries to make an example out of him. "How dare you try and make a fool out of me on my territory."

"This isn't your territory." I wonder if the Jägermeister has his gun on him. Within seconds both men back down and are gone someplace else. Mo seems proper panicky. The Jägermeister departs with a booming: "You're going down sonny! Mark my words! And by the way...your bar's a dump!"

Somehow the whole confrontation seems to backfire on Mo. The punters don't like seeing Mo try to humiliate the Jägermeister just because he's drunk. If anything the Jägermeister comes out of the display victorious. He's quite simply more popular amongst the locals than Mo ever will be. In truth, he's the most magnetic leader I've ever met.

After their fallout the Jägermeister uses all his charisma to turn everyone against Mo. The Jägermeister seems to boldly make enemies - it's almost as if he relishes living in this deadly web of risk. But he knows how to make friends too. Nevertheless there's no camaraderie here anymore. There's no longer a Voodoo fellowship of any kind.

Mo's spell is broken. He's driven deeper underground. Only a couple of months after opening Voodoo Lounge appears grotty and altogether passé. The Jägermeister damages Mo's business. Mo won't forget about this fracas in a hurry.

Mo put something in his partner's cocktail, of that I am sure. The wretchedness of that drink-spiking moment haunts me. Is Mo then responsible for spiking November Foxtrot's drink as well? Has he raped her?

November Foxtrot is a first-class friend of mine and she's haltingly good-looking.

"I had my drink spiked one night in Liechester."

"Really? Where? What happened?"

"I find it difficult to talk about this Buddy?"

"Just talk. I'm listening."

"Ok. I'm not sure where it happened. We were bar hopping. We went to 'The Lock Inn', we went to 'Voodoo Lounge' and we went to 'The Variety'. But I know I'd not had that much to drink and suddenly…well suddenly…I just can't remember much about that evening at all. Something happened. There's a big blank gap in my mind about that night. That night out was dodgy Buddy. Feel cursed. Feel stained. Vulnerable. Robbed of something. My whole life feels ruined. I'm nervous now…lost my confidence." November Foxtrot's eyes begin to fill up. She cries. I hug her. Then I look at her. I can tell by looking into her eyes that she is in some way broken. "I hope yuh gonna be alright." As November Foxtrot confides in me it's like she's unburdening the core of her heart. This incident wounds her and certain questions are left unanswered. Of course it's possible there's more than one spiker in this town, but if Mo *is* responsible for this monstrous deed, then he deserves to be hauled over the coals publicly.

Not surprisingly the Jägermeister walks away exultantly. He leaves on extremely bad terms, owing Mo and Mo's family money, but he's not bothered in the slightest bit. The Jägermeister just leaves the common riffraff to do his business for him. They tear Mo's dealing apart. This doesn't do Liechester's race relations any good, I can tell you.

Within a few days, the Jägermeister is already managing another bar. It's a place that offers him protection from the enemies he's made. He somehow gains the confidence of two wealthy and notoriously hard Liechester based businessmen. They've opened up a new bar called The Blue Hole. He must feel like a cunning brat feels, you know the kind of cunning brat who assumes the title of No.1 top boy in school, the kind of cunning brat who somehow convinces everybody that he's the hardest even though he isn't, the kind of cunning brat you somehow find in every playground.

I'm curious. I lay awake for a while in my attic bedroom. I've spent so much of my time working underground lately, that it's kind of refreshing to hear the noise from our open-air world. That night the autumn wind outside whirles and rattles noisily. The Victorian slate roof tiles sound like giant dominoes toppling in fitful gusts. "Whoossh…topple…tumble…jingle…jangle…plonk..whoo…" The eavesdropping clatter distracts me for a burst-of-time. Therapeutic it is. Puts heaven and advent calendars into my head. For a while. Soothing. Like an angelic airstream. But my mind soon returns to Voodoo Lounge. Mo slinks away without any rigorous chastisement.

14

Is there no longer any law and order in this country? Is this depravity simply to be ignored? You know I'm glad to break away from Mo's furtive world. He's infected me. He's poisoned my mind. I fall asleep feeling discoloured and tainted with thoughts of ill-omen. Coiling.

I've fallen into something deadly serious. I'm like an embryo of gangland Liechester. I want to lift the roof off this villainous darkness and let the sunlight pierce Mo's twitching hole in the ground.

I'm under the impression that Muslims consider alcohol to be Haraam (Haraam is an Arabic term meaning forbidden). This means they're fundamentally against alcohol. Not wanting to drink it. Not wanting to be associated with it's evils. Nevertheless, in this case, it seems certain rules, even though they're religious ones, are there to be ridiculed and broken. Religious order, whether it be Muslim or Christian or whatever, is often speckled with hypocrisy, isn't it?

"Eeeny – Meeny – Miny – Mo - a rat is not a human."

There's a whole heap of speculation associated with this man, most of which is related, in some way or another, to drugs and terrorism. There's plenty of stuff the public never get to hear about. Plenty of facts go unreported. Undercover military intelligence officers are implicated. My well-bred boss is one of them. But how long can this scandal remain underground?

The Jägermeister's request that I come and work with him in his new found Blue Hole venture has the force of a command: "You're coming with me Buddy," he announces as if he owns me. "Yuh wot!?" The bar war has begun.

CHAPTER 2 – THE BLUE HOLE.

"I look towards this man's staring, murderous eyes. I know what he stands for. He wants to turn the world upside down."

I've got shabbiness on my side. I'm a scruffy bugger; a likeable misfit. I think my down-at-heel appearance and laid-back attitude enables me to penetrate their crooked organisation to the core. Moreover I've the Jägermeister on my side, haven't I? Not that I'm really trying to infiltrate their dealing you get me? Just living a bit precariously - that's all. At first I don't seem a threat at all. Think they trust me. Even like me. They accept me into their hole.

The bar's domineering atmosphere envelopes me. There's no order, as I know it, to life down this jitty.....where The Blue Hole sits portentously. It's October, 1999. The prevailing urban atmosphere, what with the millennium and all, is chirpy with expectation and fervour. The pressure for a serious revolt is heightened due to all the millennium hysteria. Expectation simmers. For months there's a certain uneasiness in the air. It is, after all, seen as a propitious moment in our history. Perhaps it's unavoidable; a decreed uprising? Perhaps its the right time for dramatic social change. Morpheye's revolution terrifies me. I wonder if everyone's ready for this brash war. I seriously doubt it.

Liechester has an especially large ethnic make-up. In point of fact, it's the first town in the country to actually have an ethnic majority. A prevalence which leads to an intense racial clamour in the town centre, especially at weekends. The predominantly 'white' Blue Hole fraternity is beginning to feel marginalized. They think the time has come to make a united tribal stand. What culminates is a blue explosion of cultural territoriality. In The Blue Hole it appeares the management reserve the right to do whatever they want.

There's something unnatural about this place. Architecturally the bar is industrial. Clinical. It's completely devoid of artwork and traditional pub paraphernalia. There's no dartboard...there's no pool table...there are even no beer mats. In fact it's as minimalist as a bar can be. The mood in The Blue Hole is similarly clinical. Icy. This place will bring nothing but more darkness to our fickle community.

There's something dodgy going on here. The 'dodginess' in the air makes me feel inquisitive. "It's just a bar after all?"

"Well, I don't know about that."

"Heh?"

"More like a seriously organised criminal brothel I'd say! It's worse than you think here Buddy!"

The Jägermeister is surprisingly forthcoming. His enlightening response is enough to put me well on my guard.

Always known Liechester is a gritty rebel town. Never realized *just* how hardnosed a place it is until now though. There's an undercurrent of terror disseminating across this old market town. The atmosphere in Liechester is volatile. We're on the brink of anarchy. My gut is telling me so. The character of the locals is partially to blame. They're easily tamed. Most people have nothing. There's little hope here. No dreams achieved.

Liechester is full of crazy geezers and blue army hooligans.....all desperate for some kind of recognition. There's also a handful of dangerous extremists living and breathing here.

The Blue Hole's a murky business. This is where a regime rich in hate is bred. This is where the extremists like to hole out, like thirsty, furtive pests. It has a forbidding wrought iron gate. A narrow 1860's cobbled entrance. It's doused in neon blue light. It has all the hallmarks of something quite sinister. The smell of fear is here too, just like in Voodoo Lounge, but in this edifice it's a little more crisp and radical. The management appear ultra anxious, which in turn makes others anxious, including me.

The Blue Hole attracts hordes of regular punters. It doesn't take long for The Blue Hole to be teeming with shady underground figures. Many local people find refuge in The Hole. It's a corrupt but popular brotherhood. There's a sense of family here. Isn't easy for these twitchy townies to organise themselves into congenial groups you see. They find temporary sanity in having this windowless boozer as their local bolt hole. The mood in this place tells me everything. Loyalty does exist here. It's a working-class faithfulness born out of drudgery and mindlessness. This irrational loyalty is like an out-of-control reproducing germ.

The Blue Hole is the voracious local hub of criminal activity. It's a popular place for ex-offenders to drink. Once they've left prison, The Blue Hole is one of their first boozy ports of call. They've got to go somewhere. Their dodgy deals seem to be overlooked. The unlawful go unchallenged, so they continue to go about their business.

There's often the same crowd of familiar gangster faces in The Blue Hole. These mugs are full of flattery and fake humour. They provisionally pretend to be my friend. However they're flattering to you only when it suits them. They'll just as easily turn on you. Full of fake affection and disingenuous drivel they are. I don't trust this bunch. They're violent men with violent histories. They've frail minds. Indeed their blighted minds are almost gone....lost 'em to drugs and binge drinking. Lost 'em to Morpheye's infectious crusade. Many a punter pays The Blue Hole a fleeting visit. Like contaminated parasites they come and go. Tainted Liechester's now ridden with feeble blue vermin.

During one of my first bar shifts this guy called Gregory Ball comes into The Blue Hole. "Hi Greg 'aint seen you for time mate – since college in fact. Wot yuh been up to?"
"I've been doin a stint in the army, believe it or not, but like a twat I've only gone and gone AWOL."
"What....?"
"Buddy, have you any idea what you're getting yourself into?" He declares delicately. Fearfully even.
"I'll be alright."
Gregory swiftly drinks his pint of lager. Then leaves. His entrance and exit is like an apparition. Feel puzzled. *What have I got myself into?* Maybe I should listen to Gregory's symptomatic words of warning. Whilst keeping his own back safe, he is, I think, trying to advise me to get out whilst I still can.

My Dad doesn't openly disapprove, but he's unhappy about me working here. He doesn't say much. He never does. Then again he doen't have to say anything, his denouncing frown says it all.

At night the atmosphere is charged with a serious consuming tension. By day the place is still tense, yet it's also unnaturally hushed. There's always an oppressive chill in the air.

Whilst I'm working, my mum comes to visit me. I don't invite her to come - she just comes of her own accord. Early afternoon it is. She gets as far as walking halfway down the tunnel-like entrance. She becomes overcome with a sense of trepidation. She turns around and leaves. She has a foreboding nose. Others feel the same. Fear lays breeding in this tunnel like a plague of rats. I'm just kind of playing detective really. I mean I know there's something sinister about this hole. I can smell it. But I don't truly realise the dangers that lay ahead.

Funny isn't it, whilst they refer to me as *'proper'* I consider them to be utterly improper. *'Proper'* means you can be trusted. They often say to me *'your're proper'*. Like I say, at first they kind of welcome me into their untitled brotherhood. It's like a bellicose gang really. We've military epaulets on our pale blue uniforms, which are branded with the square inside a square Blue Hole logo. Ironically, we look like a UN peacekeeping force.

From behind the Blue Hole bar....this is what I see. In front of me there's a blue sea of thirsty punters. This swaying sea has a seemingly unquenchable taste for lager. As a snapshot in my mind it's a murky blue nebulousness. Tempestuous. Dangerous. Lethal. This 'blue' crowd has a fanatical character and it urgently needs a release. Every day they stand before me, lurching and flitting furtive looks over their shoulders. Some of these overindulged barbarians are heading for one hell of a comedown.

It's primal in here; one can smell the testosterone a mile off. This isn't just a gang though, it's a codified organisation. There's atmosphere all right, more than just a whiff of atmosphere. It positively reeks of lawlessness. The place is full of crooks old and new. If you aren't a crook already then you soon will be if you keep on coming here.

Crooky is Morpheye's main henchman. He's a real tough guy. He's also appointed himself resident comedian. His humour's crude. Full of taunts. Doesn't tell jokes. Just macho jibes. "...and then this punk, who's proper kissing my ass like, said 'your a dangerous guy', and I said 'how come you say that', and then he said 'coz you fight alone, like a warrior', and then I said 'well yeah, I don't need nobody to do my fighting for me...I 'aint rehearsing when I'm taking someone's head off!" Often there are rounds of spiky laughter, led by Crooky. Their laughter is predictable and semi-orchestral...like some kinda discordant gangster chuckling ensemble. Everyone tries to laugh when they're expected to. I don't. Never been one to go along with the crowd. I'm not going to feign laughter. Why would I? Sometimes feels like I'm back in a school playground in this joint.

The bar itself has a confrontational feel. The second you walk in here you're a target. Everyone's eyeballed in this place. Everyone's under suspicion. Even so, it's still the place to show off one's form on a Saturday night. Many of the local females seem somewhat enticed by the 'rogue' element. Yet the smell of perfumed flesh is replaced by the smell of alcohol and mistrust, as the neon nights unfurl.

The Blue Hole bar provides an affordable slice of glamour for the disconsolate working classes of Liechester. All of a sudden it seems the 'working-class' have gone up market. The criminal underworld in Liechester has become a tad more alluring and accessible overnight. That is what is really happening. The upstairs room becomes the venue for other things besides selling alcohol. Exchanges are made. Surreptitious meetings are held. Criminal business deals are struck. This is where it's all going down. I'm granted instant respect just for working here. The illegal recreational drug scene and this spurious sense of respect go hand in hand. I don't have to pay to get into any of the local night boxes and when I'm in I rarely have to buy myself a drink. It's an utterly phoney existence really.

Morpheye's an extreme socialist. He's red but his bar is blue. He greets and treats his special guests as fellow 'comrades'. These criminal forces need to be indulged from time to time and Morpheye sees to that. I can feel the pressure of a proletarian force here, like some kind of perversion of socialism it is. The underdogs are rising up. There's a lot of fluttering around special guests; a lot of fuss is made over certain individuals. In typical mafia style exquisite bar snacks are offered to The Blue Hole regulars and some particular 'special' guests. People that are or could be of use to John Pudding and Morpheye are treated well. They are looked after.

The place is filled with Morpheye's cronies. The bar's propped up by men with dusty faces and sour mashed spirits. They're Morpheye's men. They huddle together at the bar in clusters, like dumb beasts. They always seem to need a fix. Like I say, years of alcohol misuse and the dabbling abuse of cocaine has mutilated their minds. There's an abundance of cocaine and ecstasy floating about the place, but there's a lot more to The Blue Hole than just an illegal drugs affliction. This is about domination. Nevertheless, cocaine and ecstasy use do actually cause many young people in Liechester, particularly young men, to become disaffected blue insurgents. You often see bleary-eyed looking figures emerging from the tunnel. They're obviously high on something. Or you'll get groups of lads looking like they've just scored. Clients often duck into the bar and then you see them leave a few minutes later all jubilant looking. Even so, drugs are everywhere. The problem is widespread. Certainly isn't a predicament unique to The Blue Hole or the streets of Liechester. Illegal drugs and the despair they bring are just part of the overall quandary at The Blue Hole.

Having said this, one particularly evening, there's an especially turbid atmosphere in the hole. The punters all seem really tangled up in the blue-smokiness, even more than usual. Clutching hold of each other they are. It's like a big orgy is about to take place, either that, or a big fight. Apparently there's a potent batch of Charlie on the loose. At closing time, on that particular evening, there's absolute human carnage.

What we have here bears all the hallmarks of a mighty and unique underground revolutionary force. While the ethical do-gooders have been daydreaming, Liechester has become a corrupt police state. Religion is at the backside of this power game. I feel the force of both Catholicism and Protestantism. There's a shadowy theology going on; a religious-brawling politique. The battle is really between the Jägermeister and Morpheye. There's mysticism in Morpheye's green eyes as he scuffles on with his Catholic conquest. The Jägermeister's blue eyes appear haughty, royal, prepared and....well anglican to put it bluntly.

Pudding and Morpheye are the two owners of this bar cell. Many of their fiendish plots are hatched here. They're middle-aged tycoons. They're two of the town's most notorious crooks. They're in it together. Pudding and Morpheye are the big beasts of Leichester's underworld. The Blue Hole is their organization's 'front window'. They've their own property developments and their own insurance companies as well. The hole whispers of dirty money. To be fair, it stinks of the stuff. Of course the bar trade is a cash-intensive business. It's therefore ideal for laundering money from other sources. This is what I've been led to believe at least. I doubt there's a method sophisticated enough to crack this. But *perhaps* there is?

Morpheye has many aides. He's a wartime opportunist after all - he needs adherents. As a proficient military gang leader, his aim is to create a criminal power, a mafia if you like. Indeed, The Blue Hole serves as his mafia headquarters - it's the epicentre of a divisive cultural and sectoral uprising. Morpheye has a disturbing animal-like awareness. Like a warlord in a warren he is. "Join the club" he often says...roguishly. I get to know his tribe intimately. They've hard, killing faces. They grin at me as I stand behind the bar. *How delightful* - I muse. Incidentally, there's also the local Chinese triad mafia living and breathing alongside this whole set-up. Morpheye has strong links with the Chinese underworld. Having the local triads on side make him even more resilient. The Blue Hole is home to a fearsome criminal dynasty. Don't get me wrong these guys aren't unpopular. Indeed they are very popular, but that doesn't mean what they're doing is right. They're popular and what they're doing is wrong. Indeed, they're dangerously popular.

I've rented a flat from Morpheye. Naive? Maybe. I'm sharing it with the Jägermeister. This way I'm in their clutches, although of course, I don't think of it like this. I keep my head down. I'm smart enough not to ask offensive questions. Don't want to attract too much attention to myself do I. *What could possibly go wrong?*

Liechester's a small town, but it's at the centre of big things, big blue revolutionary things. The women of the town are talking, but that's about all it seems they can do. People keep approaching me. Asking me provocative questions: "Hasn't he got another business that Pudding guy?" "Aren't they a bit dodgy...the owners of this place?" "Something funny about this place Buddy!" "What's it like living with the Jägermeister?" I don't feel safe. I don't know who I can trust. Certain people tell me 'You should get out of Liechester.' This tainted Blue Hole grip's getting tighter....more radical.

I'm trying to pursue a career in journalism. Yeah - it's my new thing. One day Pudding pays me an uninvited visit. Comes round to my flat - asks me what I'm up to. Knew he was dodgy as hell. My Dad warns me not to live with the people I'm working with. I ignore him. Foolishly. What does he know? Think I know better than my Dad don't I. Suppose most youngsters do? Right? Anyhow, the Jägermeister allows Pudding into our flat. He starts pacing up and down in our lounge. Strutting his stuff he is. In his usual inflated way. But now he's acting even more territorial than normal. There's something really bothering him. He's invading my own private space. Feel infuriated. Feel like I'm onto something. Then the big man speaks - was wondering if he knew how: "Ay up! Oweyuh mush? Wots aull diss-a-ear bout yuh dowin interviews wiv people rown taahn? Eh? Eeeh?" *What on earth does it have to do with him?* I reply. Sarcastically: "I'm trying to enter the intrepid world of journalism." Try to be as nonchalant as I can be. "Uuuh - well quit stickin yuh beakin, un stop-yuh-gawkin! Yuh-get-meh? Yuh curiociteh uuull killyah.....yuh-get-meh? Stay proppah wont yuh Buddy..."...is his eloquent verbal retaliation! I appear unruffled. Still have my youthful cloak of invincibility. Pudding on the other hand is deeply rattled. The way he acts, when he finds out I've journalistic aspirations, exposes him. He keeps scratching his head. In exasperation. Clearly has something to hide. Doesn't like me snooping. Indeed, seems to find my mere presence discombobulating. The man Pudding is up to no good. I can tell you that for sure. Leaves *my* pad with another: "Quit stickin yuh beakin. Yuh-get-meh?" Followed by an uncouth: "Eyuhgorrit?" Once he's finally out the door I mutter to myself: "Primitive simpleton." Makes me feel better. Momentarily.

Things are going to start getting tricky. I can feel it. Nevertheless, I'm not going to let these nasty crooks ruin my chance of having a career as a journalist. Am I? Pudding blatantly doesn't appreciate my stirrings. Of course he doesn't. Know there's something 'big' here to uncover. Know 'cause I feel suppressed. Wanna expose these bastards. Wanna expose the truth.

(Before the opening of The Blue Hole, the Jägermeister, Morpheye, Pudding and a guy called Tony all go on a mysterious trip to Cuba. Their trip to Cuba comes up in conversation one night. Out of the four - only the Jägermeister and Tony are present in the bar that night). We're tucking into an after work feast of crispy coated chicken and french fries. We're also drinking copious amounts of rum and coke. These guys are still in holiday mode by the looks of things. That jaunt abroad seems to have gone to Tony's head. So has the yellow label Havana rum. Collectively they've managed to bring crates and crates of the stuff back with them from Cuba. I'm intrigued by their saucy Cuban recollections. Drinking the rum is bringing the not so distant memories of their vacation flooding back. They talk of riotous binge drinking, motorbike chases and wild nights out, but I'm left thinking I haven't heard the whole enigmatic story. Clumsy looks of concealment are constantly exchanged. After plenty of symptomatic laughter, there's suddenly a mood of repression in the air. Get a feeling I shouldn't be here. Or maybe I just don't wanna be here no more. Their laughter is more like a series of venomous guffaws...lacks any real sign of merriment. For sure, certain facts about their trip are purposefully not reminisced upon. *Why the sudden secrecy? What's the real reason for their trip to Cuba? Was it really just a holiday?* I wonder. There's a lot more to it, of that I'm certain. I already know these guys have connections with the Chinese Triads. Now it appears they've also some kind of dubious links in Cuba. Shady links. Links they don't want to talk about in front of me. These guys are as bent as they come. They've clandestine dealings and international ones at that. There's no doubt these guys have real influence, an influence which is extraordinarily corrupt, an influence which needs to be exposed and brought to a standstill.

There are many different bouncers employed at The Blue Hole, yet many of them look and behave quite similarly. Individuality doesn't seem to exist in the esteemed and taunting world of doormen. Most of the time these idle men just stand there flexing their muscles or scratching their groins. One of the bouncers makes a habit of throwing half eaten apples at me as I turn up to work each evening. Amazeballs. He's an absolute moron. Don't appreciate having gnawed cores thrown at me. It's degrading. Don't know why this bison of a man has resorted to throwing fruit at me. *Perhaps this is just what tough guys do? Whatever next?* The bouncers wear dour black and grey clothing. Like steel gorillas they stand there night after night guarding The Blue Hole tunnel. They're silent and mindless and blind. The mood outside the entrance to this neon blue burrow is bleak and forbidding. Surely it should be warm and welcoming? There's a lot of talk about fighting. To be fair these doorblocking guys never stop bragging about their own violent conquests. It makes them feel superior. These bully boys will never grow up. Pudding often mingles with the bouncers at The Blue Hole's glowing gate-of-entry. In his own dodgy way he makes sure they're looked after. He slips them a few E's or gives them a few lines of coke. Keeps them happy. An inky dimness lies beyond them. Some dare not enter. I'm allured by its brutishness. Perhaps its the poet in me that evokes this spirit of enquiry. Whatever it is, I'm drawn in. I'm entranced. I'm fascinated. I'm enthralled. I'm both disgusted and intrigued at the same time. I've an inquisitive gut. I'm watchful. I'm eager to inscribe. I'm also very worried.

I want to expose this scandal for what it is. First and foremost though, I'm determined to survive. I'm an observant servant but I'm not the only sharp-eyed spirit around. One time Morpheye comes up to me and declares: "Keep on watching Buddy!" As always he leaves his sentence hanging. There are racial rumblings of discontent in Liechester. We're living in racially toxic times. There are as many black people as white people here. Sadly this means there's serious trouble brewing in this town. Morpheye knows that a local racial conflict will be good for his business. Sicko. This is the key to The Blue Hole's success. Scandal sells. Especially in a macho-town like Liechester. A colourful aspersion will create a thirsty inquisitiveness amongst the thick-headed local folk. After all anarchy is Morpheye's core pursuit. He's determined to stir matters up, even if it means trading on racial hostility. Morpheye's working to destroy the fabric of our society. Only a few can actually see what's going on.

Morpheye loves building and construction for all its primitiveness. The Blue Hole is his bold creation; the birthplace of his revolution. It's a building of raw brick and not much else. The bar is a reflection of the man; it lacks pretension and chills your blood. The smell of wickedness is oozing out of the walls. Morpheye ducks in and out of the bar prolifically. He's always full of activity. He hates idleness. He hates phoniness and hypocrites. He hates English snobs and posh tarts and those loyal to the crown. He loves fighting, lawlessness, insubordination and heroism. He loves his job. He loves being busy. Morpheye's an intuitive rebel and he's fizzing with ill temper. He's adored in this lacklustre town. Morpheye has the ability to rouse the rabble with a few carefully chosen and mischievous words. He stirs up the common people to hate. Hate like him. He knows the Liechester streets and so he fights dirty....he's a real streetfighter. Almost everyone is afraid of him.

Morpheye's mindset is scarred by the hardship of his ancestors. He's staunchly republican. He wants Ireland to be a free island. The Blue Hole is a bastion of republicanism really, but there are moles and agents within its walls. Morpheye's every move is resolute. He's a tyrant after all and most tyrants are unwavering in their wishes. His suspicious and urgent green eyes tell me so much. Here's a man determined to change the course of history. Morpheye is the only person I've ever come across who appears even more single-minded than my own Dad.

Morpheye's ever-expanding building enterprise and his damaging influence on the fabric of society means that he's a man of consuming interest to the British armed forces. He's the local commander of a revolutionary force so secret and devilish that it happens to expand with no name. The Blue Hole bar is his obsession, his pride and joy. He has built it after all. Perhaps then he has a right to be so territorial whilst he's here. In the bar at night Morpheye's eyes glint with mischievousness as he looks around at his thriving conception. It smells of death and desire. He knows exactly where he's going whereas most other folk in Liechester have little direction in life. Morpheye has made himself president of his own world.

The president is prone to bouts of frenzy. One day a punter pulls the hand-dryer off the wall in the toilets. I don't really think the guy realizes who he's up against. Understandably Morpheye isn't too impressed. After all, he has fixed the hand-dryer to the wall himself. Nevertheless, what ensues is quite disturbing......"Keep watching Buddy!" Morpheye declares pre-meditatively. It's mid-afternoon. The bar is subdued. Morpheye becomes rabid. His busy, glassy eyes widen and turn telescopically towards me. He fixes a 'you'll be next' glance on me, before making a beeline for the punter. He plants his forehead on the other man's face with barbarous venom. It's a savage head butt, as savage as I'm likely ever to see. I can't avert my eyes.

Morpheye sets about the poor guy. Manhandling him mercilessly. Going straight for his eyes. He proceeds to tear him apart with his bare hands. This is seriously messed up. Morpheye is in the act of blinding another man. The tips of his fingers are like bloodthirsty maggots...searching for the eyes. You can see his hands feeling across the other man's face. Searching before the gouge. Soon his out-of-control fingers are in the other mans eyes. Gouging. Damaging. Digging away. I see blood pour from the man's eyes. Seeing the blood unnerves me. I stand behind the bar watching with terror, through what were once innocent eyes. I mean I've seen fights break out before, who hasn't? But this is different. The look in Morpheye's eyes is not the look of a man who merely wants to inflict pain. This man is a killer. I watch this spectacle with curiosity and horror.

The victim somehow manages to escape before the blood splattering gets too messy. His mustard coloured shirt is streaked with blood, blood from his own eye sockets. He reels off along the cobblestoned passage like a man demented shouting: "You don't know who you're messing with!" Benjamin Mooring, a Blue Hole adherent curtly informs me: "I don't think *he* knows who he's messing with!"

Morpeye's caustic gaze shifts fleetingly back towards me. Then he's gone. In a flash. Makes a wild and bloody exit. Like an agitated cat he clears the back-alley wall in a second. He's extremely agile for his age. Needs to get away for a while...doesn't he. Of course Morpheye has his very own escape route. He's designed the building with the back-alley escape route in mind. He'll be back though.

This is human behaviour at its most controlling. Morpheye's been looking for an excuse to scare the shit out of me. This is his way of warning me of what he's capable of. This is a forewarning of what might happen to me if I'm not careful. I certainly don't want to be the next to feel the full fury of Morpheye. That's for sure.

Now, I wonder. I'm really wondering what the hell I've got mixed up in. I wonder if that man can still see properly. The punter was a bit wayward looking, but he didn't deserve this sort of sadistic treatment. No way. It's a ghastly experience I'm sure the unfortunate soul will never forget it. Morpeye's a savage. Won't ever forget this violent performance. I know already I won't be able to unsee this image. I have, quite simply, witnessed something I wish I hadn't of witnessed. It's just one of those memories...one of those snapshot memories you take to bed with you each and every night. Witnessing this dreadful occurrence evokes feelings of guilt in me. Must I run to the police and report it? That will get me into more trouble I fear. Perhaps I'm weak and uncaring like everyone else.

There's an air of silence in the bar afterwards. I mean the bar is always quiet in the day, but now there isn't much sound at all. Some of the customers are more horrified than others. Keeping silent seems to be the most popular course of action. Those who have witnessed the confrontation are content to let the conflict pass by unchallenged. This is typical of the apathetic nature of the locals.

Is this how Morpheye usually vents his anger? Or is there more to this? Is he really making an example of this man in front of me? Does he have something particularly horrific to hide? For the moment it's enough to persuade me to tread carefully. After all, I want to be able to see. I want to keep my eyes where they are thank-you very much. My mind is a void consumed with fear. From what I hear on the rumour mill, Morpheye has been involved in other violent acts in the past. Robbed people of their sight before. It's his street-fighting trademark. Morpheye's reputation is built on violence and extremism; he strikes fear into men with his apoplectic blinding rages. Well, I don't need this acute, working-class hero crap. This is excessive use of force. This is a deleterious act. This is a fanatical act of terror. There's blood on Morpheye's hands. I don't see him after his vicious splurge for about a week. Normally he'd be in the bar at least once a day. Obviously he needs to keep his head down for a bit. All I keep thinking is - *society needs protecting from this man.*

The Jägermeister sometimes refers to Morpheye as 'the eye-plucker'. He does this cautiously. Morpheye has certainly built up a reputation as a blinding brawler, and without doubt, he's the last person I'd choose to pick a fight with. His violent actions only reinforce the clannish sensations that are starting to emanate from this republican ghetto. You can almost smell the ruinous revolution in the air. Morpheye is guilty of grievous bodily harm, sedition, inciting fear in the workplace and a whole lot more. Shows no sign of compunction. Sad fact, but Morpheye's vicious aggression makes him victorious. The treasonable dreadfulness has only just begun. That poor guy isn't the only punter I see reeling in horror down the cobbled tunnel. I see other unfortunates....from the upstairs bar window. Morpheye, along with his fiends, can do as they please in the gloom of their self-built emporium, and do as they please they do. I see men lurching away in complete terror, looking like they've just come face to face with the devil himself. Stuff happens in the Blue Hole passageway: words are exchanged, items are trafficked, deals are struck, bones are broken, blood is spilt and sanity is lost. The Blue Hole passageway is poisonous. Deadly.

To begin with The Blue Hole embodies a different prospective for both its owners. Whereas Morpheye's intent on revolution, his business partner Pudding is preoccupied with making money. Pudding's in it for the dosh. Anything else is an offshoot. Of course Morpheye's in it for the money, but from the outset, he's very much in it for the power too. In Liechester they're equally feared. Their violent reputations and their criminal connections mean few people are prepared to publicly denounce them. But if anyone has the upper hand, it's Morpheye.

They seem very sure of their place in the world and they seem to break all the rules. It really bugs me. They wine and dine for free wherever they go. They just do what the hell they like. Together they cruise around town in their chunky black warrior jeep. Edging stealthily along the streets like a gigantic tarantula. They're our local militia commanders. They've assumed this position. We've not chosen them. Nonetheless, we've not condemned them either. The Blue Hole is their space. They create their own world; a world in which they think they will feel criminally comfortable.

Pudding has too much money and too little shame. At times he appears quite mindless. Morality doesn't seem to exist in his world. He's unflinching in his lust for fortune. Over the years he's unwittingly become a bit of a posh chav.

Pudding's good at making money. Primarily it's all he cares about. It isn't that he's any smarter than the rest of us you understand. He isn't an educated man. Far from it - he's an ignorant dunce. He has no principles. That's it. Will just try anything to make a buck. He's nothing to lose. There's no sense of dignity to be overcome. He simply doesn't know any other way. Nevertheless, with time and with the manipulative influence of Morpheye, Pudding begins to develop a depraved hunger for power as well. This is disconcerting. There's nothing mysterious about Pudding. He's by far the least intelligent of The Blue Hole trio. Despite his lack of brain cells, he does somehow begin to wield a position of power too.

Pudding's a sour-faced hulk. I don't think he knows how to smile. He's in his mid-forties. He's an excessively podgy and materialistic businessman. Whereas Morpheye tends to scuttle in and out of The Blue Hole, Pudding tends to corpulently wade in and out. Morpheye has vigour. Pudding has sluggishness.

Pudding doesn't seem to have much of a neck. His head just sort of sits on top of his body like a small, cold, oval vase on top of a beer barrel. His hands are meaty squares. His fingers sizeable sausages. He's actually immensely proud of his bulk. If you bother to stop for a moment and stare at him, it's almost as if he's swelling. Plump in size and plump in pocket he is. Many refer to him as 'Big John' and that can only be because of his colossal size, can't it? More often than not Pudding just stands in the bar posing and drinking cola laced with Bacardi. He's a predominantly vain man. Stands around at the bar like a King penguin....bulking out his bulkiness....in self-admiration.

Pudding has built up a reputation as a dangerous bully. He bears personal grudges. He spends most of his time skulking around The Blue Hole making his obdurate presence felt. When he isn't in The Blue Hole feeling all safe, Pudding spends the rest of his time encased in his protective warrior jeep. I can't stand this self-glorifying rogue. He's predictable and egotistical. He also has very bad taste in music.

Pudding's got a muddled up accent. It's a Liechester drawl, but there's also a strum of Scottish in his grim enunciations. He's proud of his Scottish streak of ancestry. He's also fixated with the theme tune to the film 'Brave Heart.' A dance music re-mix of the tune has just been released into the music charts. Pudding absolutely loves it. Without fail, every time he comes into the bar he goes up to the DJ booth and plays this whining track. Like a man possessed he is. Likens himself with William Wallace. Think he's a vanquisher now. Growing fond of the idea of dragging England down. His repetitive behaviour is maddening. If the theme tune to Brave Heart is pounding out, you know Pudding is in the hole. *Before long, with a bit of luck, the CD will wear thin* - I say to myself. I grow utterly sick of this song. This

29

guy is suddenly on some sort of fanatical crusade. It's ridiculous. His conquering lust comes quite literally out-of-the-blue. He swiftly harbors delusions of grandeur, which is strange, because there's nothing cultivated about his character at all.

Pudding stands with his arms planted wide. He always takes the same defensive position. He's posturing to be noticed and noticed he is, yet not as the impressive warrior he wants to be, but simply as someone with a wearisome musical obsession. This man is no warrior poet. Pudding often strikes a meaty posture before approaching me slowly. Expansively. Repugnantly. He routinely moves towards me like this. Like some sort of ritual display of masculinity it is. He uses his immense size to try to be in command. As he wades up to me I feel half the size of him. His framework is all encompassing. He often stands there before me for a while. Says nothing. Just allowes his physical presence time to overwhelm me. His words are predictable. I always know what's coming. "Buddy......be good!" he goads mechanically as he stands there blocking my path. Too-close-for-comfort he is. Doesn't say anything more. Just wades off, as if an entire day's work is done.

Whenever I'm working, Pudding always mutters 'Buddy', then pauses for a few seconds as if he's waiting for some kind of psychologically imposing effect to take place on me and then he says 'be good'. It's his terse way of saying: "you be careful what you say and do." It's his subtle way of warning me. Every time he says: "Buddy............be good" he's actually warning me not to defy him. Weird it is. They do say all bullies have a cunning. These few words, 'Buddy.........be good,' must be his cunning. In short, behind his beefy barricades, there's a spineless nothing.

Pudding is territorial over his hole. He has an oppressive sense of space. His self-possessed and shielding body language spells out concealment. What does he have to hide? What dark secrets lie beneath his blubber? What's he trying to cover-up and bury? He plods around with his fists scrunched up. Thinks he's indestructible. This is his time.

He runs another dodgy business besides the bar. Selling hotdogs is his pride and joy. Picture in your mind a hackneyed and overweight hotdog stall owner and you'll be picturing Pudding. The Jägermeister sometimes refers to Pudding as the hotdog hulk. He designates nicknames to everyone. I often wonder what the Jägermeister calls me behind my back. Anyway Pudding's got his sausage-like fingers stuck in a few pies. He's a multi-millionaire, yet all his business connections seem dubious. He's made most of his money from selling junk food and dealing cannabis and ecstasy. Impressive. I don't think so.

Pudding preys on the weak. He exploits vulnerable members of Liechester's ethnic community. He pays his Bosnian and Albanian illegal immigrant employees a pittance. He drugs them with speed, so they work longer and harder for him. Sometimes he even lures them to work for him for more than 14 hours per day. Can't believe he gets away with it. Can't believe he isn't wedged behind bars. No one dares to stand up to this man, that's why. Local folk are too scared. Along with Morpheye he terrorizes this pitiable old market town. I, for one, am not scared of him. I want to stand up to him. I can tell that deep down he's a coward...a yellow belly. He won't even fight his own battles. He doesn't have to. He can afford to hire other people to do his dirty work for him, you see. He's growing virtually untouchable.

I meet both of John Pudding's sons. I feel sorry for them. They've been in and out of trouble with the law from early on. It isn't their fault, it's their Dad's fault. One of his sons, 'John junior' tells me: "Saw me Dad munch on eight (ecstasy) pills once in a club. Weird it were seeing me own Dad so off his head in a club." John junior also tells me: "Me Ma used to deal weed from our Skeggy 'ouse when we were little." Don't suppose Big John Pudding would appreciate his son sharing this information with me. But I'm glad he tells me. Feel somewhat enlightened now...my suspicions all confirmed. Helps me put things into a proper picture. They've been born into a life of crime. They don't know any different.

Not surprising then is it that he doesn't like it one little bit when he hears about my journalistic intentions. No wonder Pudding's so controlling. Wanna expose him. Now more than ever.

February, 2000. Pudding is staring dim-wittedly at The Blue Hole food menu. "Oweyuh Buddy? Wots gud t'eat?"
"That is something you are going to have to decide for yourself!"
It's a penetratingly sarcastic reply. Pudding turns an ugly grey. He's dumbfounded by my effrontery. He stands there, now with his hands on his hips, dithering like a bemused and mardy little boy. His eyes wince at me, but he can't think of anything witty to say. There's no clever comeback. All those happy pills have mushed up his head. I'm waiting for a: "Don't-disrespeck-meh Buddy" or at least something like, but alas....nothing. Bullies often go into two minds when they're

confronted, don't they? Pudding's rattled. I'm proud of my insubordination. My insatiable curiosity matches his insatiable greed. But on top of all this, now I'm getting sassy as well. This makes Pudding abhor me. Well now he's watching me all the time. Now he really is on my case. While I work, he prowls - like a loathsome, shuffling lump. *How peachy for me!*

One evening in March there's a rather hostile looking man in The Blue Hole. Gurning he is. In the corner. Just sitting there. Grinning obscenely. By himself. His pupils are wide...like vinyl. He looks a right mess. Quite disturbing it is....seeing someone so out-of-control. 5 E's he's necked. In one session. He's spilling his pint of lager. He's rocking frenetically backwards and forwards on his stool. In ecstasy. Momentarily he probably feels good. He doesn't look good. Looks like a psychiatric patient on a buckaroo horse. Pudding's responsible for this human wreckage. He's pocketed £40. The other guy's pocketed nothing but a head full of paranoia. By dealing these happy pills Pudding makes-out he's doing the world a favour. His excuse: "just like tuh see me mates injoyin 'emselves." Thinks he's the Godfather of love or something. That poor guy will end up a cabbage if he keeps necking Pudding's pills like that. Pudding ploughs his dirty money into his legitimate business. The Blue Hole allows him to deal drugs and launder the profits beneath a veneer of semi-respectability.

Pudding's nephew is a local copper. His name is Sergeant Wilson. These guys like to keep it in the family. One day Sergeant Wilson comes into the bar in police uniform. Asks me if Pudding is around. "Where's the big man?" Whilst my mind races, I reply as coolly as I can: "Haven't seen him yet today I'm afraid."
"Tell him his nephew called in will yuh?"
"Right you are."
"Tar." He aims a conspiratorial wink at me. Then leaves the bar.

That Wilson wink stinks of corruption. Leaves me all perplexed. My whole world suddenly seems dreadfully lonesome. This town is claustrophobic. This town is hideously bent. Muscle is all that matters in this alpha-urban settlement that I can no longer call home. I feel like 'the boy who knows too much'. Can't get that wink out of my mind. I find my mind gyrating with thoughts of a most unforeseen nature. *What the hell have I gone and got mixed up in?* Despite these feelings, I continue to work at The Blue Hole. I work there in terror. I want to. Like an alarmed madman I feel it's my duty to investigate. This feels historically significant. Must confess, have already contemplated - *how am I going to escape from the tyrannical clutches of my bosses?* However, now isn't the time to let terror prevail. Or is it? I'm only a young man. It's too early to be thinking so much about my demise. Isn't it? Perhaps not.

Some woman keeps ringing the bar. Asking for the tax details of the Pudding & Morpheye partnership she is. This twists my head in. Members of staff scribble down several messages on a pad next to the phone from the same probing woman. Guess she's just doing her job. She's already rung a few times that day. Phone rings again. I answer. "There's no one around who can help you with that at the moment. Should be in next five minutes or so though." Anyway, a few minutes later I explain the phone message to Morpheye, which is an ordeal in itself. Say to him (as courteously as possible): "She will probably ring again soon."

"Listen Buddy, if this woman rings again, just tell her to fuck off!" *Can I quote you on that?* I think to myself. Then the phone rings....with a ferocious cat-like purr. We look at each other. Hate these moments of eye contact. Never in my life have I met a man whose eyes can do so much. Forbid, endorse, disapprove, applaud, intimidate, dictate. Yeah this kinda shit - with his eyes. Nonetheless, there's no way I'm going to answer the phone and say that to her. Even though that's what Morpheye's icy eyes are expecting me to do. After my act of non-compliance...he charges over to the phone. Answers it himself. Low and behold. "Don't ring here again you fucking slag." Same woman again I presume. *Thanks for another exclusive and unabashed abusive quote* - I think to myself.

Morpheye has little respect for women. Indeed he seems to abhor women as much as he abhors the fabric of British society itself. "Women just like it up 'em!" Morpheye exclaims opprobriously one day. Just words? Perhaps when read on paper they may not seem that menacing? But if you could hear his delivery, then you too may well be ruffled by villainy.

As twisted as this might sound, to a certain extent I find working at The Blue Hole compelling. You know I can't resist dishing out a bit of backchat, but I'm also always conscious not to be too discourteous. There's an art to this kind of underground banter. Morpheye and the Jägermeister revel in it. They seem to enjoy the banter. They're expert mockers. Both intent on outwitting each other. Pudding on the other hand is baffled by it; the art of mockery is lost on him.

Morpheye speaks in riddles. So does the Jägermeister. I'm well equipped to deal with their irony-laced quips. My Dad brought me up on a diet of sarcasm and satire. Derision is a game I understand. "I'm not a clever man...," Morpheye taunts. "Well, that's debatable," I retort scurrilously. First thought that springs to mind...Innit? I might sound disrespectful. Don't mean to sound disrespectful. Challenging maybe. Controversial even. But not disrespectful. Morpheye isn't use to this sort of backchat. Nobody usually dares to challenge his authority. Possibly I've said the wrong thing? Dang. Perhaps I've offended him forever? All I know is that The Blue Hole mind games have well and truly begun. Now he doesn't *really* know if I think he's a clever man and I don't *really* know if he thinks he's a clever man. He continues wryly: "...but don't you think it would be a good idea to put this champagne in the fridge Buddy." Blighter. He's right. As always. Always on the ball. Always on the attack. Someone has carelessly left six bottles of Bollinger on the floor behind the bar. Without a moment's hesitation, I deal with it.

Morpheye often says 'I'm not a clever man'. Whether he means it I'll probably never know, but I'm pretty goddamn sure he knows how shrewd he is. He's merely being: sarcastic, misleading, authoritative, challenging, confrontational and modest at the same time. That's all. Moreover, he's as suspicious as they come. Morpheye feels he can't wholly trust anybody, not even any of the bricklaying souls in his mob. If he mistrusts everybody, thinks he won't make mistakes. *Bet he even sleeps with one eye open* - I think to myself. Morpheye ridicules my journalistic ambition. Finds my efforts highly amusing. It's clear to me that he's the real sage behind this revolutionary movement.

Despite being somewhat tyrannical, Morpheye is undoubtedly a clever man. Now I know it doesn't take a rocket scientist to run a bar, but at least Morpheye's ideas on how to run *the business* always seem reasonable. He's a practical and knowledgeable man. Pudding's suggestions on the other hand always seem futile or unsophisticated. For instance...this one time Pudding insists that I put a slice of lime in a customer's glass of Scottish malt whisky. He's inexperienced in this kind of trade. Indeed, he's utterly unrefined in all matters relating to beverage etiquette. Of course the customer doesn't want a slice of lime in his single malt. All Pudding ever drinks is Bacardi Rum. 'Aint prepared to try new things - that type – know what I'm saying?

Now Morpheye is a hugely popular bloke. His popularity is one of the fantastic aspects of his character. His reputation stems from his genuine sympathy for the working classes. Local people admire him for this, particularly young men. Furthermore, as the working classes rise up, he'll be right behind them, encouraging them all the way. At times it does actually seem as if the Orwellian oppressed are becoming the oppressors themselves. I for one feel subjugated. Already.

Morpheye knows Liechester like the back of his hand. He has, over the years, built up a successful property empire. Has access to so many different habitats and haunts - he can flit as stealthily as a shadow about town. Has no difficulty in finding a place to hide. If he needs to lay low for a while he can do this. Effortlessly. Stylishly even. His crooked copper connections lend him a hand and a wink in his revolutionary battle to outwit higher authorities. His downfall: improbable.

Pudding is above the law. He parks his bullet-proof jeep wherever he likes, and for as long as he likes. Whereas the average member of the general public is somewhat distraught if they receive a parking ticket, he isn't concerned at all. Just rips 'em up and chucks 'em away. He's no intention of paying *any* of the abundant amount of parking tickets that I've seen him acquire over the months. Just doesn't seem to care. By his very nature, it's as if Pudding feels obliged to break the law.

Anyhow, Morpheye and Pudding are the men Liechester embrace as their figurehead fathers. They are the flinching fathers of this neglected town. They are the Liechester Mob.

One typically gloomy April evening at The Blue Hole in Blighty I hear Morpheye discussing a recent trip. He's just got back. He's been to the wailing wall in Israel. I overhear that much. Step in and quip: "Is that where the expression talking to a brick wall comes from?" Not purporting to be the next Ross Noble or anything like that, but on this occasion the quip comes out razor sharply - like a flash of lightning from Elvis's finger it is. Quite chuffed with myself. Wanna give myself a pat on the back for a rare moment of quick wit. Inablitz...

Don't get me wrong. I've nothing against the Jewish. Not at all folks. Indeed, some of my family and best friends are Jewish. It's just a comment that springs to mind and that's it. Might be the only spark of humour I've ever expressed in Morpheye's presence but I can tell by his reaction that he's impressed. His face rarely shows agreeable emotion, nonetheless, on this occasion there's a glimmer of delight, even a mild affability about him. He wrenches out a wry half-smile. Blimey O'Reilly - the first time I see him smile. At least it shows he's human. I suppose. It's as if I've gained some last minute trust. 'Twas a curious moment of camaraderie.

Israel is quite an unusual place to choose to go on holiday...isn't it? Although I'm keen to know the truth behind Morpheye's mysterious trip to Israel, I never probe him. Never ask: *'Why Israel for a holiday?'* There's no need to. One of Morpheye's building buddies starts blabbing in The Blue Hole one night. He's drunk. There is a whole lot more to this trip. Just as I suspect. It's a business trip, an unsanctified arms deal business trip! Morpheye's every move is controversial. Am both fascinated and frightened by him.

Each night I'm responsible for stashing their dirty cash. It's my privileged Blue Hole undertaking! Don't like this part of my job - at all. Am accompanied all the way to the safe by Morpheye's most trusted henchman....Crooky. Always. What I mean to say is Crooky is always there behind me. Directly behind me. This habitual security measure is over-the-top to say the least. To get to the cash safe I have to: go through a door, along a corridor, through a door, down a winding underground staircase and then through another two more doors. The safe is set like a prized possession on a podium in a tiny cavernous room...like the gangster's equivalent to the crown jewels or something. There's nothing in this room...except the podium and the safe. It's a nerve-jangling chore. With this big hulking man, who's twice the size of me, trundling right behind me....I fear the worst. As time goes by our snug nightly errand becomes more and more dispiriting. *What on earth am I doing here I wonder? What on earth am I doing hanging out late at night with some chap called Crooky, deep underground?* Me and my sense of adventure heh?

During my time here I become entwined in many different furtive encounters. A sense of dodginess and entanglement is always present at The Blue Hole. Everything feels all wrong. Everything feels all illegal. Need to get out. Need to get out of this unholy place.

Late April, 2000. The Jägermeister cunningly positions three £20 notes right in front of the CCTV cameras. I pick them up and put them in my pockets. I've been caught on camera. The cameras are on me. Watching me. Seizing me...as I stuff the dosh into my pockets. Look guilty. Proper guilty. The truth of the matter is - I've been artfully framed. Morpheye still owes me £100, doesn't he? Doesn't he? I've paid a deposit for the flat. The Jägermeister's now telling me: "Morpheye isn't going to give you your deposit back." Doesn't ring true. Not at all. Somebody's playing games. Somebody's being hideously two-faced. I can feel it and in my opinion - there 'aint such thing as a fake feeling....

Suddenly there's this complete breakdown in communication and trust. Nobody believes what anybody is saying. Nobody seems to even hear what I'm saying. At least, nobody wants to hear what I'm saying. I'm just a small fish 'aint I? The Jägermeister's twisting their minds. He's facilitating this mood. He's turning them against me. The Jägermeister casts himself as a hero....me as a thief. Can imagine what he says to them behind my back: *"If Buddy's willing to pinch £60 from us, perhaps he's been stealing money out of the till for months. Worse still, if he's willing to steal from us, perhaps he's willing to proper stab us in the back! Seems like a bit of a loose canon to me...seems like he doesn't give a shit..."* Well send me to prison! I'm £40 down. Turns out they're worth hundreds of millions.

I've been fed a red herring. Morpheye never said anything about my £100 deposit. The Jägermeister's shit stirring and feeding me devil baked porky pies. Never met such a double-crossing weasel in all my life. He's attempting to turn me against them and them against me.....for Queen and country. Bastard. It's simple to plant the idea in Pudding's pliable head. Pudding doesn't like my wannabe journalist exploits anyway and now he thinks I'm a tea leaf aswell. It's enough. He turns against me. Morpheye, on the other hand, is livid in disbelief. He can't understand my behavior, not at all, yet his patience with me is growing thin. Now he doesn't even allow me to talk to him properly (if you talk to someone and they don't acknowledge you, it's like talking to a brick wall). With an accent of heavy admonishment in his voice Morpheye just keeps declaring: "Don't think you're getting your old job back." Certainly Morpheye and Pudding are both confused by my boldness, outraged by it even. They aren't use to this kind of warped insubordination. They don't like to be made to look or feel impotent. This is psychological warfare at its most destructive - nothing is straightforward in this game. Who is going to outwit who? More to the point, who is going to survive? The thing is there's stuff they don't know about. They don't know everything I've been through. They don't know the half of it. They don't the bigger picture...

Nonetheless, I'm out of my depth. Don't want to be part of this dodgy-as-hell, dissident power game anymore....but I'm already in too deep. I've witnessed things. Been part of things. Unsacred things I can't put out of my mind. Some things I reckon you never forget......they just stay with you forever.

It's the beginning of May, 2000 - our conversations are completely defective now. The snap of wit in the Blue Hole air - utterly sour. We're making each other ultra paranoid. Their verbal exchanges are laced with perverse sarcasm and I'm getting an underground ear bashing from both directions...*Buddy...be good! Don't think you're getting your old job back!* These words stir in my brain like a tormenting verse...keeping me awake at night. It's like being entrenched in some kind of mafia madness. At first there had been some sense of comradeship here. Now: acute mistrust. The atmosphere has always been sinister. Now: sinister and aggrieved.

On one of my last shifts....I'm wiping down the bar area....acting all casual like. Feel nervous inside though...utterly angst-ridden if I must admit the truth. Anyway, this thug draws back his arm. As he plunges to pick up his bourbon and coke, he kinda accidentally on purpose skims my cheekbone. With his fist. Marvelous. Absolutely bloody fucking marvelous. Feel intimidated. Massively. Who is this ruffian? Has he been employed to do this? Am I now a prime target for assault and battery? I don't know this punk or have a problem with him, until his ham-like fist touched my face that is. Even the punters are now turning against me. My time here is drawing to a close...

The fact that nothing *seems* to faze me really bothers them. In this game, being unpredictable is almost the same as dissension. Nevertheless, they're about to crush my aura of invincibility. There's conflict here, not just between me and a bunch of other men, but between me and myself, and me and the world. It's difficult enough to survive in such a crooked world, let alone remain invincible.

One safto some sort of concrete decision is made. Morpheye is surrounded by his hard-hitting and dangerously compliant, *red* bricklayer cronies. All of a sudden they've proper ganged up on me. They're clustered together in complete silence, some sitting, some standing. There are eight, maybe ten men. I dunno. All I can see is the outline of a united lynch mob. It looks almost as if they're just waiting there to have their photograph taken. But they aren't just waiting there to have their photograph taken. They're waiting there to scare the shit out of me.

I'm standing in the tunnel. I look hard at them. They look hard at me. I continue to stand and stare. They do exactly the same thing. Then my vision goes all kinda fuzzy. Feel like I've placed myself in a nebulous time machine. Can't focus on anyone of them. Go almost deaf and blind with fear. I'm in real danger. They're still all grouped together. I can make that much out. They're still all just staring right through me - like a skulk of demonic foxes they are. Nothing more, nothing less. These are Liechester's premier villains. They're overconfident here - in their hole. The Blue Hole is *their* bar. They've built it. They're proud of it. Their sweat and souls are ingrained in its **red** brickwork. The sign above the entrance confirms that it's *their* territory. But who can really lay claim to this place. Whose soul really belongs here? Whose heart is at the core of The Blue Hole? Whose? Not mine, that's for sure.

Morpheye approaches me. Comes up real close. Asserts for the very last time: "Buddy, don't think you're getting your old job back!" *Why thank-you for the genteel euphemism for terminating my employment.* Yet again he leaves the same snarling words hanging. They're like the words of a tormentor announcing victory over my spirit. It's the fifth time he's growled the same line at me today. Morpheye chooses his words carefully. It's his warped way of saying: 'you're fired, now fuck off!' Normally he's so ruthless - God only knows why he doesn't just say that. There's a deadly vibe between us. He wants me out. There's a severe flash in his eyes....I now know what people mean by Morpheye's mad glint. My reaction. Well I just laugh out loud....don't I. Crazy I know but that's what I do. I say laugh, it's more like I'm letting out a stark mad squawk more than anything else. But it's a laugh, all the same. Shit I'm petrified. Too petrified to answer back. For once in my life I'm lost for words. More to the point, my mind goes blank. Blank with fear. Completely. I've laughed at him. I've laughed at merciless Morpheye. I've laughed at the eye-plucker. Right in his face. Worse still I've laughed at him right in front of his cronies. Like I say it's a beastly laugh, a laugh that breaks from deep within me. Yet my laughter is not an expression of jocularity. You get meh? Of course it isn't. But he doesn't know that does he? Morpheye 'aint gonna stand for this insolence, is he? Is he? Have I just cackled in the face of my executioner? This is his domain. He's meant to get the last laugh.

I walk away trying to maintain some sort of dignified composure...sure my heart has missed a beat or two. This kinda fear 'aint good for a man. I'm all wobbly. Reeling. Lurching. My pace quickens uncontrollably as I stagger down that neon blue cobbled passageway for what's surely the last time. I strive to take everything in with quick terrified glances. In reality I'm half blind. As I leave, in my fluorescent flurry, I can feel the foxes eyes following me down the jitty. Hostile. Pushing. Bludgeoning. Bulldozing me away.

Seems like a particularly long cobbled passageway, as I make my lumbering exit. Nightmarish. Elm Street-like. Like I'm never going to get out. Like I'm caught in the jitty. Like I'll never make it to the outside world. Ever again. Walking. Stumbling. Against a tsunami wind. Getting nowhere.

My heart is thrashing hard. As I reach the wrought iron gates, I emerge like a traumatised mole into the white daylight. Never known daylight like this. Never seen such brightness. Retreat isn't an option. Gasping. Bursting. I've made it.

It's like I've seen everything there is to see. Like the world outside has nothing new to teach me. I leave the bar convinced I'll never return.

Feel like a man of experience. But in a ghastly way. I've suffered something. The outside world is breezy. Heavenly. The wind has never felt better as it blows in my face. I even open my mouth. Let it all in. I walk aimlessly for a while. Never turn my head back.

Although I'm now free The Blue Hole still has a devastating clutch on me. I'm gonna try my best to expose this blue clandestine cell. There's horrific violence and corruption in there that I cannot forget. Feel Iike I'm running scared. I once read: "the real test is to know how and when to exit gracefully." Well, I've stuffed that one up – I well and truly overstayed my welcome. Left the premises laughing like a madman didn't I. My exit: far from graceful. I'm glad to escape the horror and manipulation of Morpheye's regime. The gloom was killing me man. It's almost as if the bar was built to depress. I'm plagued with dark and disturbing mental pictures of blue. I soon become dazed by loneliness and utter confusion. I go into myself. I mean, after all, who am I to stand in the way of one man's pursuit to corrupt society? They've evidence on me, substantiating evidence that will stand up well in a court of law. Not that they ever want it to come to that. That will break their revolutionary wave. They've too much to lose. They want their reputations to remain unpublicized. They want our misapprehended affiliation to stay underground. I'm a nuisance for them....like a bitch-of-knot in their neck. Like I say, they've evidence on me. The only evidence I have on them is 'in my head', but this, at least, is something. I've transgressed. I'm no longer *proper*. I'm no longer part of their regime. But I'm not a thief. Not really. In hindsight perhaps some of my remarks were a little too crisp and cocky. But heh I'm just a guy making his way. Anyhow I've departed...leaving the owners rattled. They're worried that I know too much. The problem is: they don't know enough. They're paranoid. Lacking knowledge. Lacking wisdom. You know, they make me feel disloyal. They make me feel like I've defected. The duplicitous Jägermeister of course gives the impression of being totally in control of a muddled situation. He's really stirred things up. I think - *you fools it's not me, it's him you want. He's the one who's not proper. He's the deviant one. He's the real intelligent bastard!* Life for them would be much simpler if I was gone, and yes, I mean gone for good. Is an accidental death on the cards? I'm sure the thought will cross Pudding's butter bean brain. The worst thing is feeling that no one wants to talk to me. People fear being tainted through association. People are distancing themselves from me. All I can see is a bunch of shallow yellow bellies. I hate this nasty mob for all the pain they engender. I learn who my real friends are. I also discover how fickle people can be. One-minute people I don't really even know are shaking hands with me. Hobnobbing with me. Saying stuff like 'safe bruv' to me. Suddenly I've some kind of phoney respect. Respect gained from my blue-hole backdrop. The next minute I'm completely ostracized.....as if nobody would even care if I just shrivelled up and died. They adopt a 'if you're not with us - you're against us' mentality. Brainless. Goddamn brainless it is. They make me be their enemy. Feels like I didn't really choose to be involved in these covert dealings. I wonder how I ended up being surrounded by such shady characters. I didn't mean to get involved. I just kind of fell into the hole....with a bit of a wily push. Retrospectively I can now see that I was coaxed....even dragged into this messy blue world by the Jägermeister. The memory of The Blue Hole is imprinted on my mind. My senses feel altogether trounced by it all. Don't like feeling so overwhelmed. Don't like feeling so entangled. I've been drawn into a movement that is wrong. Extreme. I've been unwittingly radicalized within the clinical confines of Morpheye's blue box. So far they've remained unchallenged. Somebody has to turn on these guys. Of course that somebody is me. I've discovered secrets of a grim world, secrets I wish I'd never espied. But I've got out of there with my eyes intact and at least I'm still alive. There are local cries of anti-terrorism.

Bizarre. I know. *I don't take kindly to the word 'anti'. Isn't it far better to stand 'for' something, rather than 'against' something -* I ponder? More often than not in history those who have been anti something have actually been the terrorists themselves. Haven't they? Just throwing it up into the air – know what I'm saying? One way or another I have to bring to light the dreadful goings on at The Blue Hole. I want to uncover Morpheye's mafia madness and leave it exposed for all to see. We shouldn't have to live in such a furtive and corrupt society. We shouldn't have to live in fear. An inner voice tells me to get away, as far away as possible from the blood and the horror. I have to go some place else. Somewhere I can breathe. Somewhere I can ditch these Blue Hole echoes that are clinging onto the very fabric of my soul. I've left them with a ticklish problem - rumour. Rumour spreads speedily here and the murmurs are already swarming in and out of The Blue Hole, like mosquitoes in a prison. They don't know for sure whether I've any hard evidence on them. **They don't know what the Jägermeister has been up to behind their backs. They don't know about his betraying lies and intimidation.** I certainly sense I've got under their skins. I've nothing on them really, but they don't know that for sure. I only know what I've seen and heard…and smelt. Rant over. Out.

A few days after my escape from The Blue Hole, I see Morpheye standing by his glowing gate-of-entry. Has his henchmen alongside him. As always. I sit like a frightened spy on a bench in the middle of the pedestrian walk. He doesn't see me. At least I'm pretty sure he doesn't. He does not blink an eyelid and just keeps on staring. I don't think he's looking at anything in particular, yet his wild eyes bulge with fury and confusion. It's the face of someone with murder on their mind. Morpheye won't let himself be outfoxed, although he looks more demented now than ever. I look towards this man's staring, murderous eyes. I know what he stands for. He wants to turn the world upside down.

CHAPTER 3 - WHY DO WE LIE?

I have flashbacks sometimes, childhood memory flashbacks. This is one of my most vivid childhood memory flashbacks....

When I was younger my Mum would say to me: "If you keep pulling those faces Buddy, when the wind changes direction you'll stay like that." I believed her. I also believed in Santa Claus, the tooth fairy and the raggle-taggle gypsies. It was hard when you were a kid not to do something you liked doing. I liked pulling funny faces, so I'd pull them in the bathroom in front of the mirror where there was no wind. I could spend hours pulling faces in front of the mirror and it didn't take me long to work out that I could pull funny faces outside for hours too, even on the windiest of days. I could do it for as long as I liked. I could do it in any direction, even for ten minutes looking in the same direction, with the wind howling all around me whilst waiting for the bus to come. My mum was a liar. My mum had taught me how to lie. Could I ever believe her again?

On Saturdays my mum and me used to catch the bus into town. We used to buy all sorts of things from the market where they would shout things out really loudly to me like: "Two pounds of carrots 40p" even though I didn't have any money and hated carrots. Then they would say it again, sometimes even louder as if I hadn't heard them the first time.

Anyway when I was younger I hated carrots. I would have preferred it if my mum had bought twice as many cherries and no carrots at all. Believe me I tried my best to convince her not to buy them. "Rory Humber's Mum doesn't make him eat carrots!" I would say, but she insisted that we need a balanced diet, a little bit of everything to grow up to be big and strong like King Kong. What I couldn't understand is why she wouldn't buy me a wham bar on the way home after what she had said. "But you said a little bit of every…"

"Shut up Buddy." I couldn't believe it. I was being told to shut up for trying to look after my own metabolism and gain a healthy, more balanced diet!

Anyway, when I was younger I hated carrots. It's funny isn't it when you're younger how you dislike certain things, but as you get older you'll eat absolutely anything, even things like pumpkinseeds in salads and spicy parsnip soup. Worst of all you won't just eat it, you'll talk about eating it to everyone you know. All of a sudden it's like all the stuff you hated as a child suddenly becomes exotic and bouncing with flavour and you become fascinated with how many different dishes you can make with one single vegetable.

Anyway, when I was younger I hated carrots. I hated the smell, the colour, the shape and even the sight of them. I'd always leave them on my plate at mealtimes or even scrape them off my plate and on to the tablecloth, discreetly of course, and then shove them with my thumb under the rim of my plate. It wouldn't do me any good hiding them though. My parents would always catch me sooner or later and make me eat them. I hated carrots and I hated my parents for making me eat carrots.

Then one day my Dad alleged: "If you don't eat up all those carrots you won't be able to see in the dark." This really captivated me. At first I thought it was a lie, but it couldn't be. My Dad never lied. He was the honest type through and through. I thought - *gosh I'd love to be able to see in the dark, that sounds thrilling.* So, I ate up all the carrots on my plate, pinching my nose so as not to get the full taste, and quickly washed them down with a glass of milk.

Then a while later my brother and me decided to test Dad's theory. Even though I hated carrots more than any other vegetable, the thought of being able to see in the dark meant a hell of a lot to me. We ate three large orange carrots each, the orangiest ones we could find in the pantry and we ate them raw with butterscotch flavour angel delight to make the aftertaste go away.

It was 21.37 on my new digital watch, which could tell the time with no hands. It was already pretty dark. We waited for another 15 minutes until it was pitch black outside and then decided to see if we could go for a wee in the outside toilet, which was at the bottom of the garden, without taking a torch or switching the light on.

I got a smack off my Dad for peeing on my brother's pyjamas. When I told him it was his fault he smacked me again. I ran away in tears shouting vindictively: "Liar liar your pants are on fire."

Was my Dad really a liar? His nose didn't look any longer. Maybe we hadn't eaten enough carrots. No, I thought to myself, I couldn't have eaten any more......and this is the end of this particular childhood memory flashback of mine.

Maybe we're all liars. We are, aren't we? We're all liars. People everywhere, from all walks of life are liars. My favourite teacher was a liar, the Prime Minister Tony Bliar was a liar and the Presidents of the United States lie occasionally too. Even The Jägermeister lies sometimes!

There are liars in all the different countries across the world. Even in Inner Mongolia people are lying. They're lying right now. They're lying through their teeth and their noses haven't got any longer and their tongues haven't turned black.

At the time of my childhood memory I was only five years old and I thought I had discovered the meaning of life. I also thought - *if it's ok for my mum and dad to lie to me, then it's ok for me to lie to them.* This spelt out trouble. This spelt out deception.

Sometimes I reckon a little white lie is better than telling the truth, if it means someone will benefit from it or if by telling that lie someone will be prevented from getting hurt. So then, maybe sometimes it's good to lie. Sometimes though I reckon it's really bad to lie.....

CHAPTER 4 – THE JÄGERMEISTER'S APPRENTICE.

"You can't blag a blagger."

The Jägermeister

The Jägermeister is an exceptional individual. He has taken on this death-defying role, yet even he sometimes finds it tricky. I find his oddities fascinating. They make me feel like he needs help. They also make me feel more human as I can see something in him in me. Even when I finally see him at his most outrageous, I still somehow feel surges of sympathy for him. The Jägermeister is compassionate about society and because of this compassion I can't help feeling compassion for him. I try, in the best way I know how, to offer my sympathy. I don't think he knows how to cope with my intuitive concern. No one it appears has ever truly understood him.

He has a distinctive royal profile. Indeed he's deceptively pretty. He moves about with majestic assertion. But is he as venerable as his statuesque demeanour suggests?

On one occasion he tells me about a one-night stand. "I was flabbergasted Buddy…she tried to stick her finger up my arse! She's a rough bugger!" He can be hilarious. Furthermore he's exceedingly posh. Well, perhaps to be more precise, his posh accent make his utterances sound funny. Don't get me wrong, his utterances are comical. They're just made to sound even more amusing because of his posh delivery. "Look at the fun bags on that beauty, absolutely marvellous!" he pronounces, as this lone female struts towards the bar, boobs-a-bouncing and all.

For sure he's witty. I'll give him that. And you know, other people actually seem to want to be witty like him. In their attempts to match his wit most people fail. Miserably. They only make themselves look foolish. The Jägermeister renders them witless and himself the wittiest. It's his unassailable wit that enables him to infiltrate The Blue Hole to its crooked core. I kind of relish the bravado. I've been bred on the boastful stuff. Brinkmanship is in my blood. But even I am outmatched.

The Jägermeister spends much of his time mentally undressing women as they parade themselves in The Blue Hole. He scans the crowd of punters, looking for someone who catches his fancy, searching for a female to *roast*. His search habitually becomes a targeted inspection for sexual possession. He often asks me: "Buddy would you roast that?" It's a vulgar line of questioning really – almost as vulgar as the word vulgar itself. He has more than his fair share of sexual conquests. He's a bit of a romancer and that's putting it politely. The Jägermeister's comments are often derogatory towards women: "Here comes the beast of Liechester! Is that a woman or a man? She's got the ass of a hippopotamus! Hoorah! Here comes Coco, god it must be demeaning to look so much like a clown!"...these are just some of the remarks he whispers to me about women as they saunter into The Blue Hole.

In an attempt to create an appropriate atmosphere the Jägermeister dims the blue lights in the bar in the early afternoon. He does this even though most of the time it's still light outside. I think the lighting makes the place seedy and sinister. He thinks it makes the place sexy and seductive. He always insists on candles being lit. He also always insists that there is one on each and every table. Even on the tables where two gentlemen sit together.

Nobody seems to know very much about the Jägermeister. Nobody seems to even know where he's from. He tells me he's twenty-seven. I don't believe him. He looks as if he's well into his late thirties. The Jägermeister has an incessant ability to invent. He's a born raconteur. Quick to make friends, even quicker to discard them.

The Jägermeister has a lust for life that matches mine. He's ready for anything. He goes through his day as if his life is at stake. Perhaps it is? He has a look of supremacy about him; an undisputable presence. At The Blue Hole he gives an air of respectability to an otherwise untidy mob of bricklayers. The Jägermeister is a capable man. He's coolly derisive and always responds smoothly to individual probes. He can be savagely eloquent. His tongue can cut you down, like a scythe to a sapling it is. Sometimes he speaks the evasive language of the underworld, because sometimes he instinctively feels the need to conceal his intellectual verbal skills. Of course he doesn't want to come across as too highbrow.

Here's someone who is a dynamic and charismatic mastermind but who also has a real feisty temper. Indeed sometimes the Jägermeister comes across as a ferocious megalomaniac. I've my suspicions. Despite his aristocratic prowess he's a cripplingly lonely figure really.

47

The Jägermeister welcomes everyone, even those he loathes, with a brisk handshake. To see him in action is a bit like watching a politician drumming up support. This guy is not a politician though. He is......well, he is The Jägermeister. Always scheming. Always manipulating. Always spying. He has an astute awareness of the different human layers in society; a distinct class-consciousness. He expects to be obeyed. The Jägermeister adjusts his chat depending on who he's talking to. He manages to communicate to people in their own parlance. He's rarely himself. He's slowly weaving his two-faced spell on this multi-cultural town.

Quite remarkably the Jägermeister, the lord of The Blue Hole, is working undercover. At first I find it hard to get my head round the fact that he's in the pay of the palace. He plays the 'bad boy' to gain these mobsters trust. Astonishing. MI5 has been looking for a way to penetrate the Morpheye circle for years but surely playing the 'I'm a bad boy, I'm a racist' card is too dangerous. Too irresponsible. Well anyway. I manage to find my way into the Morpheye mafia circle with ease.

Is the Jägermeister so desperate to die gloriously? *His actions could cause more harm than good. He could make an unstable situation even more volatile* - I think to myself. Is our world in such a state that certain individuals have to appear to be bad in order to do some good? How long can he wear this mask of badness? When you sort of get to know the chap, you begin to realise that there are actually several; the Jägermeister has many different masks. On the one hand, he can appear both generous and gentle. On the other hand, he can appear both ruthless and violent. I suppose he *is* juggling with a rather dangerous assortment of rogues. Maybe the end will justify the means. To most he's an inaccessible individual. A few think that the Jägermeister might be an undercover agent, but they don't *really* believe that's the case. Some think he's simply an ebullient extrovert. Others merely have him down as a disillusioned drunk. I know he's a British spy.

Morpheye is equally curious of this majestic man's performance. He can smell the blood of an Englishman, can't he? He knows the Jägermeister is a man with some imposing secret, doesn't he? Doesn't he? At one point the possibility of collusion crosses my mind. Will Morpheye and the Jägermeister join forces? But the more I think about this concept, the more ludicrous it seems. They are poles apart. My true loyalty isn't with the monarch or the mob. My allegiance lies someplace else.

I fear the Jägermeister is trying to manage the unmanageable. I believe his mission is unattainable. Pudding can be brought down, but he won't give in without a fight. Eye-plucking Morpheye will fight his cause until his death. Yet it's the state of racial affairs in Liechester that's the overriding problem. This covert operation is exacerbating the problem of racism and terrorism.

Anyway, there's a spy in our midst. I'm gripped. It's a lonesome and gruesome fascination. The Jägermeister always seems busy creating a scene. Most of the time he feigns conviviality. He also feigns frostiness and recklessness. Come to think of it he spends most of his time feigning. After all, he is, in a way, feigning life itself. Distinguished by day. Demonic by night....and he's trying to drag me down with him. His convincing bad boy image does enable him to gain the mobs respect. They adore his bad behaviour. Encourage it.

The Jägermeister wears his shirts partially unbuttoned. One's eyes are drawn to his extraordinarily bearded chest, which cascades over his shirt collars. His chest is festooned with thick, whirly, dark and unruly hair. Like seaweed stuck on his torso it is - very Bond like. The sight of such untamed hair is actually quite distracting. The Jägermeister is hairy and proud and all pumped up with purpose. He certainly has the appropriate look to carry out his double-dealing espionage.

Outwardly the Jägermeister is always well groomed. He has a fake tan, aswell as a fake character. What's more, he has the uncompromising weight of the world on his shoulders, and its beginning to take its toll. He's lonely. You can tell by the look of melancholy on his face. Something unusual is festering in this man's mind.

The Jägermeister exercises a remarkable and inimitable way of communicating. It's not just his carefully chosen words but his intonation that grants him power. Sometimes he cunningly lowers the tone of his voice. It insures what he says is heard. His tone of voice makes people take him seriously. Sometimes he talks menacingly close to you – only a hairsbreadth away. It's unnerving....not really the way you expect your boss to talk to you. Occasionally he speaks to me in a rather intimate manner. His voice becomes confidential, nothing but a delicate, crafty whisper. Having the gift of the gab enables him to get people to do everything for him. Perhaps it's easy to get us to do everything. After all we *are* paid to do as we are told. We're not paid to think. Thinking is dangerous in the hole. The Jägermeister's voice is often charged with pleasantries, but I get the impression that he's only ever half listening. His mind is elsewhere, more often than not. He refers to me as his blue chinned comrade. But if anything, I'm more 'red brick' than 'blue chinned'. Nonetheless, he bestows loyalty in me.

The Jägermeister's English accent has a conspicuous aristocratic lilt. He's poetic at times. "You can't blag a blagger!" he proclaims flamboyantly and with twisted tongue. It's certainly no idle expression. 'You can't blag a blagger!' is probably his most notorious expression....his catchphrase. The Jägermeister rarely speaks but when he does his words are cursed; that is to say the words he utters place a curse on you. I for one never forget what he says and his words often re-sound in my mind: "You can't blag a blagger! Buddy would you roast that? It's them and us Buddy...them and us!" He fancies himself as 'the king of comebacks'. He speaks in volleying one-liners and has this remarkable way of answering questions with questions. The effect places the attention on his inquisitor; landing them in the spotlight. He makes himself feel safe....makes those asking the questions feel exposed. He parries their questions. The Jägermeister has an answer for everything.

One day I jauntily decide to quiz the Jägermeister: "You're always taking the piss aren't you?"
"My mask is a hideous, hideously mocking one. Now don't even think about mocking the mocker!" He replies clashingly. I'm left visibly subjugated. I quizz him on another occasion too: "You're unbelievably cryptic you are – aren't you? "That's just the way it goes Buddy, I'm afraid to say, when you're deep underground!"

As the months drift by the Jägermeister's voice becomes more clinical. He rasps: "Ignoramus" on occasion. It's another of his customary choral eruptions. He also acquires the habit of repeating himself. His favourite cliché 'You can't blag a blagger' is constantly employed. I on the other hand acquire the habit of listening to, but not quite believing, everything the Jägermeister alleges. The Jägermeister is a man at pains to remain mysterious. You know, he is rather good at *pretending* to be a landlord! I'm censorious inside, but give nothing away. I have, you see, detected, that the Jägermeister knows something that the rest of us doesn't.

Sometimes he absolutely revels in making an exhibition of himself. He also has a petulant talent for self-promotion. Cracking

50

open bottles of champagne seems to be his favourite diversion. He slides from partner to partner. By his side: a forever-changing selection of stunning looking women. From the outset he's a poster boy for Conservatism, but because of the people he's mixing with, and trying to engage with, he attempts to give the impression that he has solid socialist values. The Jägermeister is playing his part as the charismatic community tribalist (at times you can actually smell tribalism asserting its dominance here). Really though, he's an aristocrat pretending to be street, a blue boy trying to be red. Like I say, he has many different faces. He's a chameleonic character really.

Now the Jägermeister is good at getting what he wants. He has a powerful sense of comradeship. He can be extremely hospitable and charming when he wants to be. Above all else he's enchantingly obscene. He has us wrapped around his blue-blooded fingers. Like biddable puppets we are. I'm in thrall to the Jägermeister just like all the rest of his staff are. Somehow he persuades us to do more than the usual. He stretches you or manipulates you that little bit further. We're more like his personal slaves than his personnel. He has a certain manner of ordering people around you see. If you question or refuse to do what he says, well then you kind of know you'll quickly be without a job. He doesn't care at all....well aware he can easily recruit new staff. In the first few months of a new bar opening, the management are normally inundated with people wanting jobs. No one's irreplaceable in this boozy game. He has people running around after him left, right and centre. He has people doing *everything* for him. He doesn't have to lift a finger. He really doesn't. The Jägermeister doesn't want to be seen to be *working*; he's above all that. That would kinda break his spell. He even gets one of the bartenders washing and ironing his shirts for him at our flat...like some kinda domestic whore. I can't believe it. Admittedly, he does throw in little cash incentives or bribes of some description, but really we're just running around after him in submissive slavery.

Suddenly and unexpectedly the Jägermeister announces in an accentuating tenor: "You're not here to play *hanky-panky* behind the bar. You're not here to *investigate* or participate in convivial games of Chinese *whispers*. You're not here to *skulk* around with your jaws dropped. You're not here to be *sour* or to *scavenge,* and you're not here to prop up the bar or to *sniff other people's flowers*. You are here, *boys and girls*, to serve drinks, *POLITELY*." The Jägermeister's rather denigrating 'You're not here to' speech reduces us all to a zombie-like obedience. Everyone is under his condescending curse. Everyone succumbs to his requests. If they don't - they're gone. He somehow inspires an almost fanatical loyalty. He's adored you see.

So for a while he runs the show. He overwhelms me with deceptive titbits and treats. He buys me burgers. Plies me with free booze (especially shots of Jägermeister). Slips me the odd tenner. Keeps me happy. On side. He welcomes my down-to-earth servility. I suppose. At times I feel like his unassuming adjutant.

There's this one bartender however, who's so obliging, that it's actually laughable to see him in action. He's round and chubby and has skin the colour of milk. His name is Martin. He looks like a Moomin. At least that's what I think of every time I lay eyes on him. To put it mildly, he's an overly helpful oddball. Down at the Blue Hole he literally dances attendance. At the click of the Jägermeister's fingers he does what he's told, with an affectionate hop-skip-and-a-jump. He always answers with the musically docile words *'Yes boss'*, before pronking off like a Springbok to do his next designated chore. I'm nigh on convinced that 'Martin the Moomin' has some kind of learning difficulty, such is his lustful acquiescence.

I'm lucky compared to most, and I know it. So do the other staff, some of whom refer to me as the Jägermeister's 'golden boy'. I've a relatively easy ride for a while. He makes me feel like I've been *selected*. But does he want something in return?

The Jägermeister takes an avid interest in what I do outside of work. You know he can be strangely paternal at times. It's hard to imagine someone who can be so courteous and yet so scheming at the same time. Anyway, it's considered a privilege to be one of the Jägermeister's 'blue boys'. The Jägermeister is fond of indoctrinating those who dare to enter his fanatical zone. So for a while I'm the Jägermeister's golden boy........I'm the Jägermeister's Apprentice.

Suddenly and unexpectedly the Jägermeister summons me with a rather waspish leer. Then I get this: "Buddy....heh buddy my boy....You've got to be ultra careful. They're going to get moody. The mob is a moody movement." *Thanks for the warning* - I think to myself.

He says stuff. Intense stuff. Stuff that stays in my head. "Expect the unexpected."
I know how to read between the lines...

He takes an unremittingly keen interest in me really. He's like the big brother I never had. Sometimes he beckons me, but not with his finger, with a hiss. His hisses rattle through his teeth. Then they rattle through my brain. "Sssssssssssss." They're indoctrinating and puckish hisses and I'm privileged enough to be constantly bombarded with them!!! He often leans forward and quips: "It's them and us Buddy...them and us." There's something temperate about his declarations. This guy knows what he's doing. At least it seems as if he has some kind of seriously suave plan. The Jägermeister doesn't say 'it's them and us' to anyone else in this goddamn hole, but he whispers it to me on several occasions. Why me? I'm plunged into a 'whose side are you on?' state of mind. To me there's much more to life than simply the Irish versus the English or the working class against the nobility. I'm going to buck the Jägermeister's 'them and us' theory and splash a curve of colour into this blue military brothel. Not in an act of awkwardness, but in a critical stance for individuality and liberty.

On another occasion the Jägermeister enquires cryptically and with a degree of wit: "friend or foe?" I reply with a slightly uneasy chuckle, but declare nothing. He's riding a solitary wave but needs some kind of comradeship. That is to say, the Jägermeister requires *me* to join him in his undercover quest. The Jägermeister is out alone on a bluff *most* of the time. However, there is this attractive mystery woman. I chat with her, just the once, for a while, as she sits perched on a stool at The Blue Hole bar. Blonde. Attractive. Intelligent. She's drinking Sancerre and wearing a grey suit. Sophisticated. Serious...."Very pragmatic isn't he? Seems to have a contingency plan for everything!" she utters, nodding her head in the general direction of the Jägermeister. Her crafty words make me think - *the Jägermeister already has some sort of backup. Perhaps he isn't quite so all alone. After all.*

The Jägermeister is committed to redeem his country from the seizing grip of republicanism. One day he hands me a small blue butterfly brooch. It's a strange gift; an odd accessory to give to another man. But is it significant? Is he planting incriminating evidence on me? Or is he trying to tell me something? Cryptically? Maybe this is his way of telling me to get myself out of this blue mess. Maybe I'm in real danger? When he hands me the butterfly, this is what ruptures through my mind - *Fly away Papillon. Go now. Before its too late. Fly away. Liberate yourself. Release...let loose...go.* Silly really. It certainly seems as if the Jägermeister is trying to teach me something though. Why can't he just be goddamn normal? If he has something to say to me, why doesn't he just come out with it straight? This is like living in a blue hell. Am sick of his perplexing riddles, his weird shit. Am beginning to feel slightly brainwashed actually. Well anyway, I do want to get away from The Blue Hole, and if I could, I'd fly away right now. Yet sadly, I think I would fly away as a somewhat tainted butterfly, and not a fine-looking, colourful, and freethinking one.

I know I've ventured into murky waters. I've penetrated the Liechester mafia core. So has the Jägermeister. It's staining us both. To most the Jägermeister is mystifying; like a sorcerer. But really, at least for the time being anyway, he's a trapped and skirmishing figure. The Jägermeister is fighting an obscure battle. The forces of darkness are extremely strong here.

The Jägermeister often slams his tumbler down in a delinquent manner. It's unusual to witness such a refined looking man behave in such an uncivil manner. His actions seem to signify an imminent sense of dread or even finality. It's as if he's trying to warn us, that there's an abominable conflict on the cards. "Rack 'em up," he brusquely demands on occasion. This is his way of asking us to prepare him an alcoholic beverage. Immediately. Even the manner in which he goes about something as simple as this is quite extraordinarily brattish. "Just an aperitif!" His comical excuse, as he joyously downs his third shot of Jäger within the hour. For much of the time the Jägermeister is quite entirely drunk and gets away with it. He knows what he's doing though. He isn't like a drunken, bungling sort of fool, if you know what I mean. Actually, he spends even more of his time acting drunk, and gets away with that too. "I'm not really *sooooooooh* stormy you know?" My intuition already tells me that he's playacting most of the time. Nevertheless, despite his bogus drunken behaviour, there is, beyond all reasonable doubt, a 'real' storm brewing.

The Jägermeister eats enormous meals. He never prepares them himself. Like royalty he signals for a round of drinks to be sent over. If truth be told, he conducts himself like a tyrannical prince..."Let's have a proper spot of English nosh," trumpets the Jägermeister one inconsequential day. He's proud to be an Englishman. Typically he divulges very little about himself. On this occasion though he's showing his true colours. Mind you he only lets you know what he wants you to know about him. He demands in stentorian voice: "Let's have a roast! A proper roast dinner with all the trimmings! For all my handsome staff." The chef bends over backwards to fulfill his request. It's a Wednesday. A roast dinner is the last thing he's considered cooking. Morpheye and Pudding aren't around. He often curries favour with his personnel when their backs are turned. He's a shrewd character. That's for sure. Our requisitioned roast turns out to be a delicious feast. "Magnificent! Absolutely hunky-dory!" the Jägermeister exclaims affectedly a couple of hours later as our Sunday beef banquet, on a Wednesday, is placed dutifully before us. His greedy eyes widen to the size of the Yorkshire Puddings on his plate, and then, with an imperative royal nod, he grants us permission to begin dining with him....as if it's a special privilege. Nonetheless, we do actually eat like Kings. To a certain extent our hearts and minds are won over by our blue-blooded boss. He gets to us through our stomachs. He indulges and cajoles us.

"Are you absorbing the protocol, Buddy?" The Jägermeister is rhetorically jocular, but his inquiry is also laced with an underlying gravity. Feels like I'm being indoctrinated by a frivolous hypocrite. I'm actually being groomed by a secret service intelligence spy.

As time wears on I begin to notice contradictions in his character. I wonder what bullshit he's been feeding Morpheye and Pudding. In the midst of it all their attitude towards me suddenly changes. Is their dramatic change in attitude towards me exclusively because of my interest in journalism or is it also because of some slippery mistruth? Have they been misinformed by the double-crossing Jägermeister? I'm the Jägermeister's most potent weapon. It's not pleasant being a human weapon; being wrapped in another person's fate. The Jägermeister is dragging me down with him.

He calls me 'Little Buddy'. It's amusing at first, becomes grindingly belittling in the end. 'Little Buddy' is what the Jägermeister calls me. So 'little Buddy' is what I'm stuck with. This is emotional dwarfing; an attempt to cut me down in size. His language is often asymmetrical in this way. "Little Buddy - you're sensitive. That's what it is, you're sensitive like me. You and me have that in common." I kinda fall for his mock tenderness. He talks about me 'having potential', several times in fact. Well my 'potential' doesn't get me very far does it? To him I'm like someone he's chosen. Someone he's recruited. Moulded. Apprentisized.

The Jägermeister claims: "I've taught you *everything* you know." He hasn't. That's a lie. He definitely teaches me one thing though - how to be insincere. I'm no longer fooled by his flattery. I begin to start mistrusting *everything* he says. That is from the precise moment that he claims to have taught me *everything* I know. Of course he hasn't taught me **everything** I know.

Everything he says now sounds spun. All that champagne and *Jägermeister* I assume, is starting to cloud his brain.

The Jägermeister doesn't walk to work, he marches. Seemingly without a friend in the world, he battles on to salvage this loutish town, striding powerfully as he goes. He walks fast, astonishingly fast. Everything marks the Jägermeister out as someone important: his resounding voice, his bulging wallet, his 'for Queen and country walk'. He is far too conspicuous to be a spy. Isn't he?

Popularity can be bought. That's how it is amongst this capricious crowd anyhow. The Jägermeister has many acquaintances down the hole whom he regularly plies with free shots of his trademark tipple. His generosity appears overwhelming to the credulous folk in this town. They are easily seduced. Being popular is easy isn't it? Well, I mean, he just pretends to like everybody. To stand up for what is right. To choose to be the black sheep. Now that takes real guts. Doesn't it? Whilst the Jägermeister is sucking up to the regulars, he's also whispering stuff like this to me: "There's brokenness here...little Buddy. This place attracts bandits. Navigating these water's isn't simple. But whilst I'm at the helm I expect you to carry out my orders. Most of these punters should be condemned to the slammers. But our prisons are already brimming with rogues. Infectious this joint is....Buddy me boy. I assume you understand me. Now rack 'em up!" *What utter hypocrisy.*

This one time I get a right bollocking from Morpheye because I arrive late to work. I'm on the morning shift. Have to be at The Blue Hole at 10.00am sharp. Arrive:10.10am(approx) Morpheye proper flies off the handle. It's an intimidating occurrence. I can tell you. Morpheye is volatile. Believe. Anyhow, the thing is the only reason I'm late is because the Jägermeister was running late. That particular morning the Jägermeister insists that I wait for him to get ready at the flat so I can accompany him on the way to work. Strange really. This isn't the only time this happens. Sometimes the Jägermeister seems as if he's totally paranoid. Feels like he requires me to be with him. It's almost as if he's scared to walk alone. Weird it is. Later on in the day, When Morpheye is calmer, I explain about my lateness. Morpheye hears me out. Gives me half a lager...his way of smoothing things over with me. He's a dictator...but he can be tender. We are both on to the Jägermeister.

On another occasion....I'm walking to work with the Jägermeister. The Jägermeister is literally dragging his latest 'air hostess' girlfriend along. Stunning looking she is. A prize. She pleads: "Slow down. Slow down. Why do we have to walk so fast? I don't know why you have to walk so fast?" "Oh just hurry up." He bellows stubbornly. He has no time to talk. He's too busy walking....in the extra fast lane. The Jägermeister's mind is set elsewhere. The young woman can't keep up...has to run. It's ridiculous. I mean I'm a fast walker, but even I have to break into a trot now and again to keep up with the Jägermeister's astonishing pace.

The Jägermeister attracts trouble. One Saturday evening after work he invites some absolutely cracking looking ladies back to our flat. There's nothing unusual about that. There's a different selection of gorgeous women hanging around our apartment virtually every weekend. These particular girls stay up all night giggling along at the Jägermeister's jokes - like excitable ducklings they are. Then for some reason, at the crack of dawn, they leave our apartment and go off with my girlfriend's coat. *Big slip-up!* Have they stolen it? Or have they just blunderingly taken it by mistake? My girlfriend Petronella is livid, and of course I'm the one left to absorb her enraged seething: "Where's my fuckin coat Buddy? Where the fuck is it? Get me my bloody coat back. If I don't get it back...well you can just forget everything." She's stressing me out. Big time. She wants her coat back and that's that. She gets all hissy. Then goes into obdurate mode. This somewhat petty incident places a strain on her entire world. Petronella's coat it seems is more important than our relationship. Would she really dump me over this? Is her coat actually more important than me? It isn't my fault after all, and you know it isn't even a particularly nice coat. Could do without all her shit; all her pig-headedness. I hate it when she does this. She always seems to get her own way. Like a doddering boyfriend, I reluctantly harry the Jägermeister to make some calls...to see if he can somehow retrieve Petronella's dearly loved coat. Eventually the parents of the girl who took Petronella's coat return it to The Blue Hole. They apologize profusely on behalf of their daughter. To be fair I never thought we'd get it back. I thought it was going to be 'the day my girlfriend dumped me over her honey-coloured, fake leather, zips-a-plenty, Top Shop number.' Pheeeew. Anyhow, the strangest thing about this whole coat commotion is how apologetic this sticky-fingered girl's parents are. They're excessively remorseful. Indeed, they're virtually pleading for forgiveness. In fact, if truth be told, they're acting all terrified. The Blue Hole organization has this effect on people. Why are they so worried? Do they fear some kind of reprisal? Why do these men at the hole seem to command so much respect? This episode heightens my misgivings. There's simply no need for the parents of the girl to be quite so repentant. Extraordinary.

My relationship with Petronella is tempestuous. Our somewhat phoney affiliation is over before it begins. She could be a bundle of joy, but she could also be a bundle of misery. "We're more like soulmates than lovers," she claims. I disagree. Soulmates is stretching it a bit. Romance of any kind seems inconsequential, what with all the heavy shit churning through my mind and all. Now just isn't the time for me to give my heart to another.

One evening I return to our flat. Find the Jägermeister riffling through a bunch of documents in a silver trunk. He seems surprised to see me. His cheeks turn crimson. He reacts all funny, like a little boy caught in the act of doing something naughty, like stealing a cookie from the cookie jar. It's rare to catch the Jägermeister off guard. There's something dodgy about that silver trunk. Or at least, something dodgy inside it. Is there some incriminating evidence in it? Is the Jägermeister's true identity hidden in there? There are secrets in the bowels of that silver trunk.

There are cinematic promotional posters of James Bond films all around the lounge in our flat. The artful Jägermeister has put them all up. Painstaking work. It really is quite some display. One of my mates says: "Ay Buddy, bloody obsessed with James Bond ain't eh your flat mate?" He's got a point. Is the Jägermeister trying to tell me something? Something I already know.

The Jägermeister's need to keep everyone close to him under surveillance is acute. He even installs a bugging device and a CCTV system in our flat. Don't know why he has this system of surveillance. Don't know what he's trying to expose or who he's trying to ensnare. But I do know one thing for sure: that the Jägermeister is being conspicuously controlling. What's more, it's getting worse. Never ask him about anything he's associated with. Don't think I'd be in the circumstance I'm in if I was questioning him all the time. It's my laid back and unquestioning nature which has got me this far. The Jägermeister's got enough on his plate without having his right hand man asking probing questions all the time. I'm intuitive enough to recognise this. I remain as blasé as I can.

I notice that the Jägermeister spends half his life on his mobile phone. Not that that in itself is of any particular significance, it's merely an observation of mine. Nonetheless, his mobile phone is like his companionable other half. Always seems to have limitless free phone calls on it. Never minds any of his staff using it. Could be a way of keeping track of us. I suppose. Of course, he'll have the dialled numbers of anyone who's used his treasured phone stored on the call register. Should have anyway. Could use a scanner or a cell tracker to sneakily listen into our conversations at a later date. See if he can truly trust us. Wouldn't put it past him. Phone hacking that is. Wouldn't put anything past him. This man is capable of anything.

This one time there are two troublemakers in the bar. Off their heads they are. Causing a real fracas. Upsetting some of the Blue Hole regulars. At first we're having difficulty making the louts leave the premises. Eventually the Jägermeister becomes incensed by their insolence. Fishes his beloved mobile phone out from somewhere within the cool lining of his beige corduroy jacket.....and pretends to call the police...doesn't he. Even acts as if he's talking to the police in front of them. Horror-struck they are. It's enough to make the chisits run. The Jägermeister just stands there, as cool as a cucumber, plops his companionable other half back into his pocket: "That takes care of those juvenile delinquents." This is a typical *agent provocateur* manoeuvre from the Jägermeister. He's a slick blighter. Of course he doesn't want the police to come, that would reflect badly on *the business*.

The Jägermeister doesn't really trust anybody. He doesn't really let anyone into his life. Mortals come and go but never get close to him. The staff turnover at The Blue Hole is very high (must be breaking some kinda record). Now I realise the bar industry is renowned for high staff turnover, but rarely do people work here for much more than a couple of weeks. They leave of course for an assortment of reasons, but in the main they leave because they realise there's something sinister about the place. I, on the other hand, carry on working here....because I've got a screw loose, no doubt. I'm even mad enough to move into a flat with the Jägermeister. Tom, one of the other barmen, also moves in at a later date. Tom is, incidentally, another of John Pudding's nephews. Like I say, they like to keep it in the family at The Blue Hole. Pudding wants to know, more than ever, all that is going on.

The Jägermeister's behaviour is inexplicable to most. Outwardly it's as if he has feelings of culpability that are tearing him apart. The life of a secret government agent must be a crushingly lonely one....when you stop and think about it. To feel like a culprit but to try and not act like one must be a tremendously complex role. To be someone you're not is just like living a lie, isn't it? Nevertheless, the Jägermeister has almost everyone fooled.

"About time we went out on the lash again isn't it little Buddy?" The very next day we're on a train down to London. Just for a few cordial drinks! It's the Jägermeister's liquid loosening idea. Our liquor laced binge starts at Harvey Nichols Bar in Knightsbridge. Couple of double measures of Woodford Reserve down the hatch. Quickly followed by half a dozen Yo! Sushi!' conveyor belt dishes. It's only 11.15am. A rather unsettling brunch. The Jägermeister *kind-heartedly* settles the bill. He pampers me. He butters me up.

Here, inside smoky Central London the Jägermeister tells me his father is dead. Has he forgotten? Just the other day he was talking to me about his father as if he was still alive. Why would anybody lie about the death of their father like this? What a bungled attempt at emotional blackmail. Now I'm on high alert. The lies are getting on top of him. Think he must know he's losing control.

At first I think the Jägermeister is out of the ordinary. Now I know he's a snake. So, why the inconsistencies? Why is he lying? He's attempting to gain my sympathy. Attempting to control me in order to control Pudding and Morpheye. Play me off against them. Manipulate me. Like he manipulates everyone. That mendacious day quickly becomes one big drunken stupor. I stumble into some of London's swankiest bars feeling disillusioned....feeling like I don't want to be drunk....feeling like I don't want to be hanging about with this misleading man. My faith in humanity takes another blow. *Who can you really trust?* - I wonder cynically to myself.

Few days later...I'm in the tunnel. "Take-it," he bellows in an imperial manner bordering on the despotic. The Jägermeister often has this urgent tone of voice. He can be very manipulative with it. He hands me a tightly wrapped and compact brown paper package. The curious package is about the size of a video tape and about as heavy as a bag of sugar. The Jägermeister informs me it's viagra. *Maybe there is viagra inside the package, but it could be anything?* "Take it to our flat. Put it behind the tv in my bedroom. Run along now little Buddy," he hisses. I'm oscillating..."Just do it"...I'm in a panicky whirl..."Don't stop and talk to anyone" is his parting forewarning. It's obviously important to him. Could it be cocaine? Is it heroin? Has this 'product', whatever it is, been intercepted? Is this always his way of getting dirty shit off the streets before it reaches the black market? I've got too involved.....not got out quick enough. I do as he commands. Feel like a freak. The deed is done. Package safely deposited. Behind tv. As requested. I am after all the Jägermeister's apprentice. Part of our working agreement is that I do what he says. Isn't it? After all, he is my boss. It's my job to do what he tells me to do. Isn't it? I'm submissive - feel like I have to comply. Compliance, of course, is just what he's looking for. He's exploiting my deference. My obedience. My naiveté. Feel like a drug mule. Feel like a subordinate puppet. I am The Jägermeister's docile stooge.

Later that evening: "Don't expect me to do anything like that ever again." I declare, and I mean it. This is the moment our *friendship* evaporates.

Is the Jägermeister testing me? Don't want to be his scapegoat. His mule. His human weapon. Do Pudding or Morpheye know about these dealings? These errands? Pretty goddamn sure they don't.

Later on the Jägermeister slips me a tenner. A tenner! Tries to keep me all sweet with a tenner! "Sssssssssssss. Pocket-it." Money can't sway me. No money. My pockets remain empty. I know that I can't take much more of this. I want to get out of here. Need to get out of here. The Jägermeister is choking me with his hissing and his grooming and all of his dodgy shit.

The Jägermeister is trying to maintain some sort of control. He chooses to sit disturbingly close to me on the sofa that particular evening. He's too close for comfort. There are two other perfectly comfortable armchairs in the same room with nobody sitting on them. So why doesn't he sit on one of them? He then looks at me in a way that nobody has ever looked at me before. His eyes claim me. He acts as if I belong to him. He can sense my loyalties are drifting and when you're stuck in a regime like this your loyalties aren't meant to drift. Feel crowded. His closeness whirls improperly around me. He infringes my personal space. My masculinity is maimed. I no longer want to know this man. He interferes with my space to have power over me. To control me. To invade me. To be in charge.

Bang. I freeze in place. I am dead......

I'm not dead, but I might as well be. A blinding white wind blows through my mind. Surrounds me. Encapsulates me. There is now a trigger inside my head. Panic is blown into my brain. The impact is death threatening. I'm not prepared for this. Not at all.

I'm taking a shower late at night. It's all over in a matter of seconds. The door to the bathroom flies open. The Jägermeister appears. There are two other unfamiliar men there, one on each side of him. He's brandishing a gun. He's pointing it right at me. Can only be 2 metres away. Then it happens. A massive explosing bang. A detonation takes place right in front of my face. It splits the air, drowning out the sound of running water. The noise is deafening in such a confined space. I'm like a deer caught in headlights - I'm in a state of paralyzing bewilderment. Have you ever been unsure if you are alive or dead? The skin on my body contracts. It's as if my skin has come into contact with something corrosive – like a flesh eating acid or something. Feels like I've shrunk. Then my colour drains away. Instantaneously I can't see or hear. Magnesium. Everything bright. Everything White. There's ringing in my ears. Can't hear my own voice. Am in a deep state of panic and shock - as if I've been momentarily disembodied - as if I've been fleetingly incorporeal. Feel detached and frozen to the spot at one and the same time. It's as if I'm trying to get away but my body isn't letting me. My senses are possessed. Incapacitated. Everything seems still. I am still. Like the passage of time has come to a sudden halt. Seconds of stunned silence pass. Start to howl out loud just so I can hear myself. Scared that I've maybe gone deaf. Unsure of whether this has just happened I pinch myself real hard. I begin to wince, shutting my eyes tightly for a few

seconds and then opening them again, hoping to just wake up in bed.
Everything is still very white. I glance towards my feet, looking for
signs of blood in the water, but there's nothing. I've not been hit with a
bullet. There's no blood, no discernible wound. I am still here. Minutes
pass and the door stays closed. My eyes are fixed on the door, as if
waiting for the same collision to happen again. For a while I am an
ensnared wasp trapped under an overturned glass.

The world moves on, but I am left standing still, unable to
move on, for a while. Feel freeze-framed. Crippling it is. Stepping out
of the shower is like coming out of suspended animation; as if I've
momentarily been stuck in a time warp. This moment, which lasts no
more than ten seconds, is stuck with me now forever. I re-live this
moment over and over again.

Shit I'm scared. I'm now alone in the flat, wondering what the
hell has just happened. The Jägermeister's gone out after his impious
deed. But when will he be back? And what will he do next? Our
relationship has been detonated. He has detonated it. To put it mildly
I'm overwhelmed. I'm frightened into a silence. I feel transformed,
altered somewhat. I stand there unmoving like a dummy in the shower
for a post-traumatic while. Too long. 30 minutes or so, without hardly
moving an inch.

Terror can do strange things to you. Part of my brain, I fear,
has stopped working. Don't know for sure. Perhaps some damage may
have been caused. Have endured an unusually intense adrenalin rush.
Debilitating. Consuming. Numbed with terror. It's as if the world has
closed in on me. Confusion has struck me like an irrevocable poison.
These kinds of events do not explain themselves. I can't really make
any sense of what is happening. I'm demented with fear. I'm left in a
kind of limbo. I don't know what to do. My confidence, my spirit,
wrenched abruptly from me. The Jägermeister *must* know that the
warning shot has hit home. I wonder sometimes if he ever blasts a gun
at anyone else? And if so, how do they react? How do they cope? I
would like to know.

I manage to get myself into my bed which is just a single
mattress on the floor. I curl myself up into a stiff ball of resistance. It's
as if I'm trying to make myself undetectable. I lay there rigid, frozen in
a foetal position, wishing I'm back in my mum's womb, wishing I'm
somewhere safe. Am as soundless as a human being can be. Am as
quiet as a dead man. I say my prayers. Silently. Still have some kinda
faith. Somehow. Clutch my hands real tight and pray like mad. Am

scared to sleep. Fear he might kill me in my bed. Am like a stiff rabbit ready for the pot. Something dies in my brain that night. Manage to fall asleep though.........somehow.

Morning. My whole body - stiff as a stake. Never been this stiff before - the new me. At a snail's pace I unbend myself back to life. Feel unfleshy - as if I've been turned into wood. Slowly endeavor to unfold my limbs. Can't unfold my mind, that's like a fossil set in stone. I carry it like a stunned burden inside my skull. I'm a remnant of my former self. Punctured, flat, traumatised, heavy, jumpy, slow, stressed, and stunned – all of these things I am.

The world's like an entirely different place now. I'm so stunned I feel disfigured. Less nimble. Tense. Stare at myself in the mirror. I *am* still alive. A bewildered grimace is planted on my face. My face feels like it's been set in a mask. To reassure myself that I am actually still alive I roll my tongue, whilst looking wide-eyed into the mirror. My eyes are frozen, wide with shock. They look disturbingly darker...like the eyes of a wary owl. My feelings have taken possession of my face. Don't like the way I look. Don't want to look at myself anymore. His gun has dishonored my flesh.

Was he trying to kill me? Or is this just his way of letting me know that he *could* kill me if he wanted to. Feel muted. Feel ashamed.

The echo of the gunshot comes back to me in waves, like a distorted and malignant techno sound. I don't protest - too traumatised, too shocked, for that. For some time I do everything without talking. Remain relatively uncommunicative.....for years. Avoid situations where I may have to speak. Lost my voice 'aint I. It's not healthy, I know, but I'll survive, and be back. Just give me time.

It's a gross injustice. A blatant infringement of my human rights. This is man-on-man domestic violence. Extremism, if you like. I've been acutely acquainted with death. I've become *too* conscious of how easy it would be to simply be snuffed out. My life has been taken away from me; now my life is not my own. A 'whose behind the door' kind of fear exists in this abode now......exists in me. I have to get out.

It's an unusual case, a case that will probably never go to court. I take it as a warning to say nothing - to keep my mouth shut. Might just as well have cut off my tongue or sewn my lips together. From that moment all my mum's years of dedicated nurturing destroyed. My cheekiness. My golden invincibility. My smile. Gone. A senseless halt. A senseless halting of an innocent man. I plummet into an expressionless world....a hushed tragedy.

Now he's reverted to speaking to me through the barrel of a gun. Aren't his oratorical skills up to scratch anymore? *How masterful of him! How courageous!* - I think. Are his actions coerced? Are his actions governed by a higher authority? Is it a masterstroke of military might or an ungallant act of lunacy? Couldn't he just have had a little chat with me?

Have been his 'apprentice' for almost a year and now he's terrorizing me. Now he's trying to defeat me. Is he scared himself? Is he scared that his true identity will be exposed? Is that more important than my well being...my life?

I used to walk without any real consciousness of *'self'*. In actual fact, reckon I had quite a confident swagger. Now it's as if I've become *too* conscious of myself. My self. So much so that I appear rather awkward. Guilty even. The composure that I was once unaware of possessing has been lost; it has been taken from me. Now I feel like an angry flatfooted buffoon - all clumsy and doubtful and scared. I am different now. I have changed. He has changed me.

I sense things are coming to an end at The Blue Hole, never dream it will be quite like this though. Suddenly life seems full of unanswered questions. What should I do now? Should I get out of here? Is curiosity getting the better of me? Am I just a victim of circumstance? Or am I bringing this all on myself? Do I deserve this? Do I somehow deserve to be shot at? Do I deserve to feel so stunned....so guilty? Am questioning everything? Am more philosophical now than ever.

What is really bizarre is that the Jägermeister did this with two other men alongside him. Who are these men? Do they think the gun was loaded with a bullet? Perhaps they think I'm dead? Why has he chosen two men to witness this? To impress them? To jolt them aswell maybe? To prove to them what he's capable of? To let them know that they might be next? To kill two birds…three birds with one blast?

The Jägermeister is, like I say, a clever and manipulating bugger. I wonder if his actions sit heavily on his soul? I wonder if he's doing more harm than good? I wonder if he *really* knows what he's doing? I wonder if he even has a conscience at all? I wonder...

"Drinnnnggg...drinnnnggg."   It's   the   Jägermeister.
"Drinnnnggg...drinnnnggg."   He's   calling   me!
"Drinnnnggg...drinnnnggg."   Am alarmed, to say the least.
"Drinnnnggg...drinnnnggg."   I answer. "What's happened to your

tongue little Buddy?" His voice is pitched differently. Sounds psychopathic. What's happened to his well-bred charm? Well I suppose charm can only take you so far can't it? Indeed, he now speaks in traumatising taunts: "Where are you little Buddy?"(*What business is that of yours?* - I think to myself)

"I'm in a youth hostel."

"You can meet some very strange people in places like that little Buddy.............let the spy probe begin. SSSssssss." he hisses rabidly down the phone. "You can't blag a blagger," he clips. Then hangs up. His way of saying goodbye. His way of getting the last word. I guess. His words come back to me like a sanctioning boomerang...'*You can meet some very strange people in places like that little Buddy...Let the spy probe begin...You can't blag a blagger.*' His words reverberate in my mind. The Jägermeister has a clutch on my senses like an evil giant. I'm being controlled. I need to get away from this control. I need to reclaim my own mind....my own life.

It's the beginning of May, 2000. It's the day after the Jägermeister shot at me. I'm in the capital of Wales of all places. I check out the prices of some local bed & breakfast guesthouses in Cardiff - they're too expensive for me. So instead, I stay in a youth hostel. At first the hostel seems ok but after the Jägermeister's call, it seems like a creepy place to be. Deadly.

Why Wales? Well, the next day is a very big day for me. I've an interview at Cardiff's school of journalism, arguably the best school of journalism in the UK.

I'm lost in thought, too busy replaying the scene in my head from the night before. Can't concentrate on anything. Let alone this. My performance at interview is poor. Exceptionally poor. I know I've blown it. Am in the worst state of mind ever...when I need to be at my best. Can't forgive this man...this terrorizing man. Worst luck heh? I tell you what this guy teaches me...he teaches me to feel, dread, know, that somewhere out there, brutality is hiding, waiting, to pounce on me again.

My hair appears to have been streaked with grey overnight. The slightest unexpected noise now startles me. The sound of a drunken wolf whistle, the honk of a car, even a mobile ring-tone is enough to make me jump out of my skin.

I've been stunned. When I *finally* tell my friends about what has happened they're stunned too. My trauma seems to make others a bit traumatized. *Abuse* is contagious you know......can have infectious consequences.

Comments from my mates like: "Buddy mate - yuhinna trancelike state mate! Look like yuv seen a ghost or summit" and "Yuh look right shattered Buddy mate!" and "Why the sudden silence?" don't really help matters. It's obviously written across my face. I know I'm in a terrible state, but some things, I guess, just can't be undone.

One of my closest friends asserts: "Buddy man dis ain't ow it was meantuh'be." A compassionate, yet curious statement. This is exactly how it was *meant* to be. I wonder how he thinks life is *meant* to be. I never ask him. Don't want to bother him. Anyway, whether it was *meant* or *not meant* to be, my life is pretty screwed up.

Another pal tells me: "Don't worry. Someone bigger and harder always comes along." The problem, I believe, is that there isn't anybody bigger and harder than Morpheye. I've seen the violence he's capable of. I've seen him fight. And he fights like a pitiless animal. Worst of all he believes in violence. He believes his vicious acts are, in some way, justified in the eyes of the Catholic Church. This in turn makes me fearful of what he might do to me one day.

Why don't I just get the hell out of here and go straight to the police. Well, I don't trust the police here. Most of them are wrapped around Morpheye's little finger. Besides, I think most of them are racist pigs anyway. I believe our local police force is institutionally racist. Believed this for quite some time. Liechester is a bigoted police state. It has all the deceptive accoutrements it needs to be wholly dogmatic yet outwardly upright. I certainly don't feel like I can turn to them for help. In any case, I do keep on living in the same flat as the Jägermeister, and I do keep on working at The Blue Hole. Crazy. I know....but that's exactly what I do. I do ask myself - *Are you mad?* What can I say. I'm a passionate guy: young, wild and curious. Serious even. This is a writer's dream. Isn't it?

I need some freedom – some breathing space. Essentially I need some time to write.

Now let me recapitulate for a moment. Morpheye exercises a shadowy, but all pervading influence behind the scenes. He purposefully avoids the spotlight of publicity. He's a mercurial man with a violent temper. Above all else, fear is his debilitating weapon. Morpheye is always hovering. Always watching, like a hawk in the sky he is. He's the brain behind the bricks and seen by many as a local hero. Morpheye is a man for the underdog; an honourable rogue. He modestly attempts to conceal his success and wealth (One time he even pretends he's on the dole. His theatrical endeavours are incredibly convincing). Nevertheless, let there be no doubt, Morpheye is an extremely powerful man in this town. He's cunning. He has cunning blood. He'll be dreadfully tricky to topple. Even the Jägermeister is finding it virtually impossible to bring him down. Let's not forget just how influential a man Morpheye is. He's super alert and without equal in sheer gutsy determination. He hates the middle-classes. His boozer is absolutely brimming with rogues and rascals. Morpheye's sense of radicalism seems to be spreading, not just amongst his regular punters, but across the entire township. He has single-handedly shaped a local have-not mood bordering on hysteria. This working-class settlement is now plagued with a climate of fanaticism. In Liechester there are neon blue cafés, restaurants and bars popping up all over the place. Morpheye is responsible for this neon blue surge. There are revolutionary pockets of insurgency everywhere in this town – Morpheye's expansion is rampant. He has his own insurance and financial organizations as well. He wants complete power and he fiercely resents British interference. Morpheye can dictate with his eyes, and his eyes are on the Jägermeister and me like never before. Morpheye wants to rule. Nothing will stand in his way. Does everyone share his selfish dream? I don't think so. It's a tainted, egotistical vision. This town is being reorganized according to an Irish/American blueprint, but most people are indifferent to it all. In their ignorance they allow it to happen. In their ignorance they allow Morpheye's blue insurgency to spread. He controls the pavements and the working class people of this town. He even has the police in his proletarian pockets. Indeed, the flames of revolution are already here, blowing in the wind, blatantly and victoriously. It seems he controls everything in Liechester, except the Jägermeister perhaps, and me and my pen.

Believe it or not I'm still useful in this barmy situation. The Jägermeister is flinching. He's losing his nerve. Things are getting too hot. He uses me to take some of the focus away from him. The shooting saga is radical. To Pudding and Morpheye I suddenly seem rattled, shady even. Suddenly I'm the centre of attention. I take the lime light away from the Jägermeister, especially now I'm acting all dodgy and shifty as hell. In this regard I'm helpful - as a human distraction. I make the Jägermeister's espionage less conspicuous. Crucially though, I take Morpheye's vigilant eyes away from him for a while. In their ignorance Pudding and Morpheye suspect me, they think I'm the problem.

Liechester is full of racists. To a certain extent the extremists reflect what many folk think. Some of the locals are better at hiding their prejudices than others, but the bigotry is here. Anyhow, racial tension is strained enough as it is, without Morpheye irrationally whipping up peoples hatreds even more. Liechester has been termed a multicultural melting pot, but it's fast becoming a multi-cultural boiling pot. There are white only and Asian only 'ghettos' emerging across Liechester. Like I say, Morpheye and his clan are building neon blue divisions as fast as they can, and nobody dares to challenge them. This is an insurrection driven by Morpheye. This is the front line for global terrorism. He's determined, at all costs, to bring this society down. Can the Jägermeister stop him? Well, I wonder about that...

There are moments of unwarranted celebration. Some locals are hugging me, kissing me and slapping me on the back in public, and for what? For keeping my mouth shut? For staying silent like a mouse? These Liechester folk are like blind sheep. Now isn't the time for merriment and celebration....Is it?

Am I being a coward by keeping my mouth shut? Or is this the best thing to do? Am I allowing something monumental and ghastly to take place by remaining silent? I'm kinda haunted by this moral dilemma.

It appears the racial Armageddon many fear is upon us. There will be carnage on the streets soon. There are shocking cries and rumblings of terrorism and anti-terrorism in this town. The Blue Hole isn't an anti-terrorism cell, is it? Is it? Well, that's what some folk are saying. The notion that these bully boys are anti-terrorists is mind-boggling to me. The suggestion seems scandalous, unforgivable even. They're the bloody terrorists themselves. Aren't they?

Suddenly and quite unexpectedly I'm approached by this tall stranger. I'm just walking down the street, minding my own business, when he comes up to me. He's a pensive and unsmiling man. Rugged. Pallid. Looks like he's been spending too much of his time lurking in other people's shadows. That type. Know what I mean? He kindly informs me: "There's a lot more to this than you realize!" Should reply: "Thanks for your illuminating words of wisdom but there's even more to this than *you* realize - you goose!" but my old cockiness fails me. I react with a simple and submissive:

"Oh right. Eeeerh ok. Cheers then." Feel a bit besieged. As if I don't know there's more to this. *Does this man know everything or something?* - I speculate. Flippantly. Of course he doesn't. I tell you about such specific details because I believe in their significance. Their significance to this situation is, I believe, unveiling. Nonetheless, at this specific moment in time, I still feel stunned and confused. Am I being monitored? Followed by obscure mortals – murky mortals I can't see? Will I ever be free again? That beleaguering afternoon I contemplate an entire life without human freedom? For sure this guy is working undercover. For someone. But who's side is he on? And what am I supposed to do now? Weird innit?

Their sinister operation isn't going according to plan. It has become a bit of a calamity. Nobody is singing from the same hymn book. The blame has to lie somewhere...

Let's not forget that Pudding & Morpheye are unaware of the Jägermeister's harsh actions towards me behind the scenes. What I mean to say is....they don't know that he has scared the living daylights out of me in the shower with a gun. I'm not meant to leave the hole so soon, that isn't part of the arrangement. They think that if they look after me well enough, I'll have no reason to leave, let alone be their enemy. But this kind of terrorising gangster flash lifestyle signifies nothing to me - absolutely nothing.

Morpheye thinks I'm a thieving scum bag (I've taken £60 off his premises - don't forget). In light of these circumstances...he forces me to flee. This is his patch. He wants me off it. Pudding on the other hand seems nervous and hunted. He's always been suspicious of my journalistic intention. Now he's particularly paranoid. Pudding would get rid of me, if he could do so without too much of a fuss. But that would be way too difficult. The duplicitous Jägermeister has built me up to be well-liked. Too many people know me for Pudding to get away with that. Reckon I've actually lent the Jägermeister some credibility as well. Nonetheless, even before the Jägermeister blasts a gun at me, I'm well ready to leave the hole, been growing sick of the gloom 'aint I. Now I'm keen to make tracks whilst I am still....well, whilst I'm still alive.

I'm doing my best to gather my scrambled wits together. I know I have to get away. Away from my old job at The Blue Hole. Away from the barbarian banter. Away from the violent hustle. The lies. The deception. I know I have to get as far away as possible from this erroneous town.

I've a more than fervent itch to call on a dear old friend of mine in San Francisco. Right now, I urgently need his friendship. This contest is growing too large for me. It's engulfing me...ruining me. I will leave The Pudding & Morpheye partnership and the Jägermeister to sort out their differences alone and unhindered. Liechester 'aint big enough for the four of us...*'Buddy...be good! You can't blag a blagger!* ***Bang I am stunned*** *I'm not a clever man! Don't think you're getting your old job back!*

I decide to take the fugitive trail to San Francisco. I head for the West coast of America possessed with bewilderment and outrage.

CHAPTER 5 - ESCAPE TO SAN FRANCISCO.

"A colourful past means a colourful future."

Blue nailed gipsy woman

So, its May 2000. I take a plane from London to San Francisco. In an attitude of rebellion I reach the other side. "You can't blag a blagger!" I proclaim with a mouthful of satisfaction as I set foot on Yankee soil. I'm now in the United States of America, and that in itself is electrifying.

My friend, Taige Shine, is living as an illegal immigrant in San Francisco. He's apprehensive about coming to the airport to meet me. So, when I touch down after my taxing 14-hour flight, I make my own way over to his apartment feeling slightly disorientated. Relieved to have made it over here. Relieved to have escaped my past. It is, of course, also splendid to see my old buddy Taige.

Taige is one of my best friends from secondary school. We grew up in each other's pockets, in a valley somewhere in the middle of England. We have a lot of catching up to do. 'Ain't really in the mood for chatting mind, but needless to say, we get blind drunk together that evening. Just like old pals do.

Taige is a bartender at an Irish swing-door bar called Cassidy's. He plies me with booze all evening until everything is nicely out-of-focus. By midnight I can hardly stand up off my bar stool without falling over, what with all the Guinness in my gut. Like a gun-dazed fugitive I run into the arms of America. Well, to be more precise, I run into the arms of an Irish school friend of mine in San Francisco. What I need is to get out of my mind, and so begins my spirited swirl into oblivion.

I drink like a maniac (Think if I drink enough my memories will drain out of me). Of course my alcohol induced attempts to forget don't work. I keep on remembering. Spend much of my time re-living Blue Hole moments. Can't help it. I'm disaffected. I now see the world through polluted eyes. The phantoms are here, like an exasperating neon blue screensaver in my consciousness.

The sofa I crash on is shabby. Possibly the shabbiest sofa in the world. I'm pissed most of the time, so I manage to sleep on it like a floundering dog. It's my bed. It's where I lay in lethargy. Hiding. Surviving. I'm safe here. Away from it all. Away from the blueness.

The morning after my arrival....

I wake up with an over-fried Francisco omelette head. The searing feeling in my mind - a beastly consequence of our heavy drinking session the night before. I peel myself off my makeshift sleeping arrangement. Decide to have a bit of a hazy nose around.

Taige's home becomes my San Franciscan squatting base. It's a hippie's hang out; a pad fit for vampire habitation; a place untouched by daylight. Hangover lodge is a refuge for rebels really. Taige and his flat mates don't want any sunlight to come into the lounge. They are hiding too. The colourful tie-dye curtains are always drawn shut at hangover lodge. It makes the place debased. Despite the insalubrious conditions, life seems relatively safe here.

The apartment is smothered with a prominent layer of dead skin. There are half-dead cannabis plants scattered around the joint. The pad purely reeks of weed. The tangy scent is deep-rooted; smells like the stuff is growing out the walls. These crazy kids absolutely love the bong. A pipe full of neat green is thrust upon me the moment I arrive. That's just how it is here.

The kitchen is speckled with grease and grime and encrusted pots and pans. The loose ends of a hundred drunkenly prepared meals are strewn about the cooking area. It's a grim sight. Around me there are hordes of empty beer bottles, a Jenga tower of pizza boxes, big fat empty gherkin jars, empty coffee jars, a variety of bread crusts and a box of coco-pops.....a box of coco-pops with a single coco pop in it. Being surrounded by this contaminated mess makes me feel half-demented.

Inside the fridge....nothing but half squeezed tomato puree tubes and lidless rancid condiment pots.....*an adventurous assortment of sticky mid-morning hangover appetisers. Mmmmmm...Suppose I could have horseradish sauce on one of the loaf ends for breakfast or maybe mint sauce on toast......then again.*

My next decision...which of the full ashtrays should I sit next to in order to consume the first solid scraps to pass my lips in 2 whole days. I decide to eat standing up....as far away as possible from the ash trash. *Bon appétit,* I say to myself as I hungrily bite into one of the chewy chunky pieces of bread. I choose to eat it *au naturel* having looked through the entire stash of Freddie Francisco's gastronomic flavoured accoutrements and found nothing that tickles my fancy.

I must brave the toilet next, however destructive it might be to my health. The toilet bowl, like the ashtrays, is as good as full. Delightful. It contains the remnants of a sleep all day, party all night, philosophical existence. Whilst *flower-power* means something to me, *poo-power* means nothing. I'm out of here.

After my stomach-churning trip to the lavs, I smell my armpit, as you do sometimes when you know you smell. *God I stink.* I haven't eaten curry, but my armpit smells of curry. The tang is strong enough to smack down a rampant bull. I need to have a wash.

Hangover lodge bathroom - not much better. After my quick dip in a scum stained, pubic hair hogging bathtub, perhaps I'm marginally cleaner. I look forward to my saunter to the local corner shop, if not only for the chance to breath in and out without fear of catching some squalid unidentified disease. It's a germ-infested apartment but sure as hell its better being here than where I was before. Grateful...indebted to Taige for his peace loving generosity.

As I open the front door the Wild West sunbeams burn right into my eyes. To avoid loss of sight, I squint my eyes. After the muted blue of the hole in Liechester, the sun here seems lethal. Not use to brilliant sunshine, but glad of its presence. Feels revitalizing. Californian. Despite the strain on my eyes the streets of San Francisco look magical, what with the purple, yellow and red houses and all.

San Francisco doesn't disappoint. I experience anonymity in this flashy City. I'm touched with a fairytale feeling, similar to the one I fantasize about. This rainbow coloured, up and down picture-book settlement is charming. Will stay here for as long as I can.

We are situated just off Haight Street. It's an intriguing area of San Francisco known as Haight-Ashbury. Hippies flocked to Haight-Ashbury in the 60's. It's where the hippy movement originated. The hippy movement reached its peak with the 1967 Summer of Love. Apparently. The area around Haight Street is still a bit of a hippy ghetto in the year 2000. Let's have it.

I guess I want something supernatural to happen here. When I click my fingers I want Opal fruit candies to come splashing out of the sky and make my mouth water or I want my pockets to suddenly fill up with nothing but orange smarties. You know, something like that.

Well something colourful and rare does happen here. Not something supernatural...............something salvational.

My stay in San Francisco is an occasion for breaking away - an occasion for drunken reflection. I keep myself to myself. I give nothing away, not even a sound.

I'm massively alone. I just sit in Cassidy's and drink. Taige plies me with Guinness, Pear cider, Bourbon and looks of bafflement. Back home lager is my usual tipple, but I'm happy to just drink whatever Taige gives me. So long as it's on the house, how can I complain. Beggars can't be choosers and all that. Nothing loosens my lips though. I tell Taige nothing about my recent skirmishes and he's one of my closest friends.

It's as if I've been silenced. For a while Taige remains uncertain about what the hell is going through my mind. For some reason, I start questioning my own conscientiousness. I keep asking myself - *how responsible am I?* I know I shouldn't feel responsible for what's happened, but I still do. I'm an angry man. I fear I won't be able to disguise my fury for much longer. Here at least I don't have to. Here I can just do as I please. Can't I? San Francisco is just the kinda place I can flash my fury and ditch my reticence. Isn't it? In reality destitution is written large upon me. Like a wild animal I've gone astray. I'm traumatized. *Too* conscious of my own mortality. It's a time of rootless inebriation. I do the drink thing. I do the drug thing. I do the sex thing.

I've no itinerant plan. I just sleep wherever the party takes me. Which is anywhere and everywhere. I'm a *proper-dirty-stop-out*. I know I can crash at hangover lodge, if I need to. I know I can rely on Taige. I have a lot of meaningless sex. It's like I've fallen into some kind of inadvertent form of prostitution or something. I mean I'm not doing it for money but I'm not doing it for love either. Certainly it's not your average kind of mating. I sleep with a lot of women. Money never changes hands. I accept freebies from women: lines of cocaine, tokes on skunk-pipes, liquor laced drinks, pizza, butties, but I never take money. I sleep with them for their shelter. Their companionship. Their reassurance. It's a bonus if I get some breakfast. I prostitute myself. I prostitute myself for bed and breakfast. I prostitute myself because I'm so fucked-up.

I keep waking up wondering where the hell I am, hoping I'm at least still in San Francisco. Why've I stooped so low? I'm living on the edge. I mean I look real messed up. I've no job. Little money. Little hope. I'm losing it. Feel like a piece of meat, what with all the mattress hopping and all. Like a blob...unhuman. The unhuman blob. I'm aghast with myself. I guess I'm just trying to survive.

I'm living out of a suitcase. Always thinking - *how can I stay here and make this place my home?* Often I sit with my head in my hands, like a degraded mess. I suppose I'm a bit like a refugee. I don't want to go back to Liechester. I'm all intoxicated and loose. I'm living off Guiness. I'll soon be completely out of funds. But I'm not thinking about tomorrow. That's too much. Just living each day as it comes and each day is a decadent escapade here. I walk through the streets with a stunned head. Silent - thinking all kinds of foggy town thoughts. I let myself roam for miles and miles in this kinda hazy daze. 'Tis almost as though I've lost the plot completely. I strut around the streets of San Francisco. Endlessly. Wearing out my boots. Must have already covered half the 'up-and-down town' on foot. Gives me a sense of distance. Marvel. Exploration. Need to be outdoors. Need space. Need to feel free. Whilst walking I study the flamboyant urban pretension. I absorb as much as I can. I watch scores of people pretending to be something they're not. Despite my situation, my condition - I'm entranced by it all; suffused with intrigue.

Culturally, life is lived differently here, different to life in middle England anyhows. The streets near to hangover lodge are jammed with weird and wacky shops: ear-piercers, tattooists, hair-twisters, fortune-tellers, Eastern-Asian joss-stick traders, sex-shops, fancy-dress hirers, techno-cyberspace cafés, out-of-the-ordinary eateries, a myriad of second-hand clothing dealers, booksellers and music merchants. There are also countless effervescent brothels...boozers with the heartening stench of sweat and beer reeking out of them onto the multi-coloured boulevards. All in all there's an embellished tang of subterfuge in the air. I allow my imagination to become embroiled in this hallucinogenic mish-mash.

The area around Haight Street is like one big masquerade. Where *anything* seems likely. Even the architecture here is astonishingly ostentatious. Even the people with 'I love San Francisco' T-shirts on, seem to be having rather an untamed time. Nothing dull about this place. Routine doesn't exist here. There's an element of 'otherworldliness' about the place; a magical spiritual feeling going on. As I walk about, it's like I'm strutting in a dream, a multi-coloured rainbow and Californian-curving dream. However I'm always left wanting more. Wanting something unearthly to happen. Wanting to escape. Completely.

Am deeply impressed by what I see. I've found a scene that's wildly inspiring. San Francisco is a place where a bewildered creature like myself can feel at home. Certainly don't need a guidebook here. It's a measureless existence. No rules. No convention. No alarm clock. And dangerously strong Jack and Coke's.

The fact that Taige is an illegal immigrant in America does no one any harm. If anything, his presence in San Francisco actually enhances people's lives. He makes people laugh you see. He's a humourous soul. Taige is here illegally, but no one can really call him a bad person for discovering a less oppressive life for himself, can they? He adds to society here in his own special way. He's a harmonious blighter, really. San Francisco is a place where Taige truly belongs. He fits in here. His heart is certainly not in England. He's half English half Irish and that can make a man feel rather unsettled I reckon.

There's no cosmic reason behind him being here. There's no mythology. He just doesn't want to be in England. Let me tell you about it. Taige has a particular disdain for snobbism. He's anti-establishment. That's to say he's anti British establishment. In his mind he is an influential anarchist, but really he has no commanding political status at all. He philosophizes about meritocracy and its importance in society, but really, despite all his political ramblings, Taige Shine is a hippy at heart. If he is meant to be anywhere, well then he is meant to be here, in San Francisco.

When I see Taige for the first time in almost six years I'm shocked at how emaciated he looks. He'd always been thin, but now he looks raw-boned. Angular. I take the time to look at Taige and I mean really look at him. What I see is a weary and trembling rack of bones. A human skeleton stands before me…a cider drenched, smoky set of bones. Everytime I look at him I picture white and black images of cadaverous x-rays. That's what he makes me think of. I also notice that his eyes are blank with malnutrition and grief.

Taige is an off-the-wall bohemian with a bourbon-raddled brain. His blood is permanently diluted with liquor. He's been toppling in and out of an alienated state of consciousness for a number of years. In other words - he's an alcoholic.

Taige Shine is witty as those scarred by hardship often are. His father died when he was seventeen. The love of his life dumped him a year later. It was enough to drive him to drink. He's been living on the edge in San Francisco ever since. He's a fugitive figure in constant distress. Fears exposure. Fears being hurled back to England.

Taige looks nomadic and hippyish; like someone you'd expect to emerge from a wigwam or something. He's a man, there's no doubting that, but he often has a womanish look about him. I mean, I intermittently see a zany feminine figure prating about in front of me, but that's just Taige in thespian mode.

Despite the glorious Californian sunshine Taige's skin is a tainted blue-white. It appears as if it would be stone-cold to the touch. It's the skin of a clandestine. As I look at the colour of his skin it makes me think he doesn't have long left, and he's only twenty-four. Life in San Francisco has sucked away his human colour. Spends the bulk of his time indoors and misses much of the San Francisco sun. Shuns the daytime hours to avoid being spotted. Taige is as close to a real life human vampire as you can get.

Another remarkable thing about Taige is his hands. They're bigger than Sylvester Stallone's. At least, they're bigger than the hand imprints that Sylvester Stallone's left on a cement wall outside the entrance to the San Francisco Hard Rock Café. Taige's gargantuan hands are white, blue-veined and semi-transparent. He has prominently sharp knuckles, and his fingers disseminate outwards in a sinewy manner, like the roots of a long-haired celeriac.

When Taige is able to talk his voice is smoky and throaty. Indeed his voice appears to tremble somewhat. His words are coarse. Guttural. It's as though they've been put through some kind of scathing American language grater before reaching my ears. Sudden bursts of foul language are flanked by conked out words of civility. It's as if he's in some way brokenly apologising for being himself. "Fucking bastards uuuh. Always scrimmaging about. I'll get 'em for dis. I'm sorry it's just eeeeerh they're…it's all bullshit. Bollocks, aaaaah sorry, I can't help it. I'm Mmmm. Mmmmmm. Marvelous to see you old comrade. Back of the net!" There's a sham American accent in there somewhere. Whatever he's trying to say is hugely critical, but also hugely curtailed. His rancorous efforts to talk are often eclipsed by cavernous coughing. His sentences are seldom complete.

Talking is painful for Taige, not just because of his deadly cough, but because he's still in mourning over the death of his beloved father Leonard. I knew his father well. He was a real saintly treasure. Out of respect for his father Taige feels like he shouldn't stop mourning. Perhaps, out of respect for his father too, Taige simply can't be altogether arsed to finish what he's saying. Perchance, he's holding a few words back, in bereavement.

Taige often coughs and splutters in the corner of his grubby lounge, proving, I suppose, that there's still some life left in him. The death of Leonard affected him badly; almost killed *him*. Certainly drove him to drink. You know, I think he's actually convinced himself that he's gonna die young.

One day Taige discoveres a round, cyst-like lump on his arm. He keeps touching it. In fact, he can't stop touching it. Believes it's part of his father. Blimey. Superstitious-reincarnated–human-globules – whatever next? Finds it reassuring to feel. By caressing the lump he feels in touch with Leonard again. "It's a cancerous swelling, you know?" Well, that's *his* morose self-diagnosis. There's a tinge of sullenness in Taige's voice when he decrees: "I can still hear Len!" Poor chap. His father died years ago and he's still in serious mourning. It's like he is trying to stay sad...like he's always trying to be in a state of grief. 'Tis the only way he knows how to hold on to his deceased father. If he doesn't appear sad, then he feels guilt. So. He appears sad most of the time. Taige will never forget his Father Len. Never. "Do you miss your Dad?" I ask him. "I want to be with him." The thought crosses my mind - *By Jove...he's going to drink himself to death so he can join his father in heaven.*

Most nights he sits sprawled in his grungy armchair. He sits there hugging his guitar. Doesn't have a girlfriend to hold. Doesn't think it likely that any girl would want to hold him, at least not for the time being. Doesn't even bother going to his bed at night. Just dozes off, half-buried into his chair. "Goodnight Da." Doesn't brush his teeth. Sleeps in his clothes. Life is simpler for him this way.

Taige wakes up late in the afternoon. He never gets up in the morning. He arises moodily and his frame of mind is in some way infectious. Whilst Taige gets ready for work, everyone in the apartment knows about it. There are always a number of defeated looking souls strewn around hangover lodge. They provide a bothersome audience for Taige, as he prepares himself psychologically for another demanding bar shift. The work he does is strenuous, but not *that* strenuous. Yet for Taige, in his state of sorrow, it's a *real* laborious challenge. Anyway, somehow we all end up sharing Taige's anxiety-ridden arousings. Each day, shortly after his time of awakening, the coughing begins. In between coughs Taige paces up and down the room like a cranky old pirate. The clattering search for

79

his snouts begins. Makes me feel seasick just watching him. Eventually he finds his fags. Tries to thwart his coughing each day by lighting up a cigarette. Taige's life is full of absurdities. He sucks his cancer stick in an attitude of complete contrariness. "Marlboro reds ...khuh...knuh...khuh...don't yuh just khuuuh love 'em!?? Khuuuh." His coughing is so bad that he can't even string a sentence together. As he sucks I watch his cheeks go inwards....like the cheeks of a dehydrated child sucking juice through a straw. He takes hungry lungfuls. Smoke pours raggedly from his nose as he exhales; gushes out in streams. Tobacco invigoration is an indulgence he takes seriously. Momentarily, to my surprise, the act of smoking does seem to bring his coughing to a standstill. But then, minutes later, we're exposed to the noisy elements of his cavernous choking again. Indeed, we're consumed by his frenzied spluttering. It really bugs me. For some reason, the whole experience makes me think about what it might be like if you were stuck in bed in a hospital ward, right next to someone who persistently mutters barmy stuff in their sleep like: "Who put my false teeth in your soup!?" Just want him to be quiet.

In between coughing, he grunts with effort like a decrepit old man, as he haphazardly gets ready for work. Our ceaseless cries of complaint - "Will you please just shut the fuck-up Taige!" seem redundant to his ears. Taige's breathing adopts the pressurized pace of time. His chest wheezes and clatters, like an old wind-up clock, as he flings on a few too many layers of clothing. His breathing is full of conflicting crackles, and rattles, and rasps. During his hour of awakening he coughs up grasshopper-sized splodges of phlegm. Spits 'em into scrunches of toilet tissue. Then just plops these phlegmy paper parcels down, ubiquitously around hangover lodge. There are dozens of them. Wherever you look you can see one. Bright green and brimming they are. Taige does as he sees fit. This is, after all, his pad. I mean, who am I to judge him in his own home?

Taige's deteriorating health is tragic. All I can see is a dying man before me. This is upsetting, because this fading man is my friend, and he's talented, and he's still so very young. Taige needs booze to be able to start functioning properly; alcohol is his remedy. Although what he really needs is a personal nurse. Before going to work, by way of preparing himself, Taige calls in at the An Bodhran Irish bar on Haight Street. He downs two pints of pear cider. Hastily drinks his first pint in painful looking gulps, as if it's something he has to do, as if the cider is a bad tasting medicine that he has to consume.

Within seconds he appears to have gathered his wits, and is an altogether different creature. The second pint of cider is put away merely as back up liquid courage. These moments are like the urgent moments before a film star goes on stage. Always tips the barmaid obligingly. Every day. He's dutifully generous and for this reason, and not this reason alone, he's well-liked amongst the Irish bartenders in San Francisco. "Pop down Cassidy's for one later! Won't cha..." he says, time and again.

Taige arrives at Cassidy's all cocky, and confident, and tipsy. Yet he denies that he's tipsy, even though his face is, in point of fact, crimson with tipsiness. He convinces himself there's nothing wrong with downing two pints of cider before starting work. He feels safe once he's back behind the bar at Cassidy's where he was only hours before. It is after all a place where there's alcohol, and alcoholics find it reassuring just to be close to alcohol, don't they? His excuse for a curative shot of bourbon on arrival, is that it helps soothe his dreadful coughing. Taige makes Cassidy's his therapeutic second home. Taige lives in his own comfort zone. Hangover lodge and most of the Irish bars in San Francisco are part of his comfort zone. He seldom ventures out of this consoling social orbit that he's shaped for himself. As an illegal immigrant in San Francisco he's reasonably safe here.

Taige is a wild child from a wild family – they're all on the joy juice. He was already boozing with conviction in his early teens. Nevertheless he only really latched permanently onto the bottle in his late teenage years. Once this happened though, he never let it go.

One day whilst I'm sitting next to Taige in Cassidy's he actually admits that he's an alcoholic. I nearly fall off my bar stool. His confession isn't at all conceited, but rather humble. "Alcohol is something I will never retire from!" He takes a slurp of his Cosmopolitan. "The man takes the drink and then the drink takes the man!" he professes with a philosophical belch. Taige then buys a round of drinks for his large circle of friends. "Here get these down yuz necks – you bunch of tossers!"

Cassidy's is a disheveled Irish bar in downtown Folsom between 7th and 8th. It's a real hive of activity. It's situated near a fleapit youth hostel. Attracts a young and somewhat bedraggled crowd. Cassidy's has a certain cosiness. It's an unpretentious and comforting joint. At Cassidy's a menagerie of characters gather together for a good time, which means having a good hard gargle. Cassidy's is a bar where the punters joke, laugh, sway and sing in an elated and boozed up way. There's jubilant drunkenness in abundance here. Indeed most of the punters are in a rocking and enduring state of rapture for the majority of the time. They're here to pretend to be anarchists, to get drunk well into the night, and to just get all comfy and cosy. That's all.

I go down to Cassidy's almost every evening that I'm in San Francisco. I sit at the bar and breath it all in, whilst Taige pulls hundreds, maybe thousands of pints. It's a reasonably busy Irish saloon and most of the customers give him a dollar tip for each pint he pulls. He's absolutely raking it in. This Irish saloon's his drunken stage. This is where he belongs.

Each and every evening along comes the urging Irish persuasion: "You should just get a few pints down yuh neck. It will make you feel better – I'm tellin yuh." In my fragile state of mind I'm easily influenced by Taige's relentless hospitality. I mean, what else am I going to do in an Irish bar but get drunk? "Oh go on then, if you insist, pour-us-a-pint-a-Guinness." I sit there. Perched on my bar stool. For a long-drawn-out while. Pint of Guinness. Firmly clasped in my hand. I'm in an utterly catatonic like state. However, within a few hours I'm gorged with a complimentary tummy full of the black stuff. Am emboldened by Taige's generosity. With the free booze in front of me, life appears bearable. It is of course only superficial courage I'm feeling but I kinda need it at this moment in time. Cassidy's feels like a discreet hideaway. Seems like the perfect place to hang out, whilst things cool down back in Liechester. As a boozer, Cassidy's has a taste and tenderness I'll never forget. There's a snug family feel to the bar, real Irish blood in its timbers. It attracts a colourful crowd of bandits, misfits, musicians, travellers and urban adventurers. In particular it seems to be a refuge for skunk pipe tokers. They hang outside the Wild West saloon style swinging doors getting mellow and enthused. I'm not one to turn down the chance to get stoned for free. So, when the pipe comes my way, I give it a good draw and get frazzled the Francisco way. For an hour or so I stand outside the yellow and green swinging doors feeling like I've taken a step back in time. I'm glad to be here and not back home in gritty Liechester. *Everybody must get stoned.*

Outside Cassidy's you often see helpless youngsters squatting on the pavement, and homeless crack heads casing the joint. Sometimes the crack heads try and rob the tip jar from the bar. The bartenders at Cassidy's all have their wits about them though, and they chase any marauders out of the bar, and back onto the streets.

We spend a lot of our time on Taige's rooftop, howling like real life lost boys. We sometimes spend entire nights camping out on the roof, getting high and boozy. Taige has lots of friends here, and they often join us on his rooftop - for a jam, for a sing-a-long. There's nothing extraordinary about the roof itself, but it's flat and perfect for lying on. We often look up at the San Francisco skies, catch a glimpse of a shooting star or two. I find comfort in seeing the shooting stars in the night skies. Makes me feel like there's still some kinda life out there for me. Injects me with hope. The view of the city below, all wrapped up in a wispy looking fog, isn't bad either. The other surrounding rooftops are like rosy patches on the blanket of fog below. Trippy – it is. Sometimes we just sit on the roof talking and dreaming until it's dawn. I've fallen into a bohemian circle that I don't want to leave. *Get off the roof at dawn. Get on the road forlorn.*

I'm a stranger here, but Taige's friends quickly become my friends. I make myself at home in their disordered world. I fit in here. I recognise myself in them, in their scruffy appearance, and in their rebellious antics. I can relate to these socialites and their hippy mission. They wear their hearts on their sleeves and welcome me with open arms. It's the people that make a place. Isn't it? I mean why is San Francisco called San Francisco, after all.

After a few weeks I stop wandering meditatively around San Francisco, and adopt Taige's wallowing way of life. We begin to live parallel lives. I no longer see the sunny San Francisco mornings. I start to get up later and later into the afternoons. I start to take on Taige's somnolent routine. It's almost as if I'm becoming Taige. We're like brothers. There's a connection between us, an alleviating affinity. We spend much of our time in a drunken comatose condition. Most nights we're at Cassidy's until 05.00am playing killer pool. Together we're like creatures of the night. We sleep during the day, and are up all night, like lost souls, drifting in what now seems to be a meaningless world. I feel wretched. Unbalanced. Feel like a scrounging and bloodsucking vampire.

When we're moderately sober we're grouchy, and lost in literary thought. When we aren't at Cassidy's, we spend most of our time on the couch, nursing hangovers. Recovering. Surviving. Our mutual friend Gaynor, who's also a bartender at Cassidy's, is aware of my languorous transmutation. She becomes genuinely concerned about me, and my downward spiral. Gaynor knows something drastic has happened. She's no fool. She wants to help. So she bombards me with husky throatfuls of adulation: "Hey up gorgeous! Looking good! Check you out! Looking hot" Stuff like this. It's just flattery, but it's kinda beneficial for my confidence all the same. She's also nuturing. "There you go my love," she avows in her affectionate voice, as she places a glass of freshly squeezed orange juice under my nose. A break from the Guiness will surely do me good.

"A penny, Buddy!"

"What?"

"For your thoughts?"

"Huhguuh!" I let out an awkward and rather absurd melange of sound – 'tis something somewhere between a guffaw and a word and a hiccup.

"I beg your pardon?"

"I know I must seem like I'm lost in thought. Well I am. But not now. If you don't mind. Not now..."

"Yes – ok. Sure." She chuckles sensitively. Sincerely. "Now drink up my love."

Gaynor's a beefy and full woman, like a well-stuffed sack of potatoes. Her warm alcohol induced laugh fills the boozy air. There's a real family ambience in Cassidy's thanks to her chummy presence. She looks at me protectively. Adoringly. My emotional eyes drop to her immense breasts. They become anchored to them for a bit too long. Her breasts are like consoling udders, which I can't touch, but from which I can feed. Nourishing. Maternalistic.

At Cassidy's Gaynor dominates the dark old wooden bar. I've never met her before, but she's exceptionally familiar. It's as if she's a relative of mine, that I've not yet discovered. Turns out she's from Jersey, one of the Channel Islands where many of my ancestors were born and raised. Gaynor's a real Jersey bean, and a brazen one at that. I find her genuine Jersey-ness reassuring. She can see there's something troubling me. She can see I'm all tangled-up-in-blue. One evening Gaynor rubs Jersey black butter on my forehead and whispers soothingly: "Let the devil return to its hole." "I'll try." I respond auspiciously. I know the island of Jersey well, so I know what she's up to. Her friendly black magic is a shortcut to a place of pride and wonder. It would be lost on most people.

The next day she takes me on a ride on a San Francisco cable car. She also treats me to a salmon and cream cheese poppy seed bagel lunch in the French quarter of San Francisco, just off Bush Street. She knows how to cheer me up. That afternoon Gaynor exclaims: "I just wanna see you smile. Goddammit you godda beautiful smile." I smile again, which prompts her to announce: "I'm gonna take you to see Bob Dylan."

"As if!"

"I'm gonna get us some tickets to see Bob Dylan live in concert in Oakland. Goddammit!"

And you know...she does. And it's the best.

Suddenly and unexpectedly Gaynor hands me a green coloured cap. Don't think the colour of the cap is of any particular significance, yet it is, I must say, a splendid gooseberry green. The cap is also festooned with a rather frayed looking brown and white feather. "Here my love. If you're gonna walkabout you're gonna need a hat. You can't walkabout in this Francisco sun without a hat." Her words are spoken with a mixture of kindheartedness and forewarning. To me she's like sanctuary and safety. Gaynor is a motherly figure and at this point in my life I need mothering. Thank her tenderly for my gooseberry green cap. I become attached to my slightly scruffy, yet kinda groovy adornment. In some silly way it makes me feel complete. Like I belong here now. I simply love its gooseberry green colour. Perhaps the colour is significant? It becomes my favourite color anyhows.

Every Monday Taige plays an acoustic session at Cassidy's. His long, nimble fingers come in very useful for playing the guitar. Whereas I can only just stretch my fingers comfortably across three frets, Taige can stretch his comfortably across five. He's an exceptional guitarist. I only have to glimpse at his mind-made-up-fingers to see that he's gonna try to strum his way out of his melancholy. Taige has a gift. Playing the guitar is his gift. Whenever he has a moment to spare he plucks away at his Freshman acoustic. It's his number one diversion. When he plays, it's as if he's showing off his floating fingers, as much as anything else. I'm just glad he's found something useful to do with those lanky fingers of his. You know they're so astonishingly long.

On Mondays the girls normally arrive in a carnival-like flurry. Bejewelled and garlanded and wearing poppies in their hair, they hop and skip their way into Cassidy's. They always make quite an oscillating entrance anyhows. Taige has quite a following of female groupies. His followers all wear an abundant assortment of flower power accessories. You know jellybean necklaces and friendship bands and stuff like that. They like to dress up, but the real reason they're here is to see Taige Shine play his diamond folk music.

I scrutinize Taige during one of these acoustic sessions. Before the performance his fingers unfurl, and claw back up, like the talons of a primitive cat. They then unfurl, and then claw back up *again*. It's as if his fingers are slowly awakening. It's if his fingers are limbering up for the performance of a lifetime. That particular Monday evening he plays a couple of mesmerizing folk songs of his own creation. He stops playing halfway through the third song, and walks casually over to the bar. He somehow manages to attract the attention of all the punters; I mean all the eyes in the boozer are on him. Then Gaynor pours a generous shot of Jack, straight from the bottle, into his mouth. The crowd love it. Taige Shine wipes his mouth dry of head numbing bourbon, then starts to pluck at his guitar once again. Defiantly. Cheekily. Belts out a Johnny Cash cover. Goes down a storm. "I hear the train a comin'....It's rollin' 'round the bend..." This is entertainment with a touch of acrimony. This is musical bitterness. This is an underground artist in full swing....

There's this house in San Francisco that partygoers call the *lopside*. The house parties held at the *lopside* are legendary. The *lopside* certainly has character...a crooked, slanting kinda character. This tilting house is always full of hippy-folk. When I go there I see hordes of men and women cavorting in and around the entrance, and a cluster of wired looking rockers camped outside on the pavement. That night the place attracts a swarming, and pleasure-seeking throng. There are hundreds of hippies outside, and there's banging techno music pulsating its way from inside the *lopside*. It's just my kinda thing. Have one of the most sybaritic and unbalanced nights of my life there. People are free to come and go as they please. It's like a scene from 'Dogs in Space'. It's always like this. Apparently. The *lopside* is a squat.....for certain party animals. Yeah people do actually live here. I wonder what it must be like to live in a house that is so totally askew, and so totally dedicated to hedonism. One day, for sure, the revellers will just dance this wonky house down to the ground completely. The next day, I still feel wobbly, all catawampus like.

Taige and I are in our early twenties. We are both already quite nostalgic men. We have history in our pockets and in our minds. I'm a poet and a scribe. Taige is a songwriter and musician. He understands the world around him better than most. He's a strikingly pensive character and has a conspicuous taste for times gone by. I guess he's just fascinated in History. For him it seems the past is as great, if not greater than the future. Taige would have been happier if he'd have been born a century or two earlier. Taige has mounted several sallow photographs of various different San Francisco street scenes on the walls of his grubby lodge. As I look at the photos I notice flannel-sized cobwebs in the corners of the room. The photos themselves are black and white and a yellowish-orange. They're obviously of bygone times. Creatively Taige is trying to make a statement to me, and his other friends, and to the world. He's trying to teach us something. The framed photographs, each with its own coating of dead skin dust, look down on us. Profoundly. There's dignity in those fading images. Real Spirit. They remind us, not just of the past, but of the present too. They look very old, but in terms of our long history, they're not really old at all. The photographs make me feel like I should make the most of now, but they also tell me, rather maddeningly, that I should be more responsible. Suddenly I'm in some kind of sepia induced state of seemliness. Suddenly I've been transported back in time - to a time of aristocratic respectability. I can hear the judicious bearded voice of my paternal grandfather in those fading images saying: "think before you act." Like a reckless delinquent, all I want to do is party - cataclysmic style!

It's almost as if Taige is waiting for something bad to happen. Perhaps he's waiting to get caught and put in prison? Perhaps that's what he wants? Possibly he just doesn't care. Life might be easier for him that way. He certainly has a live-fast, die-young attitude.

You know, he wears the same jeans every day. They're adorned with a slogan. This slogan reflects the daisy-chain making side of his character. He's sprawled it on them himself with brightly coloured fabric paint. Don't know if they're his own words, but they're just like something he would come up with. Anyway, whether they're his own words or not, doesn't really matter. What matters is that this is his declaration to the human race. This is what Taige Shine wants the world to know: "JESUS IS SOFT LIKE A FLUFFY BUNNY RABBIT."

Like I say Taige is a drained and famished soul. The drink, the drugs, and the suspicion have made him rakey and fragile. He wears layer upon layer of clothes, to compensate for what is, like I say, nothing but a rack of bones. Yet he still looks wafer thin. Taige has a complex about being too skinny. He wears a pair of trousers under his favourite jeans to try to make himself look stockier. He's so self-conscious about his weight that even in the summertime, despite the Californian heat, he still wears two pairs of slacks, aswell as several tops. The life of a withering alcoholic can be very lonely. Indeed, Taige seems alone with everybody.

I never see Taige take a shower and he rarely eats. It's like he has a unique eating disorder; an eating disorder all of his own. He lives off a diet of bourbon, cider, apple juice, beef jerky and cigarettes. Seriously. That's pretty much it. He admits that he's an alcoholic, but it still seems to me as if he's somehow in denial. Perhaps there's something else bothering him. Perhaps there's something he can't talk about or admit to? Maybe there's something I can't spot or identify?

Anyway, one evening Taige surprises us all. He hastily cobbles together a concoction of tuna, pasta, a random tin of tomato soup he finds buried at the back of his grimy pantry, and a rather extravagant slop of hot peppercorn sauce. Reminds me of my student days. It's the kinda dish that has to be eaten when you're blind drunk to be fully appreciated! "There you go...chicken-of-the-sea-surprise!" Just as we're about to tuck into our spicy gastronomic bombshell, Taige's drunken friend Paul comes stumbling into hangover lodge. His timing's perfect - has he cunningly smelt out the food? Or what? Paul sometimes collaborates with Taige down at Cassidy's on Monday nights. His stage name is '*The Drunken Uncle*'. He calls me Buddy California. Don't know why, but I kinda like it. Anyway Paul's out of breath. Looks like he's seen a fearsome ghost. He's obviously distressed about something. Refuses to sit down. Begins speedily recapping his skirmish to us in a thick Irish accent (sometimes it feels more like I'm in Ireland than America). He paces neurotically around the lounge as he speaks. Find it difficult to decipher what's being said. "Gone...gone. Here. Meelastbita green." He pats his pockets. "Meelast five0 – taxed. Gone. A-been-shredded. Here. By dare" He points. "Dare....just darn dare." Gutted. From what I can gather, he's been taxed. Taxed of his last $50. Just down the road. On the corner of Page and Scott. Mugged of his last bit of cash. Paul seems proper petrified. He's salivating at the mouth. Appears to be on the edge of madness...only just holding it together. He paces, and he burbles, and he drags us all in. "Goddamn yuz. Goddamn motherfuckers. Gone tis orll gone. Jesus H Christ." He isn't so upset about the money, that can be replaced. His illusion that San Francisco is a peace-loving place has been shattered. Stolen. That's whats really pissed him off. His illusion can't be replaced.

Paul appears a little too clever for his own good. You know one of these crippling characters you rarely meet, but when you do, you can almost hear their angst-ridden minds analysing the world around them. The whole occurrence has left him struck with misapprehension. The poor chap is close to tears - I feel close to a dishevelled genius. Taige is now pacing around in despair. Paul's pacing is apparently contagious. Taige has one of his fingers coiled around his bottle of rolling rock. He's clutching hold of it as if it's a cigarette. He's out of sorts, because Paul's out of sorts. That's the kinda guy Taige is. But there's nothing any of us can do, to remedy this situation, I mean. The assailants will be long gone by now. For sure. Paul's left blatantly wounded.

I sit in hangover lodge with my fork clenched firmly in my hand. Am playing with the hot peppercorned food on my plate. It looks rank. My appetite is gone.

Despite what's happened to Paul my mind is elsewhere. I'm reliving my shooting incident. This often happens when something, anything goes wrong. I begin remembering all the wrong stuff that's happened to me. Wanna block all the bad stuff. Wanna stop remembering. Wanna put closure on it all. So I suck on a pipe and get absolutely battered....

I'm deeply stirred by the sheer number of homeless beggars here. There are tramps everywhere on the streets of San Francisco. Many of these shelterless shabbies push supermarket trolleys full of other men's junk, up and down the undulating rows. When I confess: "I feel close to being one of these trolley tramps myself." Taige just laughs. He dismisses my comment completely. Holds me in high regard you see. Too high I think. But my comment is spoken in earnest. This is how lost I feel - am close to destitution. Can this town, renowned for its fog and frivolity, really carry me?

I'm in Cassidy's *again*. It's a Wednesday in June. Could be anyday. Isn't a day to be celebrating. Anyhow I'm busy drowning my sorrows in a seemingly unending flow of Guinness. I've been in this boozer every day since I arrived here. And yes, *again* I've consumed another gutful of grog for free. It's only 18.00, and my head is already swimming with booze. A destitute wench approaches me, looking for some breed of friendship. She's off her head. She's vaguely gothic looking, and is wearing an enormous tilting beret. The most noticeable thing about her though is her slate coloured eyes. They're watery. Bloodshot. Her hat is velvety and is divided into trivial pursuit style segments. There's a black segment and then a coloured segment. The hat alternates like this all the way around. There are pastel segments of orange, pink and green. The colours on the hat are faded. The beret would have been much brighter once, I think. Her hat looks as if it contains all of her worldly belongings. Quite possibly it does. For she has that air about her, that air of a woman without a real place to call home. Certainly there's *something* bulging underneath her oversized beret. She carries a 'buzzbag' around with her. She opens it up by loosening a baggy black chord. Looks just like a mermaid's purse. With a mischievous look, she invites me to look inside her precious buzzbag. It's crammed full of drugs; a multi-coloured assortment of illegal highs. I look at her uncomprehendingly. "Why didn't you know? This is where all the colours of the rainbow come from." Blimey. She's trying to be enchanting. Or something. Trying to be the very opposite of enchanting, I reply: "Oh, is that right." Her 'buzzbag' seems to be the hot topic of conversation. In effect, it's all she can talk about. Her ecstasy eyes are wide and syrupy. They're coated with false love and commotion. This 'aint the supernatural girl I've been waiting for. Buzzbag woman is in cloud cuckoo land. There are plenty of people like that here. Taige warns me not to go off with her. The thought hasn't even entered my mind. I mean, maybe I'm loose, but I 'ain't crazy loose. Despite being inflamed with booze, I still have my wits about me. I can see that this queer fish is impecunious and utterly chancy. I need to get away from her. Actually, I feel a break from this boozer altogether will do me some good. At this moment in time it's crucial for me to be alone. Feel rude, but by Jove, what the heck....I'm out of here. Make a sharp exit. Go for a Buddy Rioux style walk. Won't forget about buzzbag woman in a hurry though, especially her desperate grey-blue eyes. Doubt she'll remember me.

I find that roaming along the flamboyant terraced streets here is perfect for a while. Fixes my craving for solidarity anyhow. Nevertheless, I know I will eventually become sick of my own company. So I arrange to meet Taige later on, after his cocaine fuelled shift at Cassidy's is over. We meet outside an Ethiopian restaurant. It's a good place to meet because we both know where it is.

Taige Shine is a clumsy exhibitionist. He was always spilling his tea round at my parent's house when we were kids - earnt him the title 'Sloppy Shine'. My Mum even made up a song about him, such was his notoriety for sloppiness. It went a little something like this: "Sloppy Shine, Sloppy Shine, he slops tea all over the place." She was always making up songs. Aaaaah me Mum - love her to bits. Whilst I'm busy wondering why Taige is not on time, he comes stumbling out of the wispy fog, all dirty, and drunk, and late. "Taige is the name, entertaining is my game!" Granted. He is quite the consummate entertainer. Taige's legs seems out of control with his body as he staggers towards me. He's pissed as a newt.

I knew Taige would be late, and I knew he would apologize profusely for being late. I also anticipate a drunken exhibition. He looks like a Dickensian character, as he emerges from the ground clouds, and he pongs of pear cider. The smell of cider is literally oozing from his pores. If truth be told, he stinks like he's been marinated in the stuff. He falls at my knees, and theatrically pleads ruefulness: "Sorry I'm late, khuuuh, sorry I'm late governor, khuuh, please forgive me for my tardiness!" He's clutching an empty bottle of cider affectionately, and just lies there like a sprawled gothic relic before me. He needs companionship.

As he lies there I notice that the zip on his 'Jesus is soft like a fluffy bunny rabbit' jeans is undone. "Taige mate, you're flying low!"
"The cage may be open, but the beast is asleep!"
"Straight in there."
"Back of the net mate!"
Taige is always eager for a bit of embellished banter when he's been on the sauce (which is everyday).

Taige is elastically expressive. He articulates with his body, especially with his lanky arms. Like a tipsy Frenchman he is. For some reason that particular evening, as he speaks, he also gesticulatingly flings his words at me in a sonic boom fashion. In a rather unusual, and it must be said, quite effective way, he's trying to be entertaining, I suppose. As we walk along, he keeps shouting stuff out from the Street Fighter computer game: "Spinningbirdkick" and "Flapjackwhirljack" to name but a few. Kinda contagious it is. Pissed out of his head he is. "Shawyuken" and "Hadooken," come up more than just a couple of times aswell - complete with hand gestures. The booze has certainly helped loosen his throat and tongue. Now he communicates with passion and impact and cider. Seems like he's having the time of his life. So I join in. Well now we're both walking up and down the rows late at night imitating StreetFighter arcade characters. Sending sonic booms, and the like, into the dark. Just flinging 'em out there. Kinda therapeutic it is. We could be up to a whole lot worse. I guess....

As I walk, and Taige stumbles, (still well and truly in street-fighter mode) we happen to pass by an obesity medical center: "At least I'll never have to pay that place a visit!" Taige jests with an 'I'm not in denial about my skinniness' goony frown on his face. Hilarious. Taige is a wit. Always has been. His attempts at humour are more comical than mine. In his company, I often sense my blood turn green with envy, in the heat of the slapstick moment. Time and again I find myself thinking – *damn, how come I didn't think of that.*

We continue, without direction, along the streets of San Francisco. We cuss and clip each other endlessly, as good mates do. It's just a spirited exchange of insults; a harmless game of rhetorical rudeness. It is, I suppose, our attempt at comedy on our real life stage. There are always lots of 'yeah mates!', 'shut ups!' and 'as ifs!?' going down. He disagrees with everything I say, and I disagree with everything he says. We rip each other's philosophies to shreds, until laughter takes over our verbal tête-à-tête. Then, after the laughter has dispersed, we sit together on a bench in a companionable silence...like a pair of old codgers. It's a reassuring silence...for a while...

"What's your beef Buddy?"

"Where are we Taige mate?"

"San Fran mate!"

"Straight in there!"

"Back of the net mate!"

"Yeah mate!– no but really – what's this area called?"

"You only happen to be in one of the most flamboyant areas of San Fran, and you mean to say you don't even know what it's called!?"

"Shut up now. Where the fuck are we?"

"Nob Hill mate!"

"Shut up. As if!?"

"Nob Hill mate. I shit you not. Nob fucking Hill."

"As if!"

"Shut up......you Nob Hill head."

"aaaaaaaaaaaaah-shudupayaface."

"Yeah mate."

"Nob Hills-a-nice-a-place-aaaaaaaaaaaaah-shudupayaface."

"Back of the net mate!"

Taige always likes to get the last word in. This is how it goes. This is sort of how it always is, when we've had a few.

Anyhow, I *still* don't *really* know where we've ended up walking to, but it doesn't matter. Later on, in the small hours of the night, Taige just flags down a yellow cab, and we head back over to hangover lodge. Taige charitably insists on settling the fare.

We can sit and drink a pint together without feeling the need to talk. I find Taige's silent company somewhat comforting. I 'ain't in the mood for talking too much, but I need to have somebody by my side. My memories are still far too vivid, and still far too blue. Indeed, they are perpetually branded on my brain. I try to drown them out with booze, but these memories 'ain't shifting. I'm not going to be able to just blot them out.

To forget, I know I have to forgive, but to forgive, I will have to stop seeking revenge. There's an agonising struggle going on inside of me. Incessantly.

One sun-drenched, San Francisco day, I find myself roving alongside a stream on John F Kennedy drive. I have, for some reason, roamed a little further out of town, on this fine afternoon. Come to think of it, I'm feeling *particularly* lost in thought. Seems as if my mind just allows me to dreamily saunter out-of-the-way. An hour or so later, I stumble upon a buffalo paddock. I stray into Golden Gate Park like a rootless oddity. Without warning, here, right before my very eyes, is an entire herd of buffalo. I am in shock and awe. These American bison have substantial dread-locked mains. In contrast to their milky brown bodies, their mains appear to be a dark chocolatey colour. Their hairdos make them look like the Rastafarians of the animal kingdom. They have firm and full looking bodies, which are shaggy and patchy in places. It looks as if somebody has started to shear them, and has just decided to give up on their strenuous furry undertaking halfway through. By looking at them I can smell and taste their meaty flesh. I find myself tucking into a pack of beef jerky that's been sweltering away in my pocket. Suddenly I'm a hungry man. The whole buffalo experience seems a bit illusory, yet strangely uplifting. With my visual senses stirred, and feeling that life is altogether surreal and fantastic, I find myself whistling my way down to the pub. Another evening of hardcore boozing lays ahead.

At Cassidy's I find myself bragging about my buffalo encounter. Of course, it comes as no surprise to the locals that I've seen a herd of buffalo in Golden Gate Park. They look at me with bemusement, as I breathlessly recite my beefy buffalo tale. Perhaps I need to get off the pavement a bit more......

I become possessed by a spirit of recklessness; unruliness is alive in me. Dangerous it is. I'm still living out of a suitcase. My life is one hell of a jumbled up mess. *Where will I sleep tonight?* - I wonder. I'm behaving hot-headedly, and I know I must look a wretched sight. I'm acting entirely out of character, but I'm unable to do anything to help myself. I also have a gripping feeling that I'm being followed.

July, 2000. I whistle to myself as tunefully as I can, as I smooch alongside Fisherman's Wharf. I've been whistling to myself a lot lately. Makes me feel free and delicate. Somehow, it makes me feel less like I'm being followed.

I gaze over one of the piers, and see a gigantic pod of lazy walruses. Blimey. Wasn't expecting that. There must be at least 40 of them. "I am the walrus, goo goo g'joob, Semolina pilchard, climbing up the Eiffel Tower....." springs into my mind. Beautiful. I stare at these flippered mammals for a while, with that Beatles song in my head. Timely. The groaning walruses take my mind away from stuff momentarily, but I soon grow agitated by their monotonous company. So, I continue walking alongside the wharf, looking for some other, spur-of-the-moment impetus.

I'm on the edge of the world, down in Alcatraz Bay. I feel like nothing really matters. Not even innocence. Or insincerity. However, a voice inside my head tells me - *Keep on walking.* So I do. The fishy smell of clam chowder emanating along the quayside, gets proper caught up in my nostrils. Appetizing. Reminds me of a seaside childhood holiday in Skegness. Or was it Bognor Regis? Can't remember. Whatever. Makes me feel all wistful and homesick. I miss my mum's cooking. Enormously. There's an incandescent sky, a dazzling sun, a few smoky trails of cloud, and a refreshing sea breeze. Life could be worse. I suppose. I stay on the water's edge until sundown. Get's all chilly. It's a stunning sight watching the fog roll in across the wharf from the shoreline of the bay. The Golden Gate Bridge is already shrouded in a nippy mist. San Francisco just sits there, waiting to get smothered in fog.

Eventually everywhere seems coated in ground clouds. The steamy vapour rolls uncompromisingly into the bay - channels its way through the colourful avenues. The white wispiness seems to want to brusquely swathe this settlement. The bright boulevards are instantly filled with nature's atmospheric fluff, like brandy snaps squirted full with cream in a wink. Well, it's a bit like that anyway. The wraithlike weather works furiously, as if in a pretentious cover-up. It's a breath-taking natural phenomenon. Love the fog I do. Especially here. So the San Francisco cotton wool curtains are drawn yet again, meanwhile, day turns into night, and that means more here than most places. I for one, never know what the night will bring....

Marty craves adoration and he's obsessed with filming. As far as I can tell he's Taige's best *American* friend. Marty's originally from Seattle, but is now at University in San Francisco studying film. This Seattleite has a childish chuckle. He looks chubby, and a bit dumb, but he's as charismatic as Steven Spielberg. Marty wants to be a film director, and everyone around him wants him to be a film director. Marty 'the movie maker' appears destined for the top.

Wherever Marty goes he always takes his digital camcorder and a crate full of Budweiser. He has an unquenchable thirst for the stuff. Incidentally, Taige is also a budding film enthusiast. Whenever Taige clutches Marty's video camera it vanishes inside a cocoon of fingers. Oh and before I forget – Taige also likes Budweiser.

I've kept it all inside me. It's too much for me to take. Taige and his mate Marty are here with me. I guess I somehow feel comfortable with these guys. I'm wildly drunk. I've taken on board a gut full of booze - nearly a whole box of buds. Then in the early hours of the night, I break down crying. Had to happen sooner or later. My bottled up shock, runs out of me. I cry hysterically. I'm *feeling* too much. There's been a commotion growing within me, possessing my soul. Within minutes my eyes turn a bloodshot red. My eyes let other people know there's something wrong with me. Emotionally it's as if I've erupted. My tears are induced by almost 8 litres of beer, but triggered by trauma. They're tears from the stressful riot within.

Taige says very little, as I slowly dissolve. Think he wants to crack a joke, but he doesn't. It's a deep cry from my heart, I can tell you. That night I give vent to *alot* of my suppressed emotion. I sob for some time, but of course I can't just sob it *all* out. There's still a niggling wisp of agony inside of me - still want revenge. Taige is concerned by my bawling release. Poor Marty doesn't know whether to laugh or cry. It's as if I'm ridding myself of a lurking demon, a demon that's been festering in my soul for too long. I cry uncontrollably in their company, but I also laugh uncontrollably in their company. Reckon they save my sanity. "Buddy man....was that for real. I 'ain't ever seen such a raw expression of human emotion before." Now Marty likes to dramatise things a little, but on this occasion there's a stroke of sincerity in his words. I know I've let myself go. I've bottled stuff up for too long you see. It's a cry for help really. Not that they can actually help me, but they do help ease my suffering a bit. Feel kinda embarrassed. Of course they tell me "Don't."

Marty has a fascinating way with words. When he talks about film he's inspirational. "Watching a film should be a spectacular treat. The importance of film is to grab the viewer's attention and keep it, touch their souls...cause them to melt and move. Entertain them. It's about diversion...about rerouting the human mind...making it rise...yeah it should be emotional. Emotional yeah...laughter...tears....and of course it's about challenging society and its conventions....and all that."

"What's your favourite film Marty?"

"E.T."

"Really?"

"Got a problem with that?"

"No...you just surprised me with that."

"What's yours?"

"Don't know...Jaws. The Lost Boys....maybe"

"Love karate kid aswell.....wax on....wax off."

Marty knows I'm interested in the little differences between life in England and America. Marty's full of ensnaring social comment - here are just a few of his poetical pearlers:

"Heh Buddy, don't ever look down on 6th Street."

"Here - it's not what you are - it's what you appear to be!"

"Well Buddy, in the States, it's not eat as much as you like, it's eat as much as you can, you got it!" He persistently repeats the same lyrical lines. Most of the time, Marty comes out with witty figures of speech, though with him it's definitely more about how he says things, than what he actually says. His facial expressions are the most amusing I've ever seen. His Seattle twang is just too funny for words. He's got this eye-poppingly hilarious delivery. He's a captivating guy. I'm telling you. He also constantly exclaims: "Bless my bottom!" At first I think he's cracking on to me, bearing in mind San Francisco is the gay capital of the world and all. Then I began to realise this is just Marty being freakish, and engaging, and just a tad contentious, all at the same time. Marty also likes to rap. Never met anyone who likes to rap before. Seems to be Eminem's biggest fan. That is, at least, where he gets most of his inspiration from, for rapping that is. Marty pulls it off without a care in the world. Oh, Marty likes to beat-box aswell, randomly, in hit or miss outbursts. What an enchanting geezer! The enthusiasm this guy has for life, and the passion he has for people, helps pull me through the lowest ebb of my life. I'm on a bit of a death wish. I've hit the bottle. I'm drinking whatever I can get my hands on. Yet Marty seems to be able to make me laugh. This laughter is indispensable right now. His compelling commentary really tickles me. Marty makes my stay in San Francisco extra fascinating.

I adore San Francisco, yet it's no paradise. There's squalor on many of the streets here. 6th Street, off Folsom, is a prime example of this foulness. It's strewn with drug dealers, prostitutes and fiendish looking desperados. It's parasitically arresting. I decide not to drift down 6th Street again, for it's disturbingly unsafe. The squatting faces I see on this urban stretch, are like grimacing fancy-dress shop horror masks. Their features are fraught with tragedy, and they're snarlingly too close for comfort. It doesn't take me long to grasp Marty's message of warning: "Don't ever look down on 6th Street." You have to keep your wits about you on this scowling skid. You can't afford to look down, not even for a second.

Suddenly and unexpectedly Taige and Marty invite me to go with them on a trip to Santa Cruz. They wanna cheer me up. It's early July, 2000. We hop on a Greyhound, and are there a few hours later. Santa Cruz/Santa Carla is where they filmed 'The Lost Boys'...one of my all time favourite films (Santa Carla is the fictional name the directors choose for the vampire infested town in the film.) The Lost Boys is certainly the film I've watched the most times - for some macabre reason. Whilst we're in Vampire Ville we stay in a cheap motel called 'Rip-Van-Winkle' motel. It has a swimming pool, and it only costs $10 per night. Most motels are flanked by pools in the States, even some of the cheapest ones. A night at 'Rip-Van-Winkle's' seems like the bargain of the century to me, but really it's just the Big American norm. We stock the motel fridge up with bottles of Budweiser. We want to continue our drinking binge back at Rip's, after our night out vampire spotting. We plan to party all night long. Love it here. Will never forget it. I see the Santa Cruz mountains and the Santa Cruz boardwalk. I walk around where the 'Lost Boys' hunted their prey. It's here in 'sleep all day, party all night' territory, that I experience one of the worst outbreaks of suppressed merriment imaginable. A day or two after I've flooded them with tears, I almost laugh my head off. I don't know why really, but I just can't stop laughing. I guess it's because I'm in therapeutic company, and I finally sense that I can relax. Maybe it's just part of some kind of healing process. Have suffered for too long, from too much suppression. Now seems like a good time to let it all out. I say let it all out, in reality some sort of side-splitting force has taken over me. I can't contain myself. Is there something strange in the air in Santa Cruz after all? I laugh so much that I actually start scaring Taige and Marty. "Well you invited me here." They think I'm proper losing it for a while. It's an indispensable release. I've never laughed so much in all my life. Laugh so much my ribs hurt. "Never invite a vampire back to his hometown." For sure, it is fun to be a vampire for the night.

This one time, back in San Fran, I wake up on a desert like beach. My hung-over wooden head is splitting with lightning aches. I 'ain't cured yet. I arise wincing into the glare of a pitiless white sun. I can see nothing but a blinding blur of sun and sand. The uncompromising rays of a colossal Californian sun are thrashing down on me. Feels like they're zapping my last layer of energy. Am in trouble now. Am still fully clad in my going-out-clothes. Look overdressed for the daytime. Look like a bamboozled human stray. My throat isn't working. Can barely manage a croak. I'm as dry as the sand beneath my shoes. Gotta stop boozing. This is no morning glory. I'm close to death's door. The combination of a Jack Daniels/pear cider/Cosmopolitan hangover and this ball of fire in the sky is proving to be almost lethal. I need water. I know I have to move now or I'll be a gonner. I'm partially blind, and rocking like an old age pensioner, as I clamber up out of the sucking sand. I stagger across the encumbering dunes. Minutes later I fall into a 1950's style beach café and hang myself over the counter. Slap a tatty $1 down. Plead for water by raising my cup shaped hand to my mouth. Luckily the waitress understands my gesture.

Think I'm in the Sunset District area of San Francisco. Doesn't strike me as a particularly affluent neighbourhood. Wherever I am, it seems very much like I've somehow ended up in the outskirts of San Francisco. I notice a few car wrecks. There are lots of gypsy like folk traipsing the streets, looking like they don't really know what to do with themselves. Maybe it's me. Maybe I don't know what to do with myself. Apart from this I fail to notice anything else of significance. I'm not my most observant self. Need to rehydrate. Need a proper bed.

Turns out I've got sunstroke. I've learnt the hard way that hangovers, and the Californian sun don't mix. Wish I'd had my gooseberry green cap. From now on, I'll take it with me wherever I go. Sometimes, when I'm feeling really worried, I say a little prayer. Don't do this very often. My prayer that night went like this: "Dear God.....if you can hear me, please help me get through this. Feel like I'm dying. Don't let me fade away." The sunstroke makes me delirious.

Lately I've been hustling for cash. I have to. Mostly my hustling takes place around pool tables. I'm always on the lookout to earn a dollar or five. I run the door at Cassidy's on several occasions, which is mostly when the fat-ass bouncers can't be arsed to turn up for work. Have to sit outside the swing doors and check the ID's of anyone who looks under twenty-five. Then just welcome the punters in. It's easy work. Some jobs are, aren't they? I must be the least intimidating doorman in San Francisco, but I'm happy to do this, whenever I get the chance, for a bit of cash in my pocket. I just hope there's no trouble, because if there is, I'll probably do a peace-loving nothing. Every now and again, when it's heaving in Cassidy's, I wash glasses and serve the odd pint behind the bar. I've become part of the furniture. Also, out of respect, I always help Taige clean up the bar at the end of the night. It's the least I can do. He is, after all, harbouring me for god's sake.

Taige is the first person I confide in. He's not the sort of person to be easily shocked. If anyone can handle it, he can. I tell him all about Mo and The Blue Hole. I tell him about the shooting altercation. "Think I've got post-traumatic stress or something." I waffle on about racism and terrorism and police corruption and drugs and undercover military intelligence work. But in the end...

"Taige mate, I can't guh back to Liechester just yet. Need your help mate. Wanna stay here for a bit longer. Need to..."

"Ok sure Buddy."

"You sure Taige?"

"Sure shank redemption sure."

"Yeah but...."

"Sure as figs are figs.....you can stay."

"Well, I'll do what I can to help and..."

"You can stay ok. It's perfectly fine. Now just shut the fuck up."

Taige has been living illegally in San Francisco for years. So, as I'm sure you can imagine, he's seen some pretty screwy stuff. But even he doesn't know how to take my news. The stuff I tell him about makes him look all bemused and pensive. Sad even. Kinda makes me not wanna tell anyone else. Taige thinks this shouldn't have happened. To be more specific, he thinks this shouldn't have happened to me. It shouldn't. From Taige's point of view I'm not the kind of person who deserves to be threatened with a gun. I'm not (not that he thinks there really are many people who do mind). "I could tell summit wuzzup.

You 'aint been yuhself Buddy mate. Yuve thrown all yuh old caution out the window. Yuve come ere un done nothin but fill mah 'ead with all this unbelievable shit. Now ere, get this down yuh neck." Booze is something Taige has always latched onto. So, he thinks that whenever anyone else is in trouble, all they need is a good hard gargle. Perhaps I'm easily led or something, but deep down I do at least know that the Joy Juice won't help matters in the long run.

I'm destitute, and with a little bit of arm-twisting persuasion by Taige, I'm boozing to ameliorate my distress. Really this is sheer self-indulgence. Sheer debauchery. Sheer delusion. It's a bit of a miracle really, when I win the killer pool tournament at Cassidy's. Just when I'm flat broke aswell. Maybe I come across as some kind of proficient hustler, but sure as hell it's luck really. I don't really know *what* I'm doing. I just happen to be playing some of the best pool I've ever played in my life, whilst the other finalist seems to have lost the ability to hold his pool cue properly. In a casual manner I've won $100 in a Californian pool tournament. Can't believe it. It's enough to put a gainful grin on my face.

One of Taige's flatmates is called Tim. He's a strikingly good-looking Irish man. His face is like a chiselled woodenheaded sculpture. He smokes with a wise gesture, and has the malicious eyes of a swindler. Tim's a rugged and severe man. He's a perceptive and hardened explorer. On his travels he sustained a serious knee injury. He now hobbles around with crutches like a proper hop-a-long-Cassidy. Since his knee injury he has become a stumbling and bedraggled alcoholic. Hop-a-long-Cassidy often staggers in late at night nursing a bottle of liquor. He's always mumbling something or other. He has a strong Irish twang. It's difficult to understand what he's trying to say, or at least I find it difficult to decipher his wilful words. One evening he burbles: "Aaaaah Buddy me lad, aaaah wanyaa as mah drinking parrrtner, aaaah I do. Yurrr deadly." Characteristically he barges into hangover lodge and makes his drunken presence felt. This one time he lurches over to the sofa, gouges his leg on the corner of the coffee table, and knocks his knee out of place yet again. His clutches go flying. He lands on some vagrant, who's sprawled out on the grungy sofa in a half unconscious condition. Hop-a-long-Cassidy lets out an almighty 'I've-had-an-absolute-skinful' howl of agony. "Aaaaaah-Ooooooh-Naaaaay." Somehow he makes it to his feet again. He stands there swaying on one leg in front of me, whilst the vagrant just rolls over and carries on kipping. A Richard Ashcroft CD is playing in the background. Whilst stumbling around the place like a crazed amputee on a catwalk, Hop-a-long-Cassidy makes an out-of-tune, but heartfelt attempt to sing along. "I got you on my mind in my sleep. Yeah...oh...yeah. Got you on my mind in my sleep. Yeah, yeah, yeah." Bad singing. Hilariously bad. It's a memorable performance. Hop-a-long-Cassidy really is a complete riot.

One day Hop-a-long-Cassidy cooks a much called for Irish stew. He insists that Taige joins us in our Emerald isle feast. "If yah starve yeeself down anymore Taige Shine, you'll disappear me lad, now ear get this inta yah." The Irish stew is thick and gunky and packed with rustic vegetables. I feel full and sleepy after devouring my bowlful. *That will keep me going for a while* - I think to myself as I fall into an Irish stew food coma. It's enough to keep Taige's bird-sized tummy going for a week. Hop-a-long Cassidy keeps saying 'lush' and 'deadly' whilst he's munching his stew. To him everything seems to be either 'lush' or 'deadly'. He has no table manners whatsoever, but who cares – he cooks a damn fine bit of nosh. I say 'table' manners, we're all slouched on the sofa whilst we're scoffing our stew. When Hop-a-long-Cassidy munches, it sounds as if his teeth are loose. He chomps like a goddamn horse.

Hop-a-long Cassidy is a compassionate fellow, but he's also a hopeless drunk. He's an intelligent man at desperate odds with the problems in the world. He's quite timid really, and during the daytime he mostly likes to keep himself to himself. He hobbles into Cassidy's on a daily basis, props up his crutches, pulls up a stool, straddles it, and then tucks into a liquid lunch of Guinness. Once the drinking starts there's no going back. One pint leads to a ten pint plus Guinness drinking binge, and well, well you can just imagine the rest.

One day a guy I recognize from Liechester walks into Cassidy's. He's on his own. Must admit, I'm completely taken aback by his entrance. There's something predatory about this solitary wolf. Makes the blood in my head gush and freeze. For a flinching moment I think I must be seeing things. Can't believe my own eyes. What on earth is he doing here? I recoil into my barstool.

Now I know the world is a small place, but it seems a little too small at this moment in time. Chummy Gaynor eyes Toby Marshall with suspicion. Maybe my gripping feeling that I was being followed had been real.

The force of Toby Marshall's sudden presence really hits me. The anonymity I've found in this far-away state falls away from me.

It's as if my part of California is crumbling from beneath me, and will now be lost forever. In a self-delusionary effort to disappear - I close my eyes. I ephemerally wish I could just be floating away on a small coastal crust, with my feet dangling consolingly in the pacific blue. Right now, this is what I want more than anything. I wish that I could just float all the way over to Honolulu safely, and regain my anonymity again. This is my wish. I open my eyes. Fuck. There, right before me, is mischievous Toby Marshall. I'm scared. If truth be told, I'm shitting my pissed stained pants. It's an uncanny encounter...a little bit *too* coincidental.

To my astonishment Toby Marshall asks about John Pudding and Morpheye. It's a real bolt from the blue. Feel rumbled. Feel this is the end. A contaminated picture flashes across my mind, the moment he mentions their monstrous names. I ask myself - *what exactly is motivating this man? Why is he talking about Morpheye? Why is he talking about John Pudding? What's the craic? What on earth is going on here?* Here I am thinking that maybe I've escaped all this Blue Hole shit. Thinking that maybe I'm just starting to get over it all a bit, and now, now there's some dodgy geezer right in my face, probing me about it. Why? Has he been following me? Has he been spying on me? Has he been sent to get me? Is he going to kill me?

Toby Marshall has the face of a butcher. He's a Liechester man, born and bred. He speaks with a tobacco nurtured huskiness. Really, his voice is like a gangster's grunt, more than anything else. "You used to work for the Pudding&Morpheye partnership didn't yuh?" I could really do without this. This is the last thing I need.

"Mmmm. Eeeeerh. Yeah."

"Ow was it? What yuh make of um?" I swallow hard.

"They're nasty bastards." I speak my mind. Surprise myself actually. My tongue is all loose, what with all the Guinness in my gut and all. False courage innit? My words don't seem to startle Toby Marshall in any way though. He says nothing else. Just starts circling the bar, like a shark.

My first thought is that Toby Marshall is a Mafia hitman – a Mafia hitman who's been paid to silence me. I whisper cagily to Taige: "This guy's after summit mate. He's ere to slice me up. How mental is this?"

"Pretty fucking mental mate!" Taige replies restlessly. Despite his own unease, he somehow manages to calm me down. "He 'ain't here to kill ya...coz if he was he'd probably 'ave done it by now."

102

"What's he after then man?"

"Dunno."

"Shit man."

"Stay on your guard mate, maybe he's after some sort of information."

"Like what Taige. I'm already well on my guard man."

"Dunno. Politics innit."

"Can't cope with this Taige."

"Just be wary. He could be attempting to ascertain your orientation, if you catch my drift?"

"No. I don't catch your drift???"

"Whose side your on. Your political orientation." He utters vigilantly.

"I 'ain't on anybody's side. I'm on my side – I'm a bloody individual – call me a misfit if you like." Feel panicky. Feel powerless. Feel massively re-ruffled.

"Then again – maybe you are jinksed Buddy!"

"Whaddya mean?"

"Maybe you are damned! Doomed for the plughole-of-death, Bud!"

"Oh don't say that – don't bloody mess about Taige!"

"I 'ain't messing. Can tell this is serious. Oh I don't bloody know do I..."

Toby Marshall certainly doesn't hang about. Does a few circling laps of Cassidy's, and he's gone. But I have a feeling he'll be back. I'm constantly looking over my shoulders now, just in case Toby Marshall happens to be lurking somewhere in the shadows. Feel jumpy. Feel chronically suspicious. Shame, my life seems doomed wherever I go. Am I imperiled forever by my Blue Hole past? Is there no escaping this wretched entanglement? Bloody seems like it. Yet my instinct for survival tells me to stay in San Francisco for just a little while longer. So I do.

A couple of days before I'm due to leave San Francisco I find myself having a somewhat tongue-tied, but reasonably cordial pint, with Toby Marshall. We're in Cassidy's. It certainly isn't something I predict, or plan, or desire. Over our pint, he asks me politely whether I'll post a postcard for him at the airport. This strikes me as an unusually odd request. Why would a full-grown man be asking me to do this? Surely he knows there are loads of post boxes scattered across this City? It's not as if a postcard will get to its destination any quicker by sending it from an airport, now is it? If it's just a goddamn postcard, what's the urgency? Is this an attempt at entrapment or something? Certain individuals, get other ill-fated folk, to do some awfully unlawful stuff at airports, or so I've heard. Can't help thinking that if I post Toby Marshall's postcard for him at the airport, I'll end up in a real grim spot of bother. I simply say 'no' to Toby Marshall's request. Then I point out a post-box to him on Folsom, between 6th and 7th street. "Thanks," he says in a disappointed tone.

Well, I don't really know much about these kind of things, but what I do know, is here's a bloke, who isn't really my friend, and he's quizzing me about personal stuff, and asking me to do weird shit. My head hurts. Toby Marshall is up to something. Toby Marshall is not my mate. Toby Marshall isn't a hippy. Still fear a contract's been taken out on my life. If I'm honest, I'll admit it to you, that's what I'm thinking. It's my inner-most fear, and yeah, I know it's highly unlikely, but it's there, in my froggy mind. Bewildered with alarm, I draw as much attention as possible towards myself, in fear that my own life is at stake. Cigarette in hand, and with my lucky second-hand red shirt on my back, I stride around San Francisco like a walking warning sign.

My head's all chaotic, but I'm trying to put on a valiant face. Fortunately, down at Cassidy's that evening, one of Taige's pals suddenly has a bountiful supply of weed on him. Apparently some dude just gives it to him! Unusual. Nobody's ever just given me a bag full of weed for nothing. It's a big bag full an'all. Anyhows, I step outside Cassidy's, and have a toke on his freebie weed. Wanna at least try and keep everything nicely in perspective – don't I. This is one of my last evenings in San Francisco. Suddenly, I start hallucinating. My hallucinations are of the afterworld. As I look around Cassidy's, everyone begins to look like vampires from hell. No shit. I now know it's time to move on. Need to go, before I too become a doomed soul. Got to get out of this place. Goddamit. Turns out the dope we've been smoking is a powerful psychedelic form of East African grass. This grass, which *miraculously* appears on the scene as a cadeaux, is staggeringly strong, nigh on toxic even.

I stay in San Francisco for as long as I can, that is until the very last day on my ninety-day tourist visa. I'm not looking forward to going back home. Not at all. Just thinking about it makes me feel rattled. I know I have to return to Liechester though. I think to myself - *I can't go out like this. I've got to be more, well, more like me.* In San Francisco I've been acting unlike me. In fact, I've been acting more like my abuser. I strangely start to imitate the Jägermeister. You do here people say that the abused become abusers themselves. There's a lot of truth in that I reckon. Well, I can at least understand the concept of abuse ricocheting. Still, I would never fire a gun at somebody. Taige is well aware of my reluctance to return home. Deep down though, I think he knows I will eventually go. Liechester is waiting for Pudding and Morpheye to get their comeuppance. Liechester is waiting to be liberated. I want to try my hand as a journalist. Now's the time. Simply have to go back. Have to get things fixed.

The day before I leave the vibrant charm of San Francisco, I find myself standing on a corner of Haight Street. I'm doing little else but exposing my senses to it all. The atmosphere is typically vivacious. Then a hunched old woman, who looks like a decaying gipsy, comes stumbling up to me. Her facial skin resembles a walnut's shell, and she smells of mothballs. Yum. *Perhaps she spends her spare time hibernating in wardrobes or something* - I muse. Anyhows her mothball pong is nauseating. Smacking me. Making me feel as if I'm starting to decay. The decrepit woman's eyeballs are like opaque white marbles. She's as blind as a bat. At least she appears that way. She clutches hold of my wrist with her scrawny hand. I notice that she has long, bright blue fingernails. Chique. She drags calculatingly at one of her saggy eyelids, and exposes a cold looking white eye globe. Yuck. She stares at me. It's a penetrating stare of nothingness...blindness. Feel sick. Still clinging onto me the blue-nailed gipsy woman voices these spellbinding words: "A colourful past means a colourful future." Then she let's go. It's a hypnotic collision. Wish it hadn't happened. Won't forget this moment in a hurry. Her gaudy quotation stains my mind. Then I see cold-blooded, half-human/half-digital wild beasts, scavenging the streets. I see delinquent colours flooding my brain, the skies and the world. Next I see blue.

It's a good idea to get away from Liechester for a while. Time allows my temper to calm down. Don't whole-heartedly wanna go back, but I'm compelled to. To me San Francisco will always be Taige's town. I can't stay here. I have to go back to Liechester to face my mainframe demons. Taige on the other hand is asking me to stay. "Stay with us. You've made it all seem real." Until I pop into Taige's scene, he's just been drifting through life like a boozed-up banshee. The day his father's heart stopped beating, a part of Taige's heart also died. He's actually been doubting his very existence. He has. Life hasn't seemed real ever since Leonard passed away. Yet Taige's life feels particularly unreal in San Francisco. The drink, the drugs, the foggy decadence, have all been clouding his mind. In truth though, Taige's fading existence, somehow gives me a flicker of hope.

On my last night in San Francisco we have a farewell gargle at Cassidy's. I'm touched by their affectionate send-off. Hop-a-long-Cassidy is singing out-of-tune in a rich Guinness voice. The thing I remember most about this evening is that *he* slips me a $2 note for my trip home. It's an approving gesture, as if I've past some kinda test, because up until then, I do wonder whether he *really* likes me or not. He hugs me and says: "Your deadly."

"Good luck with everything Tim...hope your knee gets better soon."

The next day, just before I depart, Taige smiles at me stiffly. It's painful for him to see me go. His face is white and worried and sad. Then he hastily turns his back on me. He'll miss me and I'll miss him. Taige doesn't accompany me to the airport. He's an apprehensive soul.

So, I leave my companion's salient City. We were 'alone with everybody' together that summer.

As I set foot back in Liechester the hissing, haunting voices return...*You can't blag a blagger! Buddy.....be good! I'm not a clever man! Don't think you're getting your old job back!* And then...**Bang...goes the gun...in my head.** It's like suddenly the voices come on again, as if somebody has re-dropped a needle on a badly scratched record. As for the bang from the gun, words cannot adequately explain how that impinges upon me.

I hate this gritty town. Just days after returning from America, I walk edgily past The Blue Hole. My mind is full of fear and curiosity. Is it still open to the public? Are those nasty bastards still around? Low and behold Morpheye is stood outside the entrance, but he looks ailing. His complexion is drained of colour. He's lost weight and appears frailer. Have I ruined him? Has he cracked? Luckily he doesn't notice me. I fear that if he does he may well go for me. What I mean is, he may well lash out at me in one of his infamous fits of rage, and try to blind me, or worse still - kill me. But Morpheye looks slightly weaker. His look makes me sense I'm stronger. I've not forgotten a goddamn thing. A few days pass by. I begin to feel restless.

One of the first things I decide to do on my return to Liechester, is pay The Blue Hole crowd a visit. Crazy I know, but if I don't stand up to them, who will? A close friend accompanies me. As I enter the upstairs bar, I catch sight of Morpheye in my peripheral vision. I rapidly refocus my eyes. He's lurking, like a viper in the corner. His face is awash with incredulity. There's a look of bewilderment in his deadly eyes. The fact that I dare to come back here, must make him feel he's losing his fearsome touch. I can see him grimacing in his red brick corner. Are his fingers thirsty for blood again? Is he already contemplating the gouge? He certainly appears ready to molest me. He suddenly lunges forward - only to be barred by the rock-solid arm of the Jägermeister. The Jägermeister stops Morpheye from attacking me. How audacious of him! Does the Jägermeister feel responsible? Is the Jägermeister really trying to shield and protect me? I'm sure the Jägermeister doesn't expect to see me here either. I'm sure this isn't part of his plan. The Jägermeister is probably even more surprised than Morpheye to see me back in the Blue Hole. He's astounded by my effrontery and foolhardiness. (The Jägermeister might just have saved my life. Who knows what may have happened if he hadn't stopped Morpheye from attacking me? Imagine. There could have been a real blood bath. Maybe I would have lost my sight. Maybe I would have lost my life). Nobody's stood up to Morpheye like this before. He isn't use to such resistance. Perhaps he's losing his grip; losing his power. Anyway, I don't stay for a drink. I've done what I want to do. I'm fizzing with rage. I'm more defiant than ever.

CHAPTER 6 – THE JOURNALIST'S DEADLINE.

"Is it not better to die trying, than to let fear of what might happen, rob us of our bravery and paralyze our souls?"

So, why the crusade? It's my blue entanglement that drives me. I'm up against the Liechester mob. This town's been absorbed in a blue-boxed life of its own for far too long. It's my duty to 'flag it up'. I believe I've good reason to raise the alarm. The longer they go unchallenged, the more their arrogance will grow, and the more their arrogance grows, the more dangerous they will become. This is what I'm fighting against inside my moralistic mind. This is why I have to expose them. It's a heartfelt pursuit. I'm startled, but determined. I'm determined to defeat this blue beast of a wave. It's like I've been preparing for this all my life. It's a job to die for! I'm a young man with blistering ambition. I'm dying to be heard, but also petrified to speak.

There are many unanswered questions on my litigious mind. I'm sure this Blue Hole fixation isn't just an exclusive perception of mine. I'm looking for answers that are difficult to find, but what I can feel is more than just a convoluted journalistic hunch. It's real, and extremely dangerous. I want to probe more, but I don't really have the appropriate power to investigate this dastardly scene any further.

There's a mendacious atmosphere in the Liechester Echo newspaper office. Should be an atmosphere of sincerity and seriousness. Ricochets of laughter are bouncing off the disingenuous walls. We're meant to be fact finders, but we're always being told: "bring out the colour in your copy. Find something juicy. Where's the spice?" We aren't here to merely entertain the reader, we're here to inform them, aren't we? Seems to me like we're being encouraged to produce a scandalous distortion of reality. We're persuaded to create and churn out lively fact stories. I persistently wonder - *who's pressing the press*?

Dreadful things happen, and I witness reporters getting all thrilled, because it means they've got a front-page story. I think to myself *"Gas pipes sabotaged along the golden mile. Thousands of Asians lay at home freezing, whilst journalists in their cosy warm office get all excited,"* would make a candid and interesting headline.

It's a bit perverse. Here are all these *allegedly* intelligent individuals, waiting for something bad to happen, so they can get a 'spicy' story, and make a name for themselves. At times it's almost as if they're hoping that something bad will happen, so they'll have something juicy to report. Sick really. They aren't much better than the criminals themselves.

I'm surrounded by a bunch of whingeing scribblers. Most of them seem to know little about the complexities of life. Most of them don't know how cruel life can actually be. The bulk of them are bookish and lonely nobodies, who are soon to become backstabbing, sewer scavenging scumbags. Why are they so desperate to make a name for themselves? If they want to depict the truth, they should be reporting about what's happening to me and my family, but none of them, except for some dude called Julian Sparks, has a clue what's going on.

"I wonder" Sparky muses obliquely. He has the ability to see things others can't. Here's someone who can get near to exposing the truth. But then is that really what I want? Do I want the mess my family's in to be plastered across the newspapers and shared throughout our community? Do I want our trauma to be pooled? Course it isn't. What good would that do? When something bad happens to you, the very last thing you want to do, is share your misery with an entire community. Journalists should take the time to think about what I'm saying. People generally don't want to share their grief in public. I mean if something tragic *were* to happen in their lives, how would they appreciate it if a bunch of hounding reporters and photographers turned up on their doorstep, looking for a scandal to spread across their newspaper? Sure as hell they wouldn't appreciate it. Most reporters are just looking for a colourful story in order to bolster their own career. That's the saddest thing.

As I look back and remember, ever since Pudding learnt about my journalistic aspirations, there was a distinct change in the atmosphere at The Blue Hole. The mood became staggeringly claustrophobic. This must have meant something. Pudding still thinks I'll squeal. His mission is to keep my tongue still and my hands tied. However, I don't want what's happened to me, to happen to anyone else. I don't want the innocent to suffer. This is what my conflict-ridden mind is telling me. I've become this scared, but passionate bag of nerves. The boys at The Blue Hole suspect I'm plotting something. They've good reason to. I know they suspect me. I can smell their suspicion. The problem is, they think I'm a malign force, while at the same time, I'm thinking they're the malign force. These guys are driving racism underground. They're winning the propaganda struggle in Liechester. By shrouding their own corrupt military, political and business operations in an underground murkiness, they're managing to thrive and expand. I, on the other hand, am exposed to the harsh gaze of our community. Incroyable.

I'm close to physical collapse, I can tell you. It's like I might just fall to the floor at any given moment, and just no longer be me. *People should be protesting, but nobody is.* I'm finding it virtually impossible to protest. My silence may well be interpreted by some, as a sign of sympathy for Morpheye & Pudding's divisive regime. But it's not. I want to expose them. I'm accused of being an agitator. Some blame me for fanning the flames of revolution. Some blame me for exacerbating racial friction in Liechester. I've become a scapegoat, a convenient propaganda scapegoat. They're trying to pin this one on me. All I'm attempting to do is expose a truth. Am *trying* to be an assiduous activist. The last thing I want is to become a human rights bogeyman.

Have you ever felt like a nuisance? There are searing feelings of persecution developing inside of me. Then, out of the blue, at some point in the autumn of 2000, I receive a text message. "He knows no fear, he knows no danger, he knows nothing…you only laugh twice." The sender is nameless. Nothing but the number 1111 is assigned to the text. Seems as if I've rattled somebody's cage. Somebody is nervous. Who is this Joker? I receive a constant barrage of curious text messages. Sparky's sure they're from the police. The same thought's already crossed my mind. I've given up showing them to my friends, through fear of being labelled a lunatic.

I think I've a rather unique and liberal way of thinking because of my mixture of French and English blood. I certainly have a different way of thinking to the majority of those around me in Liechester, but that doesn't mean I'm wrong.

This town's plagued with rumour and fear, yet the truth remains censored. Why am I so concerned with the fate of this wayward town? It's my home, my birthplace - perhaps that's why I'm so concerned with the discrimination and injustice here. Having said all this, at this very moment in time, this town is suffocating me. I wonder hard to myself - *Is it actually possible to expose the truth within the choking confines of journalistic law?*

Resistance against tyranny comes naturally and logically to me. My struggle is arduous, but rational. It's something I just have to try and do. I'm desperate to expose the truth. We all want to influence the world in some way, don't we? I want to be a journalist, so I can 'hang' these troublemaking pigs. I'm prepared to stick my neck out, many aren't. And so my whistle-blowing plight begins. I believe it's in the public interest.

October, 2000. For the first time in a long while, I don't fall asleep whilst reading the newspaper. Whilst I'm studying to be a journalist the Liechester Echo, the local daily rag, reviews The Blue Hole as: 'The safest place to be in town, bar none'. Bullshit. I'm flabbergasted by what I'm reading. It's enough to make me leap out of my chair, and start pacing round the room in a rage. Those demons at The Blue Hole obviously have some of the press under their weighty thumb. Later, as I continue to flick through my newspaper, all I can see is vulgar commercialism. It makes the whole world seem senseless. It makes me feel sad. Our local paper has become a propaganda machine for Morpheye's regime. What they're churning out is laughable, but effective propaganda. Am I fighting a losing battle? Is there no end to the corruption of these wiseguys? They even controll the press. Then I get this feeling again, this blue gutter feeling of mine. This place just isn't the same. Can't ever really call this place home again. Of course, they're reluctant to allow anyone to peer behind their mask. They'll do anything to preserve their reputation. They're wise enough to fool the majority, with their twisted misinformation. I plough on with my ambition, nonetheless. It's as if my concern for humanity is being put to the test. How much do I care?

Instinct tells me to give it all up in order to survive, but for a while I ignore my gut feeling. It's them this time who are being warned. They didn't envisage that a 'kid' would try and run this show. I need to draw as much attention to myself as possible, before they put me down. Rumours around town are reaching fever pitch. Of course there are always rumours going around town, rumour is everywhere. However, this one sounds so extravagant, that folk believe there must be some truth in it.

Become asphyxiated by my own inner liberalism. It's killing me to keep quiet, but I genuinely sense that my life is in real danger. Fear if I open my mouth, something terrible might happen. Know I can't keep it up for much longer. Need to talk. Need to blow the whistle. I'm inconsolable really. No one here can really help me. This is corruption at its highest level, and I'm the unfortunate bugger who's unearthed it. So, I have to live with it. It's not something I want to boast about, like some old men delight in bragging about their wartime misadventures. I prefer to keep it to myself. At first I despise it when people ask questions. After a while though, I begin to appreciate it when people begin to probe, especially when they're genuinely concerned. If I do start to tell someone about my experience, then I feel they deserve to at least get the entire picture. So I begin my disturbing monologue, which lasts for some time. Already feel half dead, but to have my past denied is be soul destroying. A wise man once told me – 'Its denial which assures the wound never heals.' That makes sense to me. Besides I'm sick to death of keeping quiet. Why should I suffer in silence and deny all of this? I'm not going to let this go. I'm not going to let my trauma disappear into the mists of time.

I'm walking faster than I used to. Often experience surges of panic as I pace about town. Sense the devil himself at my heels. Wonder when he'll be back - what he'll do next. Now isn't the time to be silent. Now's the time to protest. But I'm struggling to find my voice.

Subterfuge is something Morpheye is more than familiar with. Nothing's too devious for him, if it means maintaining control over his enemies. An accomplice of the Morpheye movement has moved in next door to our family home. He's planted bugs to listen into my family's chatter. The Blue Hole partnership want to know whether I've gone blabbing to mummy and daddy. They need to know, what I know, and what my parents know. We're under surveillance. I'm ashamed of myself for what I've gone and got my family mixed up in. My Dad's a distinguished political figure in Liechester, with a faultless reputation. He's also chairman of the local police authority. It's quite an influential position. If I tell my Dad about what I've got caught up in, all hell could break loose. Worst of all, he may turn his back on me. Besides, my Dad and I never talk about anything, so why should we start now? Morpheye doesn't know about my tight-lipped relationship with my Dad. There are some things even he doesn't know about. Morpheye wants to know what I'm up to. I got too close to him. Now he wants to control me. Now I'm paying the price. In his own special way he keeps an eye on me. It's his capability to snoop, and his elaborate network of spies, which allows Morpheye to conduct his revolutionary mission. He has a hacking hold on this godforsaken town. His knowledge is his power. He's a clever man. He presides over - everything.

As I train to be a reporter, I've this constant feeling that things are going to go hideously wrong, and go hideously wrong they do. It's like there's a large black cloud constantly hovering over me. Like I'm being shadowed. Like somebody is constantly watching me. As I say, rumour is rife, as always in tittle-tattle Liechester. People are beginning to gossip about The Blue Hole. They're good at that here, adept at it in fact, gossiping that is. There is *talk* of terrorism, and *talk* of anti-terrorism about town. These seem to be fashionable terms to describe violent men who go about their business without restraint.

I'm having a real hard time of it. I go out-on-the-town one evening. I'm quite simply trying my best to have a pleasurable time. During the evening I'm tripped up, spat at, and have a pint chucked over me. These incidents are all perpetrated by people I don't know. The culmination of this nasty evening, comes at around 1.00am. As I'm walking out of 'High-Spirits,' the bouncer tries to cripple me by stamping on my ankle. I've done nothing to warrant this violent assault. It's a completely unprovoked attack. He makes a vicious connection. Do I have *'kick me I'm a trainee journalist"* written on my back or something? Perhaps I just have one of those faces? I amble around like an ostracized cripple. For months it's painful to just toddle about town. Feel detested. In an attempt to avoid passing The Blue Hole, I eccentrically begin taking illogical routes across town, such is my fear.

On another night-out-on-the-town, a guy seizes my forearm in a nightclub called 'Havanas.' The Jägermeister's standing alongside him, summons the guy to grab hold of me. A remix of Jaydee's plastic dreams is propelling its way around the cavernous club. I can remember that. Kinda lost in music when the guy grasps my arm. I pull away. Spectacularly. My reaction: superfast and powerful. Actually, can't believe my own strength. Even though I'm immersed in the music, I'm ready and waiting to be attacked. The Jägermeister, and his latest impressionable subordinate, just stand there, simpering and acting all macho-like. Outwardly I play it cool. Inwardly, feel like an excessively restrained Spanish bull.

To me news is *something* that someone, somewhere, wants suppressed. Anything else is just embellished advertising. Well - I'm suppressed. I've some *real* news, but I can't report what I want to. Can't report that suppressed *something*. Think a lot about free will. On

113

the other hand, think a lot about state control. Come to the conclusion - I don't feel like a free man. *If we're not free to write what we want, we're not free at all* - I'm thinking. Want to tell it how it really is.

Entering the world of Journalism is a reactionary calling. I quickly learn it's difficult to report the truth, and the industry's more about money than morality. Course it is. What was I thinking? Nowadays in terms of what sells newspapers, 'successful journalism' is, more often than not, 'bad journalism'. As a nation we're becoming celebrity obsessed. Lewd and licentious stories sell newspapers. Ethical stories tend to be dragged into the digital recycle bin, and left there. Indeed, digital media, appears to be going down the same route. It's just as bad, if not worse. I'm dismayed at how the journalism industry operates. The UK journalism industry is in an unacceptable, if not wholly intolerable state. I hope the world of newspaper reporting might liberate me, if anything it chokes me. The fact that I'm now limping around with a swollen ankle, doesn't help matters. I'm unconventional, I suppose. In this world of journalism I've been sucked into, there seems to be far too many conventions. Originality and vision are stifled, strangled even. True opinion and spot-on depiction of events aren't allowed, in what seems to me like a legally repressive industry. God only knows what the term 'free press' means ???? ????? There's no room for my philosophical reaction in the papers anyhows. Can't report the truth. Journalistic law sees to that. The notion that I'm a truth-seeker seems ridiculous. This isn't the right line of work for a writer like me. I'm more of a poet I suppose. Not a reporter. Don't quite realise this though at point of entry. For sure, I want to write, but this definitely 'aint my scene; I'm not cut out to be a newspaperman. Find it all very unenlightening and disappointing really.

So, I spend my time limping around, scavenging for a spurious story. Whilst all the time all I can think of is the harrowing experience I've gone through, and am still going through, but can't document. I want to write about my coup, not about how the number 55 bus service to Chisit Heights *might* be axed, or about how Miss Cakebread's pub quiz fundraiser evening raked in £21 towards the battle of flowers parish float. Perhaps I can be classed as a writer, but I'm certainly not a puckish reporter. I've never been the interfering type, inquisitive maybe, interfering definitely not. The last thing I want is to be seen as a tiptoeing mole. But this isn't any ordinary story I've unearthed. This is a ground-breaking scoop. Want to criticise powerful people. Want to criticise people, I probably shouldn't be trying to criticise.

I've not always had this urge to become a journalist, life's unforeseen circumstances just kinda press me into it. Even so, my life as a journalist, seems comparatively doomed anyway. The world of journalism is far too contrived for my liking. Like I say, there doesn't seem enough room for 'personal comment'. Disputatious journalistic articles are not welcome. Editors want gossipy and conventional pieces of work and they expect you to churn the tame stuff out; conveyor belt style. Certainly in the regional press, anything that's remotely defamatory, or risky, is simply dumped in cyberspace. So often what you end up with is jazzy, yet phoney headlines. The headlines are then accompanied by docilely conforming copy, copy which doesn't quite seem to compliment the overly colourful headlines. The reader's often left feeling slightly duped. Why's it going this way? Could it *possibly* be because it's about advertising profit, and not about exposing the truth? Why are we misleading the general public? Is safe scandal really what they demand? In this way, are we not constantly depriving folk of a 'real' reflection of the true horrors in society. There's something obscene about the business of gathering news. I mean, I feel like I've had prurience poured all over me. Feel suddenly, contaminated by curiousness. Journalism is by no means an honourable profession. Seems like a spineless and fraudulent business to me. I certainly feel like a fraud, and I'm only a trainee journalist. Well anyway, I become swiftly disillusioned with the way in which the industry works. To be a successful journalist, it seems as if you have to be obsessed with gossipy scandal, and to be obsessed with gossipy scandal, is not a pleasant place for one's mind to be. I'm careering down the wrong path - something in my blood tells me so. With the digital age ahead...my prediction: it's only going to get uglier...

Still feel tainted by association and I struggle with obscure feelings of shame. Has my reputation been irreversibly damaged? Everywhere I go in Liechester, I can feel the eyes of someone glaring at me. Most of the time, I turn and stare wildly back. All they can see is a warped ex-Blue Hole figure, and that's enough to make me feel abhorred and tremendously sad. I'm a young man with a troubled spirit. Did destiny will this state-of-doom? Certainly I endure a kind of affliction of fate. Indeed, feel cursed by the cult of my own personality. Am cast as a scoundrel, and it seems there's no escaping my stained label. I've become ill-famed. I battle on as a hobbling unprofessional, with a cramping shame on my name, feeling half-mad. *What does the future hold for wannabee reporter Buddy Rioux?*

My family receive horrifying threats on a weekly basis. It's initiated in October, 2000, a few weeks after I start my journalism course. The campaign of terror continues...

We become the target of a blood-spattered reprisal. It's a messy onslaught. An unwelcome present arrives on our doorstep. An unsavoury cocktail of human faeces, blood, and oil is smeared on our front door. Yes, thanks to someone's sick imagination, our front door is now covered with a dripping excrement mixture. The front door of our home is darkened. The inside of our home is stained in their murky shadow. To be sure this is barbaric intimidation. *They're going to kill us* - I fear. Isn't just an isolated warning. A whole stream of terrorization ensues. Distressing cries of 'it's happened again!' are all too familiar. The filthy attacks usually come at the weekend, and I know who's to blame. *Obviously got them completely rattled!!* I'm responsible for exposing my family to the wrath of these terrorists. This is political. This is dirty. This is extreme. It's the obscene work of gangland Liechester. The dark side of the world at play.

Imagine if you had a mixture of blood and shit and oil hauled onto the front door of your family home? Imagine how hurt that would make you feel? You'd probably feel scolded and victimized. Now imagine how it would make you feel, if these vile acts of desecration continued to happen, again and again and again. Am advised to ignore it. Am advised to get away. But if I ignore this black-hearted presence, then it will never be remedied. They'll continue corrupting society. They'll go and ruin other people's lives. Besides, this is all happening on my territory. Why should we be made to live in fear? Why should we surrender to this macabre intimidation? Why should I be made to run away?

We're gripped by some kind of terror fever. As a family we're horrorstruck. They've made it their business to try and break up my family. All this bad shit starts happening because of what I know. It's entirely my fault. By-passers see the stains on our front door. It doesn't take long for the rash tongues to start wagging. The eyes of our neighbours are now upon us. They make their own minds up about what they see. It's as if a plague has denounced our family home. Find myself praying a lot. Pray to God to spare me from the mess of life.

Please spare me from the blood, the shit, the stains and the pain. What should I do? Please let me win through.

If I publish something which damages their reputation, I'll be damned forever. This is a game of life and death. Feel unfree. Am running out of energy and journalistic oomph. My voice adopts a somewhat frenetic tone. My sentences are rushed, like an impatient childs. I've gone and driven myself to the brink of mental exhaustion. I've been in this kind of terror-stricken overdrive mode for too long. I'm pressurised into not publishing. Don't know what I'm going to publish, or what I could publish for that matter. All I do know is, somebody doesn't want me to publish something. I'm not even close to publishing anything, but they don't know that, and so the monstrous threats continue to come. You know what this all means don't you? I must be onto something. Their depraved souls are anguished with the fear of exposure. At least I've achieved something.

Our lives are turned upside down. People may think I'm foolish to stand up to these guys, but in my heart, I know it's the bravest, and right thing to do. However, the safety of my family is now my main concern. We also receive a letter addressed to 'The Riouxs'. There's a razor blade in the seal. My mum opens up the letter with her finger, nearly slices it off. Inside the envelope there's a random piece of torn newspaper. It's about the size of a large postage stamp. This incident's nothing short of a terrorist assault. The police are informed. Owing to the fact that my Dad is chairman on the police authority, the local constabulary are treating these fanatical occurrences more seriously, than perhaps they would otherwise have done. Our family home is placed under-watch.

The stakeout outside our home is a futile operation. The police never witness anything. They're useless. They don't achieve anything. Of course they don't. I believe the local force are in on it themselves. Sparky, the shrewdest trainee on my journalism course, shares my suspicions. This razor blade incident puts an end to what has been an almost unquenchable curiosity...My inquisitive quest. My veritable thirst for truth. My passion to expose. Annulled. With a bang from a gun. A splattering torrent of blood, shit & oil. And a razor blade sealed in an envelope. Is this not an inhuman succession of punishable deeds? Is this not an extreme attempt to suppress? Is this not part of a merciless terrorism campaign? If it is not, then I know not what is.

I'm freaked out. There's fear in my widened eyes, fear in my soundless voice, and fear in my frozen mind. Is it not better to die trying, than to let fear of what might happen, rob us of our bravery and paralyze our souls? Yet these are men I should fear.

I'm a traumatized, wannabe journalist. I am, quintessentially, a silenced writer. I'm thrown into a crisis of conscience, to let the truth be known, or to save the lives of my family. Although inside I'm surging with fury, for the sake of my family, I do what I have to - I keep silent. Rumours are reaching high places. "What's the scandal?" - my uncle Derren asks? He works for some powerful and glorious squad of secret police officers. He's very British. Very nationalistic. Very much the 'you 'ain't seen me! Right?' type. He knows something's up. He's wise enough to work that one out. But for some reason, I can't bring myself to open up. Events are weighing heavily upon us all.

It becomes obvious to me who's running this town. It's not the politicians. It's not the judges. It's not the journalists. It's Morpheye and his movement.

I'm censored. In an attempt to subvert their overbearing command on society, I put pen to paper. *Have you ever felt like you're running out of time?* I fall asleep clutching my pen. I wake up with ink stained sheets. I'm upset, and it upsets me even more to see my Dad with his head in his hands. He's at the end of his tether. Am walking around with my fists clenched like hams in my pockets. I don't consciously clench them. Half the time I don't even realise I'm doing it. It's just a physical reaction, something my body decides to do, because it feels under attack. I sense, for the first time, that I could kill a man. I sense, I could kill another man, with my bare knuckle fists. The nervous fist clenching is something I'm going to have to stop doing.

How on earth can I document what's happening? We're limited to a 300-word limit per article - one of the journalism industries conventions. Can't possibly convey what's happening here in just 300 words. Can I? Anyhow, I don't want to spend the rest of my life criticizing, and summarizing the ill-fated struggle of others, in less than 300 words, 5 times a day. I become dispassionate about the world of journalism almost overnight. I'm not going to make it as a journalistic hero, an intrepid reporter I am not. I have no appetite for 'news'. Am questioning myself a lot lately. Who am I to expose and shame others? Who am I to play at being, some kind of valiant and denouncing infiltrator? Who am I to judge and condemn? I'm an impostor, trying to trespass on other people's private lives. What do I know about them really? What do I know of *their* struggle? What right do I have to poke around, and intrude into *their* lives? Find the newspaper industry to be a capricious business. There's nowhere near enough time to investigate matters properly. There's too much pressure to produce skimping, second-rate copy. Newspaper offices are like factories for words I reckon - they just churn out phoniness. I'm beginning to discern there's something I don't like in myself. I'm becoming duplicitous. I'm becoming more like those I hate. As a trainee journalist, I feel vulture-like. Have to halt this predatory occupational transmutation. Just isn't me.

So much goes unreported, it's quite unbelievable. *Does the public realise just how much 'news' goes unreported? I wonder?* Well, there's a whole web of tragic human experience that never gets documented, of that I'm sure. What goes unreported is what actually matters. I wonder what other ghastly misdemeanours those Blue Hole beasts are guilty of? What other heinous crimes are they committing? What have I not seen? What else is going unreported? Who else are they suppressing? What else is going on in their seedy underworld?

As I train to be a journalist I suffer from relentless intimidation. This unfurling event is monumental I deduce. It defies convention. Sadly though, my inclination to search for the truth is extinguished. *Life is just too complicated, too veritably inexplicable* - I think to myself. My youthful verve vanishes. Soon I'll have a whole head of grey hair, no doubt.

I'm badly treated, but not that badly treated. There are others who are abused in a different way, a more physical, less mental way. These guys take a different terror tact depending on their aggressor's social status. I say aggressor, what I mean to say is, any human pest that gets in their way. It's no good leaving a physical scar on a colourful, prominent public figure, but this doesn't mean they never use physical torture. A more graphic, hands on form of control, is reserved for the real social misfits. Grotesque facial mutilations send out a message of 'don't mess with us or you'll be next.' There are warning scars scattered around town. Scars that can't be washed off. Mutilated ears and noses are commonplace. What's worse, the victims don't want to talk about their disfigurements. Creates a resounding culture of dread amongst the Liechester street urchins.

There are those who can't believe I hadn't seen the danger, but life isn't always about *avoiding* danger is it? Surely a flourishing journalist is always in trouble. How long will their campaign of terror continue? Why do they harbour so much contempt? What are they so desperate to suppress? Do they really seek total chaos? I'm attempting to challenge the unchallenged. Want to write. Crave it, in fact. There has to be some kind of opposition to their regime.

I wonder what I should do, but I do nothing. I keep quiet. I write secretively in my flower-power notebook, but I don't show anyone what I'm writing. Writing is like a lifesaving device. Like resistance. Bizarrely, feels as if I might get caught, and stopped, at any given moment. For me it's a novel way of getting rid of my unmentionables. My flower-power notebook is all I have in the world. *Someone else will have to decide what to do about all this* - I tell myself. Then I feel like a yellow belly again.

When I tell Derren I'm training to be a reporter, he laughes disdainfully. It bugs me so much. Here am I, battering my head against a brickwall, trying to expose a corruption that threatens to undermine our society, and all he can do is laugh. It's almost as if he has something to hide himself. He sneeringly recommends: "If *you choose* to follow a career in journalism, then my advice to you would be *always tell the truth.*" His last few words are laced with weight. They are followed by another round of frosty laughter. Weird it is. Creepy. I wonder if he realises just how perverse a task that is. Perhaps he does, and that's why he's laughing. Maybe he's living a lie, covering something up. Perhaps he can't handle the truth. Possibly he fears exposure himself. Yeah that's probably it. Anyhows, feel massively uninspired after our brief telephone conversation. Deren's derisive counsel makes me even more off-colour. Will never forget his last laugh – was a proper cold and pealing cackle.

The world of journalism is a tricky and thorny business. Sometimes it can be exceptionally dangerous to even attempt to report the truth. In fact, sometimes it seems like it's downright impossible to report the truth. Why do I feel so goddamn responsible? I am incensed. Would the world be a better place if I were dead? Would the world be more aware? Maybe if I were gone, this terrorising scandal would be brought to the forefront of the public's consciousness? Is Martyrdom an option? Questions such as these are on my mind. You know everyday is a struggle, it's a struggle to get up in the morning, it's a struggle to remain calm when I'm bloody boiling inside, it's a struggle to keep quiet when all I want to do is scream, it's a struggle not to protest, it's a struggle to change what is wrong, it's a struggle to remember, it's a struggle to forget…everyday is a goddamn struggle.

April, 2001. They're turning my life into a living hell. I've endured another blindingly blue nightmare. In my search for 'the news,' I have in fact, become the news. To my fellow trainee hacks, my story sounds a tad too twisted. So much so, that I'm actually condemned as a fabricator. They don't believe me. None of them do. Apart from Sparky that is. He has cunning blood. They don't even allow themselves to begin to believe me. Reputations are at stake. Careers are being built. It's all a bit too treacherous for them. Well, these waters are treacherous, utterly tempestuous in fact.

The blood thrown repeatedly at our door symbolizes the desecration, the real bloodbath, that could soon follow. For months, I think of nothing but the fate of those I love the most. Find myself looking at those around me with suspicion, which in turn only makes me look suspicious. Most nights I lay awake for a long-drawn-out while, thinking - *who can you trust?* This has gone too far. This is all out of control. They're determined to teach me a lesson I'll never forget. Sparky tells me: "You're going to die before your time if you're not careful. Your conscience could end up killing you. Stop wondering. Stop investigating. Stop asking why. I'd just get the hell out of Liechester, if I were you." His words of warning, are like the words of supreme counsel. I do at least start *trying* to let go.

If I could just get at them somehow. I have to confront them again, but properly this time. To give into these bullies will make my life unbearable, but to face them is almost unbearable too. Nevertheless I possess a mental toughness - a wounding human spirit. I'm on fire inside. My blood's absolutely tingling with rage. But, all the same, an inner voice keeps telling me - *you've got to let go...you've got to let go."*

Whilst I'm walking through town one day, I spot Morpheye. A rip curl of angst sears through me when I stumble upon him. It's a debilitating kind of terror. Runs through my spine and momentarily paralyzes me. Perhaps I should ignore him? Perhaps I should walk on by? For some inexplicable reason, I'm drawn towards the blinding brawler.

Morpheye's aged slightly, but remains vicious looking. He gives me a fixed stare. His eyes are ferociously green. *They* haven't changed a bit. We're standing in the middle of a pedestrianized street. I break into a flustering sweat. I blabber out an indecipherable tale. My heart's boxing my ribcage. I rabbit on. Regardless. Frantically. I try to explain what the Jägermeister did to me in a single sentence. Of course it's possible Morpheye already knows, but I find myself blabbering nonetheless. He looks puzzled. It's obvious I'm seriously troubled. "What's gotten into you? Calm down Buddy. Come down the hole in half an hour...where we can talk things over. You can tell me all about it over a beer. The Jägermeister won't be there. I promise. It's his day off. See you inabit." Seems like he's trying to be forthcoming, but he still terrifies me in a way only he can. I'm compelled to go. There are certain things I have to get straight.

It's a Monday evening in early April 2001. It's around 20.00. There's still a crack of light left in the dark purple sky. For a moment it fills me with sanguinity. Yet hope, quickly turns back, into fear. I mutter to myself - *Come on Buddy, come on. Be brave, be brave.* I go to a kiosk to buy a pack of fags. Need to smoke. Buy ten Marlborough lights. Start chain smoking. Never done that before. Pace around town trying to decide whether what I'm about to do is the wisest thing to do. My knees, or at least some part of my legs, begin to tremble. If I don't go, don't think I'll ever forgive myself. Perhaps it's a reckless move. Yet it feels critical. I know they're mad at me, but if I can face them again, I can face anything. I have to talk to them. Even if it's on their terms. Even if it's on their neon doused blue cobblestones. *If I can prove that I'm not scared of him, by facing him properly, then I will take away some of his power. Morpheye the eye plucker, Morpheye the blinding brawler, Morpheye the murderer* - that's what's in my head. My mindset's manic. My clammy hands - tremulous. Am crushing the Marlborough light cigarette that's clamped between my fingers. The filter's gone an ugly orange. Nothing can prepare me for this. Nothing can calm me down. Cigarettes. Deep breaths. Fist clenching. Nothing. Fear can keep you alive, because it keeps you alert. Panic on the other hand can kill you, because it blurs your vision. I'm on the verge of panic. No journalist's ever been face to face with Morpheye. Deliberately. In fact *nobody* dares to tackle him. Morpheye's a hard man, a very hard man, and he's usually surrounded by other, very hard men. But I'm not approaching him belligerently am I? Am I? Now, of course, is the time for me to make my biddable peace.....

The confrontation

122

Sickness and numbness befall me. My ears begin to throb and thud. Funny isn't it, how you can feel fear in your ears? At first the thud is unbelievably fast, then it slows down to a techno-like drumbeat. Alerting. Like my ears are having some kind of dodgy premonition. Fuck I'm scared. I wait outside. Under the neon blue 'Blue Hole' sign I am. Standing. Like a dopey fly. I hover. For a dawdling second. I ask myself - *Am I mad enough to do this?* My mood changes in a flash - *Damn right I am.* In true grit mode, through the wrought iron gates, and into the blue burrow of horror I go. For the very last time.

It's hard to pull this off. A massive challenge. Possibly the hardest, maddest thing I've ever done. I'm pulsing. I'm pounding. I'm petrified. I trudge down the cobblestoned entrance, virtually paralysed with fear. I plead everything is going to be ok. To someone. Out there. Up there.

The Blue Hole feels more disconcertingly evil than ever. There are only two customers in the hole. They leave. In a hurry.

The whole situation is hideously surreal. I wonder if I should be here. Have a feeling this might be the end of the road for me. Nevertheless, this is something I have to do. For the sake of my family. My conscience. For all those concerned.

Feel sickeningly callow at the bar. I notice that the lights are excessively dim. Feel panicky in this blue murkiness. Feel like I'm in some kind of terrifying dusk-till-dawn enclosure. Claustrophobic. Ensnared. Half-demented. Worse. *Morpheye the eye plucker, Morpheye the blinding brawler, Morpheye the murderer.*

I'm there before Morpheye. Like a foot soldier I stand. Waiting for our momentous confrontation to occur. Morpheye telephones the bar.

"Yep – he's here," the bartender gamely replies..."Yep - he's alone." His call puts my nerves on ice. Just want this to be over. Quickly.

Morpheye struts in like an impatient warlord just seconds after his call. He has back-up. His mountainous bodyguard, Crooky. Crooky's a boaster and a bully. Bullying is his talent. Comes naturally to him. Everyone has the utmost respect and devotion for Crooky. Everyone laughes along with him. Everyone. Except me.

Morpheye and Crooky are standing alongside each other. They're only a few feet away from me. I stand there pale and dogged, while all the time beneath the masquerade my heart is beating faster and harder to the lyrics: "this is dangerous, this is death defying, this is dodgy-as-hell." Our spiraling eyes meet. Morpheye's green gaze is chilling. He holds his glassy green eyes wide open, in an amplifying attempt to terrify me. He does just that. Never been so scared. Feel chaotically caged in their company. Is my mind beginning to haemorrhage with fear? Feels frozen. Am I near the end? You can see the anarchy in Morpheye's face, and you can smell his menacing revolution in the air. He carries an air of urgency and guilt about him. He's a dictator under pressure. Nothing's really changed. Am worried that I might forget the precise sequence of events. Am worried that I might loose my thread of thought completely. Am worried that my frozen mind, won't do its job. I'm nervously chewing the inside of my lips. They're becoming a chomped cherry-red.

I am tremulous. They are breathing hard. I am crackling with anticipation. They stand still like back row chess pieces.

This is a serious confrontation.

Crooky begins eyeing me up and down warily. Morpheye bestows a bottle of beer upon me. With his eyes, he tells me to take a seat. So I sit. Both of them take a seat opposite me. They face me across the table. They are in opposition to me. Why are these people so tense and fearful? Why are they so frosty? Feels a bit like I'm in a police station. There's something confessional about the whole experience. Going to confession, when I was a child, always felt rather ominous. This feels a hundred times worse. I catch Morpheye's green gaze again. This time his eyes are like zapping lasers. They lock right on. Morpeye's eyes are now upon mine. I can't avert them. He leans forward conspiratorially. I experience the breath of a killer on me. Can't unscramble myself from the murderous intensity that's whirling around me, like a swarm of mini locusts. Invisible. Ravenous. It's like I'm looking death in the face. Crooky slides his impressive looking mobile into the middle of the table. They're now looking at me as if it's my move. Are they recording our conversation? I say conversation, it's me who does all the talking..."Eeeerm listen guys, pheeew. Eeerm. The Jägermeister fired a gun at me, almost in my face it were. In the flat. Yeah, and I'm 40 quid down. Yeah, I know it's only 40 quid, but hey. Yeah, ok, I took that sixty quid. Eeeerm, I took that sixty quid, because the Jägermeister told me – he told me a few days earlier, that you weren't gonna give me my 100 quid deposit back from the flat. That was unfair. Well unfair. That was bullshit, weren't it? There was nothing wrong with the flat. I looked after it. I'm the one out of pocket.

124

I mean, what do you reckon? What do you make of all this?" They don't answer me. They look interested though, engrossed even. They just sit there taking it all in. My words are oscillating wildly around me. My words are resonating off the surrounding brick walls. My words are acoustically overlapping each other, and coming out in one big jumble. Hope I'm making sense. Hope I'm not confusing them. The last thing I can afford to do is confuse them. Confusing them will only exacerbate my entanglement. I ramble on regardless..."I tried to talk to you guys before, but you guys made it impossible. He set this all up. He framed me. Huuuh. He shot at me. He pointed a gun at me and fucking fired it. Heh, he shot at me before any of this money business even became an issue. This thing about the 100 quid – that was a load of bollocks weren't it? He's been feeding me a load of shit I reckon. Reckon he's been feeding you guys a load of shit too. Pitting us against each other. Manipulating everything. Twisting it all up and....."

"Ah the plot thickens," Crooky interupts. His words are loaded with derision. Yet there's more than just a smidgen of keenness to his reply. *In a burst of blue I wonder to myself what the next stage in this perverse tragedy will be?* Of course this isn't only about money. It's about pride, and principle, and a whole lot more. All I want is for life to be normal again. I crave ordinariness. "That might explain a few things," Morpheye finally remarks with solemnity. They already have their own doubts about the Jägermeister. What I say just kinda reaffirms their own qualms. The Jägermeister *had* been playing me off against them.

Am so goddamn petrified you wouldn't believe. In a desperate and justice-seeking tone I start up again..."I don't want to be seen as a sneak or a snoop. I'm done with it all. This whole journalism thing's brought me nothing but trouble. Weird shit keeps happening to my family home. Everything's got way out of hand. Someone sent us a razorblade sealed in an envelope, and someone keeps chucking blood and shit on the front porch of our home. It's total craziness man. There's oil mixed up in it too. I want it all to sto..."

"*That* has nothing to do with the Jägermeister." Morpheye bursts out confidently. The promptness and succinctness of his reply alerts my suspicions immediately. He's grinning obscenely. Incroyable. He's *so* sure. How can he be *so* sure? The reason he is *so* sure it isn't the Jägermeister, is because it's him. He's responsible. Morpheye's responsible for the gory desecration of our home. Bastard. Terrorist.

Crooky hands me another bottle of beer. Are they trying to further loosen my tongue? We continue our conversation standing at the bar in a *slightly* more relaxed fashion. Nonetheless, the talk is still tetchy. Phoney. All three of us are choosing our words carefully. I offer to buy them a beer. They both decline the offer. They both decline the offer, by pouting their lips, and shaking their heads, from side to side, concurrently. The fact they've the same roguish mannerisms ruffles me somewhat, but it's the way in which they dish 'em out at exactly the same time, that really freaks me. "Still after that big scoop Buddy?" Crooky inquires teasingly. Maybe he gets a kick out of this kinda thing. Maybe it bolsters his ego. They wait for a wisecrack, but it doesn't come. "Put your arms up in the air Buddy." The raw red brick walls fall into me. "Hold them there." *What the fuck.* Crooky pats my jittery body from head to toe. Can't believe what's actually occurring. He's bloody frisking me. Must think I'm wired or something? God, they're so suspicious these two? Can't wait to get out of this bloody joint. A pregnant silence follows. We just stand there in a perverted hush, for a lingering moment. My senses go all blurred. My eyes suddenly cultivate a glue-like coating of skin. As I stand there, the pounding quietness begins to take possession of my ears, my soul. Think I might collapse. Feel heavy. For an excruciating moment I'm stuck in a time-warp capsule...caught in the thud of silence. Beating. Pulsing. I fear I'll never be released. Feels like this really could be the end. It's a weird flash of time. Too weird. No one's saying anything. It's as if all the 'talk' is done. I certainly have nothing much left to say to them. Maybe it wasn't such a good idea to talk? But there's a flicker of interest in Morpheye's consuming eyes. Is it possible that I knew something he didn't? Is it possible that I've shed some light on certain circumstances? Has the Jägermeister finally been busted? Then I decide to walk away.

Crooky allows me about ten paces before hollering: "Heh Buddy!" I throw a final glance over my shoulder, expecting the worst. "Lay off the acid!" Resignation is written on my face. They want me to bite. I remain philosophical. Let them have the last word. This is no time for wisecracking remarks. No time for play-acting. This has already gone way too far. I think - *ok you win. You don't win fair, but you win.* It's weird, because I feel both brave, and scared shitless at the same time.

I retreat down the dimly lit blue tunnel. Feel like running, but don't. Feel like looking back, but don't. I walk briskly, a bit too briskly, but on the whole I maintain my composure. Sort of. Somehow.

As soon as I'm out of there I puff out a colossal sigh. It's an unforgettable sigh. I converse to myself within - *that was motherfucking demon releasing.* Light up a cigarette. Fill my lungs with smoke. Start wondering – *does Crooky know Toby Marshall?*

Am unable to get this chilling encounter out of my head for sometime. To a certain extent my conscience is soothed and appeased. Feel I've done everything in my power to prevent any further threats to my family. There's nothing more I can do. Is there? Of course Big John Pudding wasn't there. Where was he on that confrontational Monday? What's he up to? What's on Big John Pudding's pliable mind? And what will they tell him? What will and won't the hot-dog hulk get to know? You know, these guys don't deserve recognition. They don't deserve to be notorious, but they are. The Liechester mob are enjoying themselves. Is this all just a game to them? If it is, it's one hell of a brutish game. Why do they do it? To these guys, life is like a series of strategic moves. They're forever plotting. They sit there, in the safety of their hole, criminally calculating who to stitch up next. It's almost as if they're looking for enemies. I'm totally different. I try to be friends with almost everyone. I'm an honest guy who doesn't want any enemies. I'm not used to lying, lying seems to come naturally to them.

These guys are in the business of breaking-up families. This is how they operate. If we don't stand up to them, nobody will. Nobody else dares to challenge them. If they get rid of us, they'll have complete control of this town. They're trying to make an example out of us. Feel morally compromised. On the one hand, don't want any of my family to be killed, but also feel obliged to alert, and protect the general public. Am I willing to pay the ultimate price of defiance? No, I guess is the simple answer. No, I don't want to be a martyr to Journalism. Now, is as good a time as any, for my parents to leave this town. Indeed, they just walk away from it all. I too, have to learn, to let go.

In the neighbourhood we're an archetypal family. Our hasty departure's gonna get the garrulous local tongues wagging, even more than they already are. It's a tragic end to an era.

Can hardly breath as this sinister interpretation of events takes shape in my mind. Some of my friends begin to feel threatened themselves. Feel tainted through association. Feel safer without me.

This makes me feel *real* bad inside. My anguish is bloody contagious. My friends become disillusioned with me. They abandon me. I hate being in my hometown where people know me. Feels intrusive, almost incestuous. Never been one for idle gossip. Now I just can't help thinking people are ignorant, and nosy as hell. Feel transparent.

This whole journalism idea seems like one big minefield. It's important to alert people to this scandal, but I don't want to cause public alarm. It's not important to alert lots of people, but to alert the right people. Sparky doesn't need alerting. Sparky's as stealthy as a fox. He's the only trainee journalist off my course who shows an interest in this ongoing scandal. All I want, is to get away from Liechester. I'll do almost anything to escape again. The worst thing, I'm still suffering in silence. Still feel freakishly muted. Know I can't keep the trauma I've been going through to myself much longer. There's nothing much I believe in anymore. Don't believe in Justice. Don't believe in the law. Certainly don't believe what the papers say.

Every good journalist should have an investigative passion and this is mine. However, my determination to overcome the Liechester mob becomes almost like a fatal obsession. On the whole, big stories like this tend not to be exclusive in newspaper terms, because they're not the sort of story you can keep to yourself. This case is different, it bucks the standard trend. In the world of journalism only me and Sparky really know about my big story, and we do keep it to ourselves - exclusively.

During Morpheye's neon revolution, the truth never is reported. Morpheye's reign of terror is never suitably exposed. Morpheye remains at large.

In my opinion, anyone with a half decent grade in their English GCSE, can write at the same level as a journalist in the regional press. Most of them are just glorified copywriters really. The real problem is to do with time. Journalists simply aren't given enough time, or resources for that matter, to investigate suspicious issues properly. The idle men in the bars might not be able to write as well as them, but they know more about what's really going on than the media folk. From a media point of view, I've little influence really. Have a few contacts from my journalism course, but they aren't *really* on my side. Most of them are in it for themselves, and are vaguely anti-establishment anyway. But people can and do change. This matter is not easy to relinquish. Deciding to knock the world of journalism on the head, for the sake of my friends and family, and for my own sake, is a massively difficult decision. Careers are important, but no career is worth dying for is it? I let go of my ambition.

She's head-snappingly attractive. What I mean is, you look at her, and then you quickly have to look at her again, before she has too much time to get out of your sight, such is her beauty. Her face reflectes her mind; both are intensely attractive. She's a rarity. An emerald freestone. A November Foxtrot. She too is bigger than this goddamn bigoted town. She feels life deeply. There's green fire in her eyes. I'm sick of everybody's accusing eyes, and now even she has accusing eyes. I've lost most of my confidence. Look done in. My wounded face is too much for her. I know she's disappointed in me. I know she hates me for involving her in all this heavy shit. I notice she's clutching her heart, and then I know I've lost her adoration. Her eyes are swimming mournfully, like graveyard marbles, as she listens. She looks absolutely scandalised when I break the news. She's wearing a cute black dress. Black seems to compliment her milky white skin. She always has an air of angelic exquisiteness, and right now she looks absolutely deadly. November Foxtrot is couture-conscious. She constantly seems to look a cut above the rest. You know, she wouldn't look out of place on a Parisian catwalk. She is, quite simply, ravishingly beautiful. November Foxtrot has a beguiling Irish charm, and her beauty is distracting me as I try to talk with her. I want to, even need to talk with her. She gracefully enquires: "Is this my fault?" "What do you mean?" I reply curiously. She laughs a nervous laugh. Proceeds to say: nothing. She knows the exact psychological moment when to say: nothing. Again she delicately clutches her heart, in a way only she can, whilst her eyes blaze away like penetrating spotlights. Does she really feel responsible for my fate? Does she know something I need to know? I know I've lost her and all her prettiness. Forever. There's a stain in her laughter now. She's disenchanted, disenchanted to the point of silence. But she's got it wrong. Whatever she's thinking, she's got it all wrong. She should remain white and angelic though. We cross each other's paths outside Saint Peter's Roman Catholic Church in Liechester, and as always, there's electricity oscillating between us. It's to be our whitest and most passionate moment, ever. It's to be our last meeting. I accept this moment of exaltation as the end of our unconcealed love, and this means I've left myself feeling half-demented. Then she let me go. It's an altruistic move, I believe. Perchance she just wants to set me free -

free from the deadly claustrophobia of this unpalatable town. Can't expect any woman to take on board all the emotional clutter I'm carrying. You always end up hurting the ones you love the most, I reckon. There's a lot I have to say to her, if she'll just give me half a chance. She doesn't know what I've been through. She doesn't know what I'm going through. It's awful really, not having the time, or a proper chance to explain. I can still see the undisguised contempt in her face, and that always makes me feel enormously sad. Like I've failed. Don't know what makes her think it could possibly have been her fault. *Infinitely not made known, anonymous artistic ambiguity undisclosed.* November Foxtrot paints a lurid black and blue picture of me. She's quite the dedicated artiste. She paints me as a double-sided character. Well part of me is, I suppose, very English, but part of me is also very French - half of me in fact. So perhaps there's an element of truth in her murky depiction. In this hazy picture, part of my face is covered by a menacing blue shadow. She's certainly portrayed me in a sinister light. It's a kind of split personality portrait; a Jekyll and Hyde representation. At least that's the elusive voodoo impression I take from it. Worst of all it's on public display in a grim local boozer. She's inaugurated my ostracism in art. I become choked just looking at it. She usually signs her artwork in the conventional bottom right hand corner with a squiggling N. Foxtrot, but on this particular piece, for some ambiguous reason, she signs it in the top right hand corner, with an eye-catching letter 'R' inside a stamp sized square. In Red.

My predatory journalistic days are short lived. I do the 'decent thing' and give up scavenging for stories. I seriously flirt with the idea of becoming a journalist, but quickly become badly scarred. In fact, reckon I become bloody journalistically scarred for life. My head's shattered, my concentration ravaged, my co-ordination blighted and vitiated. I've been successfully suppressed. Still have some adrenaline though, but it isn't adrenaline to 'find' a newspaper story. It's adrenaline to write *my* story.

Towards the end of my journalism course one of the trainee reporters says: "Well, it's not been a bad way to spend a year, I suppose." She's a proper Little-Miss-know-it-all, who doesn't really know Jack shit. For me personally, it's one hell of a bad way to spend a year of my life. It's a mortifying year of terror. It's a lonely and crushing crusade. My potentially illustrious career's over, before it's started. It's as if curiosity has eaten me whole. I am not the hunter – I am the hunted. What I really need to do is get away......

CHAPTER 7 – CHÂTEAU BRUTALE – DOING TIME.
"Watch me disappear."

One day a man, who I shall refer to only once, and who I shall refer to quite simply as *the Serb*, hands me a copy of a newspaper. He points out an advertisement headed 'Fortress Adventure' in the job section of our local rag: FORTRESS ADVENTURE - Multi-activity instructor. No work experience necessary. Work in the UK and France. Accommodation and food provided. It jumps straight out at me, like a flashy feather suspended on a line to catch a mackerel it is. Does somebody know my mind? I'm immediately seduced. *This job sounds perfect for me. This job's got my name on it.* It's easy for me to leave this country for an idyllic taste of France. My heart tells me *go for it.* For some reason I also read my star sign in the paper, probably because I'm feeling low, and need a bit of wraithlike guidance. Rather fantastically it states: "You've been blessed with a sharp intellect and a sense of adventure. You're a multitasker and need to be involved in a multitude of activities to stay engaged with the world. Another country beckons. Follow your star." So the stars are on my side. I've nothing to lose. Without hesitation, I apply for the 'no work experience necessary' multi-activity instructor position.

My interview takes place in Westminster, London. The interview room itself is leathery, timbered and exceedingly English. The atmosphere is serious and institutionalised. The whole experience is somewhat secretive. The man conducting the interview is called George Hopkins. He has a sombre tone of voice, and he makes a grand display of the fact that he owns a well polished rifle. Well that, of all things, doesn't impress me. George Hopkins's words summon my attention: "Rioux, how tall are you?" For some reason he insists on calling me by my surname. Perhaps it's an old boy British Empire trait or something. "I'm 6ft, but I-wish-I-was-a-little-bit-taller."
"Rioux, are you ready for this?"
"Ready when you are, Hopkins."

As luck would have it, I get the job. Next day, I'm on the train to Fortress Adventure, Cravenshire, for my new life as a multi-activity instructor. Romance is postponed. Getting myself out of Liechester is more imperative. In truth, they lure me away. Isn't difficult. I'm in a state of despair. Are they protecting me? Have they enticed me here for my own safety? If they have, they've a funny way of showing it. It's like officially permitted abduction. I fall into their adventurous trap, like a dispossessed foreigner.

They organise an escort for me. *How noble of them* - I think. The moment I step off the train, I'm whisked away into the undulating Cravenshire countryside. It's a circuitous journey from the train station to the Fortress. I'd never have found the place by myself. The pale driver says nothing. He has a persecuted look on his white face and he drives like a madman. Am shaken when I arrive, what with all the twists in our road trip and all. Haven't been this car sick in a long time.

I'm like a social cast off...a leper...I've no grip on my own life.

Military arrest! Absurd I know. Far-fetched it may seem, but I'm under military arrest. Somebody has an uncompromising clutch on my existence. Feel devastated. Do you know why? Feel devastated because of my inability to do anything about the tragic terror situation that's about to unfold.

Walked into this sticky snare like an ill-fated rabbit. Walked into my own exile. *They* can indeed read my fluffy and tormented mind. *They* know how desperate I am. *They* think they know what I need, at this particular momentous moment. It's a politically sensitive time. Not just for me, but for this country and the entire world. *They* certainly know my spirit. *They* cook up the perfect ploy to lure me away, in order to excommunicate me. *The establishment* thinks they know best.

Camp Fortress is an institutional place for human misshapes (non-conformists if you like), to be subdued at a time of colossal military significance. Does this mean all the other multi-activity instructors are also radical non-conformists?

Hopkins points his rifle at me as I approach the Old English Fortress. Do I have shoot me written across my forehead or something? His actions are quite uncalled for. Now, I really see them for what I suspect them to be - my pre-wartime captors. There's a big difference between us. They think I'm a national security risk, whereas I think they're a global security risk. Anyway, I've been tracked down, and ambushed, like a coveted wild animal. They're waiting for me. Expecting me. It's an extreme and well thought-out British plot, which

I guess, simply mirrors the extreme times in which we're all battling to survive. Seems like *they* know more about me, than me.

I'm enticed into exile for my dissident views. I wonder who instigates this ensnaring act. Is it the Jägermeister? My mind's racing within. An authority above him? How's this all been planned? I've become red alert. Too alert. There's a bond between the Fortress and the Jägermeister. The Fortress operation is run by one of the Jägermeister's military superiors - Victor Papa. They're acquaintances. Cronies. Victor Papa was formerly the Jägermeister's military mentor. Buried within his Fortress grounds, Victor Papa's like a spider in its web, waiting to catch it's prey.

This whole set up reeks of espionage and old imperial rule. This is an irresponsible military intelligence stunt. It's a total set-up. These guys are trained. These guys are dangerous. These guys know no limits. I'm aware that it can be deemed a serious act of defamation, to accuse an apparently unimpeachable military man of being a terrorist. But that's exactly what I want to do. My scandalous pre-wartime adventure has begun. To my friends and family I've all but disappeared. In reality I've been successfully 'removed' from the political picture. It's a legal abduction, but it's appallingly wrong. To attract attention to myself, I don't contact my family. To a great extent I hope my silence, in itself, will thunderously sound the alarm.

There's something uniquely British about this Fortress; something dominating and traditional about it. It's buried in the heart of The Cravenshire countryside, like a mountainous and proud watchtower. It's totally impenetrable, at least, it appears that way, to my raw eyes. There's an unprecedentedly strong sense of procedure amidst this enormous military operational area. An air of covertness hangs about everything here. Everything's strictly controlled. The personnel are like lead soldiers. They stand erect and are characterless. We're made to stand to attention ourselves. Makes me feel dim-witted. Manipulated. Makes me feel stiff and grey. It's mid February, 2002. The destruction of '911' still plagues my mind. The weather's typically dreary and cold for this time of year in blighty. The air around us though, seems particularly subdued. Can feel a pressing stillness...almost as if the air's regimented itself.

Whilst I'm being trained as a 'multi-activity instructor', I can see, in the anomalous foreground, others being trained in an altogether more rigorous manner. An unverified report has it - this is where MI5 carries out their meticulous training. Nothing can be confirmed here, but there's obviously militant grounding taking place. Nothing can be verified, but the brutal truth is clear. This is a place of relentless action. It's not a place where procedures are likely to be attested. Whatever's going on, it's serious and dangerous and unstoppable.

The Fortress is, above all, a Fortress of gossip. Have to be careful what I say, and who I say it to here. Try my best to remain silent. This is Victor Papa's territory. Within these grounds he has his own intelligence antennae, which enable him to find out almost everything. Victor Papa's a law unto himself. He doesn't have to prove anything, to anybody. He's our boss, our chief, our high and mighty commander. Victor Papa's the General of all Generals.

One night, towards the end of February, I accompany a bunch of fellow trainee instructors down to the local pub. The country-bumpkin style boozer is a mile or so off-site, but it's well within the General's stringent span of control. Unfortunately, this is not free-time. We're being socially supervised. Treated like irresponsible reprobates. Don't feel like socialising, but sense there's a virtual compulsion to join in.

Feel very much like an outsider. I am an outsider.

To get to the pub we're made to hike. Conga-style. Through muddy fields. In the dark. Nobody really knows which way to go. Feel foreign. Vulnerable. Misplaced. Feel like I'm in the middle of nowhere. Remote. Certainly I'm in very unfamiliar and very undulating territory. Eventually, after hours of grubby mud trudging nervousness, we turn up outside the pub, like a bunch of bemused infantry.

As I walk into the pub, it's not a congenial feeling that comes over me, rather one of abashment. I attempt to shrink into my glaring surroundings. Within seconds, I become conscious that 'The Black Sheep' is swarming with familiar faces. A load of the men who were training alongside us up at the Fortress that day, are in here boozing. They're a powerful pack. One of them approaches me: "You're looking a bit anaemic!" I'm jolted by his rather odious remark. I mean, don't feel my most ebullient self, but to be described as appearing 'anaemic' seems a little vitriolic. Another one of the brawny pack approaches me: "Fancy a pint?"

"Eeeerh. Yeah alright then. Eeeerm. Cheers." It's an effort for me to speak. I anxiously sup on my complimentary pint of lager.

Something's horribly wrong. The guy doesn't offer to buy any of the other instructors a pint, only me, for some reason. Outwardly I pretend not to be concerned, but inside I'm thinking - *what the hell's going on here?* A few minutes later, I approach the men's toilets. Another one of the hefty pack strides past me. Decisively. As he does so, he gives me an ostensibly friendly, but somewhat unnervingly solid prod, to my stomach, with his tanker-sized fist. His actions, make me feel, even more jumpy. In fact, if truth be told - feel hunted. Then I approach this random tough guy: "Hey – you're one of the guys from the Fortress aren't you? What's going on up there?" No reply. He just stares right through me. It's like talking to a blank wall. Drops his full pint of Guinness on the floor right by my feet. Then stares at me. In total silence. Can feel the rest of the pack's eyes on me too. He refuses to acknowledge me. Refuses to see me. Just stares ahead. Stolidly. Have never come across somebody who's quite so cold and unresponsive and wall-like. *Is this how all-military personnel communicate? What sort of attention-seeking stunt's he trying to pull and why?*

That evening's full of odd surprises. Indeed, it's an incredulous round of nasty encounters. I leave 'The Black Sheep' feeling strangely bewildered. It's all been *too* theatrical. Staged. All I keep thinking about is the word 'excommunication'. They're after information. Information they believe I have. They're also assessing my allegiance. Am I thoroughly disloyal? Or can I be made to be submissive? Outwardly, must just look like I'm doing a worthwhile job. In reality though, it's a case of detention without trial. Only a select few, on the inside, really know what's going on. Those establishment figures are, after all, experts at covering up. I've been tracked. Duped. Ensnared. I've also already been judged and sentenced. My face is ashen with fear. Maybe now I look anaemic.

The unreachable outside world knows nothing. Why am I suddenly being treated like such a scoundrel-of-a-subject? Why do they lay blame on me so craftily and profusely? Why the unexpected finger pointing? Why so? Is anybody here prepared to say? Is anybody here prepared to lay light on the accused?

Next day...back up at the Fortress... Victor Papa's a huge military man. He towers above me. He has this air about him, an air of supremacy. Unfortunately for me, he's on my case.

Victor Papa looks at me shiftily, eyes full of mistrust. Then he approaches me and declares: "Nothing's mightier than *my* sword." His weighty words, seize my attention. "By the way, how was last night?" He strides off, before I've a chance to respond to his penetrating question. As he parts, I notice his big eavesdropping ears. They look like antique gramophones. At least, that's what looking at his humongous lugholes, makes me think of.

Like an insatiable predator, Victor Papa wants me to know he's watching me. He makes this known to me with subtle, yet terrifying gestures. He makes this known to me, in his own *very* special way. You see, when Victor Papa enters a room, a quivering hush goes through the crowd. Victor Papa drifts in and out of the countless Fortress rooms, without saying a single word. By saying nothing, he announces his presence. This is how it is. On one occasion, at suppertime, he sits silently at the table like a proud and untoppable King. He's on the opposite side of the dining room, but he still manages to make his chilling presence felt. While I'm eating my rather seductive evening meal (it's an 'eat-as-much-as-you-can-put-on-your-plate' style buffet), Victor Papa sits there eyeballing me. His pasty white face appears gruesome. Unforgiving. Picks up his *'Mirror'* newspaper. Rustles it. Glances at me from above the pages. Hits me with a besieging look. Won't forget that fleeting glance. It's tactical. Strategic. Wounding. His blood-black eyes, are the eyes of a shark. Callous. Deadly. As he peers over his paper, his face is searching mine. Reading me. Knowing me. Whilst clutching his *mirror,* he clutches hold of my mind. And so, the psychological battle between Fortress ruler, and mere multi-activity mortal begins. I enter into Victor Papa's mirror wilderness. His intention: to urge silence upon me. I'm now one of his new-fangled wolfskins.

On another occasion, Victor Papa perches himself on the arm of a shabby sofa, in the Fortress staff headquarters. He's about 12ft away from me, and he's brandishing a foot long pickaxe. He intentionally positions himself on the arm of the sofa, so that he's sitting loosely behind one of the dim-witted wolfskins. He glances at me. An ominous shudder pervades my anatomy. Echt waar. I'm now an anathematized wolfskin. Victor Papa, by some designing means, seizes my full, and undivided, attention. With axe clenched in his fist, he proceeds to make abrupt, upward and downward movements. He holds the weapon directly behind the poor wolfskin's youthful, and beleaguered neck. Victor's guinea-pig, just sits there on the down-at-heel sofa, stuffing his face with chocolate. He's oblivious to it all. I, on the other hand, am all too mindful of what's just taken place. This is a subtle threat; a restrained and elusive warning. Victor Papa's going to teach me a lesson. A lesson I'll never forget.

During my short stay at the Fortress, I observe the true wrath of Victor Papa. This man's full of bluff and charade; an expert in psychological warfare; a specialist in denting the mind of the enemy. At all costs, he'll get what he wants.

Victor Papa's always busy overhearing. I swear sometimes, I can actually hear his brain ticking. But instead of going 'tick-tock', it's going 'tac-tic'. He has a whole bag of tactics. I can tell you. He is, after all, an almighty military man. Allow me to tell you a little bit more about this patriotic savage. Victor Papa's a pugnacious predator. He has high-flying, all-seeing eyes. He makes it clear to me that he's my reticent Cravenshire shadow. My soul's being clutched by another man. The man clutching my soul is: Victor Papa. It's a remorseless occupation. He's looking for an adventurous life, not a cautious one. He's the kind of man who does away with other men. Victor Papa believes, the essence of adventure, is war. A cold-blooded concept, for a cold-blooded man. He has a dissecting intelligence. Can suss people out quickly. He conspiringly refers to us as his 'wolfskins.' The pet name, soon becomes permanent. It's denigrating to be brandished as animals, but we can't argue with the big man.

We become wolfskins......we become wolf-like.

I know how he thinks, and he knows how I think. Problem is, I'm on his territory, and working for him. He's got me just where he wants me, right in the palm of his hand. There's nothing I can do about it. If I try to escape from his Fortress, I'll look guilty as hell. Anyhows, even if I do manage to escape, don't think I'll be able to get very far. They'll be onto me like a rash. Victor Papa has eyes everywhere. What else can I do? Who'll believe my story anyway? I mean, who am I to protest against the western world's war on terror? I crave dissention, but I also fear destitution. *Perhaps this is the safe-side?* I endure feelings of guilt. Guilt's a powerful emotion isn't it? Isn't it? Well, the guilt I'm feeling, feels gruesome, but I don't know what to do about it. *I don't know what to do.* It's not as if I can single-handedly take on the wrath of Victor Papa and his henchmen, now is it? I'm here because I know something. Something that's deemed critical for England's national security. *Perhaps I feel spiritless settling on the safe-side?* Politics heh? *They* want to get inside my mind further. *They* know how desperate I am - *they've* got that bit right. *They* think they know what I want. *They* think they know what I need. *They* think they know best. *They* know my spirit well enough to entice me onto their establishment territory. But can they keep me here? Can *they really* excommunicate me?

They've CCTV footage of me smoking bush and acting drunk. I've lost my moral authority. This is a problem for me. There's no talk of punishment. Victor Papa just shows me the recording. Then says nothing. His guilt trips are head-screwing. They make me feel disabled. Will I ever regain my moral authority? Have I lost it forever? *Well send me up river!* In an attempt to make myself feel better, I try to convince myself that this is just what most young men would do, if they were hurled into my world. However, deep down, I know, I'm on the wrong side of the law. I also know *they* have indisputable evidence to prove it. Nothing I can do will make me feel less culpable. I'm like a prostrated dog, with a bucket on its head. *Well send me to prison! They'll* only use the footage against me if needs be. It's a contingency character assassination plan, if you like. If only I'd acted more honorably. Perhaps then I'd have the courage to speak out against this American influenced, neo-conservative, beast of a wave. This war on terror is crazy man. Can't do anything to stop it though, can I? Can I? I'm just a mere mortal, struggling to make ends meet. I'm not the towering individual I purport to be. When it comes to the affairs of state, I'm a nobody. Aren't I?

I wonder - *Are the royalists and the republicans possibly joining forces, in order to defeat, what they profess to be a regime of evil?* I also wonder - *Weren't most of the American foot soldiers smoking pot, and getting all boozy, during the macabre Vietnam War? What will all the infantry do for kicks during America's war on terror? Hypocrisy innit?*

In general, the military mistrust journalists. Course they do. To a certain extent, the military machine only lets journalists know, what they want them to know. The military want the world of journalism to produce copy that compliments, even flatters, their physical war endeavours. Anyway, one thing's for sure, the press won't be visiting this place, unless they're invited. This facility is impregnable. *How convenient! How opportune!* I should be on the streets of Liechester protesting. Should be protesting - *don't get into bed with America on this one.* I'm too old to cry for help, but helps what I need. Feel detached from my parents and family. Indeed, I'm widely divergent from them. Instead of asking for their support, I just suffer in silence. This whole armoured Fortress joint is corrupt, but I can't fight it. The corruption here is unconquerable.

At the Fortress, I undergo some thorough instruction. It's military preparation really. Victor Papa insists we learn police radio procedures. From day two onwards we have to always carry radios around with us. My Golf sign is *Bravo Romeo*. Quickly become accustomed to it. At first I think having my own radio is kinda quirky, but the radios are just effective tools to control us. We're all connected. We're all guarded by our radios. Becomes a bit dystopian....

"Golf Bravo Romeo, this is Golf Echo Unicorn, message over."
"Send over."
"What's your location over?"
"I'm in the toilet. You wanna come and watch me squat? Over."
"Eeerh ok. Eerh no thanks. Eerm. Out!" Can't even go to the toilet in peace in this place.

At first the physical strain is more enduring than the psychological strain. Up at 06.00. Finish at 20.45. The life of a wolfskin multi-activity instructor is a gruelling, dawn-till-dusk, labour intensive existence. We work 10 days on the trot. At least. We have one day off. If we're lucky. Feel drained, to the point of sickness, on the days I do manage to get off.

Are they really trying to re-cultivate us in seclusion? A different rumour has it – we're being cosseted from the enemy.

The other wolfskins have nervous faces too. They seem to avoid eye contact, and have wide, starring into space eyes....like saucers. Their wolfskin faces contain shock and sorrow. I find solace in this. At least I'm not the only person in the world, with a bewildered looking mug. Who are these newfound colleagues of mine? What's under their wolfskin masquerade? Alpha Mike, to name but one of our pack, has a face of fear. He seems stunned, stunned like me. Alpha Mike has a streak of Irishness in his veins. I like him. Get on with him. Thinks the Fortress is bugged with microphones. So do I. "Buddy be wise. Be careful what you say here now. This battleground's goddamn rigged I'm tellin yuh. We're isolated here I'm tellin yuh. Oooaah it's a wretched business. For sure."

In true military style we're ordered out of bed in the morning. "Time to get up. Get up. It's time to get up!" Find it deeply oppressive. There's something tragic about waking up to another man's 'get up' bellow. There's no choice here. It's an intrusive regime. I've never been so unfree. My libertarian alarm clock is surplus to requirements. It sits next to my bed, pointlessly telling the time. I follow their instructions compliantly. I'm not here to question their regime, or dispute their methods of rule. I stick to their brutal procedure. I'm determined to win this fierce psychological battle. I can outwit them. I can colour and belie, this head-screwing experiment. This outrageous tyranny. This witch-hunt. Of course, I don't wanna be here. I don't wanna be part of their patriot game.

We've been branded as *animals*. Each of us has a pair of wolves paw-prints on our sleeve. Is this the mark of imprisonment? Is this the mark of chastisement? In a mean-spirited manoeuvre, we're made to buy our own military adventure uniforms! We're informed it's all part of the military's 'self-protective financial retrenchment scheme.' *What! Keep us out of pocket and under control more like!* My tomato red, wolfskin jacket is branded with a pair of bright yellow wolves paw prints on its sleeve. My wolfskin jacket's different to everyone else's. Why? Why the mismatch? Everyone else has identical grey paw prints on theirs. Wonder why I've been stamped with deviating yellow paw prints? And I wonder why everyone else has been stamped with grey ones? It's a stigmatising variation. Why the disparity? It's a perplexing observation of mine. An observation that gnaws at me for some time. Despite my conspicuous yellow paw prints, I've become a hidden figure, within an ever mounting pack. It's here, deep in the Cravenshire hills, that Victor Papa forms his army of gawking wolfskins. What on earth have I gone and got myself roped into now? British military intelligence wants me here. It's safer, *they* think, for an agitator (a solitary wolf like me), to be buried in the Cravenshire countryside, than to be lingering around Liechester, attempting to expose the truth.

Like I say, the Fortress is an established outfit, with a significant military presence. During the day we engage in weird training routines. We drag ourselves through tunnels and under nets along the ground. Whilst we're put through our paces on the mud-splattered assault course, we're made to chant: "I'm a wriggly worm please don't eat me!" Momentarily we are at one with the worms. "That should bring you back down to earth!" hollers Victor Papa in a nuclear tone. He stands like a British column, in the not so distant background. Follows up with a wry: "Get a wriggle on!" Puts me through a right squirming buffeting I'm tellin ya. My inquisitive nose,

141

quite literally, takes a trouncing in the mud. It's a dehumanising ritual of submission.

So, here I am, feeling all filthy and abased. Life's certainly taken a turn for the worst. One day I'm an aspiring journalist, the next, a mucky and humiliated worm of a man. Worms are ugly creatures aren't they? Well, we're made to feel like worms. Victor Papa sees to that. "Try wriggling your way out of this one!" he utters defiantly. And as if that isn't enough...'The worm of intrigue grows fat (signed VP)' is etched on my dormitory door. Doesn't help matters. Makes my mind feel even more whacked. VP's etching wriggles around inside my mud-encrusted mind. Feel agonisingly spineless. I'm stripped of my dignity. It's utterly humiliating.

"This cocooned world won't last for long!" Victor Papa remarks craftily, one brittly cold English morning. Don't feel *cocooned* here – feel insufferably misplaced...and certainly not safe. I also sense, quite potently, that there's something gruesome, and morally wrong, just around the corner. Discernment paints a nefarious, and abominable panorama of war, in my boy crying wolf, and wolf crying boy mind. Well this 21st century adventure *'cocoon'* is undeniably Victor Papa's territorial thing. It's an establishment stronghold that most never get to see. On camp there's an underground subterranean warren, where dissenting wolfskins allegedly disappear. There's also a military helicopter-landing pad. Never see it being used, but its bare presence adds to the imposing nature, of this cosseted Fortress location. Victor Papa really is a mountainous figure. He loiters around, and postures himself strategically wherever he goes. He's a gadget man. Seems as if there's nothing his mobile phone can't do. He even has his own private military plane. Sometimes he makes his presence felt, by hovering around above us, like a shark in the sky. He is overbearingly English. He is a man capable of human slaughter.

One madcap evening, we're unexpectedly led into the undulating Cravenshire countryside, on a night hike, by the big brute himself. It's completely dark. Can't see a foot ahead. To me it seems like a daft, and bamboozling pursuit. Nobody in our regiment really knows where they're going, but we keep going anyway. Nowhere. Submissively into the blinding darkness. Is this a test? To see if we'll run? We're being supervised, I know that, but is there more to this? Sure as hell feels that way. I just keep my head down. Try to allow myself to come to terms with feeling so utterly banished. Victor Papa has his accusing torch on us. I fear....death. Yep! I'm in the wrong place. Yet again. My time in Cravenshire however is short lived. Safer still, British military intelligence thinks its better to deport me to another country. An out-of-the-way corner of France beckons. After spending a few weeks buried in the concealing Cravenshire hills, I'm dispatched to a Château-with-a-curse in Flicardie, Northern France. My censorious trial has only just begun.

My maternal Grandfather was French. His name was Hippolyte Rioux, but we called him 'Papa'. He was in the French army during the Second World War. He was wounded in the back with shrapnel. Had to spend several months in hospital. He was paid a small war pension. Papa was the best gardener in the world. He grew an abundance of fertile crops including: prominent looking purple flowered globe artichokes, beetroots, potatoes, carrots, lettuces, radishes, loganberries, strawberries and luminous gooseberries, to name but a few. Papa lived from 1911-1986. I was an altar boy at his funeral. His death left a searing impression on me. I love France with my blood and bones. Papa would be proud if he knew I was going to work in his beloved country. I relish the opportunity to work in France, but not along these conniving lines. In actual fact I crave for a life in France, but not like this, not under political exile.

CHÂTEAU BRUTALE

End of February, 2002. Victor Papa flies us to our new habitat in France, in his personal military aircraft. Don't know exactly where we're going. Feel like a debased hostage. There are wisps of cloud sprinting across the light of the crisp croissant moon. There are bats flitting in and out of the black, bottomless heavens above me. The moon is by far the most eye-catching object in the night sky though. An air of impenetrability envelopes me, as we arrive at this isolated setting. We land during the hours of darkness. Makes it all the more nerve jangling and ethereal. I know little about the afflicted Château. At first it comes as an impressive visual shock. I momentarily think to myself - *could be rather idyllic living here.* It's a brief and unrealistic thought.

We're deposited in Vatanbourg, like a perilous human consignment that needs dumping and guarding. I'm locked into a life of ruefulness. They've cornered me. They've cornered the foreigner. Am going nowhere but here for a while. Victor Papa makes that decision for me. He downs a coffee, takes a protracted visit to the

Château toilette with his multi-tasking mobile phone seized in his hand, and then, after that, with giant footsteps, he climbs back into his military plane. From his cramped cockpit he barks: "These are critical times. I will instruct you." He flies off like a vulture to some other undisclosed location. Only he knows where he's going.

Now I don't *really* know where I am, and nobody I know *really* knows where I am. Of course, there's one person who knows exactly where I am, that is our very own infantry shuffling strategist: Victor Papa. So, my wolfskin way of life is initiated at the Fortress, but sustained at the Château. Feels like I've been surreally removed from the present. The Château's a place for exiles, a place to pipe down. It's a temporary residence. I guess, once the politicians make up their war-on-terror minds, I'll find independence again. Without friends or family close at hand, feel like an abandoned cast off, in some curious flat trance. Still don't feel like a free man. In actual fact, I'm caught within Victor Papa's globe brow flight path, like an insignificant soldier, in his brutal game of risk.

As I approach Château Brutale for the first time, I can smell death in the air. The Château is both impressive and grim. A morose mist exudes from the nineteenth century lamps, which spectrally line the entrance to the Château. It creates a grisly ambiance - like something from a Jack the Ripper London street scene it is. But we're certainly not in London. We're in a lost corner of France. As I move towards Château Brutale on foot, can't help thinking I'm ambling my way to an early grave. I'm geared up for misadventure.

There's a lake set inside the Château grounds. That evening I stare longingly into the stagnant water. I've no idea what I'm longing for. Have absolutely know clue how deep it is. Then I see my reflection. Slightly ripply I am. Broken. Fragmented. The hairs on my neck stand to attention. A chilling shudder cruises through my body. My reflection becomes clearer. I'm glowing in the moonlight. Don't like what I can see. Look like a yawning water wolf preparing to howl. Can feel the weight of the torpid water on my soul. Turn away, not wanting something unfathomable to happen. It's all a bit surreal. Hideously surreal, in fact. Afterwards, I think about the constant surveillance we're under. We're a private militia on tight reins. We're Victor Papa's strappingly controlled Château wolfskin troop. I think about how heavy that makes me feel. Then I begin retreating into myself even more.

The boy cries wolf and then the wolf cries boy

There's not much colour here, and there's a cold sentiment in this town, branded Vatanbourg. At dawn I'm put through my paces on the army assault course. My submission seeking superiors drill me like a dog. At dusk I'm left feeling knackered and estranged, whilst the eerie Château becomes wreathed in mist and terror. Living at the Château makes me have dark inner feelings of dread and doom.

Here freedom fights relentlessly with morality. Wanna scream: *"The American president's war-on-terror is unjust."* Wanna scream: *"Not in my name. Not for the black stuff."* Wanna escape. Wanna do the right thing. Need some guidance, but not the holier-than-thou guidance on offer here. My loyalties are being tugged at. I'm trapped in an alienating, and compromising moral maze. No longer have a choice. Become submissive. It's a humiliating submission; a soul-destroying conformity. I've been cut off from mainstream society, at a politically mercurial time. The intrusive British press can't reach me here. They pick none of this up. Course they don't. Many incidents in life go unreported, don't they? The Vatanbourg curtains are well and truly drawn on the media scavengers, and I lay silent, like a stringently religious camp. I'm submerged into a swampy ruefulness, and plunged into drudgery. Without dispute, or scrutiny, I've been forgotten about by the passive outside world. And so my laden exile begins.

March, 2002. What's left of my defiant spirit is being brutally flattened. I'm like a beast in quarantine. Who'd have thought it? Bloody mind-boggling it is. We're now in the 21st Century and I'm in exile in France. Yet it doesn't feel like I'm in France. I am definitely in the magnificent land of liberté, egalité, and fraternité, but it doesn't seem like I am. I mean, I don't see any French people for days. Do I really deserve to be banished like this? As I meditate over my macabre location, my sense of anguish sharpens deliriously. Can feel the brutal threat of death. Been spending far too much of my time thinking about death lately. I for one, don't want to breathe my last breath, here in goddamn bog land, but that's what's on my mind. I'm as good as eliminated here. My life's been repositioned. I've arrived at a surreptitious site, that's dripping with conspiracy. The surrounding environment seems tragically muted too. Muted like me. The palpable hush-hush, spells out military corruptness.

The Château is positioned in an ill-fated place. I say ill-fated, because it's distressingly close to the Somme battlefields, where thousands of men were once massacred. The First World War trenches are very near by. I can smell the not so distant horror of war. The Château was built in the 1600's, and was restored in the 1700's after the roof was damaged in the French Revolution. It was occupied by the Germans during the Second World War. Was cunningly used as a regional headquarters by them. Remnants of the occupation include swastika motifs, and German inscriptions which are carved into the stonework around some of the windows. Rumour has it, the Nazis actually shot some of their prisoners here. The Château's certainly etched with the brutal grazes of past conflicts, and the surrounding grounds are also scattered with shrapnel, and the loose ends of war. The facility is surrounded by obsolete defensive trenches, and 21 acres of mournful land. The Château has an impressive 17th century ecurie, as well as rooms dating back to the time of Louis X111. There are fine murals, and decorative frescoes on display in these rooms. All in all, it's an impressive structure, especially in these drearily flat parts. Nevertheless, can't ignore the disconcerting feeling I experience, when I step within the imposing Château walls. By day the Château affords an elegant and inspiring façade. Inside the Château there's an air of antiquity. Everything seems large and lofty. I can stand upright in the fireplace, such is its mammoth size, and the staircase is as wide as the length of a bus. There are all the items you might associate with a grand building: elaborate chandeliers, bespoke furniture, ornate gold-gilded period mirrors, intricate tapestries, highly wrought antique paintings, and like I say, giant staircases and fireplaces. The Château sure is a prominent facility. Architecturally it's by far the most striking building in the locality. The other dwellings seem diminished in size, alongside the enormity, and grandeur of the Château. They sit wedged like matchboxes in the surrounding flat fields of the Somme, appearing valueless. Yet the Château itself, has an odd feel to it. Despite its magnificence, it smells of viciousness. The cruel demise of men is lingering in the air. There's definitely *something* conspicuously brutal in the atmosphere. Could it be something reminiscent of the Nazi German occupation, perhaps? Or maybe something remaining from the Battle of the Somme? Something else perhaps? Something more contemporary? By night the Château affords a brutal façade - that's for sure. There are many brutal rumours floating amongst the staff at the Château during the evenings. It's like a twilight circuitous interrogation centre. I keep my mouth shut, as much as I can. Read enough history books to be wary of this kind of clandestine operation, but sometimes wariness doesn't count for much, does it? I mean, what can wary little Bravo Romeo, really do? Hey?

My superiors have strong royal, military, and conservative connections. They're old hat. They're overwhelmingly powerful. They're as sanctimonious as they come. In order to survive, I have to ditch my socialist leanings. It's agonizingly difficult. Little by little, I give in. I'm becoming ever more institutionalized. Nobody I know has died recently, so how come I'm so grief-stricken? Nobody I know has died lately, but there's a piercing grief in my eyes.

Vatanbourg itself is like a place drowsily waiting for an implausible change. It's a ghost town. It's absolutely dead man. My instinct warns me something's wrong. Something dreadful's happening. Suppose brutal times, call for brutal tactics, but is this a good enough excuse for isolating me so? Is it really fair for me to feel so purged by society? Segregated Vatanbourg is stuck in somnambulant ruefulness. I sustain its depressing mood. This grey town has an underprivileged air, and is consoled only by sallow Pastis. Vatanbourg is full of colourless bad vibes. Has the feel of a place lost. Elapsed. The French would call it *un coin perdu* (a lost/forgotten corner of France). Well anyway, Château Brutale in Vatanbourg is just *one* of Victor Papa's military camps. Ostensibly it's an outdoor pursuits centre for the development of young people, although very few young people ever turn up. To all appearances, that's what it is. However, I know otherwise, and so does the mighty Victor Papa. The business is a front.

My penitential trial takes place in the sleepy, out-of-the-way, nondescript town of Vatanbourg. It's a penitential path of vigilant exile. Victor Papa has his ubiquitous eyes on me. The earth beneath my feet is stained from past gory battles. This place is how it is *because of the war*. It has a *because of the war* feel. There's even a *because of the war* smell in this godforsaken town. The local inhabitants often talk about the war. According to them, everything here is how it is *because of the war*.

I've no idea how the local Charcuteries, Boulangeries, and Patisseries, make any money whatsoever. There's hardly ever a punter in sight. There's a gothic, and rather ghoulish chapel in the middle of the town, called *La Chapelle de la Saint Esprit*. It's named after the Holy Spirit. Doesn't seem like a very holy or spiritual place to me. It's covered in menacing skulls and pugnacious images of man. It's altogether deathlike. Outside there are half-gurning, half-grinning gargoyles adorned on the walls, but by far the most eye-catching external item of all, is an intricately carved bunch of hanging keys. They sit, in the stonework above the entrance, in a portentous manner. Are they the keys to another condemned world? The chapel itself is subdued, and buried in black - looks like its been entirely asphyxiated in soot. Centuries earlier, noble Parisians had been in the habit of dumping their lepers and losers here. They discarded these 'incurables' outside the chapel. Just left them to rot. This tarnishing historical detail hardly persuades me to feel privileged to be here. Indeed, Vatanbourg is still somehow associated with leprosy and destituteness. Don't really care to be part of that sore scene. What went before has left a layer of distaste across the *département*. If truth be told, it's as if a fatal illness still hangs over this sodden flat town. The chapel, and its testimonies, leave me with an undesirable echo of morbidity.

Château Brutale is sited disturbingly close to a festering marsh. It's a sombre habitat for sombre bugs and beasts. There's something truly feral about my new mosquito infested habitat. The meandering swamps are infested with mosquitoes, big fat Flicardie water rats, and some gruesomely ugly fish. There are also some ghastly looking creatures moving about in the Château lake. The inhabitants of the lake somehow manage to survive in this murky environment. These creatures of the lake surface, from time to time, to partially reveal their hideousness. The manner in which they surface, suggests they're somewhat ashamed of their grotesque appearances. They slink coyly up out of the water. Have a sneaky look. Then slink back down again. They don't show their faces for long, and never fully expose themselves. It's as if they're guilty, as if they've something to hide. Have they been ensnared in this pool of water against their will? I wonder how long some of these monstrous creatures have been lingering here. By the look of things, some have been festering here for quite a stretch of time. They're unhappy here, and would rather be someplace else. The lake behind the Château is almost permanently wrapped in a ghostly mist. It appears weirdly familiar. Am moved by it. Experience heady feelings of deja-vu down by the Château lake.

An air of mulishness hangs in our midst. It's as if the Château's unwilling to embrace the future, unable to forget its tragic past. It's a building in an incredibly bad mood. Feel encroached. Am under suspicion all over again, just as I was at the Fortress. Here we've habitual curfews. We're *occasionally* allowed offsite in the evening, but we're *always* accompanied by a senior wolfskin. We're being minded.

148

Victor Papa's military plan is obvious. Yet somehow it's incontestable. Nobody dares to denounce or question the man. The establishment forces at work here are much greater than me. Perhaps a phase of 'brutality' is the only course of action that can save me, then again, perhaps not. Have question marks of condemnation springing up all the time inside my mind. Us wolfskins are surviving in the shadow of death. We're a mislaid bunch of mercenaries with no voice. The Château site is a curious place. A place of considerable danger. It's remote. Unreal. Smells of incarceration. There are military vehicles outside the camp. Guarding. Spying. Threatening. Funny isn't it, how vehicles can look threatening? These ones look as threatening as you can get.

I become engulfed by history. For a while I'm smothered by what went before, by historical battles and past wars. You can feel the presence of countless others in this place, other long lost souls. The French *département* - *la Somme* is defined by its tragic past. War's defined it no-mans-land. The surrounding trees look like ginormous soldiers against the skyline. Impassive. Frozen in time. They are, like me, fighting for survival in this harsh marsh. The contiguous marshland is weed-entangled, and peppered with stagnant pools. The pools are smothered with mosquitoes, and an assortment of other Flicardie bugs I can't identify. In this geographically isolated marsh, wolfskin fighters are actively being spawned. The marshland is treacherous, sludgy territory. A place where certain controversial wolfskins could easily get lost forever.

We're surrounded by nothing but hundreds of flat, bare fields. It's a bit like living on a fortified island, but instead of being surrounded by a blue sea, we're surrounded by a region of earthy grey nothingness. It's a far cry from my former inner-city urban days, I can tell you. I'm surrounded by partially sunken land, and I begin to feel more than half sunken myself. The landscape appears tamed, like its almost been made to lie flat. The neighbouring woodland seems dispirited; unkeen to flourish.

Perhaps this place is a fitting place for *'moles'* to take a snooze?

Château Brutale itself is surrounded by woods. Amongst the trees, game is routinely hounded, and shot. It's a hazardous habitat for stags, roe deer, wild boar, duck, rabbit, hares, foxes, marmottes and pheasants. I often hear the slaughtering sound of gunfire, followed by harsh squawks, panicked flapping - thuds on the woodland ground. Feel sorry for these slain animals. I also feel hunted (I am not the hunter – I am the hunted). Develop a strain of sympathy for these assassinated creatures.

The boy cries wolf and then the wolf cries boy

Something tells me I'm in the shadow of war. Isn't just a tentative feeling, it's a profound feeling. It's mid-March, 2002. From the Château, I look out across the lawn towards the lake. I watch the young children running around playfully, and listen to them laughing. From a distance, the trees seem to frame the lake, making it look superimposed. For once, momentarily, it's a utopian setting; heavenly like. Then my mind drifts. My mind drifts back almost 100 years. I imagine quite the opposite to what I can see. I imagine what it must have been like on the battlefields of the Somme during the First World War. I think about the bloodshed. The chaos. The devastation. The noise. The smell of death. Then I begin to imagine scenes from the war that's about to happen, and that makes me feel sick - the thought that all our green nature could be lost forever. Like I say, something tells me, resoundingly, that we're all in the shadow of war.

The days are long. Time moves slowly here. It's a vacuous time. At the end of the day, we clamber into our chambers all deadbeat. There's zilch to do here. Yet we've no time to do anything, even if there was something to do. We've no time to ourselves. There's no respite. No reprieve. No time for quiet reflection. Relentless. Brutality.

I'm assigned a bedroom. Have to share it with another two footed wolfskin instructor. He's a Muslim wolfskin. The only Muslim wolfskin on site. He's brown skinned, asian looking. His name is Anoop. He's nervous. Talkative. Tirelessly talkative. He's my inmate. Our bedroom is a room with two single beds in it. Not much more. It's prison-like, but relatively salubrious, and comfortable enough. However, just as I'm allocated my room, a sense of disenchantment overwhelms me. Don't know what this feeling means for sure, but it's a potent forewarning. There insidious military methods of extracting information, have only just begun. This is going to be a challenge.

Anoop and I are allocated a room that's detached from the bedrooms of *all* the other wolfskins. Although our bedroom is still

150

within the same sleeping quarter, we're set apart on a completely different level. Why are we isolated? Why the segregation? Already feel like an outsider. Now I'm made to feel like a complete foreigner. A few days later we're suddenly shifted to another, similarly bare chamber. The chamber is on the same level as the other wolfskin dwellings. The unexpected shift makes me disorientated. Are we now being accepted as genuine wolfskin infantry? Are we now being received into this wayward band of soldiers? Have we moved up a rank? Still feel like a captured activist. Still feel apart.

By day I'm made to whitewash walls. By the hours of darkness I'm plagued by nightmares of blank whiteness. It's cold in my bed at night. Slightly damp. 'We get pleasure in gutting gay virgins (signed VP)', has been etched on the headboard of my wooden bed. *How Delightful* - I muse. In our new chamber there's also a tiny little drawer embedded into the whitewall. Unusual it is. Intriguing. We eventually manage to wobble it free. The secret drawer is no bigger than your average brick. There's nothing inside except a decaying smell of times gone by. *Perhaps it's a remnant of the German occupation* - I ponder. Don't know the truth about what went on here, but I can smell death in the walls. Fear I might get walled into this place myself, and be mysteriously lost and forgotten about by all living souls.

The walls in our dwellings are so white they're actually thwarting on the eyes. *Is exposure to excessive whiteness some kind of Château Brutale military tactic? Is this supposed to make us confess all we know?* - I wonder. Our chamber is lighted with an unshaded bulb. In the evenings, as I lay on my bed, I am, in effect, lying in a clinical white box. The whitewashed walls gradually begin to apply pressure to my eyes, and my culpable mind confesses all. To itself.

Anoop is wearisomely inquisitive. He asks me question, after question, after question. Never met anyone who asks so many questions. Come to think of it, never met anyone called Anoop before either. He's always asking me how to say stuff in French. "What's the word for 'ball' in French? What's the word for 'drawer' in French? How do you say 'book' in French?" And so the humdrum queries keep coming at me. I never ask him a goddamn thing. Eventually I buy him an English/French dictionary, even though I'm practically penniless. Need to try and divert his constant picking of my brain. Need to try and ease the grinding ennui. Kinda works. For a while. But soon the gnawing questions come back. Like peckers to my head. "What's the word for 'wall' in French? What's the word for 'horse' in French? How do you say 'headache' in French?"

"Look it up in your dictionary!"

"Ok – buds."

Anoop tests my patience to the edge. His incessant questions are almost too much for me.

Diligence, not inquisitiveness, is what I live by here, together with a heightened preservation instinct. Wanna be the dominant species. Wanna survive. Feel like I'm old before my time though. I'm only 25 - feel like a submissive old man. Here I am tested. Probed. Interrogated...and made to feel elderly. Keep my suspicions, and my dreads to myself. Keep 'em to myself as much as is humanly possible. Never been quite so entirely ineffectual. Still, gotta live through all of this somehow. Want my journey to continue. Also feel closer to sainthood for sharing a chamber with Anoop, without losing my temper. Have to say though, he is, at least, a gentle man. What I mean is - don't think Anoop is a bad person. A bit lonely perhaps, and for some reason, it appears he wants to learn the entire French language overnight, and wants me to be his personal tutor. But apart from that, he's ok, I suppose.

Anoop sits on his bed in our chamber scratching dementedly at the mosquito bites on his ankles. At least that keeps him quiet for a while. Not long enough mind. Then I begin to wonder - *What am I doing in this 'lost corner' of France, sharing a deliriously white room, with a Muslim man, who keeps asking me loads of questions? What is actually happening here?* - I wonder hard to myself.

We lie perpendicularly next to each other in our chamber at night; forming a human 'L' shape as we sleep. Our feet – just yards apart. In effect, we're coexisting. Never coexisted with anyone before. Not for any significant length of time anyhows. Suppose it could be worse.

There's a degree of irregularity about lying in bed in the evening, trying to get to sleep, knowing there's another man in the same room, trying to do exactly the same thing. Invasive. Deviant. Find myself synchronising my breathing with Anoop's snoring. This makes me feel perverse. The fact that Anoop's snoring sounds like the hum of a helicopter, doesn't help matters. At night time, when I'm trying to sleep, feels like I'm in prison more than at any other time. Anoop's snoring lies heavy in my mind. I regularly compose myself to sleep in an unhinged state of mind.

152

I too am forever flicking at the Flicardie marsh mosquitoes. It's a constant battle of man against fiendish little French beast. I attempt to crush them dead, before they get too comfortable, sucking away at my blood. Of course I don't always react quickly enough. In less than a split-second the biting damage is done. At least...so it seems. My arms and legs become covered in sherbet saucer style mosquito splotches. The mosquitoes remind me that I am, after all, living on swampy ground. One way or another, they got deep into my flesh. I often end up scratching myself to sleep at night. They seem to like my knuckles the best. Anyway, the mosquitoes do their thing, like only mosquitoes can.

Our chamber has a single barred window. It's no bigger than a shoebox. It allows only rueful glimpses of daylight to come in. The room itself is slightly damp. Smells of abandonment. It's as if someone lay here once before, but a very long time ago. A brutal chill strikes through me. Each and every night. Of my wolfskin stretch.

Our chambers are like attic dungeons really. At night, we lay buried in a loft-like outbuilding. Like I say, the natural lighting is scant, but in the evenings, when we need artificial light, it's actually far too bright. We aren't living in squalor, but we're certainly ruffing-it here. My bed is built for a Spaniard. It's belittlingly too small. Without a telephone, television, or even an English newspaper to hand, I've abandoned life itself. Or has society abandoned me? Don't have a clue what's happening in the world. That makes me feel sad. Secluded. I'm a military intelligence *incident*. My life's a total cover-up. I'm living in a brutal establishment, that's run by a brutal man of the establishment. Already longing for the end. But when will that come?

I adapt better than most of the other wolfskins. They all seem properly traumatized. Coming from a large family has taught me how to survive. I'm good at sharing, and sharing stuff is important here. So is swapping stuff. One time I swap a pouch of tobacco for a torch. I'm chuffed with my swap. Totally chuffed. Think it's the swap of the century. The torch allows us to see random glimpses of the woods during the hours of darkness. It reminds me of my chemistry lessons at school - when we'd look at bacteria, and other screwy scientific stuff under a microscope. It also makes me think of Halloween. Anyway, more importantly, this one time, it helps me get out of the murky woods at night-time, without falling into the deep green swampy marsh. I become particularly fond of this torch, for that very reason.

This torch becomes my precious, and reassuring other half. Sometimes you just get attached to stuff don't you?

The Château itself is managed by a man with fatuous philosophies, and a fat belly. His name is Geoffrey Partridge. Partridge is a bespectacled, short man. He's a well-stuffed, walking encyclopedia. He studied history and theology at Cambridge University, and he has a remarkable memory. He's also an officious bookworm. His mind absorbs everything that he reads, almost photographically. His mind also catalogues everything that we say and do. At times, it seems as if he's preparing a court case against us. Perhaps his absorbent brain is a little *too* big for his head. He wobbles around the Château grounds with majestic indifference. He doesn't own the Château, but he acts as if it's his. Partridge appeares to have an entrenched concept of how society should be. He's every bit the pompous traditionalist. Miraculously he can talk in great detail about every subject under the sun. But no man knows everything do they? He's something of a gastronome, an educated man with an educated palate. His engorged waistline confirms his devotion to food. He's 'embonpoint' to say the least. At mealtimes we all sit at a large round table, and it's then, I notice, that Partridge is particularly fond of his puddings. Partridge is didactic and a bit of a royal character. He's audaciously eloquent. He speaks promptly and in a disciplinarian fashion. He often challenges our code of behaviour. His power as an orator means he has power over us. He has a loud public voice and is crushingly intellectual. He makes me feel like I'm at boarding school or something like that. We refer to him as Geoffrey Partridge, although it's possible that isn't his real name. Partridge lives in a secret residence, an old military outhouse at the bottom of Château Brutale's gardens. What's he really doing here I wonder? Is he a law enforcement specialist? Or more likely, is he furtively working for MI6? Whatever his position is, it's here that he spies on us and assesses our behaviour. Partridge is an upholder of English custom and he's awfully priggish about it. Come to think of it, I've never met anyone quite so stuck-up, and self-righteous in all my life. He scuttles around camp like an overstuffed weeble - thinking he knows it all. Although he doesn't know it all, does he?

"Doctrine and discipline. That's all you need," proclaims Partridge in the manner of a talking clock. He always goes on about the two D's. "Doctrine and discipline. Obey these laws and you'll be a more manly man." It strikes me as a peculiarly preachy thing to say. I

154

walk away from him thinking - *I'm already more of a manly man than you'll ever be, Mr double D.* I also have a strong desire to call him a podgy, bible bashing ladybird, but somehow I refrain myself. I never do work out properly what his *doctrine* is, but I know it has something to do with the Church and the Bible. I do know one thing for sure, and that is that he's *exceedingly* English. Anyhows, Partridge exudes a powerful air of aptitude. There's no doubting that. But he also seems whole-heartedly disingenuous. At least to me he does. *What on earth is a man like this doing managing an outdoor pursuits centre?* - I muse? He isn't the athletic type, his belly's bursting at the seams. You know he seems so thoroughly misplaced here. And you know why? Because he's a fake and a phony, that's why. He's more concerned with *overseeing* this whole operation, rather than playing an active role in its artificial function. Not once does Partridge take part in any of the outdoor pursuit activities. He doesn't care less about the development of young people. That's all just a mock-up, a fix-up to him. All he cares about is his devious web of espionage, and having a cellar full of the finest wine and cognac France has to offer. He's a bit of a moralistic religious nut, if you ask me. Quite randomly one day, as I'm mopping the Château foyer, Partridge announces: "The spirit is always calling us to greater discernment." He sidesteps past me before scurrying off merrily. His comment seems massively out of context. Leaves me thinking - *you should lay off the spirits for a while matey!*

Another time I burst into the Château dining hall. My entrance is rather awkward. I'm a tad behind schedule for dinner. I receive a reprehensible look off Partridge. Kind of anticipate that. Partridge is, quite unsurprisingly, in the middle of one of his theological rants. Don't know what sparks off this particular divine prophesy, but this is what I walk into: "If we claim to be without sin, we deceive ourselves and the truth is not in us. I have joined myself to a covenant of the Lord into a church estate, in the fellowship of the gospel, to walk in all his ways, made known or to be known unto us through truth in..." *What!* Alpha Mike whispers: "Enjoys the sound of his own voice hey?" I chip in softly. "Must get thirsty!" Well, all this picky talk of deceit and all is enough to make me feel even more awkward, and disappointed actually. Disappointed I'm here at all, and disappointed I have to hear Partridge's attempts to delude our fragile wolfskin minds. I can sum up everything he's trying to implant into our brains in a single word, *'Peace'*. So, why on earth does he feel the need to rant and rave in such a prophetic way? I, for one, don't need a moral lesson from the preposterously pious Partridge.

Anyhow, Geoffrey Partridge wobbles and reddens as he delivers his withering moral tirades. He often goes crimson with rage, bobbles about like a spoilt chubby baby, before storming off in a fury. Every now and then he really works himself up into a right tizzy of sourness, I can tell you. The plump man leads a pampered existence, his slightest whim indulged in by a small army of wolfskin servants. Partridge screams abuse in our faces, and rages about our incompetence. He often walks away from us, when we haven't come up to scratch in our duties, exclaiming grandiloquently: "sheer incompetence, sheer incompetence!" We are all *incompetent* according to Partridge. Well, almost all of us. He has his favourite. Fanny is her name, or Foxy, or Foxtrot Hotel and I'm sure he has a few more pet names for her! He's cunningly befriended her. If truth be told, he has her wrapped around his flabby little finger. She's a constant source of enlightening information for him, and she laughs a doting and foolish: "Heeee, hee, hee," at all, and every one of his attempts at humour. It's nauseating to watch their transparent relationship unfurl before my eyes.

"Château Brutale will turn even the feistiest man into a field mouse," Partridge declares one evening. Is he endeavouring to crush me? He certainly appears to be making every effort to indoctrinate us, and put us down. Partridge's correctness and discipline are like the attributes of an emblematic public schoolmaster. He brandishes a solid wooden baton in a conjuring manner. The baton instills discipline into us lowly wolfskins. It's like the court gavel that he craves to hold, him being all *judge-mental* and all. He's every bit the demon headmaster with his stiff cane-like baton clasped in hand. His inspection of us is senseless, or at least, his inspection of me is senseless. Looking-over my life is futile. He'd be better off just asking me some more direct queries. I'd be much more willing to *talk* if I was just asked some more forthright questions. Well anyway, one day I decide to ask the righteous Partridge a bit of a blunt and challenging question of my own: "Why do you always carry that baton around with you?" (A rush of naughtiness streaks its way through my subversive blood. Feel like I've committed a gross act of insubordination). "It's an unbending instrument of tenacity in the hands of authority," is Partridge's iron reply. Told. He answers me swiftly. Razor sharply in fact. Indeed, Partridge's reply is so instantaneous, it leads me to come to the philosophical conclusion that he's already thought about what he might immediately say, if somebody, anybody, might, at some point, ask him about his beloved baton, and the way in which he continually clutches it so. Feel all inferior now, after Partridge's dogmatic vocal baton spasm. To wrap matters up...his baton is merely a repressive extension of his own bludgeoning inner qualms.

To a certain extent he himself seems imprisoned, like as if he's incarcerated by ennui or something. He's on a different cerebral plain to us humble wolfskins you see. Out here in Flicardie, there's nobody he can relate to. When he's around us he's quite simply intellectually jaded. Like I say, Partridge often goes off on these sermonizing rants. I could do without hearing these moralistic monologues to be fair. They do nothing for me. But you know he's just trying to keep himself enthused. He has a fierce intelligence, we all know that, but this is no reason for him to act like a complete arsewipe. His rants bug me. They bug me just as much, if not more than my chamber-mate Anoop's irksome inquisitions. Actually, I cannot forgive Partridge for the way he speaks to Anoop. In an attempt to pour scorn on him, he declares publicly: "Diabolical imbecile! What's wrong with you? You can hang for all I care, you good-for-nothing parasite!" Anoop just withdraws into a closed-eyed nervousness. There's no comeback. Anoop shouldn't be made to feel embarrassed of himself like this. Partridge bosses him around in a noticeably sour manner. Certainly he orders him about differently to the rest of us wolfskins. So why the deviating pitch? Why the blatant discrepancy? Could it have something to do with the colour of Anoop's skin? His religion perhaps? My funnelled intuition leads me to believe Partridge is a xenophobe. Permit me please to reiterate - yes pious Partridge, of all people, is indeed a racist scumbag.

Like I say it's an artificial existence here. We're all part of Victor Papa's military experiment really. I've always found life curious, but now my world is utterly incomprehensible. Most of the time there's a subtle, indirect kind of interrogation going on. They're attempting to urge something out of me. They're tiresomely waiting for me to speak. It's absolute craziness here man. *How fanatical life can be sometimes* - I think to myself. Anyway, Partridge puts on this simulated front. A front that's not altogether convincing. A front that he dutifully never lets up. The Château manager has one simple mission - to get me to talk. They need to know how much I know. They cage me in. They try to break my will. There's a 'do this, don't do that' thing going on. I'm becoming entangled deeper and deeper into this rueful quagmire. But you know, the last thing I am, is rueful. I'm not sorry I oppose their oil-inspired war on terror. I'm not sorry I at least try to dissent against a great wrong. I won't apologize for my resistance. They're looking for someone to frame. Demonise. They're looking for someone to blame for their clandestine military misadventure. As part of their political and military manoeuvring, they've obtained compromising photographs of me. They are surreptitious images that will damage my reputation. These guys are capable of anything. But do they have enough to actually ruin me? Do they have enough dirt on me to perpetually demonise me?

Château Brutale, April, 2002...

"Why did you prevaricate against a career in journalism?" Partridge is *trying* to be casual about the matter, but he's obviously snooping. His question is as subtle as a flying egg. My words of reply are hastily chosen: "It's too upsetting to talk about." On the spur of the moment that's what comes out. I'm not sure why this man is asking such a probing personal question. I'm not sure whether I can trust this man. To be fair, it's an utter bombshell of a question. I fear he's muckraking. The sudden stall in my career as a journalist was upsetting, but it wasn't *too* upsetting to talk about. Just don't want to talk to him about it really. He's not the right person. He's not my friend. Walk away from him whispering under my breath: "Goddamn spineless toad!" On the spur of the moment, it's the most fitting insult I can think of.

Partridge often walks with his chubby hands clasped behind his back. It's the walk of a royal. You can tell by his body language that his mind is elsewhere. He's obnoxiously self-righteous. His self-righteousness is unwarranted really. Victor Papa, on the other hand, has a reason to be self-righteous. He can abseil mountains, shoot rifles and fly planes. He's Partridge's superior. There's nobody above him. Nobody tells Victor Papa what to do. He's the true huntmaster.

At Château Brutale adventurous pursuits take place with an ever-changing squadron. Like the mysterious 'getting to know you better' river trip. Disguised as a vital team building exercise, this exploratory event is designed to get us to *talk*. I say as little as I can as I paddle down the motionless muddy river in my kayak. I have to talk every now and again. Don't want to seem like a spoilsport. Or too much of a mute. These are complicated times. Guilt can be a very powerful human emotion can't it? I feel a strong sense of guilt on this particular river trip. Feel so guilty, reckon I must even look guilty. Bet I even smell of guilt. Deep down though, I know I'm the *good* guy. I privately vow to keep hold of my thoughts. After all it's information they're after. I bite my tongue. Keep as silent as possible. It's painful. I've adopted this kind of *don't speak unless spoken to* mentality. Know it isn't a healthy existence. Know it isn't me. But I remain comparatively silent nonetheless. I'm in no doubt that my *blue* past has brought me to this crushing place.

There's something combative and obscure about my entire French adventure. We've come to Northern France in concealing camouflage. We're the wolfskin militia. We're a bunch of misplaced army troupers. Feel intrusive dressed in my tomato-red wolfskin and army style green combat pants. Paradoxically, we look hideously conspicuous, in our wolfskin masquerade. Nevertheless, Partridge insists that we always wear our uniforms, even when we're allowed off-site. Together, as a pack, we look like something out of a science-fiction film. I've always felt uncomfortable wearing uniforms, but wearing my wolfskin in France particularly aggravates me. It's like wearing an arresting skin that doesn't belong to me. It also offends the natives. This makes me feel sad. We appear like impostors to the French locals, like a cluster of dominating and rapacious wolves, what with our striking red military fatigues and all. The locals feel like their small town is being besieged by a striking alien force, as we march into town to sample the local brew (In point of fact, there's no local brew on tap, but there's plenty of regional cider, and cheap red wine). Feels like we're taking complete possession of the town. We swarm our way into the centre, like an unstoppable army of big-headed red ants. We're invading a small corner of France. We're slowly taking it over. This upsets me, as France is a country very close to my heart.

I can see that Monique, the arrogant and vigilant landlady of *L'artichaut,* is aware of whats going on. She's wholeheartedly unimpressed. She stands like a Goddess statue of Marianne behind the bar. It's as if she's just found her raison d'être. I can see a prominent alertness in her owl-like eyes. The other frenchies appear to have obedient minds. They've overwhelming looks of war daubed across their faces, and quite simply, they don't want any more trouble. Our invasion doesn't bother them too much. If anything, they're glad of the company. In their diminished world, it's as if nothing really matters anymore. Life's gonna drift over them as if it's a predetermined, and smothering grey blanket of fog anyway. No doubt, their minds have been slowly clouded, over the years, from one too many drops of Ricard. They certainly appear to be unthinking. Adulterated. Obliterated. This pallid green drink seems to be their sole reason for existence. Monique on the other hand can see that *I know*. It will be our little unspoken secret forever. Monique has passion. A passion for the Republic. A passion for reason. A passion for life. Liberté means something to her. I seem to have caught her interest. I am arrogant too.

Partridge stands at *L'artichaut* bar chewing each mouthful of his white wine. Musingly. Swilling. To try and be a bit French, he asks for a drop of cassis in his chardonnay. He's brooding over something. Is he still waiting for me to talk? Is he feeling the heat from his gruelling military superiors? *They* think I can still prove to be *useful* to them. I on the other hand don't want to be *useful* to them. It's against my gooseberry green raison d'être.

Many of the locals in Vatanbourg move around sluggishly. It's as if they have all the time in the world. They're infected with a kind of subdued fatalism. This feeling of fatalism is contagious. Vatanbourg has little to offer really, although it does have a yummy pizza parlour. The French styled parlour is managed by a somewhat somnambulant man. Looks a bit like a marmotte. The food's delicious. Still, he doesn't receive too many customers. It's dead here. That's why. In Vatanbourg that is. Geoffrey Partridge escorts us here for a *good-behaviour* culinary reward. It's demeaning. Patronising. Feel guarded. Feel like a small child. But I'm not going to turn down some quality nosh. I'm not that stubborn...I'm not that arrogant. The well-whiskered manager, who comes complete with slanting beret, carries the pizzas over to our table as if he's in some kind of sleepwalking daze. "Voila tout le monde! Bon appétit!" he croons lethargically, as he places the pizzas onto our red, white, and blue chequered table. It's gone 21.00, but it looks as if he's just rose from his pit. Despite the rather languorous service, the pizzas taste lip-smackingly scrumptious. I go for the French number with salami, artichokes, anchovies, black olives, and a runny fried egg, dumped haphazardly in the middle. I honour my pizza with a generous splash of hot chilli olive oil and get stuck in. Between slices, I also devour local side orders of grilled eels, frogs legs, snails, and a Somme bay speciality duo of cockles and mussels. For once, I'm animated. For once, it really feels like I'm living in France. This is the first foreign-flavoured food to touch my lips since my arrival here. Have been truly ravenous for this moment. Then it dawns on me. It's then that I realise how truly wrong things are.

Later back at the Château, Partridge prepares a heavy punch. How thoughtful. How generous of him! In an attempt to educate, and alert the other more meagre minded wolfskins, I call it his *propaganda punch.* My sarcasm is sadly lost on them. Indeed, my attempt to try and teach them something, hardly even seems to reach their ears. The powerfully laced alcoholic punch is designed to loosen our tongues. He plies us with booze to loosen us up for a bit of a chitchat. Plies us with booze to meddle with our measly wolfskin minds. I choose not to get all boozy. Don't want to be loosened up for interrogation. Especially not by the 'not so pious' Partridge. Black Anoop, on the other hand, gets absolutely steaming. I think he's lonely and isolated. In his drunken state he finds himself in quite an objectionable position. Rather appallingly Anoop is suddenly completely exposed. For kicks, the other somewhat savage wolfskins, strip him right down to his underpants. They take advantage of Anoop's drunken state merely for their own amusement. He becomes the centre of attention. Is subjected to a whole heap of maltreatment. Including senseless, and uncongenial prods, and hostile heckles. And this input from Partridge: "One of these days there will just have to be an accident!" Unbelievable. *He can't mean that. Can he?* He's in search of a bit of popularity if you ask me. Anoop doesn't fight back. Doesn't resist. Simply recoils. Like a defeated, and uncared for organism, he lies solitarily on the stairs in nothing but his pants. Curling up he is, into a ball. Normally he's loquacious. Now he's silent. Anoop seems to be trying to make himself as small as possible. He's reeling. He's shrinking. He's clinging onto them stairs. Poor guy's just trying to survive in the only way he knows how, in the way he feels most secure. Inside I'm sure he's pleading for this degrading treatment to soon be over, but on the outside he's like a soundless and petrified rabbit. I'm not surprised by the way he acts. He isn't the violent sort. Feel helpless in this situation. Feel momentously sad. Can see that Anoop is being shamed. Can see that Anoop is being bullied. Can see that this scandalous exhibition is mind bogglingly wrong. Above all else, I can see that Partridge actually instigates this racist human spectacle, and is now egging on the wolfskin pack. Criminal.

Later on at Partridge's propaganda party...."Come here," she whispers with elaborate provocation as she pouts her full-bodied cherry red lips. Her overzealous coquettishness arouses my suspicions. She's up to something. After something. She laughs. Dances. Swirls. Murmurs and sighs. Erotically. She flashes her penthouse suite eyes at her breasts, then looks unswervingly up at me. "My boobs are yours," she says without speaking. Her advances are seductive, but not so inviting as to be bewitching. She's fit. Sexy. Sassy. But not unparalleled in beauty. I remain wary. Is this a honey trap?

Just the once, I strike up a conversation with a female wolfskin. Lisa Lovelady is the princess of this wolfskin marshland. She's the fittest girl on site. She's a voluptuous young woman, and she's seemingly looking for a good time. She insists we call her by her real name. She isn't fond of her radio pseudonym, Lima Lima. I kinda like mine. Me and Lisa Lovelady are chatting down by the lake. She spends her time slagging off the other girls. Our conversation is lacklustre for a while. Then somehow we get onto the subject of politics. I assert, with an ounce of self-importance: "I'm from the liberal communist school of thought I guess. Bit of a lefty me. I agree with communist values and principles in theory, but I know it's virtually impossible to implement them in the Western world. Equality and liberty are imperative in politics...and the rights of the individual are paramount. These days it's essential we have variety in our society and in life in general really." The Lovelady says nothing. She just plays with her hair.

      God only knows how we end up having this conversation. Reckon I'm just in some kind of political romanticism mode. That's all. Lisa Lovelady isn't interested in politics. Don't get me wrong. She isn't unintelligent. Far from it. Just not into politics. That's all....she becomes swiftly jaded with my political monologue. Anyway, somehow my words are relayed back to Victor Papa. How so? Apparently he's at the Fortress in Cravenshire at the time of my political tête-à-tête with the Lovelady. Is Lima Lima one of Victor Papa's dedicated spies? Has she recited everything I said to her down by the lake? Why would she even bother divulging this superfluous information? Maybe she blabs to one of the other wolfskins, and they relay my irrelevant political point of view, back to Victor Papa? Maybe the marsh microphones have picked up our conversation!? Of course, it's possible, that this place has many hidden microphones. Whatever the explanation, my words are relayed from France back to Victor Papa in England. A few days later when Victor Papa flies over to the Château on one of his fleeting visits, he starts mouthing off: "I'm from the liberal communist school of thought I guess. Bit of a lefty me!" Is this echo merely coincidence? *Don't think so!* Find it hard to believe in coincidence anymore, especially totally implausible coincidences like this one. Find it hard to believe in anything whilst Victor Papa is around. One thing's for sure, you have to be careful what you say in this place, and careful who you confide in. After my head-on meeting with Victor 'I'm-a-liberal-communist-too' Papa, I walk around Château Brutale for the rest of the day, cagily assessing - *who can I trust?* My conclusion: nobody.

Let's not forget, Victor Papa's like my own personal man in the mirror. I've been bloody dragooned here thanks to him. He's trying to mirror me. Reflect me, if you like. This is his way of boldly declaring: "I've got my right-wing military eye on you, and during these extremely critical times you should choose your words cautiously." He is, with all intent and purpose, messing with my breakable mind. The General has an extraordinary capacity to dissect our character. Victor Papa repeats other little clippings of stuff I say to some of the other wolfskins. His unnerving echoes often surface a day or two later. Why bother with these military mind games? Why bother regurgitating stuff I've said? Hasn't he got anything better to do? Why doesn't he go out and slaughter some enemies for instance? He's trying to completely suppress me. He's making me fear him even more. He's making me think twice before I open my mouth. Like that's necessary! I'll tell you what I'm thinking - *I'm thinking something's intolerably wrong.*

Would like to open up to someone, but find it difficult to trust anyone here. Sense I can't trust Lisa 'cherry-lips' Lovelady anymore. Shame. Know I can't trust Foxtrot 'kiss-arse' Hotel. She's about as discreet as a woodpecker on speed. She loves to talk. She loves to talk to Partridge. Foxtrot Hotel is naïve to what's going on. I never pay her any attention or talk to her. For this reason she decides, feeble-mindedly, that I'm weird. Don't talk to her because I don't trust her. Certainly not going to open up my heart or confide any of my secrets to her. Word always seems to get back to the Partridge. Somehow he gets to know about everything, from pouches of tobacco going missing, to more demeaning, but perhaps more useful gossip, about who's shagging who. He grills every one of us, until he gets what he wants. I'm alone with everybody. I'm alone with everybody again. It's a brutal loneliness actually. Maybe I am weird? Maybe I deserved to be shot at and silenced? Maybe I deserved to have my home desecrated? Maybe I deserve to be here in this pitiless military setting? Maybe I've got this war on terror thing all wrong?

Victor Papa's like a giant spider lurking somewhere in the background. Us lowly wolfskins are all tangled up in his warlike web, like speckled human morsels. The martial set up at the Château is perfect for extracting juicy information. It's an encroaching misadventure; a brutish game. We've little privacy. I wonder if any of the other wolfskins, within the Château walls, feel quite as impinged as I do? Perhaps they've all been caught up in extraordinarily hostile events. Most of them certainly appear somewhat unhinged. Perhaps they even feel protected here.

Victor Papa run's this operation with an iron fist. The warning of his imminent presence evokes a bizarre human oscillation among the wolfskins. "Quick! Victor Papa's coming!" a wolfskin cries. We then scatter, like panicky ants, into an absurd mime of labour intensive activity. It's as if he has us all under an adventurous military spell or something. Quite remarkably we make ourselves look busy. How painstakingly convincing we wolfskins are. If you don't do what's expected, Victor Papa will get you. Only our own brutal imaginations can tell us what this might entail.

Many of the wolfskins are from Liechester. When you stop and consider that the instructor positions were advertised all over the country, this seems surprising. It's a conspicuous coincidence. Liechester's not a huge place after all. Is it more than just a twist of fate? Was it orchestrated? Why's Liechester suddenly become such a place of significance? Does it have something to do with The Blue Hole? Does it have something to do with terrorism?

Tango Unicorn has chiseled good looks, and biceps like tortoises. He's always clean shaven. Always meticulously groomed. His profile is like the human targets you find in a shooting gallery. He looks a bit like Guile from the Nintendo game streetfighter. He's perfectly formed. Tango Unicorn is as hard as a rifle, and always ready for action. He's a lean, mean, fighting machine. He's a comparatively clever wolfskin, but he's more brawn than brain. He walks like he's had a hot stoker shoved up his ass, with urgency and stiffness. He always does as he's told. He's especially dutiful. Think he's the kind of wolfskin they're hunting for. Obedient. Unquestioning. Super fit. Tango Unicorn is engrossed with the whole soldierly setup. He does everything that's expected of him, and more. There's a perverted 'selection process' taking place at Château Brutale. Almost all of the wolfskins are looking for adventure brownie points from the General, Victor Papa. I'm not.

Juliet Whisky, one of the other wolfskins, is never at ease. She's bitter. Twisted. As hard-bitten as they come. She's more like a witch than a wolf. She's never content. Consistently whinges. Her whinging is vigorous. Callous. Reliable. She's worse than a mordant child, who always gets their own way. Juliet Whisky is both insecure and conceited....a curious and dangerous mix. Something bad has happened to that poor scathing creature. I can tell. Don't know what exactly, but life has really got at her somehow. Don't know how she's going to survive all this. She isn't the kind of wolfskin Victor Papa is hunting for.

Alpha Mike's one of the more percipient wolfskins. Earthy looking. Above average intelligence. Probably too intelligent. One day he hands me a book: *'Going to the wars'*. Think he's trying to tell me something. Think he's trying to tell me something I already know. We will soon be going to war.

I don't quite fit Victor Papa's multi-activity mould. Don't think I'm martial enough. Too much of a lefty! Victor Papa's aim is not just to twist my wits and terrify me. He wants to physically exhaust me into submission. Despite all, I'm strong emotionally. However, my physical fitness is slightly defective. Life is arduous on my joints here. This brutal misadventure is seen as a reprieve for us wolfskins, like a sympathetic stay of execution. We need to be kept occupied in these critical times. If we're kept busy, we'll stay out of trouble. If we aren't kept busy, we'll probably be stirring up anarchy. At least that's what *they* think. At least that's the excuse *they* use to keep us here. The state thinks it knows what's best for us. The state thinks it's better to suppress. I'm made to surrender my individuality during a time of national crisis and global uncertainty.

Do *they* honestly believe that I'm a real threat to national security? In their attempt to *deal with us* have *they* not considered a more diplomatic or suave approach? It's here, at Château Brutale, that I experience the full wrath of state control. *They* are testing me to see if I'll commit sedition. I'm caged. There are no chains or shackles, but there are hidden recording devices and cameras, and the Château's seething with hacking informers. There's a commanding *'Big Brother is watching you'* mania going on. Like I say, this place is conducive to gossip. Nevertheless, I still try to be reticent. I'm biting my insubordinate tongue. We're living together. Working together. Socialising together. We do everything together. We're like a family. A family of wolfskins. We have to try and get on. Inevitably we grow tired of each other's company. Victor Papa's a clever man. I'm not sure if he's a good man. He wants us all to talk. He wants us all to gossip. He keeps photographing me.

Have you ever felt like you're not living your own life on your own terms? Have you ever felt incarcerated? Château Brutale is a place where free will does not exist. It's a place where virtually all of our requests are refused. It's a place where you need permission to do anything. Access to the internet is denied and our calls and incoming mail are subject to audit. Victor Papa's regime is designed to remould dissenting characters. It's a regime designed to crush individualism. *Their* excuse, just in case anybody does ask them, is that *they* are shielding me, and re-educating me through labour at a critical time of national uncertainty.

DOING TIME

My time at Château Brutale is like a guilty-until-proven-innocent prison sentence. However, this is not time spent in prison. This is time spent confined within Victor Papa's military capsuled world. I've limited liberty. My human rights are being infringed. Our wolfskin existence is dominated by work. We toil like enslaved ants here. I'm working 100 hours a week, and I've nothing to show for it. I'm living on site with several disturbingly unpredictable wolfskins. I don't know hardly anything about these volatile people. I do know that Victor Papa's trained them to shoot rifles, and I do know that the majority of them are notably unhinged.

Alcohol is banned at Château Brutale. This probably works to my advantage. Occasionally we get tipsy. Secretively. But we rarely have the time to get drunk. Besides, most of the time we're all too knackered to even consider getting all boozy. A break from the sauce will do my liver some good.

I'm a writer but I cannot write.... At Château Brutale I never have any quality private time to scribble down my thoughts. This aggravates me more than anything. Am aggrieved I don't have time to document stuff. Makes me feel like a wounded wolfskin. They take my truth-seeking writing time away from me. Intellectually it's an intolerable time.

166

At least once a week I have to take up the responsibility of being DIE (duty instructor in the ecurie - *ecurie* is the French word for horse stable). The DIE shift is a shift that none of the wolfskins look forward to. It's unlike any other shift here. It's massively draining. As part of my slave-like list of chores as DIE, I have to do a night check of the Château grounds.

I'm patrolling the Château grounds in the darkness. I notice a towering silhouette figure lurking under some trees. Deer God! The large shadow starts approaching me. Silently. Am shitting myself. Do I really need to be feeling so afraid? Is it a Stag? Is it an intruder? Is it the Grim Reaper? It's Victor Papa. The General's wondering around like a masterful wolf, attentively watching its next feed. "Whatsup?" I quiz him. Enigmatically. Nervously. He has a savage presence, and appears bloodthirsty. Victor Papa doesn't say anything. Well, for a number of seconds at least he doesn't reply, and I can tell by his facial reaction that he doesn't appreciate being harangued, especially not by such a lowly wolfskin apprentice as me. He just stands there. All mighty. All territorial. Then he booms: "All part of my military objective! "
"Hey?"
"Don't like hunting animals...prefer to hunt after men!"
Nothing else is said. The mood between us is palatably spiky. We just get on with our eerie business. Victor Papa's military objective is to keep his eye on me - keep me under control. He's a fearsome bugger. His prowling presence is there, even when he's not. It's like a mighty shadow biting at my heels. Making me crave freedom. Making me mad.

The following morning after the longest DIE shift ever, I do actually see a Stag. I spot it in the middle of the lawn, inbetween the Château and the lake. The Stag appears unspeakably magnificent. Motionless. Like a statue. Can't keep my eyes off it. Astonishing it is. During that misty snap of dawn, everything is silent. Still. Dreamlike. Miraculous. For a moment I am stuck in a Stag trance. It does move eventually. Gracefully. Steamily. I do see the Stag, I am sure of that, but everything seems surreal. Hauntingly serene. Enlightening.

I won't talk when I'm sober.

Somehow some of the girls manage to twist Partridge's uncompromising iron fist. At least, on one occasion, and by some means, our curfew is lifted. Partridge grants us the luxury of an evening off work! The girls sweet-talk me into going to some sleazy, out of town wine bar. There are four of them. Am mindful that this might be another type of honey trap. All the same, kinda feel comfortable with these particular felines. During this laissez-faire evening, one of the more moody female wolfskins challenges me to a drinking dual. Their plan: get me blind drunk. So I talk. Well after a Jäger-bomb, a few pints, and 8 double shots of tequila, I'm certainly blind drunk, and I'm sure I must be talking a right load of old codswollop, but to be honest, I can't remember much more. So, I haven't got a clue whether they extract anything crucial out of me or not. Terrible I know. Please forgive me, on this occasion - for my drunkenness. As I fade, I blurrily hear the crackle of female laughter. It's like listening to witches laughing their last laughs around a raging fire…"Aaahaha. Kah Haa Haaarhahaheeee. Aaahaha. Kah Haa Haaarhahaheeee." As I come round a solid twelve hours later I'm surrounded by silent men.

The tequila sours me from top to bottom. Am in an appallingly clammy state. My skin's a soggy pizza dough. Within minutes I've fallen asleep again, jadedly cognisant that I'm in some kind of ruinous mess. I'm an intoxicated carcass. Have alcohol poisoning. For the next three days I'm unable to work. I receive a written warning, and a theological ear bashing from Partridge; "You're a disgrace to the human race Bravo Romeo. You need to turn to the light of this world, and lead a holier life. If you choose not to, then you shall quickly fall into an agonizing Abyss. Any more bouts of drunkenness like this and you'll be out of a job, and into the deep hole of Hell!" Blimey! The other wolfskin instructor (who tries to drink me under the table), ends up in a hospital bed on a liquid replenishing drip. It's temperamental Juliet Whisky. I decide, then and there, this is the last time I'll ever have a drinking competition with a girl. It's a wholly rotten experience.

Mid April, 2002. The electricity in our sleeping quarters is out. The water supply's cut off for a whole week. There's a local poison scare. We spend 6 days without running water. There are fears the local water supply is contaminated. Our orders are clear: "Don't drink tap water from anywhere. Could be poisonous." Luckily someone finds a candle. Then within minutes, there are candles everywhere. So suddenly, we're living an adventurous, and quite miraculous candlelit existence at Château Brutale. It's a throw back to times-gone-by. Is Victor Papa *trying* to alarm us? Is he *trying* to teach us a lesson? All week I drink nothing but cold chocolate milk in semi-darkness. A few days before Partridge was ranting on devoutly about 'walking in the light'. Well, there's no chance of that now, is there?

They've plenty of time and opportunities to search through my stuff, and search through my stuff they do. I've no privacy here. One day I notice my personal belongings are all rearranged. It bugs me. The thought that they've scoured my flower-power notebook, bugs the hell out of me, to be honest. I've very few materialistic possessions, but it still infuriates me that they rummage through them. Can make you feel naked you know? I mean having your stuff tampered with. Overturned. Can make you feel all exposed like. Somebody's meddling with my stuff. Somebody's meddling with my mind. Is there a book thief about? Or should I say, is there a scrappy flower-power notebook thief about? My meditative work is fragmentary, and far from complete. Contains patchy reflections....random rememberings. Nonetheless, it still includes some important social comment. Social comment that's important to me anyhow. And for the time being I want it to remain confidential. Yet somebody's surreptitiously rummaging through my private belongings. My blood turns purple. I'm incensed.

Their establishment eyes are on me. Bastards. They let me know they're watching me. They leave pairs of sunglasses in my bedroom. All of a sudden there are pairs of sunglasses everywhere. One day they position a pair on top of my rucksack, where I keep my flower-power journal. On another occasion they pose a pair next to my sunglasses. They even put a pair in the musty secret drawer embedded in our chamber wall. I wonder – *where will they plant them next?* Each time I find a new pair of sunglasses, I hand them into the Château manager. "Greetings Geoffrey. Guess what? I've another pair of eyes for you." He shows no sign of amusement. Indeed, the looks Partridge throws at me are unceremonious looks of vilification. Being watched so vigilantly is an unusual sensation. Freakish. It is, I suppose, a bit like being an actor in a seemingly unending film. I'm growing ever more agitated.

Don't feel safe plodding around in the Château lake. Could easily get caught up in something entangling, and sink and drown. How convenient that would be, for the American and British neo-conservatives. Why do we have to plod around in the lake in the first place I hear you ask? Because Partridge wants me to pick the litter out from there by hand, that's why! "Bravo Romeo you're on litter picking duty today. I want every last scrap of rubbish removed from the lake, do you hear me?

"Loud and clear." He narrows his eyes at me...

"Just establishing a bit of moral supremacy! Look hasty now boy and remember a drop of doctrine and discipline...that's all you need...Doctrine and discipline...Good day."

"Ok almighty one." I mutter undetectably. I'm worried I might have an accident. In fact, an accident appears well on the cards. I entertain fears of meeting a brutal marsh death, of being plopped and forgotten about in the deep green marais. I think about how my body will be left to soak and swell, and go mint jelly-like. I think about how I will remain green and speckled, and undiscovered for years. I think about the possibility of never being discovered, of just being left to rot. I also think of thousands of rapacious and minuscule marsh creatures, penetrating me from every bodily orifice, to then feed gluttonously from me within. *My feet are stuck in an encumbering bog, whilst the rest of the western world prepares for war.*

When there's nothing else to do, Partridge orders us to clear up after the moles. Yes, he instructs us to shovel up the countless mounds of earth, which are left behind on the grassy verges, by our *Talpa europaean friends*. It's thought provoking work, I can tell you, for nothing but a handful of soil. Partridge is enjoying himself. I'm close to breaking point. One good thing, I get to spot a white Eurasian Spoonbill in amongst the water reeds of the marais. This heron-like bird is a rarity. It has a long beak, that's shaped like a spoon at the end. Here in Flicardie, during my time of need, the natural world has a subtle way of enlivening me.

Early May, 2002. It's a sunny day. There's a flash. I look up, but can't see anything. Then another flash. I look all around me. This time I spot a cameraman. Clicking away he is. He's on the other side of the greeny brown lake. Why's he photographing me? He snaps. Relentlessly. Seems like a professional. He's carrying an impressive looking camera in any case. Makes no attempt to converse with me. Amelie doesn't even notice. She's blissfully skipping along in an innocent world of her own. Her propinquity flurries conspicuously around me. I panic. This is all some kind of devilish set up?

There's a sea of pebbles surrounding the Château. Our footsteps give off a crunching echo as we walk across them. After our months together, we can identify each other by the sound our footsteps make on this stony sea. If we're in the Château, we can tell who's

170

approaching the Château, by their telltale footstep crunch. Foxtrot Hotel is the easiest wolfskin to identify because her footsteps are so small. She has to take twice as many footsteps as the other wolfskins. You can hear the scrunch of her boots on the pebbles a mile off, as she approaches the kitchen entrance to the Château. She always enters from this side. Don't really know why. Think she feels safe in her routine. Makes her even more easy to spot. Foxtrot Hotel is meek and nauseatingly subservient. The fact that she's Partridge's pet pal is always in the forefront of my mind. Makes me exclusively mistrustful of her, primarily because I'm so suspicious of Partridge. Can't tell her anything meaningful because she might well tell the chubby weeble himself. Foxtrot Hotel adores Geoffrey Partridge. He takes her under his wing. He swiftly recognizes she will be a cunning source of information. Foxtrot Hotel thinks I'm rather eccentric. She doesn't adore me.

June, 2002. Time is moving stealthily on by. At night time Black-crowned heron with photographic-like red eyes, stand still at the edge of the nearby Somme waters, waiting to ambush their prey. Otherwise scientifically known as Nycticorax (which means 'night raven'), these nocturnal birds, with their harsh crow like call, wreak havoc with my sleeping pattern during the early summertime Flicardie nights. The sound of the Black-crowned night Heron, can best be described as an exasperating, and cyclical 'Quark...quark...quark'. During the hours of darkness, I try my best to block out this infectious cawing habit.

We can hear an air-raid siren howling in the distance. Somebody's testing it still works. It howls on a daily basis, for weeks on end. It's a nightmarish sound. The noise adds to the dark, and oppressive atmosphere at Château Brutale. It wowls and howls and makes me wonder. Makes me think of past wars and terrors. The whirring sound is disturbing, but somehow befitting. Are we wolfskins being warned of an imminent attack? My visions are stirringly real. Again I'm momentarily transported to a ghostly past - to the time of the battle of the Somme. Images of trench warfare, and ghastly sounds of gunfire fleetingly plague my mind. There will be another war soon, of that I'm sure, but not here, not in these parts. There will be a war which will confuse us all. The howling terror has only just begun.

The boy cries wolf and then the wolf cries boy

Armed Jet fighter planes fly overhead. There *must* be a military air base in close proximity. The jet fighter planes low down presence is poignant. It tells its own story. Their presence foretells war. Their presence makes me feel sad. We play war here. We play fantasy manhunt games with plastic pellet guns. It's a gripping diversion. Some of the wolfskins take the battle too seriously. Arguments ensue: who shot who first? Swampy always goes a little bit over-the-top when it comes to manhunt. Think Swampy will be happy if there's a real war. He's crazy like that. During these manhunt exploits of ours, I wonder whether this really is an encampment where past scores were settled with guns? My brutal wonderings tell me potently that it is.

Victor Papa likes to make an entrance. He's like a soaring human predator. He flies his private plane into the Château grounds completely unexpected. And then he's on us. He can fly his plane unencumbered between Cravenshire and Flicardie. So in and out of France he flies. Hawkishly. Unimpeded. I wonder what the French forces make of all this? I wonder if they're even aware of Victor Papa's presence in *their* airspace? Victor Papa's a master manipulator. His manoeuvres are cunning. Unobstructed. He has complete physical control over all of his wolfskin infantry, and so, in effect, he virtually has complete control of our human emotions to boot. He can quickly reassign wolfskins between the Fortress and the Château as he sees fit, and shuffle us about he does. Yet I always remain in Vatanbourg. I have a fondness for France, but this godforsaken town is crushing me man. I'm mind numbingly lonely and isolated here. My feeling of solitude is like a threat of things to come – it means something. It's like a malevolent vision, an augury of death or worse still: death on an unprecedented scale. I wouldn't be feeling this lonesome if there was nothing hostile ahead, now would I? I look at Victor Papa closely one day. He stands upright, like a granite column. He holds his apelike arms behind his back. I also notice that his fingers are laced together. Without a glitch. Victor Papa often stands like this. This is Victor Papa's plotting position. As usual, he's up to something. Something tactical. Something Machiavellian.

We have stringent daily cleaning chores to perform. Often our chores are a tad *too* stringent. Here, at Château Brutale, we work extremely hard. We're made to clean toilets, and as if that isn't bad enough, we're made to clean toilets that we've already cleaned. We clean the toilets. Then Partridge inspects our cleaning proficiency. "Sheer incompetence! Sheer incompetence!" Then we are, more often than not, made to clean the toilets again. Our cyclical efforts aren't rewarded. It's soul destroying work. There are long stretches of time when there's nothing meaningful for us to do. For weeks on end we scrub, sweep and sanitise. This is how it goes. The Château becomes spotless, whilst we become disturbed. Our laborious cleaning routines enslave me. I'm living on an edge of hateful exhaustion. Have never worked so hard in all my life. The arduous hours of labour are felt most deeply in the early morning, when my muscles are unbendable. Like stone. For the first few months I am completely dead-beat. Now the exhaustion malforms into a sufferable weariness. My visage is drained. I have the look of a prisoner-of-war. One day the horror of what might face me becomes real. Suddenly there's a dull ache in the pit of my stomach. I've been mixed-up in a load of nasty trouble, haven't I? Château Brutale is a remote, hidden away facility isn't it? As I walk around the Château grounds, can't help thinking of the old iron sign that reads *'Arbeit Macht Frei'* (Work brings freedom) at Auschwitz *if I work hard and do what's expected of me, then I'll come out of this alive, maybe even unscathed*. It isn't a precise parallel, but if you take the unfolding terrorism situation as a backdrop, I'm not so far from the truth in my rumination. The fact of the matter is, this place is harsh, and it makes me think of other brutal and tragic places. Nevertheless, at least I'm not being held at camp X-ray in Cuba.

Being granted a stay of execution is on my mind. Am deep in thought, when suddenly a line of prose comes back to me, from one of my English literature classes at secondary school *'Don't let those bullies pull you down with them'*. Can't remember which book it's from, but that doesn't matter. What matters is that this thought is now in my head. I repeat it to myself. *Don't let those bullies pull you down with them, don't let those bullies pull you down with them.* Indeed, I keep repeating it to myself. Glad it comes back to me. Seems massively relevant right now. Try to conjure up a persuasive line of prose of my own, but all that keeps popping into my head is *don't get on the wrong side of Victor Papa.* Anyway, for some reason I prefer *'don't let those bullies pull you down with them.'* So I stick with that. Gives me a flicker of hope. Who says education isn't important? (My English literature teacher was a goddamn legend. He was soothing and nurturing and incredibly inspirational. They do say there can be no end to the influence of an outstanding teacher. They also say that truth can be found in Literature. All I can say is: "Three cheers for good old Bob Vincent." Amusing. Intelligent. A truly great man).

173

Do I have a right to moan? Are my bewails baseless? I mean, I'm being fed after all, aren't I? Yet I feel muted, and this mute like feeling is irrefutable. I'm cut off from the rest of the world. In truth, my soul's under military occupation. Sometimes there are no children at Château Brutale for weeks on end. We were primarily employed to instruct children weren't we? So, where are all the kids? This is meant to be a centre for the development of young people isn't it? This whole setup is hideously murky. Something definitely isn't quite right. *They* still want to keep us as engaged as possible, but it's evident they're running out of worthwhile chores for us to do. I scrape excess paint from plug sockets, and from light switches with razor blades. I polish brass that's already been polished the same day. I sweep paths that have just been swept. I've not been employed for this? Have I? I've not been employed to be made to feel so wretched and rueful? Have I?

In the summertime I'm asked to manage a bar in the ecurie at Château Brutale. The bar is an inharmonious English edifice, set in the grounds of this French Château. Hoisted behind the bar is a rather distasteful Saint George's cross on a shield. There are also two axes on either side of this white and red shield. All-set. Ready for the chop. Why can't they have the tricolours of France alongside the Saint George's cross? As a gesture of cordial goodwill? We are in France, after all. But, alas nothing.

So I spend the next few months with a Saint George's cross shield, and a couple of axes hanging over my head. My wounding stage is set. It's another of Victor Papa's repressive creations. Just part of his regime of reproof. Just part of his prescriptive plan to indoctrinate and quash. Just part of his crusade. I'm inaccurately branded. I'm Victor Papa's political prisoner. Are *they* questioning my patriotism? Well, maybe they've good reason to. I don't want to be patriotic. Patriotism's just something scoundrels hide behind. Isn't it? Like the law, people hide behind that too, pretending they've moral authority when they don't. They do - don't they? Anyhows, this architectural arrangement is inaugurated by one hell of a curious man, and I'm scandalously thrust into its spotlight. Now I have centre-stage. 'Aint I the lucky one! At the end of the bar there's an ominous medieval knight mannequin brandishing a sword. Victor Papa strategically positions it there to *keep an eye on me*. There's no chance of being caught off-guard here, that's for sure, I can tell you. I mean, what am I supposed to think with a medieval knight dummy stood facing me. It's all a bit melodramatic. Like a scene from Scooby-doo.

174

On the apex of the bar, where extra glasses are held in reserve, there are two medieval knight helmets set at either end. The entire bar area is also decked out in the most gruesome, medieval warfare-themed tapestries. The other wolfskins don't know what to make of it. Should they be captivated by this monstrously decorated bar, heavy with medieval military embellishments? Or should they be dismayed by the crusading crudeness of it? I, on the other hand, know exactly what to make of it. My French blood is well and truly stirred. I decide, without deliberation, that I detest the whole offensive setup. To me it appears phoney and hideously provisional. I'm enraged by the unfree and very unfrench trench in which I stand. Considering we're on French soil, I find the whole set-up extremely distasteful and rude. It's a dreadfully garish nationalistic creation, and I'm the poor wolfskin contained by it. I'm not the British bulldog type, far from it. I'm a European pacifist (or something along these lines), but believe it or not, they actually suspect me of republican collusion. This is turning out to be a mindboggling misadventure. Victor Papa suddenly develops a bizarre obsession with medieval relics, and he is, for some madcap reason, going to great lengths, to try and teach me something about medieval history. What on earth is he up to? What is Victor Papa plotting? What is on VP's premeditated mind?

July, 2002. The Château ecurie is transformed overnight. Victor Papa makes it his business to alter it. Now it exudes a brutal medieval austerity, and an out-of-the-way watchfulness. The knights around me are well equipped with helmets, shields, swords, axes and pikes. The past is now upon me. To a grave extent my senses are enthused with history's horrendous happenings.Victor Papa makes me look like an English patriot. He makes others see me as a nationalist and an intruding snob. On his part this is an unforgiveable act of military manipulation. Inside I feel French, but nobody knows this - nobody apart from Victor Papa that is. Victor Papa can read my mind. This is his attempt at psychosomatic, staged-managed propaganda. This is Victor Papa's way of declaring political didacticism over me, and so my course of emotional brainwashing begins....courtesy of the big brute himself. Victor Papa's exploiting history to create his own severe atmosphere. He's creating a mood to do my nut in. This is Victor Papa's contrived edifice. Not mine. It's an undignified platform on which I stand. Feel accused. Accused of some poisonous act. This is not my altar. I do not believe what Victor Papa believes.

Victor Papa imports dozens of Indonesian wooden chairs. The chairs are extraordinarily large. They're more like thrones than chairs. When I sit on one of them my legs dangle down, but don't touch the ground, such is their colossal size. Makes me feel like I've been shrunk when I sit on one of them. Feel like a miniature me. Victor Papa flies the thrones over from Indonesia himself. This man has indisputable power, and an astonishingly vivid imagination. In the newly malformed Château ecurie, there are crooked cavalry remnants scattered around everywhere. Old-fashioned curved harnesses, and warped rusty metal hooves, hang from the walls. Suddenly it seems like I'm treading my way through a bloody horse museum or something. What an immeasurably out of the ordinary state of affairs, I'm suddenly exposed to. There are large hooks aligned neatly at eye level along the length of the stables. I assume they're for hanging up saddles, but every time I catch glimpse of them, I see big foreboding, and ill-omened question marks suspended in front of me. The shutters are rigid and seem reluctant to move. In the Château ecurie hall you can almost hear the faint echoes from another equestrian era, a collective combatant cry from clashing cavalrymen and, more conspicuously, stallions at war.

At times it feels like we're living in a different era. What with the nineteenth century French maid outfits the female wolfskins are enforced to wear, and the obscure medieval tapestries that are suddenly suspended everywhere and all. This place is designed to take away my sanity. Plonked and abandoned beneath this offensive Saint George's cross shield, I'm a sad and foolish prince. I'm on display. I'm an unsightly mannequin in a shop window. I'm extraordinarily exposed. It's like a public penance. Having to work behind this ugly patriotic edifice only exacerbates my feelings of confinement. Inhibiting. Is this a tribunal for heresy? Or am I just a prisoner of my own sorrow? Whatever the reasoning, I feel grotesque and unlovable within the confines of this Saint George's Cross box.

The boy cries wolf and then the wolf cries boy

Fellow wolfskins are being relocated and dispatched at whim. Like I say, Victor Papa has total human control over his pack of wolfskins. Groups of wolfskins are continually being flown backwards and forwards between the Fortress in Cravenshire, England and the Château in Flicardie, France. Keep on reminding myself that behind every uniformed mask, of every multi-activity instructor, there is, quite possibly, an informing spy. Don't like being so mistrustful, but it's impossible not to be mistrustful whilst I'm stuck in this sham. And so, as July draws to a close and August approaches, I remain in Vatanbourg like a caged scapegoat.

Victor Papa's doing a superb job of aggravating my soul. His whole set-up is doing exactly what it's meant to - make me seethe with indignation. Feel like I'm all alone in a doomed ship out at sea. Whilst I'm working behind this particularly crude bar, Victor Papa appears. Takes a snapshot of me. Leaves without saying a word. Did he capture the St. George's cross above my head on his photographic image I wonder? What the hells this scheming man up to? I've been framed. Feel sick inside. Now I don't trust the man one little bit. God only knows what he'll do with that simulated photograph. Is he going to use it to delude the general public? Is he going to make an exhibition of me? So I stand here. Churning. Brooding. Am in some way trying to satisfy my anguish, but my French blood is boiling. I'm an angry wolfskin. Mortality is on my mind, yet again. And so is this - *don't get on the wrong side of Victor Papa. If you do, you might meet a nasty marsh death, never to be seen again!*

The boy cries wolf and then the wolf cries boy

Some atrocious incidents occurred here in the past. There's no need for a history lesson, you can feel it. *Perhaps something terrible might happen again* - are the words on my framed mind. Feel like a mortified cast-off, who's having his civil liberties culled. Can't truly account for what's happening to me, but I'm determined not to let him completely crush me. I mean it's not every day a brutal military man approaches you, and takes your photograph without uttering a single word is it? Yet this is what mighty Victor Papa does, and like a badgering bastard, this is what he keeps on doing. His actions are often unconventional and almost always confrontational. He isn't an oddball by any means, just likes to challenge convention. At least he likes to challenge my conventions anyhows. Victor Papa's a man of action. A man of adventure. He's a leader. Wants to be No.1. Needs to be No.1...Is No.1. As summertime draws to a close, Victor Papa's mirror eyes are on me like never before. Mortality is on my mind relentlessly now. He's incited me to think about my own death more than I want to.

He's incited me to think about my own death more than I need to. I'm waiting. Waiting for that brutal moment.

He knows. He knows everything. Has his sword drawn. Iridescent. He's waving it about. Irrepressibly. Today the General, Victor Papa is parading himself. Sword in hand, he makes sweeping 'I'm the king of the castle' gestures. Is he declaring war? Is he declaring victory? His enormous swishing sword speaks to me: "Whissssh...Come...challenge me...if you dare...whissssh." In this Château-with-a-curse setting he's unrivalled. Victor Papa knows nobody has the guts to confront him. He carves the letter 'R' in the air with his man-sized weapon. Stares hard at me, eyes wriggling with self-delight. *How charming his actions are. How deliberate.* He's remarkably adept at thought control. He swishes the letter 'R' again, in an attitude of defiance. He stands there with his sword in his hands for a moments silence, allowing time for the letter 'R' to speak to me.

Victor Papa is a man I should fear, and he's determined to make his mark. "Where's your sense of adventure?" he inquires conqueringly. The big bastard's got me just where he wants me, right under his spoiling for a fight nose. I'm one of Victor Papa's military conquests. Strangely, I feel nervous and consoled at the same time. I spark up a rollie. Sit there blowing smoke rings. It's a futile reaction of resistance. "That's a sign of a misspent youth." He claims with an ironic sting. As the smoke rings travel towards Victor Papa, he slices them up. Then severes the letter 'R' one last time through my Gauloise smoke. Ambles off. Like a satisfied giant. *"Mechant!"* I mutter to myself.

September, 2002. The clock of conflict is hastily tick-tick-a-tocking. Ghosty has fallen asleep whilst on night watch. It isn't the first time either. Anoop's deadbeat, snoring like an overfed walrus. We are, as usual, under a rigid curfew...

The sky's bloated with blackout clouds. My mood maddens. My mood darkens. I'm sinking with the unfathomable shutting down sky. Then the big grey Flicardie clouds take over. It's as if I'm losing control of my senses. It's as if my senses are becoming unhinged like the wooden attic doors above my chamber. I'm lying on my bed staring at the whitewashed ceiling. I'm listening to the sounds outside of the impending storm. I'm worn out. My mortality obsessed mood couldn't be much worse. Feel clamped-down. I hear the sky begin to howl. Growl. Rumble and clap. Then, as I stare at the blank ceiling a strange red blemish appears. Startled....I sit up. A convulsion of anxiety seeps

178

through me. Feel a drip on my skin. There's a soupçon of blood on the back of my hand. Wipe the drip away. Leap out of bed. I'm all horrified. Despite the curfew, decide I must seek help. I'm breaking all the wolfskin nighttime rules, but I don't care. I don't bother waking Anoop. Just leave him kipping on his snore shelf.

It's raining cords of rope outside. Throw all my caution into the Vatanbourg wind and rain. Get across the sea of pebbles without being heard. So far I'm undetectable, but I need to find aid. In my rush to report this bizarre happening, my wolfskin jacket gets caught on a rose bush. I'm ensnared. Ambushed. Temporarily. I'm just outside the Château bureau headquarters. Whilst trying to free myself, without tearing my jacket, I see something. Light. People. Action. I see their covert dealings through the Château window. I see them for what they are. Goddamn spies. I can see stuff. Official stuff. Official stuff I'm not suppose to see. "Eureka!" This really is a Château-with-a-curse.

Have you ever felt like there's nothing left to learn?

Creep nearer. Hiding. Hunching. Peeking. There are photographs of me spread out on a table before them. They're profiling me. Isolating me. And others. Turns out we *are* here under false pretences. My gut feeling serves me well. And not for the first time. They're preparing a contingency case against me. Still, they can't anticipate everything can they? Can they? They've not foreseen this eventuality. Me peering through the window during the curfewed hours of the night. So there is, after all, at least some **method** to their ministry of defence madness. This is absolutely scandalous.

I decide to investigate where the blood on the ceiling of my chamber is coming from, alone. Call me crazy, but this is what I do. Head back to our barracks. With more than a degree of trepidation, I climb the rickety wooden stairs to the attic above my chamber. Am shaking. In my search for the source of blood, can feel my own blood racing. Thumping. To my surprise I find no bloody dead body sprawled in the attic. What I do find is a red tin of paint - lying on its side on the floor. Has someone been eavesdropping and had an accident? Perchance a startled rat toppled it over? Or possibly a Château Brutale phantom has accidently on purpose spilt it? Or could it have been the wind from the storm? Well anyway, somehow the paint has seeped through the floorboards, and permeated the ceiling below. What I think is the blood of a dead man, turns out to be just red paint. Blimey...

What a howling red hour. Intense. Infiltrating. Feel naked. Panicky. Anoop's still kipping. Look's like he's slept through it all. How could anyone sleep through that storm? A crushing sense of humiliation comes over me. It's a curious feeling. But at least I now know for sure. Dirty spies. Dishonest scumbags. So I'm redeemed. Redeemed by a tin of red paint and a rolling Vatanbourg storm.

Victor Papa doesn't know everything, but he's still running the show. God only knows what they're gonna pin on me should I happen to become a little too bellicose. They're preparing a demonising case against me - I'm now clear about that in my mind. They're prepared, but they 'ain't gonna take action, unless I happen to start squealing. We're all well contained here, and I at least know, I'm not going to squeal. I've got the fear man. Big time.

There are worse realities than being incarcerated by the British I suppose. I spend a lot of my time thinking about not speaking. Indeed, only really speak when I have to. Holding out against two regimes, trying hard not to take sides, it's a lonely business. *Royalist or Republican?* - I ponder to myself. I'm convinced I'm neither. At least, I've swayed my sunny old self, to be of this opinion. I don't want to be a republican, and I certainly don't want to be a royalist. Something in my blood manoeuvres me to this manner of thinking. Still, I'm lonesome as hell here. All anomalous and all.

Early October, 2002. The clock of conflict's still counting down...tick-tock, tick-tock, tick-tock. I've been working my ass off lately, and for what? For a noiseless nothing, that's what. I'm entombed in an unbearable hush. I burrow my way into complete human darkness. I retreat into the loneliest silence imaginable. I withdraw into isolated eccentricity and ask myself - *what have I done to deserve this?* As soon as the children leave, a ghostly silence descends on the Château and its surrounding grounds. During the lengthy 'changeover' period, when there are no longer any screaming kids on site, the silence really kicks in here. Like life's suddenly been sucked out of the place. It's more silent now, than ever. It's noticeable. It really is. The town is suddenly also asleep in ruefulness, like its been dumped in some kind of otherworldly limbo. Quiet. Melancholic. Glum. Abruptness. After the kids have gone, Vatanbourg doesn't know what to do with itself. Becomes a town without a voice. In this way, it's a bit like me. It can be deafeningly silent in Vatanbourg.

The autumn bird song is remote. Pitiful. The calls of the countryside become barely audible. Even the flanking wildlife seems strangely muffled, as if straining to be heard. Could the natural world also be scared to be itself? Ruefulness settles over me like a relentless chill. I'm a fan of solitude, but now I'm too alone. A childhood memory ripples in my mind. You know, there's something terribly familiar about that goddamn lake. Every time I march by, it's as if I'm returning to an area I visited once as a child. Feel maddeningly close to death. Also feel close to heaven.

It's as if everyone knows something I don't. Everyone has evacuated away from the place. There isn't a soul in sight. Nobody in the Charcuterie. Nobody in the Boulangerie. Nobody in the Patisserie. Even the local boozer has no punters. Vatanbourg really is a sad and empty place at this time of year. All around me the curious French style shutters are creaking ruefully, in this seasonally attuned autumn environment. For some mysterious reason, the change from summer to autumn, is more noticeable here. Or am I just starting to notice things more? As I grow older? Who knows? Whatever. Autumn is now more conspicuous than ever before. As the autumn leaves fall down slowly to and fro, my oscillating mind becomes swamped with abysmal thoughts. I imagine Victor Papa shooting me dead, brutally chopping me up with an axe, and then secretively burying my bits in the festering marsh.

There's a massive October moon sitting in the sky. It's perfectly round, and absolutely monumental in size. Like an E.T. Moon. It's as if the October moon is bigger tonight than it should be. It's ablaze. Encompassing. Gapingly deep. There are creaks in the white lit night crying out *"we are still here,"* as the moon seemingly drags me in. There are sinister wolfskin whisperings rustling about the Château in France, and the Fortress in England on this full moon night. I'm defeated, and on defeated land I stand…*just*. I don't voice my inner-torment, but it's written all over my crazy moon sucking face. Mouth hanging open. Eyes wide as beer mats. The terror is etched.

The boy cries wolf and then the wolf cries boy

The October purple sky begins to turn black. Looking at the sky's like looking into a witch's cauldron. There's a tempestuous crack. There's another beast of a storm above us. That violet black night, higher heaven decides to gash out all its dregs. Feel fiery inside. It's a foul storm. I love October.

Have never questioned the concept of justice and peace so much. For some out-of-the-ordinary reason, on this bizarre purplish-black, October evening, I realise there's no justice in the world. I also realise there's no chance of peace in the world. I'm subdued. Overbearingly wasted. Life seems altogether annulled and wonderful.

As the storm ferments, the bells ring out a sorrowful chime. It's a chime of shame. Even the reverberations of the Saint-Esprit bells striking the hour sound rueful, like as if they wish time would stop still. But the clock of conflict won't stop still. Sounds like it's a straining endeavour for the bells to chime at all, but the clamour goes on, all the same. The black angels look wistful during the purple deluge. The decrepit church looks sad. Unholy. Some churches appear swollen with pride. This one appears down in the mouth. Has a purple look of bereavement. Its spire's bending down, as if it's bowing down in disgrace. Yet it still has something to say. Remorseful phonemes seep from the church's bell tower, groan their way across the old town square. The church submits a mournful echo of the letter sounds of somebody's name. The reverberation's like a droning souvenir offered to recall the remembrance of a deceased member of this cursed community. Christopher hasn't been in touch for a long while, nor have any of my friends for that matter. I wonder how they're all getting on.

Back in the 8th century, a 13ft cross floated along the river into the centre of Vatanbourg. The town became flooded with pilgrims after this curious event. The cross became known as the floating crucifix. One night, whilst I'm in Vatanbourg, a shining cross miraculously comes into sight. It's suspended between the antlers of a Stag, and is set against an orange dusk sky. I stare out at the shining symbol in the orange nirvana, in wonder and dread. For some reason, the colour of the naranja sky, makes me think the end of the world is upon us. Then, I begin to think about what it would be like, if there's a third world war. My imagination alarms me sometimes. I can see, in orange, unbearable suffering, and unspeakable carnage. The world becomes an atrocious turbid orange mess.

I pray to my master to help me to be brave through these immorally domineering times. I've been praying an awful lot lately, talking in my head to some dude who's up there, surfing in the toxic orange sky, swerving amongst the contaminated clouds. That hovering cross stains me. My night visions scares me. Am impatient for dusk to fall. Feel hunted. I lay in my chamber for a while in a posture of agony. As I close my eyes, I remember seeing the black spire of La Chapelle de la Saint Esprit, complete with distinguishable bell and crucifix. It's set starkly, like a crooked silhouette, against an orange backdrop. All is silent. All is eerie. All is orange. I make the sign of the cross, before I fall into a cavernous slumber of war.

Swampy collects nicknames. Some call him *Fish,* because out of all the wolfskins, he can stay under water for the longest. I call him *Swampy,* because I think he looks like something that's just crawled out of the swamp. He likes to be called *Chef,* because he used to be a cook, and he thinks, that if we call him *Chef,* it will grant him some kind of power over us. He's always boasting about the spectacular skills he has as a cook, but I have my doubts about that. He's one of those people who reckon they're good at everything. You know the sort? Anyway, Swampy's a somewhat crumpled, stig-of-the-dump like character. His eyebrows are like the bristles of an overused toothbrush. His craggy fingernails are furrowed with miscellaneous muck. There's nothing glamorous about this man's appearance or his personality. He's desperate for some kind of recognition. He's also a particularly foul-mouthed wolfskin. Heroism is on this wolfskin's mind. He's all alone.

Swampy sleeps with a Union-Jack flag pinned to the sloping eaves above his bed. He's shamelessly patriotic. He also sleeps with a rock the size of a cabbage under his bed. He keeps the rock within arm's reach. It looks jolly solid. He's armed. He's dangerous. He's unpredictable. Swampy's antagonistic towards me. Takes an unprovoked disliking to me right from the start. Seems harmless to most, but I know he's dangerous. There's something fatalistic about this guy. He boasts about having the 'skills to kill'. Swampy thinks his time's almost up, and he's determined, whatever impact it might have on others, to go out in a blaze of glory. Swampy's inconsolable. He has little genuine regard for his fellow wolfskins. He's in a world of his own really, and is not, by any means, a team player. His behaviour is erratic by day…what then, will he be like, during the night? Can you imagine what it's like to have to sleep in the same vicinity as such a person? I have violent apparitions of what he might do to me, in the obscurity of the nighttime. My visions are hideous. They contain blasts of blood. Night after night, I say my prayers, in a jittery frenzy. There's a dangerous streak of childishness still hovering in Swampy's psyche.

He's a juvenile delinquent, in a scrawny man's body. He really is a rare 'un. Our rooms are cell-like. When I go to bed it's like I've been closeted for the night, but Swampy could still simply walk into our room. There are no locks and keys here. Don't like sleeping in the same vicinity as Swampy, not for one minute. I fear the cabbage-sized boulder he keeps under his bed. I fear his impulsive nature. I fear what he might do with that boulder in the middle of the night.

It becomes a bit of a ritual - lighting fires that is. Swampy's become in charge of sparking up bonfires. He's the Chief Fire-Starter - for some reason. He knows how to get a good blaze going. I'll give him that, but all the same, it's kinda disturbing - his passion for fire that is.

Swampy's fire soon puffs up, and becomes blindingly orange. It's as if the fire is consuming us. Claiming us. It scorches my skin. Have to take a step back away from it, such is the clout of heat. It's a dramatic and raging fire. Its intensity reflects my human spirit, my inner mood. It glows demonically in the torturous twilight. I take the time to look into Swampy's wolfish fire eyes. I see nothing but a flaming crook. Like a band of wild soldiers we gather round the blaze. Impressionable. Vulnerable. Susceptible. We're looking for some answers, for some solace. We're a savage pack in a primitive scene. *We're fragile creatures* - I think to myself, as I stare into the unsettling flames. The thought of being consumed by the blistering heat, like an ostracized Las Fallas figurine, crosses my wolfskin mind. *What a maze life is* - I muse, as I sit there staring at the intricate bonfire. Like the bonfire, I am blazing, blazing to be heard. The flames are highlighting our wolfskin features, making us look warrior-like. What with the lush Valencian flames and all, I feel hazily seduced by suicide. Feel myself changing. Becoming more primal, even more like a real wolf. I dance around Swampy's blaze. Macabrely. I become Swampy's blossoming salsa inferno, as I prance, and weave among the flickering flame-cast shadows. The other wolfskins look at me in bewilderment. I feel relief. They feel disturbed. There's a gnarled atmosphere of both primitive release, and felonious bashfulness. If anything, we're becoming more and more feral, like cursed and forgotten creatures. Well, I for one certainly am.

The boy cries wolf and then the wolf cries boy

The nights we spend oscillating wildly around bonfires become more and more frequent. Like I say, the fires are Swampy's business. He always insists on being Chief Fire-Starter. What starts out as a comforting sociable glow, quickly becomes a raging furnace. He worships his fires. He also worships Victor Papa. Swampy likes to build big fires. He lights them in a small woodland clearing within the Château grounds. His fires are so big, I fear the flames might set light to the surrounding trees, and start a massive woodland fire. Each night the fires become wilder and wilder. There's a savage smell swelling in the air. Swampy, with his fire lighting tendencies and all, is definitely one to watch.

Swampy feels like he's been bestowed with identity here. For once, he feels like somebody. I, on the other hand, feel like I've had my identity seized away. We don't get on. Swampy wears his wolfskin fleece zipped right up to the chin. He walks around with his mucky paws stuffed right into his wolfskin pockets. He's a proud man in his wolfskin uniform, and he's ready for hostile action. He looks up to Victor Papa. In fact, he adulates the brute. He's Victor Papa's pet wolfskin. Victor Papa can command Swampy to do anything.

Swampy's desperate for companionship. He always preys on the newcomers; hangs off them like a bad smell. He often feeds them flippant untruths in an attempt to poison their minds, and turn them against me. Don't really know why he hates me so much. He's sniper-like, absolutely loves his rifles. The guy's unstable. I'm worried. Sadly, he welcomes America's gung-ho war-on-terror. This guy, with many names, also has many temperaments. On one occasion Swampy whispers to me wolfishly: "Why don't you do us all a favour and drop dead?"

"Even if I'm nice to you it's no good. I even gave you some matches so you can light your bloody fires."

"I don't need matches to start a fire."

"You see...never good enough."

"Like a funeral me. Do you like funerals Buddy?"

"So, you gonna rub two stones together then or something?"

"Do us all a favour...."

Swampy is, I fear, capable of almost anything. I constantly wrestle with his wit, or rather, his witlessness. We have to try and get along, and as I'm sure you well know, it's hard to get along with somebody you don't approve of.

Lisa Lovelady has begun to complain of cabin fever. She isn't the only one. There's a sense of hysteria brewing around this facility. We're edging towards collective wolfskin insanity. Somehow I've ended up here. Perhaps it's actually safer for me to be here than anywhere else. Certain people definitely think so. I'm politically and journalistically incapacitated. *They* are waiting patiently for my *chamber confession.* They know from their military experience that it will come. Undoubtedly my patience is wearing thin. I'm surrounded by a pack of whispering wolfskins. Gossip is humming between the Fortress in England, and the Château in France. It's a period of procrastination. *They* want to prolong my noiselessness for political reasons, but *they* also want to know exactly how much I know. The thought may seem rather inconceivable, but so much is at stake here. *I don't really know what I should do.* The clock of conflict is ticking away stridently. I'm feeling very lonely and loneliness can do funny things to a man. By some marvellous chance a charming girl is reassigned from the Fortress to the Château. Victor Papa flies her in. She seems to promptly adapt to her relocation onto French soil. She seems interested to learn French, not obsessively like Anoop, but she shows some genuine interest. I like that about her. Her radio call sign is November Romeo....Either she finds me hilarious or she's attempting to gain my confidence by laughing in all the right places. All the same, her strikingly seductive laughter, makes me feel special.

November Romeo's a mystifying wolfskin, who often chuckles. It's flagrant, yet enticing laughter that she lets loose. Sure as hell she has an enchanting laugh. Her laughter can also be mellow. Calming. Befriending. She laughs a lot, which I like. She also has a soothing voice, like the voice of a fairy godmother it is. I think she knows I like her, and so she flirts with me. She has a slightly hoarse voice, that's more than slightly sexy. Can't help being drawn in. She somehow intercepts my bashful efforts to avoid eye contact. Often get caught up in her gaze. How long can your old life follow you? How long does your past pursue you? These kind of questions are on my mind. "It's not a matter of curing, it's a matter of enduring. Real bad stuff that happens to you in life will always remain in your mind. You can't just make yourself forget. What can't be cured must be endured. Your past will always follow you." Solemn. Her words help me. Her rational words are like a charming birdsong. Nonetheless, still feel stained for life by my past misfortunes.

November Romeo passes me a cigarette lighter. "No need to snatch," she asserts, after I grab it out of her hand. I spark up. "Eeeeerh, yeh – sorry about that." I did snatch it. What on earth is wrong with me? Is my snatching a cry for help? I need to get a grip of myself. You know, this girl, November Romeo, has a gift for picking out our wolfskin peculiarities. She'd make a great psychotherapist. Or something like that. November Romeo isn't like most of the other wolfskins in our squad. She's funny and lively. We get on perfectly well. I like funniness. Need funniness at this juncture in my life. Find her interesting to look at. We've a great deal to say to each other too. 'Enthralling' is a word which describes her fittingly. It's like November Romeo has cast a spell on me. "You're not better than anyone else you know?" she exclaims emotively one day. Her curious comment makes me like her even more. It somehow gives my ego a boost. Peculiar, I know. She seems to want to hear my story. Well, like I say, I get on with this girl, and for some reason I trust her. I'm prepared to talk to her, and so I recount my disturbing tale. I tell her about Mo and his drink spiking exploits. I tell her about Morpheye's eye gouging shenaningans and Pudding's criminaly controlling behaviour. I tell her about how the Jägermeister pointed and fired a gun at me. I tell her about how badly it affected me. I tell her about my anxiety-ridden encounter with Toby Marshall in San Fran, and I tell her about the terrorizing onslaught I endured whilst I dipped into the world of Journalism. I tell her my story. I tell her everything. Maybe I'm wrong to, but I kind of need to talk to someone. She listens attentively to my troubles. She's extremely empathetic. The fact that she's been brought up in a raucous pub in Reading, makes me feel that she knows a bit about life. She worked for about nine years in that pub. In that time, she must have seen a few sordid things. Anyway, somehow she understands me. Afterwards, she just hits me with an American: "I know nothing!" Makes me smile.

I trust November Romeo, not because I think she can keep a secret, but because I think she might understand me. She has the biggeest, warmest smile. Guess I think, someone with a smile like hers is worth talking to. Guess I just need a woman's empathy. She, for one, doesn't seem to have a shred of brutishness in her; a serious rarity around here. I confide in her. It's my big unburdening. Takes me sometime. "What have they done to you. Why the silence?" She conducts her inquiries like a compassionate nurse. Couldn't careless anymore if *they* record my confession or not.

There are regular power failures at this spooky 17th century Château. We're often left to our own devices in the dark. Left to fumble around in obscurity. Left to entertain ourselves by candlelight. Our shadows splay primitive black and orange flames on our chamber walls. Dancing. Flickering. Wolfskins. Howling. Without electricity our staff headquarters become like cave dwellings. It's a fitting abode for a pack of delirious squaddies. I enjoy our candle lit tarot card séances. They're an enlightening aftereffect to the blackouts. They're instigated by none other than November Romeo. She becomes our very own on-site 'Mystic-Meg'. November Romeo has a naked fascination with mysticism. She seems to be interested in lots of things. I'm falling for her. It's as if she's been born with this Shaman-like streak within. Her mum taught her how to read Tarot cards. Intriguing. Not that I believe in them for one minute. Do find it curious that she believes so strongly in the cards power though. She's a bit like Mystic Meg in appearance, as well as temperament. As the blackouts become more and more regular, so do our misadventurous séances. So, here we all are, sitting crossed legged, each with our own candle-illuminated, traumatized, wolfskin expressions, in Flicardie, France. Sometimes I choose not to talk. Just sit there. Like a speechless silhouette. Absorbing the dappled and dreamlike mood. Shimmering. Shady. Surviving. It's a trancelike experience.

"Yuh talkin to me!" she says as if she's Robert De Niro. She has waggishness about her, that's for sure. In general, November Romeo is one of the boys. She farts out loud, drinks beer, smokes dope, and doesn't care so much about her appearance. Her shamelessness is part of her charm. She's sharp-witted. Streetwise. Down to earth. She's a hardened character, but jolly with it. November Romeo shares my suspicions about Victor Papa and Château Brutale. She knows there's something sinister going on. "Maybe, unwittingly, we're human guinea pigs in some sort of military experiment. Maybe this is all part of a rather risky armed plan." She's near to the truth, I reckon. We've certainly become a pack of loutish wolfskins. We probably would make quite vicious, and so, I guess, quite 'effective' soldiers.

She sits on her bed in the corner of the room, looking like some kind of trigger hippy gypsy woman. She's architecturally toying with her rizla papers. Somehow, even the way she skins up a spliff, is seductive. Wish she'd hurry up with it though. She looks at me and bursts out laughing. Then hits me with another "yuh talkin to me!" and then another "I know nothing!" November Romeo is acutely attentive, almost catlike in character. Indeed, she admits she's been brought up in a home teeming with felines. *Perhaps their stealth has rubbed off on her* - I think. Her eyes are bright and bewitching. They're a wonderful, almost phosphorescent gooseberry green. Perhaps that's why I like her so much. Her hair is horsechestnut brown with a hint of plum colouring. It falls down her back in thick natural waves. To me she's eye-catchingly attractive. It's like therapy. Hanging out with her I mean. Talking with her. Being with her. Is the tarot card reading a guise, a veiled artifice? Has it all been a trick to gain my trust? Get me talking? Have I finally succumbed? Has my patience been broken? Have they got the confession they need? Probably.

She gives me a look when she leaves Château Brutale. It's a look of deep admiration and hope. She's smiling as always as she goes. She maintains eye contact with me for as long as possible, as she drifts benignly away down the Château spiral staircase. Feels like a fond good-bye. Feels like I'm saying good-bye to cheerfulness. Feels like I'm saying good-bye to my box-of-delight. I never got to kiss her, but her tender farewell is good enough for me. For now. Now she's going to the Fortress in England. Victor Papa flies her away. In evening, as I lay in my chamber, I pray beautiful November Romeo is real.

Does November Romeo guard my secret? Something tells me she doesn't. Does she tell anyone else what I confide in her? Of course she probably does. Can't expect her to keep my secrets to herself forever. She's brave enough to listen, and that's enough for me. It's good to talk.

There's a black and white female cat on the prowl at the Château. She's a French cat. She's called Fremousse. Fremousse means flat face. The name suits her. She does have an unusually flat face, for a cat. She creeps around. Stealthily. Keeps her eyes on all the ongoing activities. Now and again she purrs, well thought-out and conspiratorial purrs. It's her way of letting us know she has her crafty eyes on us. She seems to be compassionately judging our misadventure. Fills me with delight.

*Our health is in their hands, and the hands that feed me taste like they want something in return.....*Quite deceitfully Partridge treats us to a slab of tongue. I attack and devour all the food I can see before me, as I'm a very hungry man indeed. In point of fact, I eat like a ravenous Roman soldier. Nothing new in that. I've a good appetite. I enjoy my food. Always have. Food's the one pleasure which momentarily takes my mind away from all this military madness. Isn't it? We're led to believe it's steak we're eating. But it isn't steak. It's a turgid, tough as old boots, slab of tongue - smothered masqueradingly in steak sauce. Bastard only enlightens me after I've eaten the entire hunk. Don't know which animal the tongue comes from. Don't even bother to ask. This culinary misdemeanor permeates the very core of my character. I'm queasy after my objectionable dinner. Just looking at Partridge gives me repellent indigestion. Then he dishes up: "Those who guard their mouths and their tongues keep themselves from calamity." What utter gush. Could pounce on him and scream vulgarities in his face. Don't give him the satisfaction of a 'Go rot in hell!' reaction though. Talk about adding insult to injury. Talk about weighing me down. Never met such a toad. Why are they playing these childish gastronomic games? Why fool around with our grub? Because by messing with our food, they can mess with our minds. That's why.

You know, I really miss cooking for myself and I truly crave certain foods. Desperately want to get back to a life where I can prepare and eat generous sized meals of my own choosing, and at an hour that suits me. I guess I'm just longing for a normal life again. Anyway, this whole tongue occurrence offends me. Feel exploited. Eaten into. Feel gastronomically asphyxiated. It's not funny. Not in anyway. It's almost like the final nail in the coffin.

That night, somebody suspends a lengthy piece of string right in the middle of the rotting wooden doorway to our chamber. It's fastened simply with a rusty drawing pin. It's just left dangling there. That very same evening, somebody also leaves a skeleton death tarot card next to my bed. I believe somebody's attempting to induce me to suicide. But I've come so far. I've endured so much. They can kill me, but there's no way I'm going to take my own life. Not now. Not after all this...

In this region of exclusion I make acquaintance with a whole variety of Flicardie wildlife: mosquitoes, spiders, owls, flies, rats and bats, to name but a few. I'm marooned amongst the insect traffic here. At night I can hear unknown noises. Distant sounds I've never heard before. Distant sounds that echo in my head. I can identify the plop of plump rats falling into the pond, the chirps and caws of golden plover feeding by moonlight, owl screams from the woodland marsh, tonsil rattling toads with their venomous croaks, and a night sky swimming with flies...they're all outlying sounds to be perceived. As the distant sounds fade, nearby, new-fangled reverberations are orchestrated. As I listen to the new night noises around me, they seem to get louder. The more I listen, the more magnified they become, until I'm inflicted with an orchestral nocturnal clatter, destined to prevent me from getting any sleep. I lie there in a brutal audible darkness. Can do nothing but listen to the sighing of the wind, and the rustling in the bone filled walls of my chamber. Boisterous. I didn't intend to come to France to lie in a death-room of darkness. I came to France for liberation and resurgence....not a concealed downfall or a hush-hush demise. Nevertheless, there are chilling, toe curling night beats here, and the distant sounds come back to me in torrents. It's like a set of Armageddon water bongo drums have been set off inside my head. For nine months during the hours around midnight, my mind is full of undulating sounds. The lake gurgles murmurs. Murmurings of murder. I hear disturbingly familiar undertones....like the soundtrack to an incurable childhood nightmare. Sounds like the night wildlife is conversing with the devil. It's a noisy cocktail. These beats set my brain on ice, and come back to me in surging outbursts. I listen to creaks and audacious mannish snores, and other alien wanking noises. I listened to these sounds, but I don't want to hear them. You can hear brutal gasps straining their way through the dank walls into our sleeping chamber; the echoes of human breathlessness. Unruly. I almost fall out of my bed once because I hear such a startling yowl. I wrestle with myself that evening. I do my best to contend with the hum of these noisy nights, by defying their rasping resonance with my silence. This doesn't work. Makes it worse. I lie there in the dark like an imitative mummy; mute and motionless in the raucous murk; enveloped - buried deep in my tomb. The wind carries the heart-rending voices of the youthful departed. They're the cries of all the deceased wolfskins who've been pressed into taking their own life. Brutally. Unforgiveably. Unamusingly. The Château's claimed many lives. It's alive with ghosts, and their rueful reverberations. The wind's investigating. Sounds sneaky. Intrusive. Sherlock-like. The bustling wind persists. Slams shut, and then re-opens the wooden attic doors above our chamber, that are only just hanging onto their hinges. Can hear these winds infiltrating the whole of our rickety quarters. Riffling through our barracks they are. There are spooky nays in the night coming from the ecurie aswell. Chilling. Omen. Try not to, but I find myself whining along with the sound of the horses, in an outlandish effort to get all drowsy. Abortive. I close my eyes. I do so with chaotic plinks and plonks in my brain, seeking to cause torment. I do so with a dominant hard-at-it croaking travelling over from the marsh. A brutal bewail it is. Must be the Flicardie frogs or toads letting out some kind of pitiless last minute mating call, I think to myself in my faintly slumberous state. It's a rather disharmonious sound, but I kind of grow habituated to it. The croaking gradually morphes into a loose synchronization, like a remorseful chorus that becomes a befitting background drone to my troopish escapade. So, I somehow learn to go about the business of sleeping, with this enormous infusing buzz going on in the surrounding deep green marsh. As I sleep at night I imagine hundreds, thousands of dead bodies rising up from the marshland and battlefields. I imagine wounded men rising from the trenches to the whirring sound of their wartime siren. At one point, not that long ago, there was human carnage here. There was too much bloodshed. We must try and avoid these kind of events in the future. There are so many brutal noises immersed in my mind at night, that I become entirely swamped by sound. As I sleep, the windows rattle, the timber creaks, and the walls continue to inject their deadly wail. Even the trees outside swaying in the wind, sound like they're begging for forgiveness. I'm bewildered by the night-time screech of the marais. The whirring mosquitoes, the buzzing flies, the clamorous chattering crickets, the plonk of frogs, and water rats plopping into the pond, the alarming cawing of the night birds, and the howling wind stricken, and pleading rue-full-ness, all mingled together, become like one full cacophony from the dead departed.

Cocorico!

Morning. It's November now. The *cocorico* sound comes from a French cockerel. It's a hideous cackling crow. It's the awakening sound of the Flicardie crack of dawn. It comes through the large gap under our decaying wooden chamber door. The cockerel sounds like it's having its baggy rouge throat cut. Then there's silence. Stillness. Everything suddenly seems masked. Timorous. Trepidatious even. Anoop's not in his bed.

Our sentences are drawing to a close. How will we all cope in a world without supervision. Some will crumble. I'm determined to survive. I want to live to tell my tale.

192

I crave liberty. Crave an unhampered existence. Crave to see a friendly face.

Sadly, Anoop is found hanging in the ecurie. He's killed himself. I'm not surprised to hear this. Not at all. But still, a feeling that comes close to horror, moves through my veins when I first hear the news. I immediately know I'm going to have to be brave now, and not guilty, because I've been nothing but friendly to the chap. I just need to blot this one out quickly, and move on, for my own well being. But I won't be able to just blot it out will I? It's just gonna be another merciless memory, that can't be wiped away. Blighter. He was a harmless, temperate guy really. This place was just too brutal for him. That Partridge is a despicable man. He victimized Anoop. So glad to be getting away from here and moving on. Today, I decide, there is no God. I put an end to my faith. To be fair, my senses decide for me. Suddenly, it seems to me, a weakness to believe in such fictional nonsense. Everything has an end doesn't it? My wofskin stretch. A piece of string. VP's sword. Swampy's fires. Partridges propaganda punch. Anoops life.

I have a cry for the deceased boy. Can't help it. Maybe he was keeping everything to himself. Perhaps he hadn't found anybody suitable to talk to. Possibly he was experiencing utter abandonment in this savage encampment. Eventually I begin to howl. Moodily. Meaningfully - like a loving mother whose given birth to a still born. The howling continues. Wildly. Uncontrollably, for an oscillating period of time, where I do nothing much more than pace around in sorrowful circles, with my palms to the sky, in despair. All I can say is: RIP Anoop - my 2002 roommate.

My wolfskin 'misadventure' is over. To a great extent my experience tames me. They try their best to institutionalise me, and their contingency profile of me is complete. Have they managed to extract the details they want? Have these control freaks considered all possible eventualities? Have they managed to sufficiently demonise me?

There'll be no more rules and regulations. No more radio procedures. No more watchful eyes. No more deadly silence. No more night-time sounds of the marais....

No more Swampy. No more Partridge. No more Victor Papa.

No more Anoop

Nine months have passed since I left Liechester. Seems a good deal longer. I've spent all of this time under the huntmaster's heedful eye. I've endured a suppressive military stretch, courtesy of the mighty Victor Papa. He has granted me a stay of 'misadventure' at Château Brutale. *How noble of him* - I reflect.

I thank Victor Papa derisively for everything: "Thank-you for everything. It's been…"

"*'Interesting'* is the word you're looking for," he breaks me up bombastically. A look of victory flashes across his face. *Splendid, absolutely splendid* - I think to myself. "So, what are my orders?"

"Orders?"

"Instructions, orders. When you dropped us here back in February, just before you flew off you made a point of saying - *'I will instruct you.'* You never did give me any instructions - well I was just wondering that's all?"

"Keep walking."

"Hey?"

"Enjoy your freedom"

"Worth it!"

"Pardon?"

"Eeeerm, nothing, ok chief...will do."

"And hey, Bravo Romeo, have a shot or two of jager on me!"

"Oh Deer God I will - mark my words!"

"But hey, don't get *too* carried away now!"

He stands near to me and says nothing more. He has his precious sword clutched in his hands. He moves it around in leisurely and triumphant strokes. Bestows another look on me, and then saunters away with his sword swishing from side to side. He's a huge man, and a master of one-upmanship. Still feel like I'm trapped under a mighty military boot. I've had enough of his egocentric exploit. I've had enough of victorious Victor in my life. I'm relieved to be leaving his establishment capsule. *Will probably drink a whole bottle of Jager when I get home* - I figure.

Can't wait to break free. It's been an interesting yet crushing odyssey. There is however something that I simply have to do before I leave. I have to look in that drawer embedded in the wall of my old chamber again....for one last time...it's something I just feel compelled to do. For some reason I run to the room. Feel like I'm running out of time or something. Feel like I know the answer is there. I'm breathless when I arrive at the tiny drawer. I wobble it free. Inside there's a fresh inscription. No doubt its from VP. This is what is scratched into the wood at the bottom of the tiny drawer: "MOGUILTY." It's written just like this...in capital letters. At first it makes me think of a newspaper headline. Then I start thinking about the carvings I remember seeing on the inside of the wooden desks at my primary school - the carvings that naughty kids used to carve with compasses, and then fill in with black felt pen. I run out of the room feeling crazy man. I hover outside the doorway. I go back in my mind to Mo's Voodoo pit. I see spiders and rats and bats escape. Ok, so Mo is guity, but what about his punishment? How are *they* gonna correct this man? How does one go about curing such an infectious disease? And what about my bruised and battered soul? Am I suppose to just swallow this deflection and simply walk away into the unknown? Possibly that's what life's all about – swallowing deflections. Then, for an instant I'm muzzled with nightmarish hallucinations. After that I become strangely flushed with a sense of euphoria. Enlightenment pops into me. Just like that. Perhaps justice does exist? Perhaps I don't need to feel like so much of a fugitive anymore?

Of course I knew this all along, that Mo was guilty that is. It's always been in my thoughts, but I'd bottled it all up for as long as I could, as if it was a reclusive pirate's elixir, that no other being should know about. Just as a hulking great big cloud carries a storm...I carried Mo's guilt...which started out, I sense, as disconcertion, yet soon infused into a deep scarred, it's-all-in-your-head-human-fogginess, and then permeated into culpability, persecution, damnation, deracination, hatred and eventually an all-encompassing-pitiless-hunted-running-around-in-circles-fox-like-feeling. My outlet...my downpour – this little drawer and perhaps, just perhaps, November 'I know nothing' Romeo. I take one last look around my whitewashed chamber. I won't miss these white walls....no siree bob!

I also have one last languishing look at the lake before I make tracks. A ghostly peal of mist is wreathed around it. It looks like a scene from a horror film. My mood maddens and sallows. I depart leaving arrogant yellow footprints as I go.

I'm peculiarly spaced out as I walk out through the Château gates. Despite our rigorous working regime it feels like I'm coming out of hibernation. *Nine months is a bit of a long time to stay in hibernation isn't it* - I surmise. At the end of my nine month stretch as a wolfskin, I'm finally being released, let out on the loose. Feel pregnant with time. Have I learnt anything? Have they learnt anything? Have I lost anything? Has the world lost anything? Are there going to be further repercussions? I'm not the kind of creature to lie low for too long. I'm not the kind of creature to remain unsung.

The boy cries wolf and then the wolf cries boy

When I leave this Château-with-a-curse I feel the absence of control. It's a potent feeling. It's like I've stepped back into a world of enormous freedom that will take some getting used to. It's almost like I don't know what to do, now that I'm not being told what to do. What I'm trying to say is that I'm overwhelmed with emancipation. I'm glad to be free, but I've forgotten how to think for myself. Feel like a captive might feel, after being unexpectedly set free from a seemingly endless prison sentence. I'm curiously mole-like.

So, I channel my way home across the sleeve of sea between France and England like a man reprieved.

Time has wafted by. The biological and chemical clock of conflict is ticking louder than ever now. War seems inevitable. But who's really caused this war? No lone wolf can be blamed. This war is like an unstoppable tidal wave. The bigger picture looks ghastly. I'm against the impending war on terror. I've no real philosophy for this way of thinking, it's just I don't unequivocally trust the Americans and hey I'm pro-peace in general anyway...a pacifist if you like. I also sense that it might well lead to global religious chaos and absolute suffering. My gut feeling is the whole war on terror is forged, and that that oozing black liquid, that most of us seem to crave so much, also has a lot to do with it *(45 minutes? sometimes I reckon it's really bad to lie)*. Effectively, this leads me to come to the speculative conclusion, that this particular war is more about profit, and power, than morality or justice. I do categorically believe however, that that man in the middle-east is up to grave mischief. Complicated innit? I'm an author – not an authority. I don't wanna push no red buttons...

One thing I do know for sure, and that is: there are good and bad white people in this world, and there are good and bad black people, and the good people aren't always that good, and the bad people aren't always that bad, and the white people aren't always that white, and the black people aren't always that black. Like within most groupings of species in life, there are a vast variety of different kinky shades and spirits. Goodness and badness flows through us all, and always will. I hope I don't sound like I'm sermonizing too much, and I hope I don't sound too much like Geoffrey Partridge, but I believe we've got to learn to be more understanding and tolerant. Now, more than ever, there needs to be more room for individuality and freedom of expression in society. Languages are important. Cultures and creed and colours *must* be allowed to flourish and swirl and combine. Anyway, another terrorizing venture in our history is just about to begin. Time is running out for some. Our future looks bleak. War is suddenly upon us.

I spend nine months waiting. I spend all of my time there waiting for that brutal moment, waiting for that unbearable brutal moment that never comes. Turns out to be a bit of a soporific misadventure. I've been holed up for a large chunk of my life. In terms of politics and journalism I've been coerced to lie dormant. I've been hidden away from the world. It's going to be difficult to adapt to real life after this other man's imposed escapade. Indeed, lots of things seem utterly futile to me. I mean, I haven't read a newspaper or watched TV for nearly a year now. I'm out-of-touch with conventional society. Conventional society seems insincere and cowardly. I wanna find something real.

The gulf between the intensity of my own experience, and the indifference of those back home, makes homecoming painful. It's difficult to adapt when I return home. My friends seem like unknowing strangers. I've been culturally divorced from mainstream civilization for too long. Somehow though, the thought of finally being able to write helps me to climb out of my state of alienation. There's a whole heap of impressions I wanna share with somebody, impressions that seem monumental. Ultimately my conscience is commanding me to write. At least I'm still alive, at least I still have my hands, and at least I still have consideration. I'll have to phenomenally reinvent myself, now that I'm no longer a multi-activity wolfskin instructor, and finally put pen to paper.

197

CHAPTER 8 –
THERE'S SOMETHING I'VE NOT TOLD YOU ABOUT:
GHOSTY AT CHÂTEAU BRUTALE.

"I've got a man called Ghosty following me to bed.
I've got a man called Ghosty camping in my head."

Ghosty was always around me at Château Brutale, like my reticent shadow he was. A period of sleuthing ensued. Ghosty had taken control of my spirit. Would I ever feel free again? *To keep me down Ghosty had to stay down with me.* Ever felt like you're a dead man? I was constantly thinking that I was going to be *'disposed'* of accidentally on purpose. Back then, in 2002, I just wanted to know when I was going to die.

Sometimes I think having other people around you makes you less like yourself. Having other people around you all the time can hideously do your nut in. I needed time to myself. I needed time to do whatever I wanted to do, in whatever way I saw fit. I needed time to be alone and I mean *properly* alone. Really I just needed time to write. I never had time to write at Château Brutale and I found this disabling. In fact, my ability to laugh at life back then had been fading. People back home were asking questions. Who was holding him? Why were they holding him? What did he know? Was he dead or alive? *I was in the grip of a ghostly melancholy. Like phantom pains the blue nightmares come every night. I just close my eyes and they come into my head. I awake in the morning feeling tetchy. Trembling...remembering...slow stages of a tragedy.*

Château Brutale was teeming with moles. Ghosty was one of them. Ghosty was one of the more sophisticated and untruthful moles. "Your time will come," he announced apocalyptically. I had my own personally enlightening and gripping ghost. How repugnantly privileged I was. There was something macabre about Ghosty. He was a tough and robust guy. I imagined he knew how to kill a man instantly with one hard hit. He spent most of his time behind me that year. I was all alone, but I was hardly ever on my own. Ghosty moved backwards and forwards between the Château and the Fortress. His mission was to pick up as much intelligence as possible, and to report back to the big man. Ghosty was Victor Papa's aide-de-camp. Ghosty

198

was one of Victor's most trusted spies. As if the ceaseless presence of Victor Papa's brawn, and Geoffrey Partridge's brain wasn't enough, I also had my very own wraithlike shadow to contend with – Ghosty.

I remember exclaiming: "I feel like my life's in danger." Ghosty replied, as if he had nothing but death on his mind:
"Ah well, we've all got to die at some point."
This was the last thing I wanted to hear. Again, it seemed like the end of my life was just around the corner. This gloomy guy wasn't here to help me.

Ghosty was a mysterious figure and he was a bit of a liar. His personality and his nickname were well matched. This ghost couldn't just simply be brushed away. We were alone in the Château staff headquarters. He made a point of showing me a painting with an SAS inscription on the back of its frame. He chose his moment discreetly. Yet to this day, I don't know what he was really getting at. Was he covertly trying to tell me he was a member of the SAS? Was he stealthily attempting to recruit me? Whatever he was trying to do, he just added to my state of bewilderment.

To my astonishment, one evening Ghosty started talking about my home town Liechester. He declared: "I went out in Liechester once." His comment seemed random. In fact, it seemed hellishly misplaced.
"Really, where did you go?" I replied with interest and a whole heap of vigilance.
"Can't remember the name of the bar, but I got kicked out of there by the doormen." I was more than a little intrigued now.
"Describe the bar to me? What did it look like?"
"It had a neon blue sign above the entrance." This really was a bolt-from-the-blue.
"Wasn't called The Blue Hole was it?"
"Yeah...that rings a bell. Now eeeerm – yeah eeeeeeeerh I think that's what it was called." He gave the impression that he was growing tired of our conversation. He glanced upwards, and began to rub his sturdy and stubbly chin. He appeared bogusly blasé. Was his nonchalance feigned? Almost beyond doubt it seemed that way. I wanted to know for sure. Ghosty might well have been an agent provocateur. Ghosty might well have been a deceitful ghost. Or perhaps he might just have been growing tired of our conversation. But I didn't think so. I knew he'd arrived in Liechester by train, so I decided to ask him: "How far was it from the train station?"

"Bout 5 minutes walk. Had a cobbled tunnel entrance. I can remember that. It was all a bit dark and sinister-ish."

"Well, it sounds just like The Blue Hole. I use to work there." My mind was racing. I tried to remain calm. I had to be ultra cautious. I was mega alert. *Can I trust this man* - I thought to myself? *Who can you trust?* Even though I wanted to talk, I couldn't. Even though I needed to talk, I couldn't. I had to be careful what I said. Luckily it was in my blood to be reticent.

"Why did you get chucked out?"

"I was just totally pissed, and was dancing like a lunatic in the outside bit."

"No way, I can't believe you got chucked out of that place."

"Why? How come?" Ghosty enquired ghoulishly. Laconically. Immediately. Hungrily. Thoughts were racing through my mind. Was this whole conversation a lie just to extract information from me? I had been approached by a number of strange characters in recent years. Why on earth didn't someone just come straight out and ask me what had happened. Why on earth didn't someone just ask me if there was anything troubling me? Anyhow, I'd got to the point where I just didn't care anymore. "They're fucking nasty bastards in that place man." I felt my throat clot.

"Why do you say that?" I felt massively besieged. Heat exuded through my cheeks turning them purple. I croaked out despairingly:

"They just were." Then I clammed up completely.

Ghosty knew I'd been on the receiving end of something. He didn't react to my comments, but I'm pretty goddamn sure he'd catalogued all I'd said. Was Ghosty part of an SAS troop? Was he working for the Ministry of Defence under a clandestine guise? Where was he going with all these little white mechanical lies? I feared this was state sponsored terrorism. Ghosty was twice the age of the other wolfskins. He was well into his 40's. We were all in our 20's or late teens. Anyhows, I don't know much about these kinda things, but what I do know, was here was an experienced man, who wasn't really my friend, and he was somehow getting me to speak about a load of personal stuff, that I felt very uncomfortable talking about.

One thing's for sure, this ghoul wasn't one to mess with. Once Ghosty said to me: "Me and Victor were gonna take Alpha Mike out round the back, and kick the living shit out of 'im." I might have been wrong, but I took this as a subtle threat to mean - *watch it, or you'll end up getting battered yourself.* Anyway, what's the craic with threatening to put individuals in corners to brutalize them? Why does violence always seem to be a solution? Is there no end to it? I always knew Alpha Mike was a bit of a rebel, but I liked him all the same. Probably I was actually a bit similar to him. Anyhows, they never did 'kick the shit' out of Alpha Mike, and I never did meet my well-anticipated violent marsh death. I couldn't beat these savages, but I would never join them.

There had been a brutal uncertainty in the air in boggy Vatanbourg, and nothing's worse than what we can imagine. I was exhausted. It was an extraordinary relief to be on my own again. My future was unknown. What would happen tomorrow was unknown, and this unknowing felt blissful. I could taste freedom, and it tasted golden, and euphoric, and overwhelmingly unbrutal.

Then a saintly figure appeared from the bottom of the garden. I was awed by what I saw. A lady from the lake, all in white, a good ghost, was walking towards me. I didn't know whether to scream or run - I did neither – I froze. This angel of hope somehow made my gruesome thoughts float away, and for the first time in years I had a pungent sense of well being. In my wonderful, way above average dream, there were two huge trees between the lake and the Château, meeting like lungs from the earth, and as their branches touched, they seemed to create an almost luminescent green heart shape.

I awoke with a rush of blood to my head. Even though it was just a dream, it had somehow given me an enormous sense of exuberance. During this sensational slumber, I had glowingly rekindled, my gooseberry green, Jersey French spirit.

It was raining real hard outside, but that didn't dissuade me from walking in the shower. The mood I was in, I don't think it would have mattered what the weather was like, I'd have gone on walking all the same. As it happens, the heavy rain made me feel alive. I didn't seek shelter. I just kept on walking in the cold, and gusty downpour, that is until my belly told me it was time to go back home, and eat anything, and everything I wanted. I was soaked to the bone, but I hadn't been this awake for a long time.

As I walked back home in the English rain, I was listening to a bad ass mellow trance tune entitled 'Rachel's song' on my newfangled MP3 player. It was part of Paul oakenfold's goa mix. It made me feel, leap, splash, laugh and cry, but above all else, it made me rise inside.

Feeling faintly liberated, I turned the track up.....I was absolutely buzzing off it. Life outside was noiseless. I could hear nothing but the pulsations of this tender trance track resonating in my waking ears. I was purely immersed in the music, and I began to feel my moral soul embolden, and start shifting. My strength of mind was miraculously returning. I was beginning to feel shrewd again. I was beginning to feel less guilty. Then for some reason this bombshell of an elucidation came to me: "It appears society insists that we have an enemy – just accept it." Reality seeped into me like an orgasmic ache. One way or another these words somehow helped me to think optimistically about what *I* should do with the rest of *my* life. These words were like door handles to my new destiny. The world around us is baffling and relentlessly harsh. I have a duty to at least try to preserve and protect myself. I believe I owe myself that much - all things considered. I guess I was ditching 'idealism'. I'm just an individual. I can influence the world, but I can't save it from war.

CONSPIRACY. RELOAD. There's no such thing as a fake feeling....I want to recover properly, but I don't know if I ever will. I am at least determined to survive for a while longer. My days are certainly now less saddled with strain, but there's still an echo in my head. Bang. I am stunned......but I am still here. Life goes on...for some of us...the lucky ones. *A colourful past means a colourful future.*

J'écris parce que je ne peux pas parler. J'étais perdu dans un fin brouillard bleu. J'ai perdu ma tête quand j'étais dans la rue..*Fin*

Lightning Source UK Ltd.
Milton Keynes UK
UKHW041507020720
365925UK00001B/147